THE HEAT BROUGHT ON
A MINI CRIME WAVE . . .

First that grunge girl, Loretta Picard, murdered two police officers, then there was a woman in Prospect Park who was waylaid, stripped, and beaten in the middle of the day. A baby, snatched from a carriage in midtown Manhattan twelve hours later, was found, unharmed, in the woods in Peekskill, New York. The kidnapper had been attempting to bury the baby alive, when someone walking up the trail startled him. By the following weekend, seventeen weather-related deaths were reported. One of the victims was a nineteen-year-old runner who collapsed during a track meet on Randalls Island. Meanwhile, concerned citizens began to take the law into their own hands, a man in Queens shooting his neighbor to death when he refused to shut down his sprinkler. Bad things happen, Emma Price thought. No one has any real control.

NAOMI RAND

THE ONE THAT GOT AWAY

AN EMMA PRICE MYSTERY

AVON BOOKS

An Imprint of HarperCollinsPublishers

This is a work of fiction. Names, characters, places, and incidents are products of the author's imagination or are used fictitiously and are not to be construed as real. Any resemblance to actual events, locales, organizations, or persons, living or dead, is entirely coincidental.

AVON BOOKS
An Imprint of HarperCollins*Publishers*
10 East 53rd Street
New York, New York 10022-5299

Copyright © 2001 by Naomi Rand
ISBN: 0-06-103124-0
www.avonmystery.com

First Avon Books paperback printing: July 2002
First HarperCollins hardcover printing: August 2001

Avon Trademark Reg. U.S. Pat. Off. and in Other Countries, Marca Registrada, Hecho en U.S.A.
HarperCollins ® is a registered trademark of HarperCollins Publishers Inc.

Printed in the U.S.A.

10 9 8 7 6 5 4 3 2 1

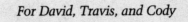

For David, Travis, and Cody

Acknowledgments

Any work of fiction is a struggle. This book was certainly no exception. I would like to thank the many generous readers who gave me help in the writing of the novel; members of my writing group who read every draft and offered insightful commentary, Nicole Bokat, Alice Elliot Dark, Kalindi Handler, Ed Levy, Deirdre Day Macleod, David Schiller, and Sasha Troyan. Thanks to Amy Bedik, Susan Korones Gifford, Asa Miraglia, and Amy Pratt for offering me your friendship, and for going beyond the call of duty in reading this work.

I could never have gotten this novel published without my agent, the amazing Flip Brophy, whose dedication to my writing, and to this novel, never flagged. Thanks to my editor, Robert Jones, whose generosity and enthusiasm make him the sort of editor all writers dream of having on their side.

Thanks to Audrea Alarcon, the most loving and imaginative babysitter I've ever seen in action. Thanks to Russell Stetler, for being the best kind of investigator, courageous and indefatigable. Thanks to my parents, Anna and Harry Rand, and my sister Deborah, for their faith. Thanks to Leo and Dorothy Braudy for reading this at an early stage and being fans. Thank you Travis and Cody, my boys, for making each day better than the last. I couldn't have written this book without the amazing pleasure of watching the two of you grow up. And finally, thank you David Duncan Fitzgerald, as always, for everything.

THE ONE THAT GOT AWAY

ON THE NIGHT IN QUESTION

August 2, 1999

N.Y. DAILY NEWS

TWO COPS KILLED IN DOWNTOWN SHOOTING

A 2 a.m. noise complaint turned deadly this morning. Officer Stewart Larrabbee and rookie Police Officer Cheri Maples were fatally wounded in the stairwell of a Stanton St. apartment house. Maples, the daughter of Randolph Maples, PBA president, was particularly unlucky. Apparently, she'd been partnered with Larrabbee that very day. The two were allegedly shot by Loretta Picard, a 21-year-old bartender at the Pit, a downtown club.

Notes from Officer Michael P. Janus

Officer Maples was found facedown on the stairs. She had been shot once, the bullet piercing her jugular. There was a towel on top of her throat, drenched in blood. Officer Larrabbee was found in front of the suspect's door. Officer Larrabbee had sustained multiple gunshot wounds, one to the arm, one to the chest and one to the genital area. Attempts to revive both officers failed. As we came up the stairs, my partner Officer Raines and myself spotted the suspect attempting to flee. Upon seeing us, she raised her hands. A physical search found no weapon present. However, the suspect's door was ajar. On questioning another tenant, we ascertained that this was said suspect's apartment. On entering her apartment and searching, we found a nine-millimeter handgun in the garbage pail, along with bloodstained pants and a T-shirt. Forensics is examining the blood on the clothing and ballistics tests are ongoing. This was the point where we apprised said suspect of her rights and took her into custody.

NATIONAL ENQUIRER

EXCLUSIVE PICTURES OF TATTOOED TEENAGE COP KILLER

see story page 7.

Tattoo artist Mick Shaeffer told this reporter Loretta Picard, currently being held in the double homicide of two New York City police officers, requested a fire breathing dragon inked between her breasts. "I worked on it over three hours and never a peep out of her. That girl was stoical," he said. Picard also requested a small heart with JJ inscribed inside and a special memorial C, inked directly above her pubic hair. The last was apparently in honor of Courtney Love. Shaeffer told the reporter that Picard said Love was her idol.

ROLLING STONE: NOTES

SMASHING PUMPKINS AND COURTNEY GAIN RESPECT IN STRANGE PLACES

Loretta Picard, the twenty-one-year-old New York City bartender who is a suspect in a double murder, confirmed reports that she had been listening to Smashing Pumpkins and Hole on the night in question. Apparently, irate neighbors called police, which led to the deadly encounter between Picard and two of New York's Finest. Members of the CSPM, the Committee for Safety and Purity in Music, a conservative action group, called for stricter controls over content. "If anyone thinks they can tell someone what to think or how to act, I mean if someone thinks music is what makes a person pick up a gun and shoot someone, that's fucking crazy and they're the ones deserve to be put away," Courtney Love responded. Billy Corgan, who is laying down tracks for the upcoming Pumpkins album, had no comment.

1

Worldwide it was the hottest August in recorded weather history. Al Roker looked positively gleeful as he predicted a full week of ninety-eight-degree temperatures. In downtown Brooklyn, Emma Price sighed, nudging the air conditioner up another notch. Then she hacked apart an avocado. The chicken, roasted that morning, was cooling in the fridge. Fresh corn, removed from the cob, stood ready for sautéing. A salad of comestible delights waited under a Saran Wrap cover, thin slices of jicama carefully sculpted into an ivory crown.

The front door slammed. Her son Liam raced in. Pressing a finger to his lips, he ducked behind the kitchen table.

"Which way did he go?" Beatriz Castillo demanded a minute later.

"I don't know who you mean," Emma said. But she indicated his position with a downward sweep of the eyes.

"It's no good protecting him," Bea said. "I planted a tracking device in his jeans."

There was a giggle from under the table, then Liam sprang out and raised his weapon. A thin stream of water hit Bea smack in the middle of her forehead.

"Now you're in for it," she said with abundant good humor.

"Outside," Emma cautioned.

"You heard your mom." Bea wiped the water off. And Emma noted how merciless youth was. Bea, Liam's babysitter and erstwhile guardian, wore a mint-green, midriff-baring sleeveless blouse and cutoffs that exposed most of her thighs. Emma's thighs were also exposed, but not nearly so dramatically. Her stomach was hidden by a blowzy Gap T. A diamond stud gracing Bea's right nostril cemented the difference. "Surrender," Bea said to Liam. "Give in to my superior powers."

"No way!" Liam waved his squirt gun in her face. "You want a piece of me, come and get me." He puffed himself up to his full four feet ten inches, saying this, and Bea lunged. Emma cleared her throat and opened the glass doors separating the kitchen from the world as Liam leaped across the pressed redwood deck, then onto the metal staircase, disappearing into the garden. Beatriz pursued. Looking out the window, Emma found her son hiding behind the hundred-year-old maple. The sprinkler pulsed on and they were both hit with a blast of water. Then Bea grabbed him, lifting him on high like a miniature avenging god.

The kitchen clock read six. Will's plane had landed at La Guardia half an hour before. He'd be home any minute. And Will was returning under protest. *I had no choice,* Emma told herself. Then she closed the glass doors against the heat, took a drink of cold water and lay down on the living room couch.

"Mrs. P?"

Someone was tugging on her arm. Emma bolted upright.

"I didn't mean to scare you." It was Bea talking.

"What's wrong?" Emma asked. The room was hazy. Was it smoke? Her nostrils twitched, trying to detect an acrid smell. Then her head cleared and she saw her mistake. She'd been asleep. In the interim, darkness had descended. Emma swallowed and found her mouth was bone dry.

"It's eight-twenty," Bea said. "I've got to leave."

"Is Will here?"

Bea shook her head. "I didn't want to bother you. I gave Liam a shower and fed him dinner." Bea shoved her hands into the pockets of her shorts. Emma stood, and her legs gave out. She grabbed the back of the sofa for support.

"You okay, Mrs. P.?"

"I'm fine," Emma said. "God, I hate naps, they make you feel sick." She took a few shallow breaths, then deeper, fuller ones. Her body readjusted. Like being in a cave, she thought, then, seeing daylight, inching your way up slowly, and dragging yourself out. She tried again and this time found her bearings. Reaching into her pocket, she pulled out her wallet and withdrew three twenties.

"That's way too much," Bea told her. "I've only been here since four."

"Take it, please."

Bea looked down at the money, then up at Emma. Her lips parted. In order to deflect the inevitable protest, Emma shoved the money into Bea's front pocket.

"You were a lifesaver," Emma said. "You didn't want to come and I guilted you into it. I took advantage of your good nature, Bea. So think of this as your reward."

Bea's eyes filled with water. "Don't say that, Mrs. P." Emma blinked. Apparently this wasn't an optical illusion.

"What is it? What's wrong?"

"Nothing." The response was too quick, an automatic denial. Bea surveyed the living room, attempting to avoid eye contact. "It's that time of the month. I always get overemotional and embarrass myself."

Apparently Will was testing her patience. It had been four hours since his plane was due. And in the time that had elapsed, there had been no phone call. Why assume this is something he can control, she wondered, because she knew where this would lead. Blaming him wouldn't banish her anxiety. Cradling the phone against one ear, Emma nudged the door to Liam's room open. The overhead light was out, but the sheet on Liam's bed glowed. Lifting a corner, she found him hunched over a flashlight scrutinizing *Tales from Wayside School*. She heard a disembodied voice scream, "it's a two-run homer. Derek's first of the series."

"Hey, you," Emma said, reaching for the transistor radio. He clutched it to his chest, defiantly.

"Not yet." He was pleading.

"Okay, but consider this your ten-minute warning."

"It's only the fourth inning."

"Ten minutes. And I can make it five."

He sculpted disappointment onto his face. Emma offered up a solid imitation.

"Just till the seventh," he begged.

"Ten minutes. This is absolutely nonnegotiable."

"But Dad's not even home yet. I wanted to see him."

"You'll see him tomorrow." She kissed Liam, then ruffled his hair. In return, he sulked. "You're tempting fate," she said, leaning over to tickle him under his armpits. "Nooo, Mooom," he sang out, collapsing in a giggling heap.

Downstairs in the kitchen, Emma found a bottle of cold beer at the very back of the fridge. Still cradling the phone, she flicked the top off and tilted it back. With the first sip, her stomach pursed.

"Jesus," she said, capping the beer and setting it on the counter. There was an open box of saltines in the snack drawer. Emma bit down on one and the soggy mass imploded on her tongue. As she spit into the sink, a chipper voice in her ear said, "American Airlines, Celia speaking, how can I help you?"

* * *

According to Celia, the flight was on time and a Mr. Will Price was on the passenger list. So his plane *had* landed safely. Emma studied the clock. She told herself there was no reason to worry. This was Will exacting his favorite form of punishment. He loved to force her into imagining the worst, a world without him. Of course it always worked. Emma saw Will in the back seat of a yellow cab, admiring his Pakistani driver's turbaned head. Then she saw the cab flip over a divider and slam into a speeding Mack truck.

Come on, Em, this is only increasing the misery, she thought. Climbing the stairs again, she removed the flashlight and gave Liam a good-night kiss.

"I can't wait to see Dad," he said.

"Me, too," she told him, trying to tamp down the irony.

Halfway to the kitchen she heard Will's key in the door. The anxiety was immediately diluted with anger. He has no goddamn excuse, she told herself.

Emma went to greet him. Passing the hall table, she saw three twenties fanned out and shook her head at Bea's foolish generosity.

The door was swinging open. Will set his duffel bag inside.

"Well, hello," she said, hearing her own peevish tone, and immediately regretting it.

He reached around to retrieve a Toys Я Us shopping bag, then shut the door. "Sorry I'm late. There was an accident on the Brooklyn-Queens Expressway. A tractor trailer jackknifed right in front of us." Leaning forward, he produced a dutiful kiss. She tasted the minty fresh odor of Listerine and underneath it something sour, alcohol based.

"I was worried," she said.

"These things happen." Will was a little too glib. "Is Liam still up?"

He's definitely punishing me, Emma thought. And I suppose, according to his lights, I richly deserve it. Over his head at work, when his shrew of a wife calls up and demands his immediate presence. Not an easy thing to manage when you're on a movie set in Helena, Montana.

Emma set the dinner on the table. Will offered her a curt nod, then pulled open the door of the fridge to grab the last cold beer. He stood there in front of her, brandishing the bottle.

"I'm not hungry," he said. "You go ahead and eat."

Emma looked down at her plate, then shoved it away. He shrugged.

"I have to take a ten o'clock flight back tomorrow."

"I thought you had till Sunday night."

He shook his head hard, rubbing in the ridiculous nature of her present position. What could be so important it couldn't have waited another goddamn week?

Married twelve years. Emma remembered how, once, she had been the one charting new, undiscovered countries. They'd met when Will Price was filming a documentary. He'd come out to the capital defender's office in Jersey in order to cover a particularly gruesome case; Sidney Routon, who was accused of murdering his ex-wife and their two children. Sidney Routon told anyone who'd listen that he was saving his children from the devil.

Sidney had told them his defense should be based on the words of God, on God's concept of sinfulness and pride. Dawn Prescott, Emma's boss and the project's chief counsel, preferred to try for a pretrial judgment of mental incompetence, then entered an insanity plea.

Dawn let Will come into the office and film, thinking the publicity might help the cause. Inside of a week, Emma Price, chief investigator and grad school dropout, became the star of this part of Will's low-budget epic on the vagaries of the criminal justice system. Within a month, they were engaged.

The film took three years to finish. Then he made a half-hearted attempt to get a distributor. In the meanwhile, he moved on, becoming an itinerant film editor on big-budget Hollywood features. They called him "Miracle Man" and mooned over him. Between the money and the adulation, he succumbed. It was so many years ago. Now she was a wife. A mother. And how they had met was just their private joke. In courting, Will managing to transform her into a minor, morally committed celebrity.

After her marriage, Emma had gotten pregnant in record time and left her job at Capital Crimes to raise Liam. She did often think about how ironic it was, meeting Will effectively sabotaging her career, the same career he had apparently been so eager to showcase.

"We started at five this morning and we still couldn't get the shot," he was saying. "There we were, with me having to catch a twelve o'clock flight. We're on the thirty-sixth take and Mitch is losing his fucking mind. Then he throws a hissy fit and says, everything is on hold until we get it right. Unfortunately, that's when I remind him I'm leaving for the weekend. So when he reminds me we're three weeks behind schedule already, plus a half a mil over budget, I tell him, sorry, but I've got to go. And he says, no way in hell I'm going anywhere. Plus, if I run out like this, I'll never get another job. There I am...stuck between him and you, between a rock and a hard place."

"You should have called to explain," Emma said, but she was unable to muster any real conviction.

"You told me last night you weren't accepting any more excuses. You said you couldn't stand another minute and slammed down the phone. You were fucking out of your mind with me, Emma. I should have called? No fucking way. Aren't you the one who must be obeyed? You expect my appearance here on the doorstep or else. Your standards, your fucking impossible standards."

"Don't, Will," Emma said quietly. "Don't do this now."

"You have a better time in mind?"

She shrugged, feeling deliberately weak and spent. The terrain was too hopelessly familiar.

"I know why you wanted me here. I had to ship myself home, so you could tell me what a disappointment I am to my face. How I'm not home enough. How I don't do enough when I *am* around. How we have a child and what kind of father do I think I am; haven't I ever looked in the goddamn kitchen cupboard? Can't I figure out what to buy without asking you to make a list? Can't I get anything right at all? Why did I take Liam to *that* movie? Why did I let him go out without his jacket? Why did I buy the wrong kind of fucking milk? Plus there's the two of us together. Why don't I ever want to talk to you?"

"I'd say it's a little past the talking stage with us," Emma said.

"Right! You want to have sex, but you also want to murder me. That doesn't generally produce the most romantic feelings."

"We've made love once in the last six months."

That slowed him down. But only for a moment. "Jesus, Em, why did you marry me when I'm such a total loser?"

"You're not a loser," she said, but was unable to hide the knowing, slightly abashed smile. He'd sandbagged her. She was willing to admit that her list of grievances were part of the problem. But only part.

Will took a breath. Girding his loins, she thought, feeling more than a little ashamed. He was right, she did complain too much, only how did you go about stopping? We've come too far to go back, she thought suddenly, and felt that fear invade her, saw what was in store. She was already the one who folded the laundry and insured that Liam's teeth were properly cleaned. She paid the bills, took care of repainting and repairs to the house, bargained for the best insurance and totted up the receipts for the taxes. On top of that, there was her job, the class in criminal investigation she taught three days a week at Fordham Law. Someone has to do these things, she decided. Someone has to keep this household running and pretend we're a family. She shivered. Pretend?

"It's true, I complain about certain things," she said. "I get resentful. But that's not all there is between us. Will, be fair."

"Why don't you try being fair yourself," he countered. "When I'm working, I have zero control."

"This is different."

He raised his eyebrows.

The girl who cried wolf, she thought. A postmodern fable. She shut her mouth and licked at the dryness on her lips. Was it really too late to explain?

"I'm tired of this, Em, tired of the hostility. Tired of shouldering the blame."

"But you had a drink at the airport," she said. "You sat there and made me wait and worry."

"I had several drinks," he said, his voice softening. "I didn't mean to make you worry. I was simply trying to figure this all out."

"What's that supposed to mean?" Emma knew though and hugged herself for warmth.

"We've been going through the motions for over a year. You wanted me home to give me the news and I appreciate that. I appreciate your honesty. You've always been better at the hard things."

She shook her head deliberately. But he kept going.

"I'm forty years old. This is who I am and who I'm always going to be. It's not just about what I have to do every day of the week. It's about liking me. You don't like me, Em. Somewhere along the way, you stopped. And a little while later you stopped loving me." He laughed bitterly. "What can I do?" he asked. It was apparently meant as a rhetorical question. She thought about throwing herself in his path, and saw her own mangled frame.

Emma reached out. He shoved her arms away. And as she opened her mouth to offer a denial, he bolted. The front door slammed shut. When she got there and threw it open, he had flagged down a cab. She opened her mouth to call to him, but it was pointless.

"Stupid," she said to herself. "Stupid, stupid, stupid." She closed the door slowly, then leaned her back against it.

2

The heat brought on a mini crime wave. First that grunge girl, Loretta Picard, murdered two police officers, then there was a woman in Prospect Park who was waylaid, stripped, and beaten in the middle of the day, the man who attacked her writing WHORE on her body in indelible red ink. A baby, snatched from a carriage in midtown Manhattan twelve hours later, was found, unharmed, in the woods in Peekskill, New York. The kidnapper had been attempting to bury the baby alive, when someone walking up the trail startled him. By the following weekend, seventeen weather-related deaths were reported. One of the victims was a nineteen-year-old runner who collapsed during a track meet on Randalls Island. Meanwhile, concerned citizens began to take the law into their own hands, a man in Queens shooting his neighbor to death when he refused to shut down his sprinkler.

On Sunday morning you couldn't even see the clouds through the haze. People moved slowly in the heat, walking in the corners of buildings to catch a small piece of shade. Lawns were brown. Trees in the city parks wore curling dead leaves and flowers in window boxes shriveled. Bad things happen, Emma Price thought. No one has any real control.

She'd attempted to speak with Will several times over the course of the week but there had been nothing but a brutal silence. Twelve years, she thought, feeling grief, and, hard at its heels, rage. "How could he do this to us?" she kept asking. And was asking it still when Sunday morning came and Will opened the front door, unannounced. "I need to talk to Liam," he said, brushing by her to climb the stairs.

By the time he finished with whatever explanation he was willing to tender, she could hear Liam's wailing. Racing up, she met Will on the landing. She had to admit, he did look heartbroken. "What can I do?" he asked. But when she put out her hand to catch him, when she tried to offer an alternative plan, he fled. Calling later to speak to Liam, his voice was so frigid, tendrils of ice snaked out of the phone.

   This is what comes of repression, she thought. The decision simmers there for so long, when it finally rises to the surface, it has the destructive payload of an entire nuclear arsenal.

That night, Emma found herself channel surfing. A weathercaster in a pink sleeveless dress was rhapsodizing about the current extreme weather conditions. An hour earlier, a tornado had landed in New Jersey, destroying a town hall and several adjoining buildings. Then it had cut a swath through the countryside, taking the roof off an elementary school and crushing a school bus. Meanwhile, Hurricane Mathilda was heading up the eastern seaboard, apparently poised to hit the New York metropolitan area sometime before daybreak. The woman noted it was the worst hurricane season in recorded history, then showed footage of the oversized surf at area beaches. She coyly added that Hurricane Norm was south, southeast of Bermuda.

   Getting Liam to sleep that night required the kind of boundless energy Emma had had as a teenager. He asked for story after story, then lay there, sullen and uncommunicative. When she tried to leave the room, he burst into tears. It was eleven when she sank, gratefully, into her own bed. As she flicked past the channels, she couldn't help remembering how Will had done the same thing, stutter-stepping over the sepia-tinted movies on AMC, then listening too long to Sports Update. Another, paltry bone of contention. She began to cry, then clicked the television off. In the half light, she shifted in her bed, trying to find some level of comfort. Her whole body ached, just as if she'd spent hours in the gym, being pummeled by a vastly superior sparring partner.

In order to fall asleep, she imagined a faceless man doing damage to her. That man stroked her thighs, then held her down and moved his hand along her stomach. When she was ready, he came inside, knowing exactly what sort of steady rhythm to use to make her respond.

After she climaxed, she drifted off. Asleep, she could feel the wind pressing against her unfurled wings. The crumpled figure left behind on her bed would fool a casual intruder. Emma soared high above the city of her birth, then headed north to perform intricate dives down the gray glass sides of the Twin Towers.

And as she practiced aerial acrobatics, an eleven-year-old boy named Delbert McConnell was playing catch-up war, waiting in a stairwell to catch the breeze from the open door to the roof. His best friend Jimmy Loman was back in the hall, cursing out Del's family. Jimmy said Delbert's mom had these nasty chicken lips. Jimmy crowed, "Nasty is as nasty does." Delbert didn't mind. It was boasting on Jimmy's part, designed to stump him. And all because he was holding the superior weapon, a fine-looking Uzi made of lifelike plastic. It could spray up to a hundred yards and had two separate containers that held an even gallon of tap water. He was pumping the action when Jimmy started coming toward him, so Delbert went scooting down the ninth-floor hall corridor to get to Jimmy and fix him, Delbert yelling out, "I'm gonna get you now, mutha fucka!" and he stuck the muzzle of his pump-action Uzi around the corner, pressing the trigger hard so that the water streamed toward its target. "Got you now, niggah." He stepped out, with the gun in front, stepped into the view of Franklin P. Edwards who at twenty-four had been a housing cop for three months, four hours, and seventeen days.

Officer Edwards leaned back against the stairwell and it was him yelling "Help!" Doors pulled open. Edwards reached down for the machine gun saying, "See, he had a weapon."

"That's not real, stupidass. Look what you've done, man. Just look at the kid. Is he breathing? Got him right in the chest. Jesus, how many rounds did you let off? Where you think you are, idiot? Motherfucking Bosnia?"

Franklin looked down at what he held, finally realizing that the hard plastic body was not real metal and then, that the liquid seeping through his fingers from the wound in his own chest was water, not blood.

3

At 3:09 that morning, Detective Laurence Solomon came off the subway feeling bruised. It was because of staring down at that kid's body with a chorus of angry voices jamming in behind, the mother sobbing and wailing. Hot as hell in the hall. That idiot Edwards leaning against the wall, looking pulverized. Solomon knew half of it was regret, but the other half was fear. Edwards slunk back in against the wall for a damn good reason. Just seconds after Solomon arrived, the kid's mom had broken free from the huddle around the body and tried beating him to death with her closed fists. Miserable things went on in this world, most of them way past imagining.

There was one thing for certain, he needed a drink. Thinking this, he made a hard right toward Bertha's Liquor Locker. Then he caught sight of Lily wearing her usual later-than-midnight outfit, a silver lamé miniskirt and tube top. Solomon crossed the street, making an attempt to avoid her. Too late for that.

"Hey, big boy," Lily called out, then floated over on her high heels. "Give me a light," she said, holding her cigarette out.

"I don't smoke, Lil," he told her, sighing and looking her over. Lily was in her late thirties, too old to be out here on the street, too worn down from her habit not to try. She had the junkie twitch going, her eyes edging back and forth.

"I got a special tonight," she said gaily.

"Don't tell me about it, Lil. I'm not in the mood."

"Why not? You're off duty. Plus, a good-looking Nubian king like yourself. Tall and dignified. Solly, you're a regular gift from the gods."

"Not tonight."

"No time like the present." She narrowed her field of vision, then added, "I know, it's cause you're already tied up. Left a whole pack of females back at your crib. What you tell them, boyfriend? How you're going to bring them back a bedtime story and a bottle of Cristal?"

"How many you think I have hiding back there?"

"A whole damn harem. You got no other excuse for turning me down."

Solomon didn't bother disabusing her of that notion.

"If that's true I'm gonna have to buy myself the entire Brothers Grimm."

"What's that mean?"

Luckily, Lily didn't really care to have the reference explained. Instead, she sidled closer. "How about I give you some nice story to warm the coldest-hearted child." She peered up at him. "Be a friend, Solly. I been out here a whole two hours. Not even a how de do for me."

"Means it's time to go home, Lil. Go on. Keep yourself dry. There's a hurricane coming."

"They're always spooking you with those warnings," she said. "Last time, the only thing we got was a few raindrops."

Solomon picked up the pace, but Lily kept up, wobbling along on those heels. He wondered, for about the hundredth time, how women could manage with those damn platforms to heaven, their legs bending pitifully. What if someone was after you, damn, what if you really had to run? Then he smiled, considering. You could take one off and use it for a needle-sharp weapon.

Bertha's lights blazed up to greet them, the sign writ large in script in the window, OPEN ALL NIGHT. The shadow inside the double-thick plate glass was Bertha herself, overflowing, her hair pulled back into a red-checked kerchief. She was staring into a mini TV she had fixed on the ceiling, holding court with her faithful attendants, bottles of Stoli and Jim Beam, perched behind her.

"How 'bout you give a girl a loan?"

"I loan you something, what you gonna do? Make me accessory after the fact. Last time you OD'd, who was it scraping you up, carrying you over to Kings and sticking you in detox?"

"You're a saint, Laurence Solomon. Baby Jesus' right hand man."

"You know I can't, Lil," he said and felt sorry saying it. "Do something good for yourself. You're getting too old for this. Buy yourself a little piece of shame, Lil."

"Got no shame to get, I'm plumb out of shame," she told him, wrinkling up her nose. "All right, Solly. You been punishing me with all those words of yours. All right. Even an old dog like me can get lost."

She turned back abruptly and when she did, he felt guilty for a second. He should have given her what she wanted or enough for at least a dime bag, cause what did it matter? Everyone flew down the same fast track, the only question, how soon you made it to the cutoff. Solomon thought how his particular appointed task was basically to provide friction, a way of slowing down that free-fall descent.

Tonight that poor boy hadn't known his death was sneaking up. And suddenly, it was too late. He was gone, with his mom mourning the loss, weeping and wailing and asking God for reasons. Just some black kid lying on the tile floor, his plastic weapon ready to be tagged. Another little hero taken down in combat.

The bell rang as Solomon walked in the door. Bertha

looked up, saw it was him, and said, "Hi, handsome," her midnight smile emerging from the collection of wrinkles at her throat. Solomon asked for a bottle of Loch Dnu and she went searching, then pulled it down off a shelf. As soon as they'd made the exchange, money for black, sweet, sinfully smooth Scotch, she turned back to the TV screen.

Back outside, he saw Lily was gone. So was the moon, scurrying behind a thick sheet of clouds. Solomon turned the corner of his own block as a lightning bolt whistled through the sky. He unlatched the scrolled metal hook on his front-yard gate and stepped inside. The block behind him was quiet, private homes drowning in sleep, the only noise the hum of air conditioners. Still, he felt the back of his neck tingle. Turning, all he saw was an empty street with a strong wind shivering the branches of the honey locust.

It was when he turned the key in the lock. The slipslap sound of feet behind him, then a voice full of squeak saying, "Give it over, asshole."

This boy approximately the same age as the one he'd just zipped into a body bag, only this one's torn-sleeved T had a stamped-on photo of Notorious B.I.G. with the words LIVE FOREVER IN OUR HEARTS printed underneath the smiling bad-boy face. He wore a pair of shorts riding low over his hips to expose his boxers. Nappy hair bandannaed back, a nothing little kid holding a snub-nosed nine millimeter. The kid had to raise his arm at an angle to aim at Solomon's head and there was a tremble in his gun hand because of it.

"Give it up, man."

"What's that supposed to mean? Give up what?" Solomon asked softly.

"Your wallet. Give me your wallet. Come on. I'm gonna shoot."

"You're gonna shoot one way or another, right? Why give

you the wallet? Why don't you take it off me when I'm dead?"

Solomon watched the kid's finger nudging down on the trigger. The boy threw a glance back to the street. Solomon looked that way himself, to take in a late-model BMW parked at the nearest hydrant.

"Your little posse? This your initiation rite?" Solomon sighed at the blatant stupidity. "Shoot me and you're dead yourself, little big man. Strikes me that I can even smell the frying. Damn but that nappy hair's gonna singe. You're gonna be cooked clean through to nothing. A regular barbecue. You like that way to go?"

Solomon had the Loch Dnu wrapped in the crook of his left arm. He shifted it and acted as if he were going for his wallet. The kid licked his lips, thinking he was home free. Solomon sighed at the waste as he let the whole bottle of Loch Dnu crash down on the kid's arm. The gun dropped and the boy howled in pain as the bottle shattered against the pavement. In sympathy there was a peal of thunder and another flash of lightning. God on the warpath, Solomon thought, pulling out his own piece and shoving it in the kid's face.

"You must really be a virgin," he said. "You done picked yourself a cop."

"Shit," the boy muttered. Then turned and bolted. It took some courage or else blind luck, because Solomon wasn't even considering firing a round. Instead he admired the mutual retreat, the kid rounding the corner while his friends in the car took off with a squeal of tires and a moan of the accelerator.

The boy's arm was probably fractured. And staring down at the mess in front of his door, Solomon just had to shake his head.

Into the kitchen to wash the Loch Dnu off his hands. The rain came down in a rush, banging hard against the plate-glass windows. Opening the fridge, he found two containers of leftover Chinese. Up above, in the cupboard, a half-bottle of red wine he'd decided wasn't good for anything but cooking. Glenda had brought it over, meaning to make a gift, but it had been too new, leaving a sour taste behind. Solomon poured himself a stiff drink, held his breath, and swallowed. Then he went to turn on the shower, making the water bracing cold. Once inside he felt every ache there was in his forty-three-year-old body, his knees beaten up from too many pickup games, the whole edifice creaking and threatening to topple.

Three messages on his answering machine; Glenda, wondering where he was as she stood there like a fool at Louise's Crawdaddy Home-Style Cooking; Glenda, at home now, telling him in a nasty, played-out tone of voice how she'd had enough and no man in the world was going to get hisself inflated, treating her like this, not you either, Mr. Laurence-damn-Solomon; Glenda calling again from home to tell him he was a lowdown skunk and a goddamn coward for not calling her. Didn't he have the decency, didn't he have any respect? A good woman like herself deserved to be respected.

Laurence Solomon let out a low whistle of appreciation, even agreement. Then he lay down on the bed and closed his eyes, hoping for merciful sleep. Just as he was drifting off, the phone rang. He let the machine answer, but the bad news was Ruiz's voice saying, "Hey, partner. We got ourselves a floater."

Five-thirteen A.M. Laurence Solomon driving through the hurricane. The rain actually blowing sideways. He couldn't see an inch ahead. Sticking the siren on the hood, he tried to hold his own. WBLS was having an early-morning Lauryn Hill fest, playing "To Zion."

Then, just as he pulled into the parking lot behind the Coney Island Aquarium, the rain let up. Ruiz's old-model Buick Skylark sprawled over two spots. Getting out of the car, Solomon looked up and realized he was staring at the eye of the storm, a funnel of white and blue tucked inside the gray mass of clouds. Warm air clung to his body. He knocked on the window, and Ruiz started awake.

"Long time no see," Ruiz said, rolling down the window. "Hope I wasn't interrupting anything." He had a facetious grin on his face.

"And what would you be interrupting?"

"You and the lovely lady Glenda doing the nasty."

Solomon sighed. "Glenda's never going to give my sorry ass the time of day again."

"Don't you despair, Solly. She'll come around. You got to think historically."

Ruiz exited the vehicle, holding a wax-paper bag in his right fist. He extracted a huge, greasy cruller and took a bite. Watching as the vanilla cream pumped out of the end, Solomon felt his stomach knot.

They walked over to what used to be the Coney Island boardwalk. Waves made huge crests, banging down angrily to leave pools behind. Solomon sidestepped the most slippery parts of the wooden walkway and they circled around the aquarium to the empty lot where the water had tossed the girl's body. She looked peaceful, which was something given the collection of humanity surrounding her, the crew from the meatwagon and three tired-looking beat cops. She might have been sleeping, going to sleep to dream on the cement that was littered with other things the waves had brought in, driftwood, plastic bags, banged-up Pepsi cans, and the body of a baby shark, pure white, flipped over onto its back so you could read the long-toothed grin.

4

The Monday morning sky was crystal blue and the humidity had lost its punch. Emma's next-door neighbor, Irva Remedios, stood on the top step of her limestone stoop, declaiming. Irva, part-time librarian at the Brooklyn Public Library, and film trivia buff.

"They can't make a movie no more, I tell you. *Independence Day,* what was that? Just a rehash of *War of the Worlds. Men in Black* was cute, but please. For me the scariest movie I ever saw was one of those fifties sci-fi flicks. Go on, guess which."

"Invaders from Mars," Emma said. "The one where the boy is desperate because all the adults are being turned into aliens. He keeps asking people for help but it turns out every one of them has been taken over. They're wearing this zipper in the back of their necks, kind of like Chatty Cathy when you think about it. Then the kid wakes up and it's all a dream, and you breathe a huge sigh of relief until he looks out his window and there's a spaceship landing. I was six. I saw it on my grandmother's TV, one of those old black-and-white Zeniths. For years after that, I'd wake up in a cold sweat. Of course, in my dream I was the kid and the zipper necks were my parents. What's your reading?"

"Your parents were aliens? I don't know about that, doll." Irva wrinkled her nose, apparently considering. "Could be. Did you see the remake?"

Emma shook her head.

"Didn't miss much. The new ones aren't ever as good as the originals. I was thinking of *Invasion of the Body Snatchers*. Remember that one? Kevin getting those wide eyes whenever he finds another one of those pods. Did you know he's the brother of that writer, Mary McCarthy? Plenty of talent in that family." Irva paused, inhaled the newly freshened air and added, "Beautiful day."

"Absolutely gorgeous," Emma agreed.

There was a temperate silence. Emma knew Irva was aching to ask about something a lot more intimate than sci-fi flicks. By now, everyone on the block had to be aware of Will's escape. If Emma listened hard, she could hear them whispering. Had he been cheating on her? Was it something else? Was he secretly gay? In a world of endless possibilities, her neighbors could endlessly amuse themselves.

And here she was, barefoot and pregnant, just like the song. Emma glanced at her own naked feet, poised on the cement steps. She did appreciate the absurdity of her situation. Human beings are the most arrogant creatures in the universe, she thought. Imagining we can plan out our lives.

Think of it this way, she told herself, you never believed you'd even have one kid. Still, she also had to admit that after Liam's birth, she'd walked around in a haze of goodwill. Having a child had clearly been the best thing she'd ever done. And Will had seemed to agree wholeheartedly, he was such a devoted father. Which was why she'd been so shocked when he firmly refused to consider having a second.

"We can't." He'd stacked up a list of reasons, chief among them their jobs and her already sizable litany of complaints.

And she had agreed, or was it that she'd simply given in. It *had* made a certain kind of sense. Plus, there was always Liam.

So Emma used her diaphragm religiously. Besides, she thought, feeling defensive, by the age of forty, half your eggs were supposed to be calcified. Certainly, in the preceding year, Will's fastidious avoidance and her own diminished appetite had put sex on the endangered list. Then, six weeks before, they'd taken a weekend off, staying in a Gothic hotel up in the Adirondacks. Had it been the atmosphere in that tower suite, or the lack of context? While Liam went canoeing and horseback riding, the two of them had made love. Late afternoon, the light slanting across the wooden floor, the coils of the bed squeaking underneath them; they'd joined together tenderly, like the old friends they sometimes were. And afterward, the three of them had dinner in a hall full of similarly happy families.

Two weeks went by. Will was off at the western front. And Emma missed her period. Tension, she decided, premenopausal symptoms. Unfortunately, her body resisted this interpretation, transforming itself, her breasts turning voluptuous, her stomach puffing out. She knew it was crazy to invest in the test kit, crazier still to take the urine sample, peeing into the plastic cup and adding litmus paper that immediately turned cerulean blue. She refused to believe, until her doctor called her to tell her about the results of the blood work. That was when her courage evaporated.

So easy to tot up the mistakes. Mistake number one, not telling Will over the phone, losing her mind instead. Mistake number two, thinking that all she'd have to do was see his face and the words would spill out, that then he'd go all limp and deed her permission, saying, "Sure, Em, let's do this again. Em, I was thinking last night how sad that this part of our life was gone forever, it was the best, the very best."

She agreeing, "Yes, it was."

As if having another child would fix everything that was going wrong between us, Emma thought, I'm only a tad deluded. She had to crack a smile.

Having a baby with Will as a partner was one thing. Because, at the beginning, he'd been wonderful, sharing the late-night feedings and bone-deep exhaustion. Not that he would have been able to do that the second time around, even if he had been willing. And not that it was even an option now, she reminded herself. Emma rubbed her eyes, trying to achieve clarity. She knew there was another wild card to factor in. Liam, who had been teetering on the brink of independence this whole year. Emma wanted to see him safely through to the other side. She considered the sort of adjustment she would be asking him to make if she decided to keep this baby. It was certainly unfair. Without Will there, Liam would demand, and deserve, her undivided attention. I can tell Will, she thought for the thousandth time. Then discarded the thought. She couldn't imagine saying it, no, every possible scenario was degrading. Get an abortion, she told herself. It's the smartest thing to do. The fairest, too. Still, thinking this, she felt a wave of panic.

Irva excused herself to make dinner. Emma knew what was cooking, a Puerto Rican version of pot roast. Over the years the smell had become imbedded in the wall that separated their two homes. During Emma's first pregnancy it had made her unbearably nauseous. This time, however, she found it comforting.

Down the block Liam was squatting near his best friend Tony as they planned some kind of bipolar street-hockey strategy. Emma took a seat on the stoop and opened the *Times,* turning to the metropolitan section. The caption read DISTRICT ATTORNEY MOSES PLANS DEATH PENALTY ASSAULT. Once again, Reggie was in the spotlight.

Emma read on. Apparently Reg was finally deserting the cause. Emma wasn't surprised. He'd only been waiting for the right case to come along. This could be it. Loretta Picard was white, disgruntled, and clearly homicidal. The sort of trial that could jump-start Reggie's move from courthouse to state house. Emma knew his tactics so damn well.

Ten years ago, when she'd been chief investigator for Jersey Capital Crimes, Reggie had been their brightest legal mind. Back then, she and Reg had been a tough team to beat; young, energetic, and, of course, idealistic.

But he'd been the first to man the lifeboats, crossing the Hudson to escape, changing from oversized Afro to a short cut, going from jeans to Armani, in other words, going over to the prosecutorial side. Up till now he'd refused to alter his position on the death penalty. But apparently that last vestige of his former morality was about to be exorcised.

"Look at me," Liam yelled. He went skating by, jumped over a cardboard box someone had left in the middle of the street and came to a sudden stop. Turning back, he put up one gloved hand to wave.

"Terrific!" Emma yelled. Tony was careening up behind him. Tony grabbed onto Liam for support.

"You two be careful," she cautioned, as they swayed, then righted themselves. Liam rolled his eyes, his typical response to her pleas for caution.

"God, Mom!" Like how could anyone be so dense. Then he skated off.

Emma sighed. She looked down her home block and saw Nesbitt on his stoop, taking in the sun. He waved. She waved back. Nes worked as a lighting designer in the theater. Now that Bea was busy with school, Emma used him to fill in with babysitting. Suzanne, Tony's mom, was his next-door neighbor and Suze had been Emma's best friend since college. She and her husband Al had bought on the block two months after Will and Emma. Liam and Tony had been born three hours apart, Suze and Emma bunking together on the St. Vincent's maternity ward. For years, the boys had spent every waking moment bonded at the hip.

It will help to live here, she decided. Then she sighed, shaking her head. Why hadn't she grabbed on to Will and hung on for dear life? Was it really because she would have had to beg him to stay? No. It was his tone of voice. Will had sounded so determined, so completely sure.

Emma unrolled the *Daily News* and scanned the headlines. The second page had a split photo, Reggie on one side looking dapper, Loretta Picard on the other in handcuffs, her tongue stuck out at the photographer. Loretta's skin-short hair did not detract from her spectacular good looks. A rock-'n'-roll princess, Emma thought, just the kind of kid you wanted to be when you were a teenager, just the kind your parents warned you against. The headline read, MOSES SEEKS DEATH.

Liam was pushing the puck down the middle of the street. Emma saw the Bergen Street bus crossing Bond, then roaring toward him. He was flailing away at Tony with his stick, completely unaware of the danger. She jumped up, waving her hands in his direction, then flew down the steps. Up at the other end of the street, Nesbitt leapt into action. He flung himself in front of the bus. Brakes squealed and the driver cursed, offering him the finger for his trouble. Meanwhile, Liam grabbed the puck, lifting it high above his head.

"Get out of the street," Emma screamed, as she grabbed for Liam, and dragged him to safety. "What's wrong with you two? I told you to pay attention!"

Liam was grinning. He poked Tony in the ribs.

"Did you see how I got the puck away from Tone like that? I'm gonna try out for the Rangers."

"If you live that long," Emma said icily. "You could have been killed. Nesbitt almost was."

"Nothing happened, hey, I said I was sorry. Sorry, Nes." He enunciated each word clearly, his eyes flashing defiance. It's enough to make you crazy, Emma thought.

* * *

That morning, Liam had woken her with an accusation. "Why'd you tell Dad to leave?" he'd demanded, leaning over the bed. She had rubbed her eyes, attempting to marshal her weakened defenses.

"That's not how it is at all," she'd offered. "Is that what he said?"

Liam hadn't bothered to respond. He'd simply stalked out. Had he decided to take his father's side unbidden?

Emma knew where this could go if she didn't take care. Plenty of divorced mothers forged alliances with their children by hand-feeding them bitter doses of information, ammunition to use against the absent parent. He'll have to make up his own mind, she decided, attempting, once again, to grab a piece of that moral high ground. Then she realized that she was deluding herself.

Great, she told herself, morally superior. And currently detested.

"Thank you, Nes," she said.

"No problem. Those boys are getting wild."

"Christ, go on you two," Emma said, ruffling Liam's hair. He ducked away and took off down the block like a newly freed prisoner. He moved so quickly she felt the breeze press her back, and was convinced those were sparks flying off the metal wheels. They settled in at Tony's house where they each took three turns jumping off the top of his stoop, before disappearing inside.

"What'cha gonna do, Emma. They're being boys," Nesbitt said. "I used to drive my mom crazy, too."

"Like this?"

"Actually, I used to pretend to be the Rose Bowl queen and dress up in this pink dress of my older sister's. Then I'd make the other kids push me down the street on a float."

"Sounds safer," Emma said.

"In West Texas?" Nes offered a harsh laugh.

She joined him. Then felt the familiar catch in her throat. Shit, she thought, suddenly fighting back tears. Loneliness, she told herself, loneliness and hormones. Except the truth ran deeper. She cursed her blindness. Emma knew her life had been based on one apparently reasonable assumption. She'd trusted Will in a way that now seemed comical, imagining a future where they would grow old gracefully, in tandem, a future where all the current tension would miraculously dissolve. Really, it was astonishing. She, the ultimate pragmatist, had been trapped by a fantasy. How did it happen, she wondered, as waves of guilt and disbelief rolled over her. They were a byproduct of Will's abandonment and a further reason for embarrassment. She'd broken down on the No. 2 train going south; on line inside the restroom of the Cobble Hill Cinema; in the middle of placing an order at Jim and Andy's, the neighborhood fruit stand. And when you started sobbing for no reason out in public, New Yorkers automatically turned away, latching their eyes onto something safe. As if you were displaying a missing limb, she thought, and begging them for charity.

Emma rubbed her eyes clear. Nesbitt reached out to hug her. "Give me a call if you need anything," he said. She felt her cheeks turn to flame.

"I'll be fine," she said, automatically shrugging him off.

"I know you will."

"Thanks." Emma felt ashamed of the degree of ice in her voice. She had always hated to display weakness. He's your friend, she told herself. Still, she turned away, climbing up her own front steps and shutting the door firmly. She leaned against it and told herself that everyone must have moments like this. The ones where you lapse into self-pity and start totting up the reasons.

Striding to the refrigerator for more fortification, Emma

reached for a beer. She took the cap off the bottle, then found herself unable to take even the smallest sip. Instead, she sat down on one of the kitchen chairs. Outside the window, the maple tree looked remarkably healthy and happy.

You can't feel envious of a tree.

A drawing Liam had made the previous year hung on the kitchen wall, Spiderman throwing his web over a recalcitrant bad guy. Will had framed it himself. Will stepping onto one of the kitchen chairs, his long dirty-blond hair pulled back in a ponytail, his green eyes twinkling. So proud of his son. So proud of everything he did. Throwing Liam a look of limitless affection. She remembered how he'd turned his gaze onto her, and knew she'd been a fool. She had thought what resided inside was comfortable and dependable.

Light streamed into the kitchen from the five-foot-high windows. In the garden, late August bloomers filled a side bed, slashes of orange lilies and red hollyhocks. Irva had drawn up a blueprint, then Emma planted the beds herself. She and Will had scraped three coats of paint off the kitchen walls, working together to turn it from infirmary blue to a brilliant white. They'd sanded down the floors. In labor with Liam, she'd walked back and forth along the second floor landing, panting like a dog whenever she felt a contraction.

That night, Emma read Liam forty-seven pages of *Aliens Ate My Homework* and made him two peanut butter and jelly sandwiches. When she leaned over to kiss him goodnight, he pulled away from her, covering his head.

She went downstairs and filled a tall glass with the rest of the half bottle of Jameson's Will had left behind. She looked longingly at it for what seemed like an eternity, then took it over to the sink and poured it down the drain. Things are never as bad in the morning, she thought, folding her body into bed and tucking the covers in, then shaking her head as she acknowledged the impotence of her own, paltry lie.

5

"I know you're there, Emma."

"Who is this?" she demanded. The ringing phone had roused her from sleep. She blinked at the clock. It was not even six.

"It's Dawn," the disembodied voice said. "Did you see about Reg? Did you see what that turncoat bastard's handing us?"

"Jesus," Emma said. Semiconscious, she was still aware of feeling ploughed under. And completely miserable.

"Are you there, Em? Pay attention because I'm about to make you one hell of an offer."

"Are you crazy?" It was a rhetorical question. Dawn Prescott had always had her own code of behavior. When she had been Emma's boss at Jersey Capital Crimes, wake up calls like this were the standard.

A fresh-faced sociology grad student, Emma had been doing fieldwork for her dissertation, its broad theme, class background and the inequity of death penalty law. First stop, the New Jersey capital defender's office, a hole in the wall in the most bombed-out part of Trenton. She'd gone there to interview their lead counsel, Dawn. By the end, Emma had been the one answering questions. About her parents, old lefties who'd paid a real price for their political views. About her own goals and how far the graduate degree would take her. Then Dawn had completely turned the tables, offering her a job. Emma had surprised herself by agreeing. At twenty-eight, she found herself stepping into prison cells in Rahway and arriving at crime scenes as fast as her VW Beetle could carry her. Within two years she was a full-time investigator, finding out more about the backgrounds of Dawn's court-assigned clients than their own mothers knew; in four more, Dawn bumped her up so that she was in charge of the entire investigative staff.

First Reg left. Then Emma. And finally Dawn. Now head of the New York capital defender's office, she was running a new bunch of brilliant young things ragged.

"I want you to come on with me," Dawn said. "It's perfect timing."

Emma walked into the bathroom, nestling the phone under her ear. She drenched her face with cold water.

"Are you there, Em?"

"You must be desperate," Emma said, dabbing her face.

"I'm excited, not desperate. The idea just came to me out of the blue. And the more I looked at it, the better it seemed. Desperate? I've never been desperate in my life."

Emma laughed. That was such an obvious lie.

"Liam's a grown boy now, so you can't use that as an excuse," Dawn told her.

"Grown? He's ten years old. And I do have a few other commitments," Emma said. "I have a life, Dawn."

"So work part time for a few months till you get everything squared away."

"You and I both know that won't suit. Your idea of part time is a fifty-hour workweek."

"I'm serious about this," Dawn said. "Is it Liam? Look, Em, you don't have to feel sorry for him. He'll cope. Everyone I know is a child of divorce."

"So that's it," Emma said, reeling from the sucker punch. "Who told you?"

"That's not important," Dawn said.

"Will and I aren't getting a divorce," Emma said.

"Really?" Dawn hardly sounded convinced. "Look, Em, most people would try to spare your feelings here, but what's the point? Kids are survivors. And this job would be the best thing for you, perfect for keeping your mind off things."

Emma wanted to slam down the phone, then realized her anger was actually dissipating, worse, she was beginning to see the humor. Only Dawn was socially inept enough to try this sort of approach. Dawn would use any tactic to make you believe it was in your best interests to cave in. It was why she was so great in court, scalpel sharp. It was also why her idea of a homelife meant sharing an apartment with two cats who got fed by a neighbor or placed in cages at the local veterinarian's office whenever she got some downtime. For relaxation, Dawn liked to set off on Outward-Bound-style vacations. Her last one had been dog sledding in the shrinking Alaskan wilderness.

"I'm thinking sixty-five to start," Dawn said. "What do you say, Em?"

"What do I say?" Emma grinned. As if Dawn would ever care to hear her honest opinion.

"You're worrying too much about that kid of yours," Dawn insisted. "He's going to do what he wants, regardless. Think of what we were like. All those days I sat at my parents' dining room table stoned out of my gourd. They never even guessed."

"So Liam's going to turn to drugs to salve the pain? Dawn, you never know when to let things drop," Emma said. Then she firmly returned the phone to its cradle.

Emma dressed, got her first cup of coffee and retrieved the daily papers. The *Times* had an interview with Delbert McConnell's mother. She and Al Sharpton were leading a demonstration to the Fulton Mall Toys Я Us. Emma turned to the *News*. This headline read: UNKNOWN BEAUTY DROWNED, and a grainy photo showed the girl's body, wet hair draped over her face. Underneath it in smaller type the headline read: ANTI-GUN PROTEST PLANS FIRST ASSAULT: page 2.

The Picard case had lost ground. On page three there was a story about Dawn's move to suppress Loretta's jailhouse confession, claiming it had been coerced. The accompanying photo showed Loretta Picard as a teenager, a girl with dark hair and an angular jawline. What a pain-in-the-ass case, Emma thought, but for a second she did consider her own approach. And for a second more, she caught herself wondering what brick walls Dawn had hit. Plenty if she's calling me, Emma decided. Sixty-five is no way good enough. Of course, that's bait. She'll be willing to go up from there. And whatever she ends up offering, I'm going to be the one who'll have to fly to Timbuktu to interview Ms. Picard's former guidance counselor. Plus, after Loretta Picard, someone else will need my hands-on attention. I'll be leaving the house at 2:00 A.M. to get to a crime scene. It was fine when I was a sweet young thing. But ten years is practically a time warp. Ten years ago my hair was naturally brown and when I talked about touch-ups, I was referring to flaking paint, not liposuction. Ten years ago, when I drank a cup of coffee, I felt as if I'd inhaled rocket fuel. Now I need it just to crawl from the bed to the bathroom. Talk about diminishing powers.

"I put that one to rest," she said aloud, turning the page. The photo of the drowned beauty confronted her. And she realized she was gazing into Beatriz Castillo's wide-open eyes.

"Are you awake?" Emma asked Suzanne.

"Barely."

"I'm coming over." She hung up quickly, not trusting her voice.

Irva had carved a brick walkway that meandered between all the backyard gardens on the block. This path made it easier for her to water and fertilize. Emma used it for more parochial reasons, as the quickest route to her best friend's house.

"What's so important?" Suzanne asked. She had on her morning outfit, a sports bra and a pair of well-worn gym shorts. She looked nervous and Emma couldn't blame her. A week ago it had been a small enough thing, Will's defection. Emma handed her the paper and Suzanne pursed her lips, squinting as she lifted the newsprint closer to her face.

"What?" she asked.

Emma breathed a sigh of relief. But Suzanne kept staring down. Then she shook her head incredulously. "It looks like Bea," she said. "Look, Em, these things lie. You couldn't recognize your own mother."

They both peered at the photograph. Then Suzanne strode over to the phone.

"I tried already," Emma said. "The machine was on. I did leave a message."

"So we'll wait for her to call back."

"I called yesterday, too," Emma said. "There's never been a time when she hasn't gotten back in touch with me within a day. Plus, I tried her cell."

"It can't be Bea," Suzanne said. Sinking into a deck chair, she nodded, underscoring her own sagacity. "That boyfriend of hers would have missed her. He would have put out an all-points bulletin."

"But if it *is* Bea, and I'm only offering up the possibility, you understand, she wouldn't have gone in the water alone. You know how phobic she is."

Suzanne's face went pale. "All right, what's the plan, Em? You always have a plan."

Fifteen minutes later, Suzanne was comfortably ensconced in Emma Price's living room. She had pulled out Emma's workout mat, dusted it off, and was bending herself into a pretzel.

"Youch," Emma said.

"It's incredibly relaxing," Suzanne told her. "You should try it."

"Sure, I should," Emma agreed. Although she really couldn't even imagine.

When she was safely inside her car, Emma flipped on her mobile phone. For so many years she'd been able to turn to Will for comfort. Innumerable times during the course of their marriage, she'd called him to complain about the irritations of daily life; including probably the most exciting story she'd had to relate, the time she'd been sideswiped by a gypsy cab and she had given chase up to Flatbush Avenue and around the park drive, eventually cutting him off at the entrance to the BQE by careening in front of a late-model Lincoln Continental. Laughing, she'd told Will that all it had taken was one look at her face to get the Russian driver to sheepishly surrender his insurance card. She'd also called to alert Will to the triumphs he'd missed, Liam's first independent steps, his first soccer goal, his bravery when he strapped on ice skates and sailed off for the very first time, without even a backward glance.

No answer. When the service picked up, she left a cryptic message. Old habits die hard, she told herself, feeling a pang.

In front of the Gowanus housing project, the police were out in force. A small group of marchers huddled together, holding a banner that read, CHILDREN ARE NOT TARGETS. STOP THE KILLING.

Emma drove into the no-man's-land near the public pool. The small community park that surrounded it was province of the scungiest group of hookers imaginable. The girls were wearing short silver miniskirts and tube tops with platform shoes. They took mincing steps toward the cars to ascertain whether they were potential customers. Not one of them looked to be above drinking age.

Crossing Third Avenue, Emma passed factories. She cruised past Fourth where the housing stock changed. Row houses lined the block. A fully manned domino game was in progress in front of the gated windows of Harry's Hardware.

On Fifth, several six-story apartment buildings mixed with smaller, two family homes. The ground floors held a variety of paying businesses, a bodega, Price Discount Drugs, and a Santeria with Jesus statues prominently displayed in the window. At 396, a Puerto Rican flag waved from a cracked flagpole. The downstairs housed a social club with red velvet curtains pulled shut against inquiring eyes.

Bea had rented the apartment two years earlier when her mother had decided to move to Florida. Back then, she'd been in her second year at Brooklyn College and had worked for Emma five afternoons a week. In addition to paying for her college health insurance plan, Emma had bought Bea a fully loaded computer system as a housewarming present. Her friends told her she was crazy, but she'd insisted Bea was worth it. Emma firmly believed that no one but a member of his immediate family could have loved Liam more.

She buzzed 4G. No response. Emma examined the street traffic. Several passersby in workday clothes hurried toward the F train. She squared her shoulders, then turned back, pressing buzzer after buzzer until some fool let her in.

The interior hallways were clean and smelled of ammonia but the paint job was several years old. A large gash showed through the plaster, exposing a corroded heating pipe. Emma climbed the stairs to 4G and banged on the door. Then she closed her eyes and did what stood in for prayer in her mind, imagining the most immediate future, seeing the boyfriend with the odd name, Chazz. Ever since his arrival on the scene, Bea had been busy, her babysitting hours decreasing dramatically, until she finally cut down to weekends and the stray emergency call. Although they'd never met, Emma had taken liberties, imagining a dark-haired boy with affectionate eyes and a hearty laugh. Right now, more than anything, she wished for his appearance at the door. Then he'd call Bea, who would emerge, still flushed with sleep, leaning on his well-proportioned shoulder, Bea offering that full-blown smile and saying, "Mrs. Price, this is pretty early to come visiting." In return, Emma would gladly extend her most profuse apology. Then they could laugh together at her fears, undoubtedly a product of her own recent marital discord, another feature of a world that was suddenly being ripped apart at the seams. Emma heard Bea saying, "You thought that was me? Oh my God, that's so terrible," saw that blend of disbelief and sympathy offered in a look.

No one answered. And Emma's anxiety grew. She pounded on the green wood with a closed fist. The hallway smelled of cooking. Pacing up and down the corridor, she was eventually able to identify the source. Arroz con pollo, she thought, ringing the bell to apartment 4R. Floorboards creaked, tumblers rolled back, and the door was pulled the length of the police lock. An older Hispanic woman with a face full of makeup and a head full of curlers, peered out.

"I'm a friend of Beatriz Castillo," Emma said.

"¿Beatriz? ¿Quién es?"

"*Perdóneme.* 4G, *sabe...una pequita...una hermosa, una linda...*" Emma pointed toward Bea's apartment.

"*Oh...sí, sí,*" The woman's eyes brightened with intelligence. "That sweet girl?"

"That's right. Beatriz."

"She is just so very nice, so nice a girl."

"Have you seen her?"

"*Sí.* Yes I saw her."

"Today?"

"*Sí, hoy.*"

Emma nodded, already smiling her relief. But then the woman slowly shook her head.

"Oh, not today, no, not this day."

"When?"

"The day before this day. All right?"

"And her friend. The boy, Chazz?"

"*¿Quién es?*"

"*¿El esposo de Beatriz?*"

"Don't know for him. Don't talk for him. You just wait. You just wait *por* someone will come. For sure, for very sure. Soon." She clucked her tongue and closed the door firmly in Emma's face.

Emma felt defeated. I should try every one of these goddamn apartments, Emma told herself. I should go up and down the stairs and bust them in with a battering ram. Someone might have seen Bea this morning, setting off to work. Someone might have waved to her as she left the building and walked north to the train, holding on to the arm of her beloved Chazz.

Emma leaned against the wall and looked around at the tile floor, at the still, empty hallway. She shook her head and thought to herself how everything in this world was suddenly unfamiliar.

Outside the graffiti-covered front door, it was terminally hot, the air on Fifth Avenue shimmering.

Suzanne had taken the boys out to a store down the street that sold morning fortification in the shape of Dunkin' Donuts. They greeted Emma at the door, waving their booty, lustrous silver cards of helmeted men with team names slashed across their bodies. The men looked brutish and slightly unkempt. Emma knelt down beside Liam. She fully understood how he would never realize that her ability to speak on this topic was a measure of her love.

During the Stanley Cup playoffs, Liam would nestle in the crook of Will's arm, their elbows displacing her from the bed, the two men in her life settling in to share bowls of popcorn and make rapid-fire, play-by-play commentary. A vision from another lifetime. Emma swallowed hard, remembering.

"We're going to trade," Liam said. He and Tony stared down at the sorted piles, then began to finger them lovingly. Taking her leave, Emma found Suzanne sitting on the deck off the kitchen, smoking a cigarette.

"I thought you'd quit!" Emma exclaimed.

"I have one now and then."

"What about that holier-than-thou, purity-of-the-body crap you always give me?"

"I figure I'm just about pure enough to tempt fate." Suzanne flicked the cigarette away. "Well?" she asked. "Do you have an answer?"

"Bea's not there," Emma said, taking the redwood chair next to her oldest friend. She looked out at the towering maple. It had been planted a hundred years ago, back when these houses were worker's homes, providing places for hired help who spent their lives in domestic service at the stately mansions lining the blocks of nearby Brooklyn

Heights. A century later, those residents had been pushed out by artistically minded urbanites and upper-middle-class racially mixed couples.

"Will called to say he just got back in town. I told him what was happening. He wanted to come over but I thought he'd better speak with you first. Did I do right?"

"You did," Emma said. She knew that Suzanne believed herself fully briefed on her best friend's current plight. She was wrong, of course. Suzanne knew nothing about the pregnancy. The last thing Emma wanted right now was advice. She slid her hands protectively over her belly, and glanced down, self-conscious.

"Will might be a help," Suzanne offered.

"So I imagined when I called him."

"He did mention that you phoned." Suzanne gave a scrutinizing look. "Call him back. Invite him over."

"And then what?" Emma asked it honestly, as if Suzanne possessed a spyglass through which she could view the future. "We don't even know if it's Bea. We're jumping to conclusions." A fairly tepid argument, but the best she could offer. "I mean, realistically," she added, "what are the chances?"

"I'm not giving odds," Suzanne said. "Will offered to help. Why not take him up on it? As far as I'm concerned, everyone gets to be an asshole once in their life. How else can they meet the person they would most hate themselves for becoming?"

"You think this is about Will being selfish and petty?" Emma asked. "You think it's some momentary lapse?"

Suzanne leaned over and gave Emma Price a kiss on the cheek. "You can't stop loving someone or needing them just like that."

"No," Emma said ruefully. "But wouldn't it make life a whole lot easier?"

Suzanne nodded, and reached out, caressing Emma's knee.

"Don't pity me," Emma said. "If you do, I'll have to pity myself. Then all hope is lost. I shouldn't have called him. It was only force of habit." She stared down at the paper that sat on the table between them. The drowned girl's face peered out of the photograph. Standing, Emma picked up the newspaper and stuck it in her back pocket. Then she turned on her heel, heading for the phone.

Three years earlier on a frigid December day, Emma had watched from the back of the room as Reginald Moses was sworn in as Manhattan district attorney. Reg had looked every inch the star in his Armani suit, with a tastefully subtle lavender tie. So handsome. So dapper. So notably African American. During the press conference afterward, he was soft-spoken, yet forceful. He'd run for election right after three out-of-control police officers had beaten a Haitian club patron senseless, landing him in a wheelchair. Reg got Jesse Jackson and Sharpton to stump for him and all the good Upper West Side liberals had voted, giving him a razor-thin margin of victory. Dawn had thought she could pique Emma's interest by playing up Reg's nouvelle villain status. But Emma and Reg had been close friends since day one.

I've always admired predatory males, Emma thought. They look great from a distance. Because Reggie was the type of man who would sidearm you to get onto the 5:16 train. Then, if you happened to fall onto the track, if you happened to die a gruesome death because of it, he would never actually know. He'd be comfortably ensconced in his seat, with his *Times* unfurled, dutifully reading all the news that was fit to print.

"Emma Price, one of my favorite people," Reggie said.

"You're making headlines," she said.

There was a weighty silence.

"I'm not calling to admonish you," she assured him. "No way am I going to start a discussion about your apparent conversion right before I ask a favor. I'm not that crazy."

He chuckled.

Half an hour later she was standing outside the door of the Kings County morgue.

The detectives assigned to the case were running late. Which gave Emma time to reflect. She was not by nature a person who enjoyed the spectacle of someone else's misery. As chief investigator in Jersey, she'd always made herself immediately familiar with all the gory details, but she kept her work and home life separate. Driving by a wreck on the highway, there were some who stared inside the crushed metal, hoping for blood, but Emma chose to avert her eyes. And if a low-flying jet soared over her, she did not wish for it to crash, leaving behind a trail of burning fuel and mangled bodies. Yet here she was now. Only one way to cope. It was the way she'd managed in the past when she'd had to make unscheduled trips to blood-spattered rooms or found herself walking into the central morgue in Jersey City or Newark.

She lied. She told herself there was no connection between her own, animate self and the body she was about to see, pulled out on a metal trolley. She pretended to be a surgeon, deciding this was a way of learning how to move her scalpel, splicing together endings, irrigating arteries, finding terminals that led to, of all things, the heart gone cold and silent.

Emma crossed her arms and leaned back against the off-white wall, wishing she had some bad habit that was socially acceptable, but she had never been addicted to nicotine. And she wasn't about to light up a joint in the bathroom across the hall. So all she had left was anxiety. It flooded her body, making her palms itch, and making her gasp. White-coated residents and blue-smocked orderlies added to the tension, racing by down the poorly lit corridor. At the end of the hall, elevator doors slid open disgorging a gurney. She pressed her body back against the wall as the attendants moved their charge directly past. The door to the morgue swung open, then closed with a vacuum-packed whoosh.

She dug her hands deep into her pockets, bunching them into fists, and suddenly wishing she was somewhere, any-where, else.

"Mrs. Price?"

Two men strode down the hall. She nodded and stuck out her hand.

"I'm Detective Miguel Ruiz and this is my partner, Detec-tive Laurence Solomon." Ruiz's palm was cool. He released hers a little too quickly.

Miguel Ruiz was an older man with pockmarked skin and a thatch of black hair. He wore a T-shirt under a plaid summer-weight jacket. His pants were cheap black double-knits. "We're very glad you decided to come down here," he said. "We appreciate any kind of civilian assistance."

Emma didn't trust herself to speak. She nodded instead, swallowing several times, then wrapping her arms around her chest for comfort.

"This must be hard," he added, offering a conciliatory look. "Would you like to wait for a few minutes? We could get you some coffee. We could talk a little first."

Emma shook her head.

"Then you're ready?" He held the door open, putting up a cautionary hand. "Mrs. Price, don't think you have to be brave." Looking up at him, she realized he was almost as nervous as she was. "What you do is, if something's getting to you at any time, you just leave," Ruiz said. "We won't think anything of it. What we're after, first and foremost, is the positive ID."

"I'll be fine," Emma said and felt grateful. His anxiety offered her a familiar role. In reassuring him, she was able to calm herself and point out, yet again, that she was one of those special people. You know. The kind who always managed to forge ahead, regardless.

Inside, a blue-suited assistant was busy making notes on the corpse she'd seen being wheeled in; the sheet had been pulled back to reveal an elderly white man with a gunshot wound to the chest. Emma made herself look him over carefully. All the body parts were in evidence. He's dead and gone, she told herself. His soul has flown off to China, no, farther than that, to the outer reaches of the solar system. He's studying quasars. He knows everything important in the world. Then she reconsidered. What if he hasn't gone anywhere? What if he's hanging around this room to see what sort of mess they make? What if he's taunting me right now, doing a jig and dancing naked on the ceiling?

"Okay, so far?" Ruiz was asking. The nervous smile flared out again. Disliking him did help. Even if it was simply a matter of convenience.

Ruiz motioned to the attendant and the drawer began to roll out.

If this was my child, Emma thought. Now that would be the hardest thing to bear. Yes, if someone threw Liam out a window, watched him fall from bone-shattering heights, watched him die without caring?

For Liam, for the child I'd been unable to protect? Emma closed her eyes and saw the solution.

You'd pick up a knife, a common kitchen implement. You'd leave the house searching for the bastard. You'd get onto an ocean-going vessel. You'd journey as far east as the rising sun. You'd find the man woman boy girl who did this and stab them repeatedly.

Her stomach wasn't giving way. That, at least, was a blessing.

"Here she is," Ruiz said. "Lucky she wasn't in there too long. She's not too swollen."

Emma noted the tag on the toe, then she began to pray. She looked up at the unveiled body slowly and saw that her prayers could do no earthly good.

"You know her?" Ruiz asked.

"Yes," Emma said.

"You need to tell us her name, honey."

"Bea...Beatriz Castillo."

Emma looked down at the floor. There were stains on the blue tile that no amount of mopping could expunge. The attendant rolled the drawer back into place and stepped away, offering her the space to mourn. She looked up again as the drawer clicked shut. Number 47...that's your number, Beatriz. Play it in the lottery. Go down to the corner and make a bet with the numbers man. Win this one time.

6

Laurence Solomon had been talking with a crank when that self-righteous prick of a lieutenant, Bernardino, charged into his office. Ruiz had been busy, too, wolfing down one of those stale cheese Danishes that Blind Willie sold out front. He'd had his eyes shut tight, humming while he ate. The woman on the other end of the phone line had been raving on about a girl named Larissa and how she was sure the no-name floater in the *Daily News* pullout was that same fucking whore. Laurence had just rolled her particulars up into a ball and was heading it for the hoop he'd posted right above his trashcan, when Bernardino stuck his face inside, glancing at Ruiz who was floating in carbohydrate heaven, then pushing his nose up close, pugnaciously letting his face measure all levels of disgust.

"Got someone from that shithead DA's office coming down to help you ID that floater."

"What are they after?" Solomon had asked. Like Bernardino would give him an answer.

Bernardino had broken out into a crushing smile. "Where'd you get that nice suit? Today's Man?"

And with that standing in for clever repartee, he'd turned on his heel.

Later they were in a private office just down the hall from the morgue. Solomon's eyes skated over the ME's personal effects; a pile full of paperwork, photos of the kids and husband. Today's Man. Sad, Solomon thought. No way would he ever set foot in that sort of lowbrow discount store. Bernardino was, and would always be, a fool.

Bernardino hated him. Why? Because Solomon had worked himself up from the ranks, street beat to detective in two short years. The lieutenant was sure that favors had been given. Bernardino came from an old-line Italian family in Canarsie but the way he talked, you'd think they'd come over in blue uniforms on the *Mayflower*. When the fact was, they'd immigrated from Sicily in the twenties, gotten their share of abuse and risen up. Bernardino didn't seem to have an eye for the parallels. More frankly put, he didn't think a "niggah" could get anywhere on his own.

Thought he was sinking Laurence Solomon by sticking him with Ruiz. Miguel already in his late forties, a career guy who spent a lot of time insuring his own personal safety. Miguel also the proud owner of a split-level in Jericho and a thirty-foot cabin cruiser named *Rosa Brava*. A flying fish he'd caught down in the Florida Keys hung over his desk. On the bulletin board he'd pinned pictures of his six kids in christening gowns and a Puerto Rican flag. The mug on a mug stand said PONCE MEN DO IT BETTER. On the left side of their shared cubicle Solomon's desk stayed tidy with one photo of his college-age son standing on a beach during spring break the only personal touch.

Cardinal rule number one, give back exactly what you get. With Bernardino on his ass, Solomon adopted and adapted the African attitude, wearing shades indoors. He took his time answering the lieutenant's questions and made sure he acted as if he was the one doing the favor. It really burned the guy up.

So exactly why were they with this Price woman, a goodwill package FedExed to them from white-bread Reggie Moses?

Solomon wondered. He and Ruiz had better figure it out but quick. Only what could Moses have in common with this no-name girl? Was she a witness gone south? Only one thing was sure, if you fronted for Reggie you might as well douse yourself with gasoline right outside, on the precinct steps, and strike a match.

Privately, Solomon had to give Reginald Moses credit. Just last month he'd arraigned two more members of New York's Finest after they beat a dark-skinned Hispanic motorist into submission for running a traffic light. Hell, he was a righteous brother, as long as you weren't a part of the other, uniformed brotherhood.

Laurence Solomon had no illusions about Reggie's final destination. He was splashed all over the media, in one record-breaking month gracing the cover of *New York, Vibe* and *Time*. Preening for at least the statehouse, Solomon thought. Meanwhile NYPD foot soldiers made smart remarks about getting a bargain-basement price for a contract on Reg's life. During his tenure as PBA president, Maples had even had a photo of Reggie blown up and sent to a few of his friends on custom-made dart boards. The only surprise Solomon had lately was when Moses decided to go for the death penalty in the Picard case. As if that was going to win him the PBA endorsement. Too little, too damn late.

Solomon examined what this woman Emma Price was wearing, a tan linen suit, fashionably crumpled, the skirt short enough to show off her legs. She had dark hair pulled back into a tight braid and there were age lines around her eyes. She wore no makeup and could have used some, but she was still attractive. Late thirties, he decided, and too damn thin. White women must take an oath never to put a piece of meat on their bones. She'd decided to forego stockings. Those bare feet digging into her black leather flats made him re-assess, moving her down a notch; from elegant to funky.

She seemed more than a little upset. It was bizarre. Try to figure this, Solomon told himself. Cover your back. Let Ruiz drive her crazy. Miguel, who was ill-suited for any sort of mental diligence, was already steaming.

"Ms. Price. You want some coffee? Let me get you something," Solomon offered.

She shook her head.

"Why don't we begin?" Ruiz asked. His smile came out like a grimace of pain. On the way down, Ruiz had been beefing about how those a-holes out of the DA's office thought they were the biggest fucking joes, how he wasn't going to bend over and let them have their way. "*Maricóns,*" he'd said, making an expressive gesture. Solomon had let him vent. Now he gave him first crack at the interview, knowing he was simply greasing the treads. Miguel was old-fashioned when it came to women, a throwback to the time when courtly gentlemen lit cigarettes and held doors open. His own wife, Diane, called him "my little pussycat." Solomon knew Ruiz was going to be stumped, torn between his desire to deride this woman, and his inability to say one bad thing to a member of the opposite sex. In fact, Ruiz was piss-poor at getting a suspect to cop. With women he never pushed hard enough and with men he took the alternate view, letting his anger lead him by the horns until the perps ended up as pissed off at him as he was at them. When they clammed up, Solomon stepped in. The old, time-tested routine of good cop, bad cop. Bernardino had actually done him a favor, sticking him with Ruiz. Luckily, he was too stupid to realize it.

"You say the girl's name is Beatriz Castillo. How were you acquainted?"

"She worked for me as a baby-sitter. She used to work full time, but lately I've been using her sporadically."

"Why was that?"

"She was in college. She wasn't as available."

Ruiz shook his head as if this news disappointed him. Then he threw Solomon a tortured look. "Just one time, give us some credit," he said.

"What are you talking about?" It was the Price woman asking, leaning forward.

"We know where you come from. Just tell us what you want with the girl," Ruiz said.

"What? Look, I told you, when I saw the picture I got worried."

Ruiz leaned back in his chair and uttered a soft groan.

"You and who else?"

She looked completely mystified, and then, more to the point, annoyed. "Detective?"

"What about your boss?" he asked.

"I wasn't aware I had one."

"Mr. Moses. The district attorney."

Solomon noted the way her face flushed. "You mean you think I'm down here at Reggie's behest?" She laughed. "It's not that way at all. He was doing *me* the favor."

"A favor to get you to come down here to ID a body. You think I'm stone-cold crazy? Coming down here when you could have called us at the office?"

"I call your office," she said, belligerence rising in her voice. "And just how long would that have taken?"

"That's just not fair. I love how you people talk, though. Spend one day out on the street and then go and criticize."

"One more time. I'm not here for Reginald Moses. I'm here because of Bea. Look, be reasonable, detective. I call and you ask me to come down to the precinct so I can give you an endless list of particulars. Or worse, roll up the name and throw it in the wastebasket. What have you had, about two hundred calls because of that photo?"

"We do our job."

Solomon looked from one to the other. Talk about a short in the lines of communication. Talk about an abject failure.

"I never said you didn't." Emma threw an exasperated look Solomon's way. He read it as, "Do something for me here. Talk sense to this guy."

A grunt from Ruiz.

"I know how you must feel about Reggie," she said. "This has nothing to do with him."

The wrong thing to say. Miguel was entirely too comfortable with the attitude he'd formed. An old dog, guarding a fossilized bone, Solomon thought. A chicken bone, to boot. The kind that splinters off in the throat and chokes you. Because the woman was holding on to her story a beat too long. It was starting to sound authentic.

Not to Ruiz. "Why would the DA send you down here to the morgue on your lonely?"

"Because I asked him to."

This was too much. Ruiz could imagine many things, but he was too old-fashioned to consider her choosing to ID a body. The more the world changed, the more Miguel clung to his ridiculously idealized version of what a woman was. Yet another deluded male, Solomon thought.

"He's doing it to you, the same way he does it to us," Ruiz said. His voice had softened. He was offering her the best sort of fatherly advice. "You're just doing his dirty work for him, but be careful. All that boss of yours cares about is himself, first and foremost."

"Maybe so," she said. "I'm certainly not up for defending Reggie. I'm here for Bea."

Ruiz shook his head. He was sorry for her now. "Whatever," Ruiz said. He crumpled up his coffee cup and threw it into the wastepaper basket. Then turned on his heel and stepped outside, shutting the door firmly.

"So, are you jerking us around?" Solomon asked.

"No."

Solomon waited a beat, just to see.

"I've been telling you and your partner the truth."

"Have you? The whole truth and nothing but?"

"Why would I lie?"

"Force of habit?"

She couldn't help smiling. He watched her tongue run over her teeth, making a final count, and felt pleasantly intrigued. "I have Bea's address," she said. "We can go over there now, if you like."

7

What do you think you're doing, Em? Leading them there like the Pied Piper? Do you think if you come back with these two men, Bea is going to magically reappear? She's dead, Emma. Get it? Dead.

The thought savaged her. Emma flashed on the corpse, so graphically displayed. And saw Bea in life, turning to her just days before, saying, "Sorry, Mrs. P. But I've got to go."

"Don't," Emma said aloud.

"What if God was one of us?" Joan Osborne asked over the car stereo.

What if he was. At least he'd be mortal, Emma thought. Then he'd be forced into pity. She swallowed hard, and started to cry.

At 396 Fifth, an overweight, bull-faced woman in a house dress handed Detective Solomon a set of keys.

"You want me up there with you?" she asked.

"It's not necessary."

"Have you seen her boyfriend recently?" Emma asked.

"My job's keeping the place up, not snooping around." The woman snorted for emphasis, retreating into her apartment and closing the door firmly against them.

As they started up the stairs, Ruiz nudged her from behind. When Emma turned, she found him chewing a toothpick. Like he's just made a meal out of me, Emma thought.

Except that just as his eyes flamed, he averted his gaze, staring at the ground.

"It's the boyfriend you're after?" he said.

She didn't see why she should dignify the question with a response.

The other detective knocked. No answer. He turned the key. Two years earlier, when Emma had stopped by to collect Liam, the living room had held a hand-me-down couch with wire-hard plaid upholstery and an old coffee table, the walls had been painted hot pink. Now the apartment was pure Gen X, aqua walls with white trim along the baseboards; the lamps in the living room wearing authentically yellowed shades with small, nasty-looking animal figures crawling up the wooden bases.

"Was the boyfriend supposed to be living here?" Ruiz asked, emerging from the bedroom. "No sign of him that I can see. Too bad for you, I guess." He had picked up a framed photo of Bea. "This is the floater," he said, handing the picture to Solomon. "Got any ideas for the next of kin?"

"Her mother and sister live in Florida," Emma said.

"They have names?"

"Castillo."

"Great. Castillo. Somewhere in Florida."

She stepped inside the bedroom, salmon sheets cascading off the bed matched the walls.

Ruiz was right. Emma wanted to find Chazz. But why? Why had she even imagined that he'd be sitting here, waiting? He could have been dragged under, too. In fact, that was more than likely. Someone had brought Beatriz out onto the sand. Someone had invited her into the water. And he was certainly the likeliest suspect. One of the absurdities of life, Emma thought, how what you fear most ends up devouring you.

Ruiz threw open the closet to expose two rows of neatly hung dresses and a huge collection of shoes.

"This boyfriend have a name?" he asked.

"Chazz."

"That short for Charlie?"

"I'm not really sure," Emma said.

"Is there anything you are sure of?" Ruiz sucked his teeth, a clear sign of annoyance. "Maybe that invisible boyfriend of hers is in here. Chazzie? Here Chazzie." He pulled open the top drawer of an antique bureau and reached in, snagging several pairs of satin bikini underwear. When he turned around to confront her, Emma stared down at what was in his hand.

"What?" he asked belligerently. Then, once again, he seemed to deflate quickly, shoving the underwear back into the drawer.

"Any idea on the mother's address?" The other detective was asking. Solomon, Emma reminded herself. Detective Solomon, the relatively wise.

"Bea would have it in her datebook. It was red, with an embossed heart." Her voice was registering too high. A sure sign of nerves, she told herself.

She wandered around the room, and found she couldn't bring herself to touch anything. Infection, she thought, is that what I'm afraid of? Or is it something else, is it acceptance that terrifies me the most?

Ruiz was sifting through the pile of books on the side table next to the bed. Emma stepped back into the living room, then into the kitchen. A glassed-in cupboard held plates and cups. She reached up and took one out to examine it. Hostile beasts crudely etched into the porcelain. Turning the plate over, she saw the artist's initials, PS, engraved on the back. The dish was slightly damp. There was also a pool of water under the empty rack. Emma reached up and touched the dish again, then worked her way back toward the glasses, noting that several of them still had a thin coating of water.

Fierce humidity might slow down the drying time, but Bea had been found early yesterday morning. Had she washed these dishes and set them back in their places two days ago? It seemed more than a little unlikely. And if someone else had been there since? Chazz, Emma thought. It had to be Chazz, who was also the one responsible for Bea's transformation, because, when Emma had first hired her, Bea had been the penultimate homegirl, her favorite outfit stretch pants and a baggy low-cut T. She'd owned four pairs of 14-K giant hoop earrings and her prize possession was a necklace with her name in gold script. *That* Bea spent her free time shopping for bargains at the Fulton Mall and was a regular customer at the RKO theaters where they ran all the bad-boy features. *That* Bea had been a working-class girl with no highbrow pretensions. And this was not *her* dream house.

If it was Chazz tidying up, removing signs of his continued and continuing presence, then why bother? Because he has something to hide, Emma decided. Because he is, in some way, responsible.

Emma sat down on the couch. It gave underneath her. True down pillows, another sign of material progress. She remembered one rainy day at her house when the kids were watching a video and Bea had settled in beside her, reaching into the ever-swelling pile of catalogues. Then she'd started to ooh and aah.

"I always wanted one of those." Bea had pointed to a three-foot-high white porcelain stork with a gold painted beak. "I'm gonna hit the lottery and then I'll go crazy." Bea picked out a lamp made of brass with a clear plastic shade, a pair of opulent white leather couches, a glass coffee table set on four silver coasters. They'd made her think money and they'd made Emma wince.

Emma returned to the bedroom, noting that the desk at the far end of the room held Bea's PC. It was surrounded by piles of college textbooks. There was another desk that was also piled high with books.

"I take it she attended school," Solomon said, conversationally.

"Brooklyn College. This would have been her last year."

Solomon stood at the desk, thumbing through the textbooks. "I had to read this one," he said, holding up a copy of *A Farewell to Arms*.

"Did you like it?"

"No. Did you?"

Emma shrugged. "The first time I hated it. The second time I cried."

"What changed the second time around?"

"I had become experienced, as Jimi used to put it," Emma said. "Or at least I was under that illusion."

"Jimi?" Solomon raised his eyebrows. "A wizard on the guitar. I can still listen. Plenty of experiences a person might wish away."

Like this one, she thought, feeling the gnawing sadness. A photo of Bea in a gilt frame sat on the bedside table. She smiled up at Emma, apparently carefree.

"Sorry about the girl." Solomon had said it. She turned and found him looking at her with what she interpreted as more than a little prurient interest. Her first response was surprise. Her second, a belief that she was imagining it. A flush spread across her cheeks, followed closely by a stab of guilt. Why, Emma wondered? After all, I'm currently separated, officially pregnant, and a mom. I should feel lucky that any male of the species notes my existence.

"What about the boyfriend?" Solomon asked.

"They'd been seeing each other for over a year. It was serious." She paused, then added, "You do realize I've been telling you the truth."

"Do I infer an insult to Detective Ruiz's intelligence?" He said it kindly, though. Emma didn't think it smart to answer. She chose, instead, a temperate silence. He was pulling out the top desk drawer. He set it on the bed and rummaged around. Inside there was the regular debris, paper clips, rubber bands, half used rolls of Scotch tape. He replaced it and tried the second, finding a bunch of letters, tied together with a purple ribbon.

"Carmen Castillo, 2 Edge Road, Saint Augustine, Florida. That sounds like the mom. Miguel," he called out, "make yourself useful. Get a phone number."

"If I get the number, you gotta make the call." And Emma heard him barking at the operator.

"This girl was your baby-sitter. You were called down through conscience and civic duty and Reg is only a long-time personal friend?"

"Yes."

"You shouldn't be here." Solomon folded his arms firmly across his chest.

"Got it," Ruiz called out. "Your turn to break the bad news, Solly."

He wanted her to accede. And she wasn't ready. So she turned to look out the window. A children's plastic wading pool sat in the middle of a courtyard planted with impatiens and marigolds. He cleared his throat.

"I'll give you a minute," he said, then stepped from the room. Emma looked over at the bookcase next to the desk. There were empty spaces on both pieces of furniture. On the side table, the books were surrounded by a thin coating of dust, but rectangular portions of the desk and one of the bookcase shelves were dustfree. Something had definitely been removed. She opened the last desk drawer and looked inside. Right on top was a diary. She lifted it out and couldn't help herself.

July 15
6:00

Dear red as cupid's beating heart DIARY,

Today I'm twenty. Some people think birthdays are a big deal and want to have fun. Then there are the rest of us who know that they're just the reason the world gives for embarrassing you.

Every year me and my mom go through this whole thing. We try to have a good time and pretend we're having a party, but really we're just waiting on Lucien. We can be eating in a restaurant and suddenly there he is, making stupid faces at us through the glass. I mean, does he have a homing device planted in his head? I think it really is like he says, that he was taken into an alien rocket ship where they gave him this one special power, the power to make my life a living hell.

Last night it was just me and my mami and Ana hiding out in the apartment. Of course, Lucien knew we were there even though we didn't answer the buzzer. Someone else must have let him in cause then he was pounding on the door and screaming at us like this demon was sinking his claws in right out there in the hall. We'd just gotten up to lighting the candles and I was about to blow them out to make a wish. Mami got up to get the door and I said, "Don't you go out there" but she did anyhow. I blew the candles out and wished he'd die.

*I wanted him to go clutching on his heart in the hallway
and fall down on the floor and moan and twitch. Then
we could bury him and I could pretend to love him.*

*Mami likes to explain how he was a good religious
man. He never even drank or smoked. Well, if you
want my opinion, that might have been a clue.*

*Ana must have known what I'd gone and wished for,
cause she gave me this look like she was half proud
and half ashamed of me. Mami had opened the door
by then with just a little gap, at least she'd been smart
enough to keep the chain on. He was talking to her
about a sign from Christ and how she had to sprinkle
me with holy water and how the devil was coming so I
should hide down in the basement where he couldn't
look for me, how I should carry my cross with me always. Me and Ana, we went into my room and shut the
door. We turned the radio on really loud. Then Mami
came knocking.*

*"Your dad wants to see you," she said. I tried ignor-
ing her. I mean, she'd already given him money. But
she started crying so hard I had to go. He smelled like
garbage and there was this yellow stain down the front
of his pants from where he'd gone on himself. He'd
grown his beard out to look like Jesus I guess. He
wanted to kiss me, so I let him and tried hard not to
wipe off the place where he'd touched me.*

*"For your birthday," he said. He was holding this
thing out which must have been a radio once. He
probably got it out of someone's trash can. I took it
and then I couldn't help myself. I slammed the door
back in his face and stood there leaning on it. The next
second I felt bad, my whole body was shaking and it
felt like he'd gone and stabbed me in the heart, so I
opened the door. There he was, just standing there*

with his big puppy dog eyes. I took two fifties of those four Mrs. Price went and gave me for my birthday out of my pocket and handed them over, then closed the door.

You can see how it would take us a while to get back to the cake. It was sitting on the table and none of us had even cut out our pieces yet. I was the one who said, "Come on now. I want some of that." Then mami smiled. She has these dimples in her cheeks when she smiles and her cake was a fine thing. It had three white stars and a yellow moon on one side, a pink heart on the other with an arrow stuck through. There was writing on top that read, "love to Beatriz on her birthday." After we finished eating, we opened the presents. Ana gave me a gold ankle bracelet. My mom gave me this green dress with this high neck that could choke you to death. I kissed her and told her how much I loved it. She kissed me hard the way she sometimes does and got all teary. She told me how I was a good girl. She said how she was lucky to have such wonderful daughters and then she started thanking God for his blessings. We all had to get down on our knees and pray.

This is my last birthday when all of us are going to be here together. Mami has made up her mind. She's moving to Florida in three months. I wonder if she's going to try to tell him or one day if he's just going to show up and there's gonna be someone new living at our place. I'll tell you what I know though. I can run but I can't hide. No matter where I move, he'll find me out but no way am I going down there to Florida. What would I do with myself? It's okay for Ana, she's still little and anyhow she really is a good girl. Me, I'm set to finish college and get myself a life right here

*where I know people. Plus there's Chazz to think of. I
could never ever ever leave him behind.*

"You about ready in there?" It was Ruiz asking.

Emma dropped the diary back into the drawer and tried
not to feel as if she had been caught doing something wrong.
A business card fell onto the floor. She leaned over to retrieve it.

"Time to go," Ruiz said. She heard footsteps approaching.
Emma didn't stop to think, just stuffed the cardboard rectan-
gle into her pocket and pushed the desk drawer shut. Turning away, she glanced at the array of photos on the dresser;
Bea with her mom, Bea and her sister Ana in the front car of
the Coney Island Cyclone, Bea with Liam and Tony on Halloween, mugging for the camera. As she passed, Emma put
her fingertip on the dresser. It came off clean.

"Is this Mrs. Castillo? My name is Detective Laurence
Solomon of the New York Police Department. I'm calling
about your daughter, Beatriz. Can you verify for me that
your daughter lives at 396 Fifth Avenue, Brooklyn, New
York? Your daughter Beatriz has had an accident. Yes, I'm
afraid...I'm afraid she's dead. I'm so sorry to be the one
bringing you this news."

Emma had to give him credit. He sounded genuinely
mournful.

Ruiz stood in the doorway, waiting. Emma threw a last
look back at the room. She imagined Bea waking up, shoving back the covers, then groaning as the light streamed in.

Emma moved toward Ruiz. At the last minute, just as she
was crossing the threshold, he put up his arm to stop her.

"What now?" she asked.

"I'm asking for consideration," he said. "I'm asking for
you to show us a little respect."

"I'm being respectful," she said. Except it didn't come out at all contritely. Frankly, she was tired of dealing with him. There were so many things so much more unfair than what he imagined her to be doing, not the least of them the fact that she would never have Bea in front of her again, Bea laughing with delight at something Liam had said, then relating it to Emma so that she could partake in her son's originality, his charm. Bea, who always saw the best in him, who brought it out. Emma felt a surge of panic. What would she tell Liam? How could he stand knowing this, especially now?

"I've got to get home," she said, worried at the thought of the difficult task awaiting her. And she shoved his arm down.

"Manny, I need you," Solomon called from the living room. Ruiz exhaled dramatically and backed away. As he did, Emma felt her own defenses falter. She felt the tears well up again. Not here, she told herself. Not yet.

"Her mother's flying in tomorrow." Solomon said. His mouth twitched a little as if he were trying to coax an encouraging smile.

"In the paper it said they found her at Coney," Emma said.

"The riptide yesterday was savage, what with the hurricanes."

"And no one was allowed into the water, right?"

"There are always those bent on tempting fate."

"Not Bea," Emma said. "Bea couldn't swim a stroke. You couldn't drag her near the ocean. We took her on vacation with us up to the Cape. She'd stake out a place on the rise, as far away from the waves as possible. Swimming? The best you could get after pleading with her, was when she'd wade up to her ankles in the pond. And that was when it was hot as hell. Someone must have convinced her to go in. It could have been her boyfriend."

"I see."

"Do you? Really?"

He shrugged. "No, but it's my job to pretend."

"Look," Emma said, insisting. "Someone's been back here since, cleaning up. The dishes are wet. There are other signs."

"What is it? Looking for a job on the force?" Solomon offered a grudging laugh. "Time for you to get back to your nearest and dearest. Otherwise, I might find myself starting to get a little annoyed."

Emma pulled over in front of the elementary school on Pacific and Third and wept unashamedly. A man walking his dog passed close to her car and glanced inside. Emma forced herself to look up, offering him defiance. He averted his eyes immediately and rushed away.

Nothing purer than grief, she thought. Nothing more personal, nothing more private, and nothing people are more hungry to examine.

God, will I miss you, Bea.

Miss things about you I can't think of now. Someday I'll step off the F train at Bergen and see a homegirl skating across the platform. There'll be this stitch in my side from excitement and I'll hold my breath when I go to touch her on the shoulder. At the last possible moment, I'll remind myself and have to slide my hand back into my coat pocket, then walk by her triple-time fast. I'll only be able to catch sight of the side of her face, that will be enough to recognize the futility. Or maybe Suze and I will be sitting at the Brooklyn Inn and I'll see a woman laughing through the plate-glass window. I'll knock on the glass thinking it's you grown up. And she'll turn, cheating me again, transforming in that wink of an eye into some other, perfect stranger.

I'll miss you, Bea. There's nothing I can do about that. I'll miss you and resurrect you and bury you for the rest of my life. It's what you do when someone you care for dies. That's your special form of payment.

Emma regained control. As she did, she searched for Kleenex to wipe the evidence off her face. She stabbed her hands into her pockets and discovered the business card. There was a graphic of a pendulum swinging above a logo for THE PIT, A PLACE OF OTHERWORLDLY DELIGHTS. Beneath that the address and telephone number. Turning the card over she read a message written in handsome bold script.

"Girl, I'd like to take you through the Pale Door."

8

The morning was sultry, sweatboxes of rain threatening to pour down from the sky. Steel-gray air in the town of Fall River, Mass. Milton Roberts stretched, made his best grunting noise and opened his front door. No surprises here. A street full of squat, red-brick houses, with neat clipped lawns in front. His lawn was Italianate, a white slab of cement, one of the first improvements he'd made on moving in. As Milton headed down his own walk to retrieve his copy of the *Fall River Times,* he hoisted his middle finger at the wizened jockey to his right. The weary metal face didn't wink. The jockey held a sign reading NO TRESPASSING in his ever-willing hand.

The Duluths lived next door. Jim Duluth liked to work his garden, which was a mass of late-summer trumpet vines and last-gasp roses, blasts of red across a green patch of lawn. He'd begged Milton not to pave over the lawn, as if it were the last square inch of rain forest left on the fucking continent. He refused to listen. After that, the Duluths wouldn't even say good morning.

Nice people up here, Milton thought. He was used to warmer climes and the only one around who didn't mind the current weather pattern, mysterious clouds full of rainwater air, shoving hot breaths of vapor over the land. Hurricane weather. What he missed most? The storms racing in, and the ocean water churning up. Sky, black as pitch. Wind currents singing in your ears. Then what happened after, blissful calm, the sun beating down. Going out on the water and getting caught in a storm, the most goddamn frightening thing that could happen. He'd been there a few times, when he'd worked the fishing boats, only sixteen then, hanging on to the swordfish some tourist had caught, holding it up by its slick sides so they could photo op their trophy.

A hot wind shot up out of nowhere, rustling the leaves on a few sturdy oaks. He missed the palm fronds, missed the whispering noise they made, the way they told secrets.

Leila used to tell him he was the last of the true romantics.

Missed Leila too, in a way. Not that she hadn't thrown him out that last time, washed her hands of him altogether, said, "good riddance to bad rubbish," and slammed the door.

The first storm had passed them by, winking up past the Cape. The paper had been full of it, trees down, flooding, vacationers rushing home over 495 to avoid the incoming natural disaster. But the second one was snaking inland. This time, they might get some action.

The wind blew up again and he saw what had happened to his paper. In the middle of the goddamn street, being scattered to the four corners of the globe.

"Fuckin-A," Milton said, opening his metal gate and rushing out. His squat two hundred pounds did a battle-ax run and he was on it, grabbing a few of the windswept sheets, the whole fucking thing a disaster. Sunday's paper delivered on Saturday, stuffed full of color folios; Seaman's sofas, Target clothes blown down the street, the business section heading in pieces for the Duluths' front lawn. He bent down, trying to salvage something out of it. *Doonesbury, For Better or For Worse,* and Prince Valiant's gleaming face displayed, ruffled in midair.

The car came out of nowhere. Not true, actually, he might have heard it idling. The lack of the morning cup of java slowed his reaction time. He leapt for the sidewalk, and saw with relief he was going to make it, crazy people out here not seeing a man bent over like this in the middle of his own goddamn street, not looking, kids out too early and gunning the motor, putting the pedal to the metal for a fucking joyride.

The front of the car hit him in midair, tossed him down onto the concrete and then ran him over, crushing his chest. He was still awake, short-circuited into the pain that was running through his body, when he heard the squeal of the brakes, the car door opening. They were coming out now to see what they'd done and there was this guy bending over him, he saw the face, moonlike above.

"What a fucking mess," the guy said. And it was then he understood what he'd been too stupid to know before. His dad had said that to him, how he'd never amount to anything, how he had shit for brains. His dad had said that all right, one hand reeling him into the wall and the day he'd hit the bastard back was the day he went off on his own to make his fucking fortune. The car door slammed again and Milton closed his eyes, remembering the sound the waves made, slapping against the shore, hot sand under his feet, even at night, how it burned off your soles, how you were thrust into dreaming with it. What's not to like, he thought, about life, that is, what's not to like, not able to say another word about that, because words had already deserted him as the car reversed and bumped back over his now still body, just in case they'd missed a spot.

9

A man was downstairs, rattling the glass in the Victorian pocket doors. Emma searched for a weapon in the half dark and found piles of dirty clothing instead. She realized she was trapped inside the bedroom closet, only all the hangers had been removed. The back slid open to reveal a weaving passageway, ending in a blank gray wall. Pressing her hands against it, she discovered it was ice cold, then she heard Liam's screams. As she ran back, the thin walls closed in on her. Her hands were clenched, except she already knew that any defense would be futile. Emma forced her eyes open. "Will, what are you doing here?" she asked.

He was staring at her, his face a tabula rasa.

"Shit," Emma said under her breath. She got out of bed and made her way, stiff-legged, to the bathroom. As she threw some cold water on her face, she experienced a wave of nausea. Leaning against the sink, she closed her eyes and tried to breathe deeply, normally. In another minute, the sickness was gone, leaving behind a very real trace memory.

"Would someone save me?" Emma whispered. She smiled weakly at her own pale face.

When she reemerged, Will was leaning against the far wall of the room. His eyes were silent and still. She felt herself, unconsciously, head his way and saw him realize what she was thinking of doing before she had even admitted it to herself. He recoiled and her hands dropped to her sides. Habit, she thought, changing direction. That's all it is, Em, twelve years of habit, which you are about to relearn. But how? How does anyone change so quickly? For example, how did he manage?

She headed for the dresser, pulled on underwear, then wriggled into a pair of jean shorts. Removing the T-shirt she had worn as a nightshirt, she threw it over a chair. It slid off, landing on the floor. Emma made no move to retrieve it. Instead she picked out a bright red Gap T, pulled it on, brushed her hair a few times, then hooked a finger for Will to follow. On the landing, he hesitated. She saw he meant to wake Liam. "We need to talk first," she said, hearing the quaver in her voice. She swallowed hard to try and control it and gave him the firmest look she could muster.

Luckily, he relented.

Downstairs in the kitchen she saw he'd prepared some of his excellent espresso and set out two cups. This was probably meant as kindness but she found it painful instead, reminding her of so many evenings when Will had taken over the kitchen, cooking masterfully, entertaining while he meticulously diced the onions and pounded down garlic. She remembered him holding court from behind the stove, regaling the assembled guests with his excellent, dryly executed stories, then feeding them so very well. Will had been the perfect host. People always told her what a catch her husband was. And he was certainly at his best when on display, charming, eagerly solicitous, apparently completely at ease and available. It was only when they were alone that he retreated. You had to be relentless to break inside. You butted away and butted away, and finally his defenses crumbled. Emma knew initially he had been attracted by her fervor, by her determination. And she had been infatuated with his *difference.* Born into a family of fighters, Emma believed every waking moment was a chance to prove your own self-worth. Will seemed so calm, so innately confident by comparison.

What a relief, she had thought. How masterful. Now she understood it had only been another cunning disguise.

She poured herself a cup of coffee and sipped at it, noting how the dishes had been washed and set to dry. Magazines formed a neat pile in the middle of the table, and its surface was wiped clean of crumbs and dust. Will sat down and crossed his legs casually, territorially.

"I've sublet an apartment," he said.

"Just great," she said, under her breath.

"I thought Liam could spend the rest of the weekend with me," Will said, adding, "I thought it might help."

"Help? In what way?"

"It could stabilize things."

"Really?" she said. "This is short notice." She felt completely enraged by his placid tone.

"I left a message for you last night," he said.

"I haven't listened to the machine." As if listening to a message would have made this any easier. There was a pregnant, hostile pause. "How incredibly easy this is for you," she said finally.

"That's not fair, Em. It's not easy. I don't know how you could even imagine that."

"I can only judge by what I see. You leave. You get yourself a little bachelor pad in about a half a minute. Now you want Liam to sleep over. And I'm required to go along or else I'm the bad guy, right?"

He didn't contradict her.

Anger gave way to despair. I've got to do something, she thought. Except nothing seemed to come to mind. She stood, grabbing up her coffee cup and taking it over to the sink where she poured out the remains, scrubbing it clean.

"Was it Bea?" he asked.

Keeping her back turned, she nodded.

"Poor kid. How did it happen?"

"She drowned," Emma said, turning to face him, adding bitterly under her breath, "I would have thought that was obvious."

"Okay, all right." He moved nearer, stopping at what he apparently deemed a physically inviolate distance. "I understand it's hard to be civilized." Emma saw that now he was adopting the guise of the patient, suffering rationalist. What have I done to deserve this, she wondered? There were things she did have to admit to, things said and unsaid. But none of them should have merited this sort of abandonment. Emma took a deep breath, then swallowed and added as evenly as she could, "The boyfriend's missing too."

"Terrible. What a stupid thing to do, he must have thought it would be a kick. At that age, you think you're impervious."

"So you think it's teenage hijinks gone horribly wrong?"

"What other explanation can there be?"

"Bea didn't know how to swim."

"People change."

"Don't I know it," she muttered.

Then, inexplicably, he stepped over and took her by the shoulders. She went to brush his hands back. But he held on and there they were, a sad tableau. Emma felt her misery, her own loneliness, so palpable, so immediate. *Tell* him, she thought. She pulled back to study him, then winced. She was seeing a stranger.

"Oh god," she whispered.

"How are we going to explain this to Liam?" he asked. "You didn't say anything yet, did you, Em?"

"I couldn't face it," she said.

Emma remembered her own progress home the night before. How she had smiled bravely, as Liam rushed toward her, then looked over his head to Suzanne, the two of them exchanging the sort of significant look that spelled certain doom.

"We should wait," Will told her. "Wait till he's ready."

"You mean we should lie."

"Lying is underrated." He met her eyes. "He can't take this on top of everything else."

"Everything else?"

"I mean what's gone on between us."

"Please, you can drop the euphemisms."

"What should I say?"

"Say you left, left us both and now you're sorry," she offered. She meant to go on, but found she was unable to beg. Or unwilling.

"I'm sorry," he said, sounding neither convinced nor convincing. She thought she could make out what lay just below the surface; his own peculiar, unoriginal sort of pride. He admires himself, she thought. He thinks he's done us all a service, acknowledging what any fool could see. Which makes me worse than a fool, because I really didn't see this coming. Even in our worst moments, I didn't imagine an ending.

Emma's anger flared up, overpowering her. A simple deliberate act of retribution, she thought. A well-honed kitchen knife jammed into his stomach. Instead, she forced herself to get up, take the coffee pot off the stove, unscrew it, and wash it clean. She filled it with new beans, added water, and turned the burner on underneath. A few more deep breaths and her shoulders finally relaxed. Amazing that she was able to use a normal tone of voice. "I suppose you want some more," she offered.

They sat at the breakfast table. It could have been the beginning of another ordinary day, except if that were the case they would have been sitting there companionably, studying the daily paper and fighting over the best sections while the coffee bubbled up.

* * *

Emma Price poured half into her cup and refilled his empty one. She added milk to his and left her own black. Sitting down opposite him, she looked at the man she had chosen to marry. Tell him you're pregnant, she thought. Let him understand what he's doing. Emma looked down at her hands and etched on her palm was an image of Bea's face, open-eyed and silent.

"She would never have gone in that kind of rough water. Nobody changes that much."

Will simply shrugged.

It was exasperating. How could he be blind to something so painfully obvious? "You think she went from phobia to idiocy, all in one easy lesson?"

"Bea didn't tell you everything, Em. She was someone we employed to watch our child. She was good at her job. That doesn't mean we knew her."

"Don't you care about what happened to her, Will?"

"Of course I do," Will said. Only the words sounded rehearsed. His apparent callousness surprised her. "Bea was wonderful to Liam," he added. "It will break his heart."

And you've broken mine, Emma thought. She tamped down tears and stalked the room with her eyes. There was a long, embarrassing pause. Finally regaining control, Emma said, "Dawn offered me a job at the capital defender's office."

"Take it," he said immediately. "I can help out with Liam."

"In what way?" she asked.

"There you go again," he said. "You really can't stop yourself, Em." He shook his head. She stared back deliberately, and thought she saw the outlines of his sadness. She felt a momentary hope that he was about to tender a better offer. But he only sighed as if she were the slowest learner in history. "Can Liam come with me now?" he asked. "I'll take good care."

* * *

"Wake up, sleepyhead." Will's voice was remarkably gentle. Emma raised the blinds and turned to find Liam giving a Cheshire-cat grin, then throwing his arms around his father and hanging on for dear life.

He loves Will more, Emma thought. And gasped.

The first five years of his life, Liam had clung to her and rejected Will completely. When he began to accept Will as a slightly tarnished substitute, Emma had seen it as progress. Then he'd begun to show a marked preference for his dad's company, taking frequent trips to Yankee baseball, warming bleacher seats at the Garden. Whenever Will got the chance, they'd go run a pick-up basketball game in the schoolyard or play hockey at the roller rink. Emma could have tagged along, could even have participated, she was talented at sports. But she was always generous enough to decline. The time they spent alone was so important to Liam. So she'd let him go, secretly noting her own selflessness. And now, if the two of them marched off, leaving her in the dust? The pain would be excruciating.

If she had asked him to dress, Liam would have dawdled, finding amusement in some comics he had thrown onto the floor, or tossing a tennis ball against the wall of the room, then diving for it. Barely avoiding lethal contact with the side of the bunk bed. For Will, Liam put his clothes on in under a minute. Emma offered breakfast, and Liam didn't even respond. He raced down to the front door with Will in tow. She was left upstairs alone, to pack.

Emma tugged the zipper shut on the duffel bag and set it on her shoulder. Standing at the top of the stairs looking down, she had a surge of fear. Would she always trail in their wake? At the door, she did manage to salvage a kiss and Will handed her a sheet of paper filled with particulars, his new address, new phone. The late-model Lincoln sent by Atlantic Car Service was waiting outside. Father and son rode off together, into the morning.

"Why is this happening?" Liam had demanded. Emma remembered the look on Liam's face, the purity of his pain.

"Because even if people love each other, sometimes they can't live together anymore. Sometimes people say things and do things that they can't take back."

"Like what? What did you say to him?"

"Nothing," Emma told him. "It's not all me," she added in what had been her only viable form of defense.

She dearly wished to apportion blame; words threatened to sail out of her mouth at the oddest times; when she was washing his hair during the late-night bath, in the morning while he demolished his carefully prepared breakfast of French toast and bacon. Yet she had managed to act like an adult, better than most adults, she told herself. And this morning, she realized the truth, her desire to hold on to the moral high ground had been a way to pretend that she and Will still had a future.

"Is he in love with someone else?" Liam demanded.

"Not that I know of."

"I think you're crazy." He'd said it firmly, shutting himself away from her, forever.

Saturday. Except it wasn't like any Saturday in the last twelve years, the house as quiet as a tomb. Emma poured another cup of coffee and unrolled the morning paper. The governor had appeared at a Republican fundraiser where he'd devoted a good part of his speech to lambasting soft-hearted liberals who wasted taxpayer dollars helping death-row criminals file writs and petitions. There were certain cases where this sort of thing seemed ludicrous, take, for example, Ms. Loretta Picard.

The *Times* mentioned Beatriz in a tiny article deep in the Metro Section under the headline, DROWNED BATHER'S IDENTITY KNOWN. The *News* gave Beatriz photo space with the same three-sentence story underneath it. They used up page two with a long news story about the governor and Loretta, adding a grainy photograph of the bar where she'd worked. The caption read, "The Pit, Picard's workplace and a fixture in the downtown bar scene." Emma took the business card out of her pocket. The Pit. There it was again. Picard and Beatriz Castillo? Where was there a more unlikely intersection? Life. Full of odd coincidences, Emma decided. She read on. Apparently Loretta Picard had used false ID to get the job when she was hired. She was only nineteen.

Emma turned the business card over. *Girl, I'd like to take you through the Pale Door.* Was it a come on? Words from a song Bea had scribbled down? Had she really frequented the club or had she been handed the card to use as a notepad? The script was elegant, stylized, it was probably not even Bea's handwriting. It bore no obvious resemblance to any of the notes she'd scratched out over the years, and no resemblance at all to that careful script she'd used for her diary entry.

Emma wandered through the living room, opened her front door, and sat down on her stoop. It was a beautiful morning with a sky full of crisp, cumulus clouds. Emma waved to Dante as he lifted the shutters on the bodega. Felix Redmond walked by with his surrogate children, a pair of two-year-old short-haired golden retrievers. He stopped to chat about the plummeting temperatures. As he wandered off, pulled by the canine pizza prospectors, Emma had to contemplate the nature of her new, strangely liberated life and its attendant isolation.

Five minutes later, she was on the phone to Dawn.

"I can do thirty hours a week and not a minute more," she told her. "Do you want me?"

Dawn grunted. "That's not what I offered."

"You said part time. That's part time."

"That's half time," Dawn said.

"Only on your uncommon schedule. Look, Dawn, it's what I can do, take it or leave it."

"Huh," Dawn said, making a little snorting noise into the receiver.

Emma examined her nails. She saw that the cuticles needed trimming. An excellent place to start, she thought, pulling clippers out of the side drawer by her bed and beginning to work.

"Thirty-seven, five," Dawn said.

"Not good enough." She pared one hand down neatly, then turned to the other.

"Half time for half pay."

"As if that were a real offer to begin with." Emma pried out a stubborn hangnail and demolished it.

"Forty-three," Dawn said.

"I'll take sixty to start," Emma told her. "And a raise if I find that you're trying to jack up my hours."

"Highway robbery."

"You're getting away cheap," Emma said. "You're the one who called me, as I remember."

"Fine, Emma, have it your way," Dawn said. But she sounded relieved. "You do have a fax at home, don't you?"

"Yes."

"Good," said Dawn. "I'll send you the Picard file."

"Why don't you start by telling me about the ID?"

A little too much time elapsed before Dawn said, "We didn't know about it. Reggie got us with that one."

"You didn't know?"

"She didn't tell us. Were we supposed to guess?"

"What about her high school records?"

"We just sent someone out there yesterday."

"Yesterday? Jesus, what are you handing me?"

"Her state of mind is an issue."

"Is this one of your subtle understatements? Let me read between the lines, you're trying for insanity. Do you have someone examining her?"

"Why don't you raise it when you see her?" Dawn said.

"You mean you haven't sent someone over?"

"There are extenuating circumstances," Dawn said.

"Such as?"

"Such as her refusal to cooperate. I brought Mel down but she walked out of the room."

"I guess you could make something out of that," Emma said, beginning to wonder if she could rescind her offer.

"I could. And I could have to. So I'm depending on you to work your magic. Good luck, Em." There was a decidedly mischievous lilt to her voice.

Should I be intrigued or horrified? Emma knew what Dawn expected: her old self, the one who worked weekends and holidays and would do just about anything to promote the cause. Dawn could never understand how that dedication had vanished the minute Liam was born. I was forced to choose, Emma thought. And there was never even a question.

Now? I'll work it out, Emma decided. Because I'm going to need some other source of income. Running the capital crimes clinic at Fordham was fine as long as Will was the major breadwinner. I'm sure he'll pay child support. And yes, he'll probably offer a decent settlement. But he hardly makes enough to support two households. Then she blanched. Jesus, Emma, she thought, I'm getting to be pretty damn cold-blooded. That was fast. Still, she thought Dawn would take whatever it was she had to offer, at least for the time being. After all, Dawn had been the one coming to her. And then Emma had a thought that really panicked her. What if Liam preferred having her gone? What if he wanted Will and only Will? She subdued that thought, put it in a holding cell, then took a hot shower, changing into a linen sleeveless dress and flats and putting on a touch of makeup. Digging in her desk drawer, she came up with a pile of Will's old production-office cards, and checked to make sure the hot print was dropping into the wire basket under the fax machine on her way out the door.

10

As she rang the super's bell, Emma thought, 396 Fifth, my home away from home. She was here for Bea. After all, someone had to keep her interests in mind. Emma tossed off a rueful smile in the face of that argument. She knew doing was always better than thinking.

She had the card and her fake story at the ready. But before there was a response, a man opened the inside door and held it for her; an older man with a thick mane of white hair wearing a smoke gray business suit and immaculately shined black wing tips. "Thanks," she said.

"Anytime, dahlin'," he told her, betraying a thick Southern accent. He gave her a fairly seductive look, the kind she used to get from an assortment of potential suitors; young burly men unloading package goods to Wall Street execs. Of course, these days her fan club seemed to have shrunk. Only men over fifty noted her appeal.

"Have a good day, now," he added, smiling warmly.

"You, too," Emma said, feeling that it was her duty to be agreeable. And he *was* attractive in a distinguished, elderly statesman sort of way.

She headed downstairs to the super's apartment, running through her cover story in her mind. People hated talking to the police or to anyone connected with the legal profession. But if you told them you were working on a film, they became gregarious to the point of exhaustion. In America, everyone was convinced they were movie star material. Emma had used this cover pose before, whenever she deemed it necessary and expedient to lie.

"Whatcha want?" the super asked, peering out through the metal grating on the top of the door.

Emma flashed the card. "I was here yesterday," she said.

"Oh, yeah, I remember you. Your partner's upstairs." The eye hole dropped down and Emma heard the sound of someone padding away.

Climbing the stairs, she wondered if she was going to be treated to the sight of Ruiz's pockmarked face. The thought was dispiriting. She was relieved to find it was Det. Laurence Solomon who stood in the doorway of the apartment directly opposite Bea's, conferring with a man in green satin pajamas. "You say this guy was living with her?" Solomon asked.

"Sure. Here all the time," the man said. "I think she wanted to keep him kind of under wraps for her mom. If you ask me, the guy was mooching off her. He was that type. One of those white boys, the ones who think you're supposed to bow down to them."

"Could you give me a physical description?"

"I just did, man. He was white, okay? A slim-assed white boy." There was a hearty, in-your-face laugh. "Anyhow, what are you after him for? I thought the little girl drowned."

"How about that physical description," Solomon said in a stubborn cop's voice, every word barely concealing a threat.

"Listen, I can't say exactly what he was like." Emma noted that the thatch of black hair on the man's head looked suspiciously bountiful. He was wearing a rug, she was sure. Plus, he sounded more than a little tired of cops and what they assumed they could get out of you. He was already edging back inside his apartment. In another second, he'd be making an excuse and slamming the door in Solomon's face. So Emma decided it was time to take the initiative, she strode over and stuck out her hand.

"Emma Price," she said.

The man stared down as if gazing at some unsightly mess. He even wrinkled his nose. "Your partner here wakes me up to give me a hard time. You cops are precious."

"Mr. Cantas..." Solomon began.

Emma cut him off, handing the man a business card. "Mr. Cantas," she interjected. "I'm not from the police. You've got this wrong. I'm in another line of work entirely."

"What's this?"

"Cyclops Productions. I've been doing research with the kind assistance of Detective Solomon. Mr. Cantas, do you realize how important realism is when a major studio begins to research a film project? And that's what I'm doing here. Detective Solomon has been kind enough to let me ride with him. Then, this case comes along and I don't have to tell you how intriguing it is. I rushed right back to the office last night and took a meeting with the other producers. We're thinking of commissioning a rewrite based on this Castillo girl's story. My director says he can see it all, the drama of the coming storm, the poor kid getting sucked down. I think he's right, it works." She turned to Solomon. "This must be a bit of a shock to you, detective."

Emma waited to see if he would blow her out of the water. The worst that could happen was a moment of confusion ending in total humiliation. God knows, Emma thought, I'm used to that by now. He surprised her, though, flinging a small, petulant nod her way.

"You're serious?" Cantas asked.

"Never more."

Cantas rubbed his chin. "You know," he said. "I'm in the business myself. I got me a band. We do gigs at clubs around the city. Let me get you the business card." He retreated, leaving in his wake the pronounced odor of Brut.

"You better watch yourself, Mrs. Price." Solomon's low growl was a threat in itself. "I'm not going to be responsible."

"I don't expect you to be."

"Plus, I can arrest you for obstruction."

"You weren't getting anywhere." Emma heard her own arrogance, and quickly added, "Give me a chance. You've got nothing to lose."

"According to who?" He looked as if he were about to launch into a lecture on propriety, but José Cantas was back, handing her the card. She took out her wallet and slid it inside with a flourish. "What about this boyfriend?" she asked.

"It's like I told the detective. He was a white boy. Blond, rough-looking, you know. Something like that kid in *Seven*. The one the girls go crazy for."

"Brad Pitt?"

"That's right. Downtown all the way. Liked to wear black. First time I seen him he has this long hair and lets it fly out like a girl. Later on he gets himself scalped. Starts using gel so's it sticks up in points. You know the style?"

"I'm familiar with it. For some kids these days, style is everything. My nine-year-old keeps fighting with me because he wants an earring."

"You speak of it, that boy had three," Cantas said. "Liked to wear tiny little red studs in them. Personally, I don't think they were made out of anything precious."

"Left ear or right?"

Cantas took a second to consider, then said, "Got to be the right with me viewing him here, in my mind's eye."

"Any tattoos?"

"I wouldn't know about that part." He laughed. "Me, I had one of a mermaid done when I was in the service."

"I've got a little rose myself," Emma said confidingly.

"Bet I know where you had it put."

Emma tried to offer a seductive smile, although she felt considerably out of practice. "Did you know the boy's name?"

"Mr. Chazz Perry," Cantas said proudly. He added, "I've got me an eye for detail." Craning his neck to find Solomon, he added, "This doing anything for you, detective?"

"You've been most exceedingly helpful," Solomon said, sounding noticeably less than sincere.

"I try my best to be good to the police." Cantas offered a vicious smile. As he turned toward Emma, he softened it. "You got yourself my card, feel free to call," he said in a meaningful way.

She nodded conspiratorially.

"I'd like you to talk to a sketch artist," Solomon interjected.

"Now, where'm I gonna find the time? I've been talking my head off to you as it is. Go ask Pedro, he's the one with hours to waste."

"Pedro?"

"Rents out space in the parking lot around the corner. That Mr. Perry put his Miata in there for safekeeping. A nice bold blue car. Treated it like his queen. Started jamming me up because I park my own T-Bird next to him and one day this scratch appears. Starts telling me I owe him for fixing it. Threatened he'd sue, even." Cantas lowered his voice. "Not that I ever gave him a nickel." He started to close the door and Emma put out her hand to stop him.

"Do you remember the last time you saw Mr. Perry, José?" Emma asked sweetly.

"Two days ago. He was pulling out of the lot just when I was going in. Him and Bea went sailing by. She gave me a wave. They had chairs, umbrellas, my guess is they were off to the beach."

"What time of day was it?" Solomon asked, moving forward to use his own body as a doorjamb.

"I left the club at ten and came back here, so it must have been close to eleven. That's morning, not evening. Is that enough for you, boss?" The *boss* was accompanied by a leer.

"That was the last time you saw either one of them?"

"Sure was. I went right to sleep and slept through to the next day, I was that tired. Go to pick up my paper in the morning and there's the sweet little girl, stretched out on the front cover."

"You recognized her in the paper?"

Cantas didn't seem ashamed. "No, man, no, not then. Later on, when they had her name on the news or something. Sweetest little chiquita, too. Never hurt a flea. I tell you, I feel nothing but sorry."

The door closed. Emma leaned back against the wall, folding her arms. "Never hurt a flea," she said. "You should remember that, detective."

He didn't look the least bit amused. And she braced herself for a firestorm.

"What are you up to?"

Emma found herself unable to dredge up an appropriate response. There was no way she could explain her arrival and her decision to insert herself into the conversation without sounding as if she were tendering an insult. The bottom line was, she didn't trust him with Bea's business. Still, right now they both seemed to want to find Chazz. We have that in common, she told herself.

"Cantas knew it was Bea when he saw the front page of the paper yesterday."

"Do you listen, lady? I was asking you a question."

"I thought your question was rhetorical. We can converse, detective. But I would hope you'd act like a gentleman. If so, I'll be courteous and return the favor. If you start in on me like that partner of yours, I'll take umbrage and that will make me even more annoying."

"What a scary thought." He raised his eyes heavenward, then turned, heading for the stairs. She dogged his steps. On the first-floor landing he spun around, confronting her. "What about when Mr. Cantas calls up and asks to be in your state-of-the-art motion picture?" he demanded.

"Mr. Cantas will be enlightened in the ways of the world. How people aren't always what they seem."

"What about when he calls me up to complain?"

"He won't call. He doesn't like you. And besides," Emma added, "he let Bea down. It doesn't take much to pick up the phone. He probably feels some shame about that."

"Does he? Are things always this simple?"

No, Emma thought, which is why I'm here. Hardly his business though. "Have you been inside the apartment again?" she asked.

"You're not going in, if that's what you're after."

"I would have thought you'd be a little more grateful."

"Grateful for what?" He let fly an exasperated breath of air, then fled.

She wasn't letting him off that easy. Round the corner she stayed in hot pursuit. No blue Miata, just an empty space where the grass had flattened and died. She stepped away while he questioned Pedro, the owner of the lot, who said he hadn't seen the car or the guy, Chazz Perry, for days. Pedro confirmed the short blond hair and triple ruby red studs. The boy was of average height and always paid on time, in cash. "Never gave me any sort of trouble," Pedro said. And he agreed to speak with a sketch artist.

"No more floaters came up then?" Emma asked it, catching up when Solomon was done. He glared at her.

"Are you going to dog me like this all day?"

"It depends."

"On what?"

"I helped you out with Cantas."

"Helped me out by impersonating someone you aren't? And me knowing? That gets out, I'm gonna be up to my neck."

"It won't get out," she said coolly.

"So you're a goddamn fortune teller." He tried walking away again. But Emma kept up. "What about the autopsy?"

"You're a private citizen. I've done my fact checking. I don't owe you anything."

"I pay my taxes."

"Do you? If you say so."

"Any signs of violence on the body?"

Solomon stopped again and offered her an exasperated look. Which she mirrored. It roused a chuckle.

"You're impossible," he said, but she could see his face relax.

"Thanks. Look, it's eleven-forty and my stomach's rumbling, detective. How about letting me buy you lunch?"

"Not a good idea."

"Lunch and you lose me for good."

She offered a full-face, eager-to-please-in-every-sense-of-the-word sort of smile, then dipped her eyes a little and ran a hand through her hair.

"Tell me, Emma Price, are you the kind who always gets her way?"

"Sure," she said, thinking, *if you only knew.*

Emma found them a booth inside Aunt Suzie's and ordered herself an iced coffee. He had seltzer with a twist.

"You're truly a piece of work."

"I'll take that as a compliment."

"Take it whatever way you want." He sipped his drink and Emma took a second to admire him. Tall, handsome, exuding the good-natured self-confidence of a man who'd never had any problem attracting the appropriate female's attention. "Tell me why you're worrying over the disappearing Chazz this morning," she said. "You weren't buying into his existence yesterday."

"Do I look worried?"

"You just happened to be canvassing the building? That's standard procedure when somebody drowns? What came up in the autopsy?"

"Is this supposed to whet my appetite?" he asked. "Or are you the sort who likes to bring up gruesome topics so you can eat your companion's meal?"

"I'm not a ghoul," she said deliberately. And she made sure to tug his gaze in tight. "The two of them got into his car and went off to the beach. You and I both know that someone was in that apartment afterward, cleaning up. If that was Chazz, Chazz making sure there was no sign, no way to track him, he ran . . . You don't run unless you feel responsible."

"You know him that well?"

"We never met."

"Well, here's news for you, Ms. Price, sometimes you run when you're afraid."

"So was he afraid?"

"Do they make a good Reuben here?" he asked. There was mischief in his eyes.

"Are you going to help Bea?"

"I'm going to help bury her," he said, lifting the menu to use as a shield.

Emma leaned over and pushed it down. "Jesus! Are you really that cold?" She saw he wasn't. He was just waiting to see if he had successfully primed the detonator.

"This is *my* case," he said.

"All right."

"So stop being a nudge." Said with the Yiddish inflection. She laughed. "There wasn't any sign of a physical struggle.

No flesh under her nails, no DNA traces left. That could be the water, but as far as we know there are no signs of abrasions that were inconsistent with her being banged up by the surf. If you have some brilliant explanation of how she got dragged in and submerged that isn't accidental, tell me."

"Why not ask him."

"Chazz Perry? The gentleman is making himself unavailable." He sucked in air through his teeth, making a thin, whistling noise, then leaned forward. "Look," he said. "I don't know what this is about. This girl wasn't really just your baby-sitter, now was she? And what kind of intimacy do you have with white-bread Moses to get you sent down to the morgue with us as gatekeepers? I've given you some hope, now tell me what's really going on."

She hated to disappoint. But she didn't have an answer that would satisfy. Is this really just for Beatriz? she wondered. Or is it for me, so I can tell myself I've done everything I can?

There was an absolute, pin-drop silence until the food arrived. When her order came, Emma realized she was ferociously hungry. She wolfed down a sandwich and fries, then sucked the coffee milkshake dry.

"How do you maintain that youthful figure?"

"I run on fossil fuel," Emma said dryly.

"Just wait a few years. The fuel option tends to give out."

"I'm forty," she said.

"I wouldn't have guessed."

"Nice to hear that smooth a lie. So how old are you, detective?"

"In the same ballpark. Roughly."

"So you're like Dorian Gray?"

"Got the painting shoved in the closet."

Emma raised her eyebrows. She'd assumed he wouldn't get the literary reference. Well, she told herself, he's certainly not the first man I've misjudged.

"Why did you come to her apartment? You could have handed us the address and left it at that. It would have been the normal thing to do, considering."

"I suppose I felt obligated."

"To do what?"

"To make sure Bea was taken care of. I'm not the most trusting individual," Emma admitted.

"I guess that's fair. Or at least, honest." He leaned back in his seat and lifted his coffee cup. Over the rim, he gave her a thoughtful look. Setting it down again, he offered her the vaguest sort of conciliatory smile.

"After someone dies it's so much like an invading force," she said. "Everything getting ripped apart. I thought there should be someone there who knew her."

"So you're giving me heat because you're the most concerned relation? Running your own little investigation so you can feel satisfied?"

She didn't answer. She was waiting for the rest of the critique, that selfish is as selfish does. But instead, he surprised her, extending his hands palms up to make the offering. "I put out an APB from the information I got last night canvassing the building. I've got myself a portrait of Chazz Perry that's been hot-wired out and our friend Pedro will add a few lines to it. If the gods are with us, we'll pick him up. Will that do?"

"It's a start," she said softly.

"It won't bring the girl back," he said. "I'm not paid to work miracles." He reached out and took her hand. Emma was surprised, and more surprised that she didn't immediately pull away. Instead, she suddenly felt lightheaded, like a teenager. "I've got to go," he said, and threw a broad smile her way. He knows what he's doing, she thought. He released her hand, dropped a ten on the table and said, "That should cover everything. I don't want anyone seeing this as a bribe. So where's your husband this morning? I'm surprised he lets you out. Doesn't he know what kind of mischief you get up to?"

"We're separated." Emma was grateful to hear the steel in her voice. "At least that wasn't going to betray her. "Our son's with him for the weekend."

"That's tough. The kids really dog you with it. My son still goes on about how I let his mom go. And it's been ten whole years. Plus, putting him through Miami U just about shoved me into the poorhouse. Funny, isn't it? How you don't begrudge them one dime? You'd give your kid the pie in the sky, if you could reach it." Emma nodded sympathetically. And he leaned over, kissing her on the cheek. Did he really do that, she wondered, reaching up instinctively to touch the spot. "Just checking," he said, then turned and strolled away.

Her hands danced around, nervous, edgy. She forced them into her lap. When she could breathe evenly, she took his ten dollars and slid it into her wallet, noting the ring of water left by his glass and the brown rim where her own milkshake had rested. Nothing happened here, she told herself. But her body was tingling, offering a convincing alternative argument.

Emma spent the rest of the afternoon back at her house, catching up on the little that Dawn had been able to dig up on Loretta Picard. Loretta's mom had had a history of mental illness. In fact, the poor woman had hanged herself inside the county jail one night, after being picked up on drunk and disorderly charges. At the time, Loretta had been fifteen and a freshman in high school. At the end of the year, she'd disappeared from Little Falls, New Jersey, for good. From the ages of sixteen to nineteen, she'd been in town. She refused to specify just how she'd made a living. She did admit she'd worked at the Pit for six months. When Dawn had pressed her, she'd denied any serious wrongdoing. Still, Emma had to assume, barring any sort of special skills, she'd either dealt drugs, turned tricks, or worked some other kind of scam to make a living on the fringes.

Loretta's ID began with a doctored birth certificate and Social Security card. After that, it was no problem obtaining a passport. She had declined to offer up the name of the skillful salesperson. Not that it mattered, Emma decided. These days, information was so thoroughly computerized, any decent hacker could come up with a way of ordering you a brand-spanking-new identity. Or if, by chance, you were still computer illiterate, you could do things the old-fashioned way, walking into the Hall of Records and offering a bribe.

They would have to start at her last and only place of employment. Dawn had already sent people downtown to talk to her boss, a man named Bill Weston. They had struck out so far. The Pit was a late-night hangout depending on the ebb and flow of clientele, which meant an after-hours adventure. Dawn had had better luck with Loretta's closest relation, an aunt named Brittany Manners who lived in Little Falls. Nothing this woman had to say was going to move a grand jury to mercy.

"Even when she was little, that Loretta always had a nasty way about her. I told my sister, but Marie, she never wanted to listen. She'd give that little girl of hers anything, thought she was the cat's meow, which, if you ask me, was the stupidest way to go. I tried explaining it to Marie, and she wouldn't hear a word against her baby. It's how she was, tender to a fault. When what that Loretta needed was a few rules and regulations. I won't speak badly of the dead, but you can see what happens if you let yourself get soft and sentimental. It's not that sort of world. And the sooner kids learn it, the better.

"You want to know the last time I saw Loretta? A week after Marie passed. She stopped over for a visit. And no, I won't tell you the rest. But I will say she wasn't setting foot in my house ever again. I mean, blood relation or no, I've had enough.

"Seeing her face like that, splashed all over the papers, wasn't a surprise. You want my advice? Put her down, that's what I say. Like a sick animal. She was always causing trouble. No, I'm not about to tell you how. Look it up yourself, if you care so much. Waste someone else's tax dollars, that's what you people do. All you want to do with these murderers is feed them and give them a paid vacation. That's what prison's like, fancy food and a cushy way of life. They got it too damn easy. The whole way this country's run just makes me sick."

Reggie's team would have a field day with her.

Brittany Manners would undoubtedly come back to haunt them at the trial. Or she might stonewall Reggie, then sell her story to the *Enquirer*. That way, prospective jurors could read it before their day in court. They'd lie as they often did with high-profile cases, pretending total ignorance.

Emma knew she'd have to make it her business to cross the Hudson. Well, at least a trip to the heartland of New Jersey always made her proud to be a New Yorker.

Dawn had faxed a short list of guidance counselors, teachers, and the name of the county social worker who'd counseled Loretta after her mother's death. As for the father? Loretta had been conceived in a certain amount of deliberate haste. On her real birth certificate, the father's name had been typed in as "unknown."

Emma went down the names and addresses of the contacts. Many still lived in Little Falls. But a few had moved on; to Atlanta, Sweet River, Alabama, Las Vegas, Nevada, one all the way to California, the Sunshine State. How was she going to manage those trips? You've taken on too much, she told herself. Still, she felt elated. The same way she'd felt earlier in the day, running the story by José Cantas. Good to be in pursuit of something tangible. So much easier than tangling with Will, trying to navigate the world of nebulous human emotions.

Then she read the initial intake interview. And began to reconsider.

LORETTA PICARD: *Who the fuck are you?*

DAWN PRESCOTT: *Your court-appointed attorney. You asked for an attorney.*

LORETTA PICARD: *Says who?*

DAWN PRESCOTT: *I must have been given the wrong information. Are you saying you want to represent yourself?*

LORETTA PICARD: *Nah. What do I care. All lawyers suck. All any of you want is money.*

DAWN PRESCOTT: *I'm court appointed. That means you don't have to pay me a cent. Listen, Ms. Picard. You're charged with the commission of a capital crime. You killed members of the police force. Right now, the governor, the mayor, and anyone else who has a political life all want your head on a platter.*

LORETTA PICARD: *Big fucking deal.*

It went on like that for a while with the two of them batting around various elements of Loretta's distrust. Finally, Loretta did agree to let Dawn represent her and signed on the dotted line, saying, "Hell, I guess I don't have much of a choice in this, it's not like I'm O.J."

Which led to Loretta's description of events.

LORETTA PICARD: *I had this coke. Some boy at the bar gave it to me. No, I don't know the stupidasshole's fucking name. He thought he could pass me the coke and then I'd give him a blowjob. Boy, was he wrong. I mean I'm not some stupidfuckingwhore you know? I got the shit home and I did a few lines and then my air conditioner, it's sort of old, Junior, the super said I could have it cause this guy left it in his place and god, it really sucks, it's so fucking annoying, well the thing broke down completely. Anyhow I had the window open to try and help with the heat cause it was hot as shit, and I had the music up a little loud cause I wanted to all right, it's a free fucking country. Anyhow this old bitch from across the hall, she's always looking at me funny, never giving me a hello like she would if she was decent and no, I don't know her name. She just fumbles with her clothes and gives me this cross-eyed stare like I'm Satan or doing some voodoo spell over her and I mean no way, I'm not into that shit. I knew it was her at the door, wanting to give me hell about the music, so I just thought I would scare her. That way she wouldn't be going bug-eyed at me all the time. The trigger must have slipped that's all and the next thing you know the cop's lying there. What was he doing up there anyhow?*

DAWN PRESCOTT: *There had been a complaint about the noise called in. They were trying to investigate.*

LORETTA PICARD: *You see. You see what I mean. A person can't live anywhere in peace.*

DAWN PRESCOTT: *What happened next, Loretta?*

LORETTA PICARD: *Well...I got scared, I guess. I mean he was a cop! Next thing I know I hear the girl coming up the stairs. So I guess it was self-defense or something. I mean, it was like I was in a war.*

DAWN PRESCOTT: *You say you opened the door and let off a round. But you hit Officer Larrabbee three times.*

LORETTA PICARD: *I was scared. I just didn't think, all right? All right?*

Dawn returned to the story several times, trying to drag out conflicting details. Each time Loretta's version was basically the same and remarkably like the one she'd offered in the transcript of the videotaped confession at the station house on East Fifth. Emma sighed, hearing her stomach rumble. At least the nausea appeared to have abated. She put the sheaf of papers into a file folder, then had an early-evening snack of barbecued potato chips. After she finished the entire bag, she tried Will's new number and was a little disconcerted when his mother, Melanie, answered the phone.

"Emma, how are you?" she asked solicitously.

"Just fine," Emma said, searching for the right tone, one that would be pleasant but bar further investigation. "Can you put Liam on?"

"Are you sure you're all right? If there's anything I can do."

"Let me speak to Liam," Emma said firmly. She was grateful to hear the phone being put down, then Melanie calling out for him, insisting that he come. It took several more minutes before Liam coughed into the receiver.

"What, Mom?" he asked, already sounding annoyed.

"I just wanted to say goodnight," she told him.

"Goodnight." And hung up before she could add another word.

She stared at the phone. She tried to laugh. It was pathetically hard. I deserve something for submitting to this, she thought. I want one of those permanently pressed white duck jackets the navy hands out. I want people to applaud when I walk past and count the medals, every single one of them awarded in the heat of combat. I want them to most especially note the three bronze stars and the distinguished service cross.

11

There were some people who swore that coincidence was predestination in disguise. Emma was not one of them. Still, there had been times when she wondered whether there was a supernatural power at work. Little things jogged this question into being. People who had slipped from her consciousness for years would suddenly come to mind during her morning shower. Later that afternoon she'd run into them on the steps of the Brooklyn Public Library. What were the odds? Better than if they'd moved to Cairo, she'd tell herself. It did make her wonder. But, if not coincidence, what? She had long ago precluded buying into the concept of God as a working deity, so Emma depended on her own peculiar mixture of science and emotion. This was what she turned to now, telling herself that the card she'd squashed into her pocket was simply a second set of reasons for making a late-night run to the Pit.

Emma got into the shower and rinsed off. In her closet there were dresses she hadn't worn in years. She settled for a black Betsey Johnson original that puffed out from the empire waist, hiding the small bulge already apparent around her midriff. She put a tape recorder, a notebook, and several leakproof pens into her leather backpack and left the hall light burning, locking the front door behind her.

The Pit opened at ten-thirty but, as with all happening nightspots, it didn't get really crowded until after one.

Emma recognized there were limits to her own perseverance. Add to this the exhaustion that came with being pregnant. She reminded herself, yet again, of the relief she would feel when she got rid of this child. But that thought threw her into a downward spiral. This was Will's child, after all, Will's and hers together. Sentiment has no place in this kind of decision, she told herself, then chided herself, knowing nothing could be farther from the truth.

She arrived at the Pit three minutes after the doors had opened.

Looking around the room, she had a hard time imagining why people would willingly leave their happy homes for this. The walls were painted maroon and someone had drawn stark black cartoon characters across the top of the hand-carved pale oak bar. She recognized Ren and Stimpy, the hapless *South Park* boy, Natasha and Boris and, was it really possible? Yes, those were the Fabulous Furry Freak Brothers. Quite the cross-generational seeding. The bartender had spiked black hair, a nose ring, two crosses dangling from his left ear, and a white T-shirt that showed off his gym-perfect musculature.

Emma ordered a Coke, stifled a yawn, then asked for the manager.

"Billy's not to be disturbed," the bartender said, emphasizing this with a practiced sullen look. But she matched him, pout for pout.

"I'm with the Capital Crimes Division, working on the Picard case. He knows I'm coming down."

"You got proof?"

Emma passed over one of her all-purpose business cards. It read EMMA PRICE, INVESTIGATOR and gave her home phone number and address. Anyone could have had one made up, but the bartender barely glanced at it, then pointed at a metal door with a round glass window cemented into the top of it. A man stood in front of it with his arms crossed.

"Tell Eliot over there what you want," he said.

"Did you know Loretta?" she asked.

"Not enough to care." He turned his back to her.

Compared to Eliot, the bartender was a 98-pound weakling. To undercut the threat, Eliot was dressed conservatively in a black suit of a discriminating Italian cut. The only flamboyance was the purple tie knotted at the neck. She flashed her card in his face and repeated her request.

"Whatcha wanna know about that girl?" he asked. "Poor Bill's been pulling out his hair over her. We got the licensing commission nosing around, threatening to close us down. But I mean, come on, the girl was freaky. How was he supposed to know? And Bill's such a good guy, really, feels sympathy for everyone."

Eliot seemed to expect commiseration. So Emma nodded agreeably. He acknowledged her good will with a half-moon smile, then led her up a metal stairway to the second floor, passing the DJ's suite and a room with a turquoise door that had a Mexican peasant art dog gracing it. They stopped in front of a silver door that boasted a submarine porthole. "Here you go," he said, knocking. When the door opened a crack, Emma inhaled marijuana smoke.

"What's up?" a voice asked.

"Billie boy, this lady here has come about Loretta."

"Not now," the voice said. The door was shoved back, but Eliot kept it open, using one beefy hand.

"Loretta's lawyer sent her."

"Oh, all right." The door swung open, permitting entry. "Sorry, I've just been in such a state."

Bill Weston had a mane of white hair and he inhabited the nether regions of middle age. A life of hard partying made an accurate guess at his birth date well-nigh impossible. Plus, there were deep lines on his face and the type of gauntness Emma associated with a long-term drug habit.

The office was small and immaculate. An expensive computer system nestled in one corner and waist-high file cabinets leaned against the far wall. Bill took a seat behind a sleek wooden desk, stubbing the joint out in his ashtray. The wall was festooned with photos; Bill with Lou Reed, both wearing shades, Bill with Andy and a young Ultra Violet, Bill with his arm round Truman Capote, Bill with Steve Rubell.

"In with the in-crowd," Emma said.

"Back when."

"Not now?"

"Now my job is hanging by a thread. And your client's responsible."

"They want you to be the scapegoat? That doesn't seem fair."

"Fair? Who said the world was fair? I'm paid to be expendable. Hell, you bounce back enough times, you get used to the acceleration principle. And the height." He winced, possibly from imagining his quick descent. "So what do you do for a living?" he asked.

"Investigate, just like it says on my card." Emma pulled out her notebook. "You had a very brief conversation with someone from our office and said that you hired Loretta on a friend's recommendation. Which friend is that? Could you be a bit more specific?"

"A friend is a friend is a friend," he said, and offered a sly wink.

Emma ignored the inference of complicity. "You can tell me now, or you can wait until the DA subpoenas you," she said.

"I can't see how this matters."

"Then why does it hurt to tell?"

He shrugged and offered up an ethereal smile. "We got her name from Penny Strider. Penny does a lot of work for us. Those cartoons behind the bar are hers. She did a tremendous job with the bathrooms. Penny's talent is so raw. Greatness seeps from her."

"I see," Emma said. Seeps? She couldn't help making a silent reference to Love Canal. "Can you remember what Penny Strider told you about Loretta to pique your interest?"

"That she knew her, knew she needed a job, and that Loretta would be perfect."

"Perfect how?" Emma asked.

"She'd fit in."

"Did she?"

"Obviously not, or we wouldn't be having this conversation." Bill raised his eyebrows dramatically. But Emma had to disagree. Wasn't that exactly the point of this sort of place? Kids coming here to pretend to rub shoulders with danger?

"Were there any complaints about her before the shooting?"

"None that I know of."

"You interviewed Loretta for the job?"

"I met with her briefly."

"And checked her references?"

"Not my department," he said stiffly. "Lisa Kravinovsky makes those calls."

Emma checked down her list of contacts. Finding the name, she circled it.

"I'll need to get in touch with her, and I'll need a number for Penny Strider, too. You might as well give them both to me now."

Bill rubbed his hands together, then spun open the Rolodex and wrote something down on a card. When he passed the sheet over, she saw he used a formal, grade-school print.

"You're a hands-off kind of guy?"

"If things flow right, you don't have to tamper," he told her.

"Words to live by," Emma said. Bill Weston was extending his hand as if this were the end of the interview but Emma sat there with her legs crossed. She didn't have to offer any further resistance. He melted back into his chair. "Was there anyone here who was close with Loretta?"

"I've got six different bartenders, forty waiters and waitresses moving around on the snack floor. Then there's the talent. I'm supposed to baby-sit them, too. Ever try to keep kids this age happy? They think they're God's chosen sons and daughters. That, by itself, is a full-time job." He leaned in conspiratorially. "Ms. Price, you must see that this Loretta was a type."

"How so?"

"Not the warmest individual."

"That was why you hired her."

"True enough. You don't have to win Miss Congeniality to be a bartender. And no, this place isn't about being sweet and pleasant. It's about having an edge. Loretta had an edge."

Emma noted that he again referred to her in the past tense. Wishful thinking, she decided. Bill Weston was the type who wished for smooth sailing every minute of the day. And apparently, rarely got his wish.

Poor Bill, she thought, he obviously needs to get back to his heavy spliff-smoking schedule. "Do you consider yourself a good judge of human nature?" she asked.

"Impeccable." He stood, cocking his finger as if it were a gun, squeezing off an invisible round. "This is the end, Ms. Price," he said. The Ms. was clearly derogatory. Emma reached out. His palm was cold. The handshake lasted barely two seconds.

She didn't find it hard to dislike Weston. For one thing, Emma had never had much tolerance for potheads. People who smoked from morning to night got fuzzy around the edges. They let the world sail on without them. Plus, he seemed the sort of man who depended on being disagreeable as a way of investing himself with a supposedly unique personality.

Weston's office was soundproofed. Outside the door, the music from the club had been a little fainter than it would be on the dance floor, but still close to deafening. She started back down the catwalk, and halfway down, an imposing body barred her progress.

"Eliot," she said.

"The boss is taking all this pretty hard. What a shame, this kind of thing happening."

"A real shame," Emma agreed.

"That girl just went crazy, you know. Went off or something."

"She was high. It might be that."

"No way. Plenty of people get high. You don't see them going out and mowing people down. If you ask me, she had to have a screw loose upstairs."

"You could be right," Emma said. "How well did you know her?"

"Me and Loretta?" He blanched as if the very thought was insulting.

"So she wasn't your type," Emma said, smiling.

"I steer clear of all entanglements with coworkers." Eliot still wasn't letting her pass. "The boss, did he say anything much to help you out? The whole thing's stressed him. He even sent a contribution to the Policemen's Fund for that poor guy's widow." Eliot stretched his arms above his head and rolled his back like a cat. Emma could make out the distinct sound of bones cracking. When she didn't respond, he added, "Where're you heading next?"

"Home," Emma said. "It's past my bedtime."

She wondered if the *Post* was tantalizing him, holding out money for some juicy secret he had to discover on the sly. "Is there anyone else here who was friends with Loretta?" she asked.

He shrugged, looking her up and down, then apparently gave up on whatever he'd been intending, and started down the stairs. He pulled the door open, holding it for her like a perfect gentleman. As she stepped out, Emma caught his eye and couldn't resist. Ridiculous, really. But she had to ask someone and here he was, making himself more than available. "Eliot," she said, leaning in confidingly, "do you happen to know a guy named Chazz?"

He blinked several times, and looked pointedly away. His tongue was tripping over his teeth, getting smashed up on those ivory rocks. "Chazz. Is that some sort of nickname?"

He does know him, she thought, and felt the surge of adrenaline.

"What's he look like, anyway?" Eliot asked, his voice a notch too high.

"Blond . . . good-looking, three ruby studs in one ear. He has a girlfriend named Beatriz."

"There's lots of guys in here I say hello to. I don't know their actual names. Chazz." He was offering a poor rendition of the thought process. "Sorry, I just can't recall."

Then he turned away, waved to someone, and walked off way too quickly, making it to the bar in record time. He leaned over to speak with the bartender. Emma counted. Two minutes, three minutes, five. Eliot never turned her way again. Instead, he stepped around the bar and disappeared into the bowels of the club.

Emma went back up to the bar and ordered a juice drink. The bartender served her without meeting her eyes. "Excuse me," she said, trying to coax a verbal response. He took her order without meeting her eyes.

I've gone invisible, she thought. That happened awfully fast.

The room was beginning to fill up with people who were half her age and looked even younger. Emma tried not to torture herself, still when she scanned the crowd there were too many attractive, limber women with no perceivable body fat. Social Distortion's new album was playing over the loudspeaker system. Two men came out and began to set up microphones on the raised stage. Emma tried to imagine Bea as a regular, and couldn't make the leap of imagination that required. The girls wore short pleated skirts, black no-sleeve and high-necked sweaters, and ugly plaid dresses that looked as if they were made out of some harsh, permanently rigid fabric. They had on too much dark lipstick and dashes of eye shadow. Their hair was graced with purple and light blue streaks. Their noses and mouths were pierced. They sported tattoos on various hidden and obvious parts of their bodies. It was a largely white clientele, only a smattering of black or Hispanic faces. And they were all a decade younger than Jesus had been when the troops up on Calvary hill stuck him on the cross to die.

Emma made her way through the crowd to find the bathroom. The door was puce. A Lambda marker graced it. Inside, a girl stood at the sink, smoking a spliff, then put it down to adjust her contact lens. The walls had been painted light blue. They were decorated with animals in the primitive style that Keith Haring had made entirely too popular. Except that this work had none of Haring's sense of playfulness. The animals were vicious, chewing off one another's heads. The mural above the sinks depicted some grotesque sun-worshipping ceremony. At the very top of the pyramid, a spread-eagled bear was being sacrificed by a pack of wolves. The artist's work was powerful, original, and all too familiar.

So it was Penny Strider who had painted the walls of Beatriz's one-bedroom apartment. Penny Strider who had decorated those aqua kitchen cabinets and left her tag on the hand-painted china.

Curiouser and curiouser, she thought. A stall door swung open and she entered. The inside of the stall was hot pink. She sat down on the toilet and read the graffiti that had been liberally added to the walls. LESLIE LOVES THE FUCK OUT OF MONA. I'M GONNA GET YOU TRACY. THIS SHIT HURTS. ECSTASY IS BEST. ACID NOT HEROIN. One piece of the graffiti looked more permanent. A frame had been gouged out, right above the sanitary napkin disposal. Hand-stenciled in black, the inscription read . . .

AND TRAVELLERS NOW WITHIN THAT VALLEY,
THROUGH THE RED-LITTEN WINDOWS, SEE
VAST FORMS THAT MOVE FANTASTICALLY
TO A DISCORDANT MELODY;
WHILE, LIKE A RAPID GHASTLY RIVER,
THROUGH THE PALE DOOR . . .

12

After eleven in Nogales, New Mexico. The Owl Diner had a sign in the window, OPEN ALL NIGHT, TRUCKERS MORE THAN WELCOME. Miriam Watkins hung her apron by the back door, slung her purse over her arm, and called out a goodbye. In the parking lot, three trucks were parked next to each other, nesting. On the other side, Pablo's car and Estelle's Jeep. Estelle had gone crazy when she found it at the police auction more than a month before, boasted how it was fully loaded and not even a scratch. Then a buddy of Pablo's had told her why. It was so neat cause it was the property of a suicide. Since then Estelle had been afraid she was driving with the poor man's ghost.

Miriam got into her eight-year-old Honda Accord. Nothing plush in there. Just total evidence of her life. Stains made by Lisa spitting up. The girl could keep nothing inside during a trip. And Cole Jr. brought debris with him everywhere, have junk, will travel was his motto. Saltines and chocolate nuggets from Milky Way bars wasted into the floor, ground in so hard that the vacuums at Bob's Auto Wash barely made a dent.

By the time she got home, Andy would be waking up for the night shift. She'd get a kiss. A chuck on the chin. She tried remembering the last time they'd had sex. Pretty much the stuff of fairy tales. Her girlfriends said that was to be expected, but she had a vacation planned. She'd gotten Estelle to commit to a nighttime sit on Sunday, and she and Andy were going to take a spare room at the Shady Rest. Something she'd read about in *Cosmo*, how to keep your marriage on track. Got herself a nice negligee at Kmart. The way she imagined, they'd stop in at Home Liquors and get themselves a bottle of Cristal. Then ease, a king-sized bed, and 317 channels off the satellite dish.

Funny how life turned out, imagining sex with your husband in a roadside motel like this was going to be the adventure of a lifetime.

Eight miles to the side road, then up the tracks to home. She bent over the radio, adjusting. Easy enough to speed this time of night, but hard with the way the car took the power. You went over sixty and it started to sound as though it was about to shiver apart at the seams.

It was the kind of night you never got at home. A tiny sliver of moon, and the stars thrown up around it, threading out in all their glory. The night sky was a curiosity, the way it shifted with the seasons, telling different sorts of stories.

Miriam felt herself about to pass into dreaming, the exhaustion tugging at her to come. One truck rushed by in the opposite direction, heading toward Nogales. Then it was still and silent. The radio was playing "My Baby," all that old-time sixties junk her mom had listened to, and Miriam tapped her fingers along to it, trying to pry her eyes back open.

Two more miles to the pulloff, a dirt road so small most people overlooked it. Then the hilltop climb. Not much of a house, only two bedrooms. But the spot? Serenity plus, the way you could see down into the painted desert, the shadows curling over the whole of it at dusk.

The car was glowing. Someone coming up fast from behind. Looking in her rearview she recognized one of those monster SUVs. The kind she'd have to get when they scraped enough money together. The way those headlights made your own car glow at night as they passed, as though a spaceship were landing right on the roof. She slowed down just a notch, to let the dangerous speed it had on it cruise by. Only it didn't, settling in behind her, so that she had to put her hand up to shade the glow away and adjust her mirror. Glancing back, she found the big truck's grill way too close for comfort. Then it punched into her, and she grabbed onto her own wheel tight, veering away onto the other part of the highway, then lost control, banging up onto the side of the road, and over into the ditch, before coming to a stop.

She smelled burning rubber and heard the wail of the other car's brakes. Then there was someone coming and she saw the flashlight beams, realized there were two of them, bent down, and went scrambling for the gun she had in the glove compartment, had it in her hand when the first one bent over and fired, fired at the light.

"Jesus Christ, lady," the man's voice said. "Are you crazy? I was coming to see if you were all right."

"Oh god, oh god," she said, muttered it to herself.

The light fluttered out there. Her hands were shaking, holding the gun. And she realized she was bleeding, there was as metallic taste on her tongue.

The light scanned the car and then a light came from the other side.

"You see her in there," the other voice said. Then both lights clicked off at once. It was stone cold dark and there was a part of her that thought yes, they were only trying to help and the whole thing was some kind of stupid accident, only how did they know she was a woman, how had they seen her and made her out, was it under the flashlight beam, there were things you could see, he'd seen her maybe. But he'd been too far, too far away, and she'd bent over. She unlocked the seat belt and slid down cradling the gun, waiting. What could she do? What could she hope to do against the two of them?

Into the silence, an owl's voice floated up. In the bed sleeping safe, Cole's arm stretched out on top, one hand jammed into his mouth, for comfort. The baby, put down on her side, asleep, too, still and lonely. Andy, already awake, waiting for her at the breakfast table, his lunch all packed with coffee in a thermos to see him through.

The glass shattered on both sides at once. And she was already pleading, words gasping out of her mouth to explain, shooting blindly into the dark, telling them that she was someone's mother, someone's wife, someone's daughter, telling them that they were bastards, howling at them and shooting until the chamber was empty. The first bullet hit her in the shoulder, the next in the leg. She still managed to drag herself out of the car where they had the chance to finish her, as she crawled away.

13

By the time Solomon dropped Carmen Castillo and her daughter off at a friend's house, it was after nine. Then Solomon went to a phone booth and punched in Emma Price's number. He felt the need for a public, well-trafficked spot. And also felt tangibly disappointed when no one answered, leaving a message as to the time and location of the funeral service, before heading home to bed.

Rising early the next day, he showered, shaved, and put on his mourning suit, a larger version of the same outfit he'd been given as a boy. Laurence Solomon was nothing if not his father's son. As such, he had once been heir apparent to the family fortune, Solomon's Funeral Home, a respectable business operating out of a Normandy-style townhouse at the easternmost end of one of the finest blocks in Sugar Hill, Harlem.

At four, Solomon had been pressed into service, his father, Arthur, bringing him home an elegant black suit and Laurence had worn it to greet the bereaved at the door, leading them inside like the good shepherd he most certainly was. There had been many kind comments from the adults about his gravity and maturity. Arthur had gathered in the compliments and swallowed them up like a deep, deep well.

Arthur Solomon. A man of the old school. He'd only say he was going to punish you once. If you disobeyed him in any way after that, he responded with lightning-quick efficiency. Arthur had had a fertile testing ground for his rigid

theories on child rearing. Not Laurence, no, it was Ralph, his
eldest, who had driven him crazy. Old women in the neighborhood said that Ralph had a birthmark in the shape of a
cloven hoof because he was the devil's own earthly son. His
best scam? Charging neighborhood kids admission to see
the nastiest bodies. Ralph got his butt beaten raw for that
one. Then Arthur locked him in with his biggest money
earner all night long.

Their mother, Patience, liked to claim Ralph was "spir-
ited." And when Arthur would try to starve his eldest son
into submission, Patience would take pity, sneaking dinner
up to him by way of Laurence. When Ralph's allowance was
docked, he could always hit his mother for a loan. Finally, in
frustration, Arthur did the one thing he could to assert his
power as supreme lord and master: he withdrew his love.

By the time Laurence was old enough to analyze what he
saw around him, he was witnessing the end result, how
Ralph and Arthur didn't speak. It would have taken a fool
not to realize that it was to be his job to make up for this, the
most burning loss in his father's life. Laurence did his best
for as long as he could stand to.

He could still conjure up the kitchen in that house with its old,
round-faced fridge and the red-and-white gingham curtains
Patience had sewn. He could see his twenty-two-year-old self
taking a seat at that same table and, with the brash arrogance
of youth, telling his widowed father that he'd had enough.

"What's this you're saying?" Arthur had cupped his hand
round his ear.

"I can't take the business from you, Daddy. I just can't.
It's not for me."

"And why the hell not?"

"I just don't have what it takes. People come in here wanting relief. It's worse than being a preacher, the way you have

to sit with them and comfort them. I don't have the gift you have, I just won't be able to provide." Solomon had thought he was being so smart, going about his defection by heaping on praise and making himself out to be weak, instead of raising his real objections, how it was ghoulish, making a profit off of someone else's loss.

"Gave you everything you ever had in life. Now it's not for you?" Arthur snorted his disapproval, then turned his face away as if he couldn't endure the shame. They didn't say another word to each other that night. Two days later, Arthur went out to get the paper, paid the newsman for it, turned the corner, and collapsed on the pavement, victim of a massive heart attack.

Laurence was the one who prepared his own father's body, then greeted the mourners and led the procession in the funeral home's black hearse to the Mount Zion Baptist Cemetery. A week later, he sold the business, sharing the profits with Ralph. That money had kept him going for a while. He thought about law school, thought and thought. But when the money ran out, he did the stupidest thing he could and enrolled at the Police Academy.

His youthful training did come in handy. He knew what to say when Ruiz stumbled as he was supposed to offer consolation to the bereaved. And yesterday, down at the morgue, Solomon had let Carmen Castillo sink against him, let her weep and pray after he'd rolled open the drawer to show her Beatriz's body. He'd given Carmen time to kiss her daughter on the cheek before wrapping her up in his arms and saying certain comforting words. Then he'd gotten her back out to the car where she and her youngest had wept together on the drive to Luke Mattiglione's Funeral Home. Going in, he'd shot Luke a meaningful look to make sure she got the best deal possible on the coffin. It was good of him to do all that, sure, but Laurence Solomon didn't do it selflessly. Long experience had taught him it was important to find a place for yourself inside the inner circle. If he'd learned one thing from Arthur, it was how, in the midst of loss, people were at their most vulnerable.

He drove Carmen and her younger daughter Ana back to Bea's apartment to help them sort through her books and clothing. On the way, he confirmed that Bea was a non-swimmer. Her sister said Bea wouldn't even set foot in the pool when she visited them in Florida. "And that water wasn't even deep," Ana added. Then Carmen broke down weeping and saying *"Oh, Dios mío."*

"Maybe you should do this later," he said, as he was helping her from the car. But she shook her head firmly.

Inside the apartment, Carmen gathered together a collection of photographs, then sank onto the living room couch. So it was Ana who took charge, heading for the bedroom. He walked in to find her sorting through clothing and emptying out drawers. She turned around to face him and there was this guilty, furtive look. He knew then she had been checking for signs of anything she might have to conceal or evacuate. "Mami, the detective's right," she said, averting her eyes. "Let's come back later." The tremble in her voice showed she was not used to subterfuge.

"When you do come back to pack up the rest, let me know," he said, walking them out.

"You're so kind to help." Carmen had kissed him on the cheek, leaving a thread of tears.

"Let me know," he said again, this time to Ana and locked the apartment door. He handed Carmen the key. There was certainly no point in telling her how he'd already dusted for fingerprints, then cleaned up the traces. So far he'd been unable to compile evidence that could move this into the realm of a murder investigation and until he did, he was acting primarily on instinct. Right now the best argument he'd be able

to forward if he got dressed down by Bernardino for wasting
time, was how he was working on finding an elusive missing
person. He'd called in a favor at the bureau, and run the
prints in Bea's apartment through the register of known of-
fenders. Of course, they'd come up blank. So Carmen
Castillo didn't need to know that or how he'd put a new lock
on the door and posted a watch for as many hours as he
could scam from another pal who owed him big time, just in
case Chazz Perry did decide to show.

Carmen got into the taxi, and Laurence Solomon waited
for Ana, still holding the door.

"We need to talk," he said firmly, before she bent down.

She threw a worried look her mother's way.

"I won't say a thing to her about the boyfriend until I
have to."

"Where is he?" she whispered. He shook his head to indicate his ignorance. "Oh, God." She gasped and then new
tears sprang up.

Her dress, primness personified; a Peter Pan collar, lace at
the hem. Her shoulder length hair flipped under perfectly.
Turning away, Solomon had totted up everything he knew
about Beatriz Castillo and thought about the starkness of the
contrast between the siblings.

The Castillo service was in the Chapel of Peace. Stepping
into the reception area, Solomon found the room full to
choking. Carmen and Ana perched delicately on a formal
velvet couch, Ana with her arm around her mother. Laurence
went up to pay his respects, received another kiss for his
trouble, then excused himself. Inside the chapel, he took a
seat in the very last row, stretching his legs out into the aisle.
One of the benefits of being six feet two was, you almost always could claim the superior vantage point.

* * *

The best-case scenario, Solomon thought, this Chazz was out in the water with his girl and she went under. Still, what kind of asshole takes a nonswimmer into demon-sized waves?

Bea's last meal had been beach food, a hot dog and fries, only partially digested, and the coroner gave the mealtime as two to three hours prior to submersion. She'd been in the water roughly twenty-four hours, give or take a little more, then gotten thrust up on land. There had been plenty of beachgoers the day before they found her body, even with the beaches closed to wading, and Solomon had sent a few foot soldiers out to talk with the regulars but, so far, no one admitted to seeing the girl or anyone resembling the sketch of Chazz Perry. Of course, if the two of them had been down at the beach after dark, it would go some way toward explaining why they hadn't been spotted. The girl had been wearing a bikini bottom when she was found. Why would anyone get into a bikini and go wading into danger in the dark? There was only one thing Laurence Solomon was beginning to be sure of. If this Chazz Perry did turn up, he was not going to be someone Solomon would be able to admire. Chazz Perry. Probably not even his real name. Solomon had been able to ascertain that the Miata had worn a New York tag, but there was no blue Miata registered to a Chazz or a Charles Perry. And no Miata had turned up in any of the public parking lots near Coney, either in its original pristine state or dismembered. Someone could have jacked it and ripped it apart by now, but Solomon had seen the same signs Emma Price had pointed out, the glasses and plates, still damp, and bald spots on various pieces of furniture. Add to that the absence of any male clothing and you got a picture of someone ridiculously tidy. Which meant he wasn't running out of panic, he was running because it was part of a plan.

Solomon had read the girl's diary. All of it foolish gushing schoolgirl stuff about how much she loved her "baby." The only specifics he'd been able to cull was a description of this tattoo Chazz had, Bea describing kissing her honey down in his private parts, then lip syncing over his mascot, a dog threaded in blue ink doing a canine tap dance above his pubic hair. The things kids did to their bodies. As if someone else's artistic sentiment inscribed on your flesh was going to make you special.

These last few months, Beatriz had neglected to make regular entries. It was what happened when you were young, you didn't think about making a record for posterity.

He recalled his own arrogance, how he'd felt superior to the work, too good to deal with the dear departed and the poor lost souls they'd left behind. Morbid? Pumping a body full of formaldehyde was nothing compared to examining an entry wound or taking in a room and noting how body parts had been rearranged, pieces of bone used as a new, rose-colored type of decor. Not to mention what it was like trying to ID a floater, the smell so thick you had to scrub off for days to get yourself even moderately fresh. He stifled a smile, thinking just how perversely pleased Arthur Solomon would have been if he could only see him now.

14

Emma Price woke up at 9:44, stared at the clock for a furious minute and a half, then reached for the alarm button, jamming it down. There was still a low buzzing noise. She threw the clock against the wall in disgust and dove into the shower. Afterward, thumbing through her closet, Emma could find only one semiappropriate outfit.

Even though she was late, mourners still jammed the reception area and a line snaked toward the door. Emma joined it, scrutinizing the crowd in the hopes of finding a familiar face, noting how the lack of her usual stiff cup of morning coffee was already having an effect. She felt the throbbing that was the first sign of a caffeine-withdrawal headache.

"Thanks for letting me know about this." A voice came from behind. Turning, Emma noted Suzanne's formal black dress, her high heels and taupe stockings. Then she glanced down reflexively at her own outfit, a form-fitting Lycra black dress from an era when she'd still had stomach muscles. She'd covered it with a dark gray silk vest to hide the bulge.

"I'd pay good money for a cup of coffee," she confided.

But then they were being pushed ahead. Emma had to meet Carmen Castillo's watery gaze. And she flinched. Luckily, her brain quickly registered all possible facial responses, settling on a solemn, slightly pained look. "Carmen," Emma said. "I'm so sorry."

"How could this have happened?" Carmen asked so

earnestly, Emma felt called upon to provide a suitable explanation. Except that she had none to tender.

"It's such a tragedy." Suzanne interrupted, taking both of Carmen's hands in her own, then kneeling on the carpet. "The only thing we can do right now is pray."

Coming from someone else, the words would have made Emma laugh, but Suzanne sounded completely genuine. And Emma knew how earnestly she believed in a mutable, amorphous greater being. The key word being mutable, Emma reminded herself. Their last year at college, Suzanne had taken up Eastern philosophy with a vengeance, and since then, she'd toppled through at least ten various phases before landing with a crash in her current Zen Buddhist pose. Each enthusiasm led to an attempt at conversion. And each time Emma would nod, smiling reasonably for as long as she could, before telling Suze to go proselytize somewhere else.

People claimed that tragedy was what cemented one's relationship with God, how in the midst of disasters, a strong belief in God was a comfort. In that case, Emma thought, I had my shot with Rosa. Her older sister had been thirty, doing postgraduate work in England. Rosa was on her way to visit a friend who was staying at his family's cottage in the Scottish Highlands, when the plane went down.

Rosa, who had inherited her fervent Marxism from their father. A belief not unlike Suzanne's devotion. And one that had been so much more fashionable in the late sixties, before the collapse of worldwide socialism. Her thesis, done at Cambridge, discussed the slave trade and its effect on the developments of sugar plantations in Cuba.

Loch Ness was supposed to be home to Nessie. Many claimed they'd sighted the serpent. Of course, in the morning, the fog was so dense, it would have been easy for a small child or a willing adult to trick themselves into believing those were Nessie's sad eyes rearing up out of the mist and her green scaly body, breaching the water.

That Loch was so deep, divers couldn't reach the bottom. Apparently, it once had been home to a glacier that had receded, leaving a cool blue chip of itself behind.

Emma had driven their parents to JFK. Pierce, Rosa's lover, had met them at the gate in Edinburgh. Later the three of them stood on the lake shore, watching search parties press on with their work, divers in wet suits and town men who did this for a living. In their time they had brought up the capsized bodies of children and tourists, even recovering mermaids who had taken a wrong turn and gotten land-locked. But they were unable to find her sister's body.

There had apparently been no sound at all, just the metal body spiraling down. The pilot had been pulled from the wreckage alive, and eight other passengers had survived. Seventeen were lost, Rosa among them.

Emma still woke in the hour between deep night and dawn and lay there, attempting a resurrection. But in recent days, she could only come up with snatches; Rosa drawing, making six-year-old Emma sit still while she worked on that clever portrait. Rosa offering her bribes; spirals of red licorice with nuggets of coral pink sugar at the center. Rosa holding Emma in her lap and showing her how to play patty cake for the camera. Rosa, cartwheeling over a hill and Emma trailing behind. Rosa shrugging her shoulders and Emma shrugging, too, making her face into a facile imitation, the two of them striding down Johnson Avenue fiercely defiant . . . ever proud.

Faith in some higher power hadn't welled up in her when Rosa died. And it didn't overtake her now. But Emma, who rarely worried over her lack of spiritual conviction, knew she was about to be confronted by a roomful of true believers and the ferocity of her own difference, her singular, vulnerable state, was suddenly unnerving.

"Poor pitiful me," she muttered, trying to make it into a joke. A deep sadness overtook her. Suzanne touched her shoulder and Emma shook Suzanne off as gently as she could.

In the next room, an ivory coffin with gold inlay sat on a raised platform.

"Just remember to cremate me," Suzanne said. "No matter what my loving husband says. I have it in my will, don't let him try and talk you out of it."

"Suze!" Emma couldn't help smiling. "There are certain things you can't control."

"You should talk, control freak number one. I'm serious, Em. I don't want people staring at me. It's one thing if you look as good as Bea. But who wants to admire some rubber-faced hag?"

"She doesn't look good, Suze. No one looks good as a corpse."

Bea wore a red satin party dress, a full-length mass of frills and bows. Her cheeks had been rouged and her lips painted. Emma moved closer to inspect the jewelry; gold earrings, and a pendant around her neck with BEATRIZ written in gold script. They had dispensed with the nose ring, skillfully hiding the hole, and Bea's hair was a cascade of perfect curls.

Suzanne tugged, forcing Emma to turn away and search for seats as far from the stage as possible. She came upon Solomon and decided he'd stand in for a friendly face. Plus, there were two empty seats next to him. She introduced Suzanne, noting how she gave him a keen once-over.

As she took her seat, Emma realized her head was pounding.

"You don't look good," Suzanne said. "Are you going to faint?"

"You're sick?" It was Solomon asking. And, she noted, not unkindly.

"Simple caffeine withdrawal." Emma knew it was more than that. Grief, she thought, exhaustion. Plus my condition. But the pain was so intense. And she realized she was shivering. I might black out, she thought. Which was absolutely too bizarre to contemplate.

"I'll get you some water," Suzanne said, brushing past her. Emma leaned forward taking deep breaths, the pain in her head immediate and overwhelming. Then she felt a hand clamp down on her neck.

"Here?" Solomon asked. He pressed down hard, pushing his fingers into the muscle. She wanted to scream. Instead she bit down on her lower lip and panted, the way she had in labor. And suddenly, miraculously, her head cleared.

"Better?" He had removed his hand. Emma reached up to make sure her head was still screwed on to her body.

"How did you do that?" she asked.

"Pressure points."

"Incredible. A true Renaissance man." Emma blinked. She could register detail again and noted the generic black suit and wing-tipped shoes. He was studiously somber, the sole exception being the diamond stud in his left earlobe. In this guise he looked, if possible, even more attractive.

"Have you found Chazz?"

He shook his head. Then she remembered that other small and decidedly unpleasant detail.

"This is awkward." She took the business card out of her purse, and unceremoniously dropped it into his hands. "I found this at Bea's."

"What?"

"It dropped out of her diary. All right. I know. I shouldn't have been there in the first place, shouldn't have been reading it either. I was going to put it back when Ruiz came in and I . . ." She hesitated. "I guess I got nervous," she said.

"How about yesterday?" he asked. "What was stopping you from giving it to me then?"

She couldn't exactly say it had slipped her mind. Emma opened her mouth, then shut it. There was no excuse. Besides, she was tired of excuses, tired of hearing them. And tired of providing them. People do horrible things to each other, she thought. Then they tender an apology and assume they'll get off, scot-free. The way the bereaved look at you, when you're sitting at the defense table and the defendant testifies in his or her own behalf, saying "sorry." They shoot daggers with their eyes. You can only try to deflect them and save yourself. A sad and ignoble truth. How nothing can ever be enough.

One of those generic men who work in funeral parlors tested the microphone with a somber and inauthentic grace. Emma imagined him cooing at the bodies as he pumped them full of formaldehyde.

"Ladies and gentlemen, friends of Beatriz Castillo." He paused, waiting for silence. "Mary Cruz would like to say a few words." And a plump woman in a brown-and-white striped dress stepped forward.

At that moment, Suzanne returned with a small paper cup filled to the brim. Emma drank, more from gratitude than any real need. And Mary Cruz turned toward the coffin, theatrically sweeping the air above it with her hand.

"*Mi Beatriz*," she said as she bent forward, settling both hands on Beatriz's face and closing her eyes.

Emma glanced at Suzanne who had her own eyes closed and her head bowed, as did the rest of the assembled mourners. Only Solomon's eyes were wide open. Only Solomon was staring straight ahead.

"Amen," Mary said.

"Amen," the assembled mourners repeated.

Mary made the sign of the cross over Beatriz's body then turned back to the microphone. "Such a beautiful girl." Mary Cruz paused to pick up a glass of water and she took a sip, all the while managing to beam out at the audience. Emma recognized two of Bea's old friends, Mathilde Reyes and another girl Bea had known since junior high school, seated next to Ana. The rest of the crowd was unfamiliar, middle aged, Hispanic, and largely female; the room a collection of heavily painted faces and low-level beehive hairdos. Turning around, Emma did catch sight of the courtly Southern gentleman who had ushered her into 396 Fifth. He was standing by the door, his head slightly bowed in prayer, a neighbor coming to pay his respects. Decent. And apparently more than José Cantas could manage.

"Sisters and brothers," said Mary, "I am so pleased to see you here today. Many of you know how Carmen and I have been sisters in the Lord for over twenty years, how Beatriz was one of her two little gifts of joy. I can remember when sister Carmen brought her little lamb to our church for her baptism. I knew then she would have a special purpose.

"Beatriz was never afraid of the power of the Lord. She never hesitated. She was our sweet little angel. She came on Saturdays to help us with our preparations, on Sundays to learn at our knee. I say it to you now, full of confidence, she knew Jesus. So I stand here in front of you today, happy because I know that Beatriz was wise, and because of this wisdom was taken, snatched up to be raised on high.

"A child so full of devotion, so tender, so loving. Today I am here to tell you that our Beatriz is happy. She's standing at Jesus' right hand and he's looking into her eyes. And do you know what he sees there? Joy. Only joy."

"Don't you fucking cut me! Get her away from me. Jesus, get the knife!" It was a man's voice. Everyone turned to find its owner. He wasn't hard to spot. He was heading up the center aisle, making for the coffin.

"Bea's father," Emma whispered to Solomon. "Lucien Agosta. He's crazy." The word hardly doing justice to the poor man's condition. Solomon shrugged. Even his disdain was elegant. She admired it, and admired how he studiously ignored her. Then Lucien squealed as if he'd been struck in the gut and springing forward, lashed out at an invisible foe. When he appeared to have subdued them, he pulled himself up to his full height, turning to face the front of the room. "Maria Cruz? Get your fucking face away from my daughter. Good-for-nothing whore of Babylon." Carmen reached for him, but as her hand made contact, he jumped away, as if a scorpion had swung out its tail. "Don't you dare," he said, and Carmen sank back into her chair, leaning her head in her hands.

"Shame on you, Lucien." Mary Cruz was shaking her finger at him in a schoolmarmish gesture. Solomon tried to stand, but Emma tugged him back.

"Wait," she said. He firmly removed her hand, then got up and stepped over to the rear exit door, leaning against it, to make himself into a physical warning.

"My little baby. You see what she did? She tried walking on the water. She never listened to her papi. I told her. You gotta be white as sugar. You gotta be like that. If the lion lies down with the lamb, then the lamb gets eaten up. She should have seen what I tried to show her. And now she's gone, just look!"

"Lucien Agosta." Mary Cruz touched his shoulder but he swiped her hand away.

"Don't you touch me, you foul-mouthed whore. I've seen

you sneaking around all over, counting your money up. My daughter doesn't want you here." He raised a hand as if to strike her down. "Get thee from me, whore! I know what you did with Rafael Sabato. You're so good, go tell his wife how you got down on your knees and sucked on her husband's cock. How you licked his balls."

There was a sharp intake of breath. Emma wondered if this came from Rafael Sabato's corner. Mary Cruz's face had gone bright red. Then Ana was walking up to him and taking him into her arms. "Papi, come on now," she said. He crumpled, turning into a bent, broken thing. She led him off to a corner of the room and there was an awkward silence. Mary smoothed out the wrinkles in her dress, then boldly raised her eyes as if daring them to say another word. She put a hand up to her hair, patting it back into place.

"Let us pray," she said, breathing hoarsely.

There was muttering. Dissension in the ranks, Emma thought.

"Let us pray," she said again, her voice firmer. "O Lord, sweet Jesus, let this girl be a lesson to all of us. She is saved, but we are still sinners. She will be next to her Lord on the judgment day, but how many of us can say the same? Let us pray that we can be with her, that we can follow in the path of her righteousness. Let her show us the way.

"For those of us who have sinned, may we sin no more. For those of us who have forsaken Jesus, let him into your souls."

Cries of "*Dios mío*" and "*Perdóneme*" broke out.

"You do forgive us, Jesus, even this poor sinner. You wash us all clean. Because you see how we loved this child. And we, in turn, see your glory. Sweet Jesus, Amen. Let us walk in the path of righteousness, let us walk with the light, and let us step out of the darkness."

Someone in the front screamed out, "Bless you, Lord."

"I want to say this now. Jesus never does anything without a reason. He has a purpose for this young girl. He wants her with him. Because we know soon there will be a call. Soon, those of you who haven't repented are going to come before him in all his glory. Yes, you are going to have to bend down at his feet and kiss the hem of his garments and you are going to have to pray, but this girl is saved forever and ever."

Mary Cruz sat down next to Carmen and pulled her close. Carmen was sobbing. Then she broke free, running to the coffin, throwing herself over it and kissing Beatriz's face.

"Quite a service. Do you think Bea enjoyed it?" Suzanne asked.

"She was probably mortified," Emma said.

Standing by the door, Solomon towered over the exiting mourners. Emma held back, waiting for the crowd to thin. As it did, she noted that her friend from 396 had made good his escape. She was sorry. She had meant to go up to him, ask him how he knew Bea, and soak up a little more of that Southern comfort. It would have been nice to see *one* friendly male face.

"Your detective friend is certainly handsome," Suzanne said under her breath, dragging Emma forward. "A pleasure to meet you," she said, reaching out to take his hand. "The pleasure's all mine," he replied.

"Are you going to the cemetery?" Emma asked.

"Yes," he said coldly, avoiding her eyes.

How much nerve do you have, she wondered? She certainly had enough for this. In the most convivial tone she could muster, she said, "Then, give me a ride."

15

"Impeding the progress of an investigation. I'd like to charge you, taking evidence out of the apartment when you were only there because I was doing you a goddamn favor."

"Evidence? So this is an official investigation?"

"I didn't say that."

Emma Price was admiring the stalled traffic on the Long Island Expressway. Out the window, a good-looking tennis type in the next car was using his right hand as an extravagant baton.

"Enough," she said, swinging back to confront him. "I apologized. I gave what I had. We're talking about a business card."

"With a note on the back."

"Admit you were doing yourself a favor then, by letting me tag along. You weren't sure who I was. Your partner had been completely insulting and you, yourself, had made certain erroneous assumptions."

"This is your defense?"

"I didn't realize I needed one. I haven't been arrested or charged, have I?" Emma reached over and switched off the radio. "My headache's back. You don't have anything in here, do you?"

"I might."

"Where?"

"Check the glove compartment."

She reached over and clicked it open. His service revolver spilled out onto her lap. Emma pulled back, involuntarily.

"Nice touch, detective." She stared down at the well-oiled piece of metal, then picked up the gun to set it between them. She reached inside again, extracting a huge bottle of buffered extra-strength aspirin and couldn't avoid reading the warning label, "As with any drug, if you are pregnant or nursing a baby, seek the advice of a health professional before using this product," then in bold print, IT IS ESPECIALLY IMPORTANT NOT TO USE ASPIRIN DURING THE LAST THREE MONTHS OF PREGNANCY. IT MAY CAUSE PROBLEMS IN THE UNBORN CHILD.

It may cause problems, she thought. The last three months. I'm nowhere near. And what does it matter? In a few days this baby's going to be history. It's the logical thing to do, and right now I'm going to become someone who is supremely, insanely logical.

Unscrewing the cap, she poured two white caplets into the palm of her hand and studied them. Just then the traffic started to move. Glancing up, she saw a sign for the rest area. Curling her hand round the pills, she dropped them back into the bottle, snapped the lid on, and set it back inside the glove compartment. She set the gun in after it, then clicked the latch. They were fast approaching a Texaco station where the man with the star waited to service and serve.

"I need to use the facilities," she said.

Solomon pulled up in front of the restrooms. She glanced over and he smiled mercilessly. He's going to abandon me here, she told herself, and she tried to catch his eye to reassure herself. Of course he refused to look her way. Jesus, men and their punishments, she thought. And they think *we're* insane.

It was the fastest rest stop in history. But when she emerged, his car was gone. "Goddamn," she muttered, scanning the area. And underneath her annoyance, she recognized self-pity threatening to well up. "Please," she said aloud and felt palpable relief when she spotted his Volvo, parked at the very edge of the lot. Hiking over, she found him studying a road map.

"Lost?" she asked.

"If I was, would I admit it?"

Why should he trust me Emma asked herself. After all, there were plenty of reasons not to, some that he wasn't even privy to. For example, she hadn't mentioned Eliot who was a possible acquaintance or better yet, good friend of the elusive Chazz. And she hadn't told him about that stanza of poetry, so carefully preserved on the Pit's bathroom wall. She also hadn't communicated her discovery of Penny Strider's interborough artwork. She wanted to share these things, but didn't know how and where to start. Tread carefully, she told herself. Was there a way to explain her presence at that bar the night before without making it into a question of her trusting his competence? Well, she could tell him the truth. And lose his trust forever. Because Emma knew, firsthand, about the blue wall of silence. Cops basically lived by the old Musketeer motto of all for one and one for all and once he found out she was working for Loretta Picard, he'd have no choice, self-preservation would demand that he despise her.

Emma imagined herself confessing, and saw the result. Solomon offering up the sign of the cross, then rearing back his hand to stab her in the heart with a finely honed wooden stake.

The man was too incredibly handsome, too aware of the superior package genetics had dealt. And obviously intelligent to boot. While I'm forty, married, well, almost married, a mom, she told herself. It didn't exactly exempt her from certain natural urges. It just insured that the fantasy would remain that forever.

* * *

The cemetery overlooked Long Island Sound. They walked
up just as Mary Cruz backed away from the grave. Other
mourners began to file past and Emma joined the line, reaching down to take a handful of dirt. She threw it in and said a
silent farewell. Ana flung two large handfuls into the open
grave, and added a solitary rose. Then Carmen collapsed beside her, wailing and beating the ground.

"Here," Solomon said, lifting her gently. Carmen took his
arm, offering him a look of the deepest gratitude.

Walking behind them, Emma noted the statues of Jesus, his
virgin mother and Saint Francis with his head surrounded by
a cannily rendered halo of granite birds. Then she leaned
against the side of the Volvo, waiting as Solomon opened the
door of the limousine and helped Carmen inside, watched
him turn to Ana, escorting her around to the far side, then
saw him slide something into her hand.

"What do you expect to get from her?" Emma asked as he
walked up.

"What?"

"Don't act innocent. Ana. Bea's little sister."

"Don't you ever stop?" he asked.

"No," Emma admitted.

A smile stuttered across his lips. "At least you're honest,"
he said.

Angels blowing horns adorned the wrought-iron gates. They
drove through, exiting onto a local access road. Emma
pulled her portable phone out of her purse to call home.
There was a message from Will saying he and Liam would
be back at seven that night, one from Dawn checking her
progress, and one from a friend who had known Beatriz and

had seen the article in the paper. Emma unfolded the slip of paper Bill Weston had given her and she tried Penny Strider's number again. The answering machine picked up after ten beeps. She assumed this indicated a long list of other callers. She left a second, hopefully more urgent message.

As they pulled onto the Long Island Expressway, a lightning bolt pierced the horizon. Rain hammered against the roof of the car and water streamed down the windshield. Solomon drove too fast, swerving around slower moving vehicles. If Will had done this, it would have provided fodder for a predictable marital spat. Emma would have asked him to slow down and he would have complied until he believed she wasn't paying attention, then the speedometer would have inched back up to seventy, seventy-five, eighty.

That was how Will was. What was the term they used for that sort of behavior, passive aggressive? Which had its charms: A partner who seemed to embrace civility, who then walked in and destroyed the illusion, all in one helter-skelter moment. Apparently, Solomon was a different sort. More like me, Emma decided. What you see is what you get. No point in asking him to adjust the pressure on the gas pedal. He'll never even pretend to comply. In fact, he probably believes caution of any kind is bred from fear.

"So what do you think that message means on the back of the card?" he asked her.

"Some line from a song," she ventured. "Or a poem?"

"Do you recognize it?"

"No." She thought of the stanza of poetry scrawled on the side of the bathroom stall. This would be the perfect time to bring that up. She opened her mouth to explain, then felt unaccountably dizzy. Leaning back in the seat, she closed her eyes, trying to regain her equilibrium.

"Are you all right?" he asked. She opened her eyes to find him staring over. Turning back to the road, he braked hard. The traffic in front of them had come to a stop.

"I think so."

"I guess we're not going anywhere for a while. Must be an accident. Why not try to rest?" He said it kindly. "Go on," he added.

She wanted to resist, but he must have hypnotized her. She didn't even have time to register her own surprise and she was asleep. Asleep she happened on the most serious truth of all. People *could* fly. All they had to remember was how to spread their wings, those delicate gossamer threads that were tucked inside the shoulder blade. They all had them, from babies to astronauts. And at night, under the light of the yellow globe of a moon, they sprouted. Emma's were filament green, scalloped . . . grand.

She swooped off the roof of a building, then soared up, banking right to admire the lights of the great island of Manhattan. She made one smart ring around the Empire State Building and singed the metal off the radio antennae clipped onto the top of Nelson and David's twin towers, then flew farther, perching like a hawk on the top tier of the George Washington Bridge. The metal was copper red at night, double spans lit up with a thousand frosted light bulbs. Emma gazed down at the city she loved. Along the Henry Hudson Parkway, car headlights splashed north and south, while she kept watch.

But even when you flew in your dreams, there were things to be cautious of. Simply put, you had to know when to give up, when to pack your wings into the duffel bag and slip down into the subway. In other words, when to stop pretending you were some sort of god.

Emma Price, though, was drunk with the power of flight and therefore was obscenely careless. Too late, she realized she had forgotten her only son sleeping alone in his bed. At ten, he still clutched his transitional object, a stuffed animal he'd named Dirty Dog. It had been washed countless times until the bold color was faded to a dingy gray. Liam slept with his body rolled between the mattress and the wall. And as he did, the dog came to life. Seeing a shadow march across the wall behind, it turned its head and stared, cocking one glass eye at the intruder. There was the sound of creaking wood, as the bastard reached into his pocket for a weapon.

Dawn was breaking. Emma was only halfway down the West Side of Manhattan. She turned out over the river in an attempt to claim the shortcut, but in that half-light where night became morning, her wings caught fire, sparks flying off the tips. There was a buzzing in her ears as they disintegrated. And as the dawn turned New Jersey pink, she fell in a dead man's spiral into the stone-cold Hudson.

"We're almost there." Solomon's hand was on her shoulder. She started, looked down at it and felt her whole body flush. "You can drop me anywhere," she said.

"Don't be foolish. I'm taking you to your door."

"You don't know where I live."

"Sure I do," he said. "It's part of the job."

Bergen Street. He made a right. Three more blocks, she thought, and wondered how to begin. She had no convenient segue. Blurt it out, Emma told herself. You're no shrinking violet. Stop thinking you can control this. Or anything. And stop imagining that what he thinks of you matters. So you like the guy. Fine. You're never going to get a chance to know him.

They were a block from home, and Solomon pulled out of traffic and into the space in front of a fire hydrant.

"What else have you got to tell me?" he asked.

She felt the flush of embarrassment at having waited so long. So he'd known. She opened her mouth to begin, then stopped because he was looking at her in a certain way. He leaned over and gave her a kiss. God, did she like the way he did it, so smooth, so practiced. Practical, too, she decided and a small sigh of pleasure escaped from between her lips. Where'd you hide that neat parcel of shame, Em, she wondered. Mailed it off, she decided, sent it to Will and made sure to charge on delivery.

"You're okay with this?" he asked, pulling away.

"What do you mean by okay?"

"You don't know a thing about me," he said.

She smiled. "Is that meant as a threat or a come on?"

"I'm only explaining the possibilities." He said it sternly. She couldn't figure out why his tone had changed. Especially when he reached out for her again. Her mind stopped functioning and her body tingled as he caressed her breasts, then moved down slowly, evenly, surely. She was giving him permission, in fact, part of her was actually pleading with him to stroke her stomach and go lower. Then reason began to prevail, a small, chiding voice. You're pregnant, it said. What do you think you're doing? Taking revenge? What's the point? Who are you ever going to tell who's going to admire you for this?

The mood fled. She covered his hand with her own, pressing down.

"What?" he asked.

"Not now, all right? Is that all right?"

He looked bemused. Shaking his head, he put the car back into gear, clucking his tongue as he did it. They rolled down the street. The light in front of them turned red and when it did, he twisted around to face her. "So you're working for Picard."

Emma drew back, as if he'd slapped her.

"How long have you known?"

"Long enough. As far as I'm concerned, she doesn't deserve the money we spend to feed and house her."

She felt completely sullied. "How could you not tell me till now?"

He didn't bother to respond, just pressed down on the gas, making the tires screech. She threw open her door and he braked the car, barely stopping in time. Then Emma was out, running down the pavement. She reached her front door, unlocked it, let herself in and closed it firmly behind her, spinning the cylinders, then cursed under her breath, asking herself, why, why did you even imagine that man could be interested?

In the bathroom, she flicked on the light. Shocking to discover the change that had occurred. Have I been sleeping this long, she wondered, because there were webs of wrinkles at the corners of her eyes. The skin around her neck was no longer taut, and at the curve where her hairline receded, an age spot was making an appearance. Vanity, she thought. How a woman succumbs.

16

M onday. The sky was dirty and gray. Rain came down in sheets, soaking New York in one of those terrific, late summer downpours. Water filled up storm drains and made rivers out of intersections. Subway service was delayed for hours and Metro North had trains short out. In Queens, cars were left abandoned in flooded intersections.

Emma drove north to Rikers to interview Loretta Picard. She inched along, peering through the windshield. The weather was distracting, but it didn't prevent her from replaying the previous night's *20/20* interview; Loretta framed in the glare of TV cameras with her face looking pinched and mean, the word RAGE clipped out of what was left of her hair.

When John Stossel had asked how she felt about the governor and the mayor calling for a death-penalty indictment, Loretta had said, "I don't blame them." Then she'd taken a piece of gum out of her mouth, rolled it into a ball, and sent it shooting off camera. "Look, when someone does something this bad, maybe they deserve to get fried. Plus, shit, I don't want to spend my life sitting in jail wasting taxpayers' money." Screwing up her face as though she were truly pondering this, she had added, "It's not fun in here, you know." Then, inexplicably, she had beamed for the camera.

Dawn Prescott told Emma how she'd pleaded with Loretta not to do the interview. After she'd gotten nowhere, she'd even tried to get a judge to grant her authority over her client. A pretty quixotic quest. It was like watching someone commit suicide, Dawn had said bitterly.

"You confessed to these murders?" It was Stossel asking.

"Look. They found the gun. It had my prints on it. Who's going to listen if I try to explain how there were extenuating circumstances."

"We might."

"Right!" She cocked an eyebrow at the camera. "The only thing your audience is interested in is whether I killed the cops or not. And I did kill them." She demonstrated then, hooking her finger into a pistol and firing a round at the camera.

"Why would you do such a thing?" Watching in the comfort of her own bedroom, Emma had searched Loretta's face for clues. Was the girl stupid? Was she insane? Was she a Mark David Chapman wannabe, thinking this was her one chance in a million to run down fame and make it her personal bedfellow?

"Why was I dumb enough to take them out?" Loretta smiled. "Would you believe it if I said it was an act of self-defense?"

Stossel made a doubting-Thomas face and she smiled wickedly.

"Didn't think so," she said. "Let's try another angle. It was the Lord working in his own mysterious way? No. Okay, then how about the only difference between living and getting taken down is if you're born lucky. Cause luck is a greedy, nasty little beast. You have to find it the right food and do up its hair in a process or else it gets mad. Now, I don't know a personal thing about those two cops, but I do know that that night they forgot to be careful. They didn't feed and water the beast. You know what I mean, don't you, John?" She leaned in when she asked, staring right into his eyes. The camera caught her waiting for his answer, then backed away as if it couldn't stand the sight. "Larrabbee came up first. Then the woman. I don't know what she was thinking. She was green, though. Just out of school. They didn't teach her enough, did they? They didn't warn her about someone like me. Or maybe it was all those rules they've tried to enforce lately. How you're supposed to ask questions first, and shoot later. Maybe that's what got her killed." Loretta paused, then gave a bold-faced look for the camera. "Or maybe that day she forgot the evening feeding? Maybe her little piece of luck went jumping out of her pocket and found a place in the basement or a poor orphan girl who would treat it better."

Stossel oozed sincerity as he asked the next question. "Are you sorry?"

"Sorry? Shit, no, how can I be sorry now? What's done is way done." Her jaw was set, her eyes frosty blue. Emma tried to find remorse. If it was there, it was hidden too deep to discover. Or there was none in residence. No remorse, no. And not a teaspoonful of pity.

Loretta swaggered into interview room C, sat down opposite Emma and asked, "Wassup?" Emma pushed forward the pack of Camels she'd brought, and Loretta popped one out, sticking it in her mouth, then offered Emma a spare.

"I don't smoke," Emma said. "I'm trying to maintain my lungs."

"Good for you," Loretta said. "Me, I don't have that luxury." She blew out some smoke and asked, "What's all that shit you've got with you there?"

Emma glanced over at the case file. "Your life."

"Well, enjoy," Loretta said. "Thank God it's your job, not mine." Then Loretta whistled. "Hey, are you some shrink? I told Dawn I wouldn't talk with one of them."

"I'm an investigator. They pay me to fill in all those little holes in your background. You know, the curious little details that could help you formulate a defense. That is, if, after last night, we can still manage to construct one."

"So you watched?" Loretta's eyes lit up. "How was it?"

"You were a little on the cold-hearted side for me," Emma said.

"Hmm." Loretta seemed to be considering the evaluation. "S'pose it could have come across cold-hearted. But I was honest, too. I wanted it to be a whole new type of news broadcast."

"So you were breaking ground?"

"Sure. A regular trailblazer." Loretta cocked her head to the side, birdlike.

"Since I'm here to help prepare a defense, I thought you might help point me in some direction," Emma said.

"I love helping people. I'm a lot like Florence Nightingale that way. What do you want? A list of my nearest and dearest?"

"Like your Aunt Brittany?"

"So you guys talked."

"We did. Apparently she's not one of your biggest fans."

"That's for damn sure." A cloud slid over Loretta's face.

"She has children?"

"You asking or telling?"

"I believe I know that for a fact. What about your cousins?"

"None of us were close," Loretta said. She pulled a cloud of smoke into her mouth, then released it, slapping her eyes away. Clearly invested in portraying herself as smart-mouthed and soulless, Emma decided. It wasn't an unusual stance. In fact, it was just a slightly more tawdry version of the typical teenager's pose. Something to look forward to, she thought. "Are we going to have to waste a lot of time with the back and forth?" Emma asked.

"Got nothing *but* time these days."

"And no pity for those of us on tighter schedules. Not that I blame you." Emma tried extending a wry, conspiratorial smile. Loretta refused to engage. Leaning back in her chair, she crossed her legs. "So what's your job like?" Loretta asked. "Are you a real detective, like in the movies?"

"That depends." Emma leaned in. "Are you a real murderer?"

"Sure," Loretta said.

"How about your job, did you like being a bartender?"

"The money's decent and people leave you alone."

"Sounds pretty perfect."

This time, Loretta did crack a smile.

"I never tried tending bar," Emma admitted. "It must have been because I have such a lousy memory. I was sure I'd never be able to keep all those really obscure drinks straight."

"All you have to do is fake them." Loretta giggled. "I have a book, *Four Hundred Easy Party Drinks*. I memorized it, like for when you go take the driving test. Go on, try me. I can tell you how to put together anything."

"Frog in a Blender?"

"You know that one?" Loretta smiled and Emma realized she had the same lopsided smile Ellen Barkin had made famous. "Easy as pie. An ounce of vodka, an ounce Midori, then add some lemonade and a half-ounce of strawberry cooler, throw in the ice, and mix. What's your poison?"

"I'm pretty basic. Scotch on the rocks."

"Good scotch though, right?"

"At least Dewar's."

"I can tell quality by what brand of scotch, it's a regular Rorschach test."

"So what about that ID, Loretta," Emma asked, sliding the heat up a notch. "Where'd you pick it up?"

"Around."

"Around where, exactly?"

"Why are you and Dawn so worried? Either way they're going to try me as an adult."

"That doesn't bother you?"

Loretta looked away, then crossed her legs and leaned back in her chair, pondering. "Too late for being bothered," she said. And for the first time, her voice sounded almost mournful.

"Tell me about the birth certificate," Emma said. "Who fixed you up?"

"Why do you have to know?"

"So there won't be any surprises later on."

"It was just some guy."

Emma rolled her eyes.

"Can I go?" Loretta offered a slinky stretch of the arms.

"Not yet. Before you got the job at the Pit, what did you do for income?"

"Odd things. I ran errands, worked off the books cleaning houses."

"You didn't tell Dawn that."

"Maybe I like you better," Loretta said, grinning.

"How about some names?"

"Names just aren't important."

"They are to me."

Loretta dropped the cigarette on the floor and ground it under her heel. "Look, I'll tell you why I wanted to work at the Pit. It was where I liked to hang. Being there so much, I figured I might as well make some money."

"Do you consider Penny Strider a friend?" Emma asked.

"Penny?" Loretta squinted, looking flustered. "Who's been giving out her name?"

"Bill Weston says she recommended you for the job."

"Oh, that." Loretta sounded almost disappointed. "No big deal. They had an opening. She offered them my services."

"So the two of you were tight?"

"We used to be."

"What happened?"

"I'm what happened," Loretta said. "I screwed it up, like always." Then she averted her eyes, deliberately.

"How did you do it?"

"Sure you're not that shrink?" Loretta made a petulant, little-girl face. Her tongue ran the circuit of her teeth, flicking them clean, while Emma played the reluctant audience. A full minute passed. "Look, I shot two cops. Why would anyone want to admit to being friends with me?" Loretta's nails beat out a fierce tattoo.

"So then there's no one out there? We need some character witnesses for you, Loretta. Some people who're actually trustworthy and wouldn't make fools of themselves in front of a judge."

"Why just a judge?"

"I would have thought Dawn explained this part. The first thing we try to do is to come up with an argument that voids the death penalty indictment before we get into the trial phase."

"How many times do you win doing that?" Loretta asked.

Emma didn't think it would be wise to say. "Are you thinking?" she asked, instead.

"Yeah, pondering deeply."

Emma chuckled. "You certainly have one fuck of a bad attitude."

Loretta gave a barking laugh in response. And then, the two of them were laughing together, a jocular moment that Emma hadn't counted on. But afterward, the tension in the room definitely faded. "So," Emma said finally, "are you sexually active?"

"I'm not seeing anyone in here, if that's what you mean. The guards have offered, but I'm deep in the declining mode. And I've got my own private cell. They separated me from the other girls for my very own good."

"When were you last involved?" Emma asked, lifting her pen as if to jot down notes.

"Damn, but the name escapes me."

"Let's sit here and try to dredge one up."

"You're getting desperate." Loretta had a mischievous look in her eyes. "Come to think of it, I took a vow of celibacy. I was actually contemplating joining a monastery."

"Were you really? Buddhism appeals to you? Or were you thinking Trappist?"

"Hadn't gotten that far yet. What about working it into my defense. How I've been looking for God in all the wrong places."

"I'll see what I can do," Emma said, grinning. "Now give me a name."

"Hmm." Loretta scratched her head. "There was this guy named Neil. Neil Charles. I was seeing him about a year and a half ago, but he moved out of town. Went to Hollywood. Or it might have been Europe. I remember him saying how he needed to scale the Berlin Wall. Needed to measure how high it was."

"Except they tore it down. I'm afraid he's out of luck." Emma bent in a little closer. "What's this about, Loretta? Why are you making it so easy for the DA?" There was a pin-drop silence between them. Then Loretta got up and crossed the room to stare out the barred window. Emma waited, wondering if she'd finally gotten through.

"Am I making it easy?"

"That interview you gave last night didn't help your cause."

Loretta didn't turn back to her. "They showed it in the day room," she said. "The other girls liked it a whole hell of a lot. They gave me a whole big round of applause."

"They probably thought you were brilliant. But you should always think of the audience. I watched some pathetic child who wanted her twenty seconds of fame."

"Is that what you really saw?" Loretta asked, turning to confront her. Emma heard the unspoken rest as, I thought *you'd* be a little smarter. Loretta smiled, indicating she thought she had definitely gotten the upper hand. In return, Emma offered a frost-ridden look and Loretta's confident smile wilted. "You don't understand how things are," Loretta said.

"Let me try."

Loretta shook her head, fiercely. Emma began to leaf through the papers again. Maybe they could find something to go on in her childhood. Were there incidents of abuse? Perhaps, but insanity·was the most difficult defense. When the fifteen-year-old who took a semiautomatic weapon into school, spraying his classmates, wasn't insane. When the nine-year-old who beat his neighbor to death, then absconded with her bicycle, was judged fit to stand trial... Emma understood Dawn's frustration. Looking up, she used her X-ray vision to peek beneath the zip-front prison uniform and found a surprisingly voluptuous body. She wondered about that, and the care Loretta was taking to protect her friends, because Emma knew that this girl was too smart, even too intriguing, to have skated through the world completely alone. Emma moved up, studying Loretta's short hair, the flesh-colored HATE.

"Want to buy? Or are you just window shopping?" Loretta asked, taking a seat, then adjusting her pose so that her feet rested on the table.

Emma smiled. The corners of Loretta's mouth twitched, then she braved one in return. Emma opened the voluminous file and riffled through it, looking for one particular entry.

"Those clothes in your garbage can in your apartment had

Cheri Maples's blood all over them. And then there's the towel. Your towel apparently. The police said no one took it out into the hall, but there it was, bunched up at her neck. It had to be you. But why, Loretta?"

Loretta's eyes widened, her face colored. "I was trying to clean up," she said caustically.

"You're tough, aren't you, Loretta? You've just been proving it to me, and you proved it to the whole country last night. Except that, if you're so mean-spirited, why would you want things tidy?"

"I'm compulsive," Loretta said, stubbornly.

"You know, once I had the unhappy duty of watching someone die. They bind you down with leather thongs, Loretta. They think they're being modern, but it looks pretty damn medieval. His name was René, René Leveche. He kept staring up at us. The mother of the girl he was accused of killing was sitting right beside me. She spit at him and it landed on the glass. He got to watch it trail down while he lost consciousness. Afterward the nurse came up to check his vital signs. Then she nodded and when she did, the mother started clapping. I never saw a face like hers. Someone so filled up with hate."

"That's supposed to scare me?" Loretta's disdain was evident.

"I'm just talking." Emma made sure her tone was completely colorless.

"You want the truth?" Loretta said, and her voice was lousy with contempt. She picked up a cigarette, lit it, and pulled in hard. "How about, I don't know how that towel got there. My bet is one of the cops put it on her. Or one of my good-hearted neighbors."

"You don't really want to die," Emma said quietly. "I think you're acting. Maybe it's because you don't see any other way to manage this. I don't know. Or maybe there's someone out there you're trying to impress. If so, do you want to tell me who's in the audience?"

"God," Loretta said sullenly. "God's keeping a lookout."

"Which god is this who so dislikes the NYPD?"

"The one who was sending me to the monastery." Loretta studied the pile of papers between them, then reached for the pack of cigarettes and shoved it into her breast pocket. As she did, Emma saw her hands were shaking. "It was cause of her eyes," Loretta muttered. "It wasn't decent. You don't want dead people's eyes staring up at you. It probably sounds nuts to you, but you've got to be nuts to do what I did, nuts or higher than heaven."

"You don't sound nuts," Emma said deliberately. "Was Cheri Maples alive when you tried to stop the bleeding? Was she saying something?"

Loretta's mouth opened. Emma held her breath. She wanted this, a moment of compassion. For who, Emma wondered? For the two of us, she realized. Only then, well, it was as if a twig had snapped underfoot. Loretta shoved back her chair and stood, looking spooked. "You think you're so fucking big," she said, shaking her head hard, then offering a fiercely defiant look. She turned to the door and had her hand raised to knock. Not yet, Emma thought. She needed to maintain this edge. But, it was a surprise when she heard herself asking, "What about Chazz?"

Loretta swung her head back immediately, as if bitten. "Chazz?" Then she regained control and mimicked someone looking thoughtful, scratching her head and nodding sagely. "Hey, wait a second. I bet I know. He was banging that Maples girl. I probably was in love with him and shot her cause I was jealous." Loretta managed to emit a little choking laugh. "Tell you what, you want to see me die, I'll make sure they save you your own personal ticket."

* * *

Out through the heavy metal doors, past three checkpoints and into the parking lot. Next stop? Loretta's humble abode. Emma checked the time and saw she was running late. Undoubtedly, this would only further endear her to Officer Janus who had agreed to meet her and let her inside, then answer a few brief questions. Her tires screeched on the way out of the lot and up onto the East River Drive. She tried to keep her mind's eye on the traffic, knowing that if she didn't, she'd end up in a serious accident. People drove like maniacs, cutting into lanes without signaling, moving their cars like steamrollers. Emma took care, but did notch the engine up to sixty-five.

Only when she pulled out onto Houston Street, did she allow herself to think. Chazz. She knew who I meant, Emma told herself, feeling a surge of confidence, then immediately distrusting it. Of course Loretta knows him, she decided. He was probably a regular at the club. Which explained why Eliot had recognized the name as well. Her current paranoid vision of the world infecting everything. Remember the context, she told herself. Chazz was handsome. Loretta probably admired him. Maybe even had a crush. And so, subduing that thought, Emma was freed. Freed to go back over the other ground they'd covered. That towel, draped over the body. Had Loretta been trying to help? Or was that simply something Emma needed to believe in order to deed her client a little sliver of humanity?

Rolling down Stanton Emma spotted her target, pulled as close as she dared, then jammed the gears into reverse, and was able to accomplish a true miracle, angling the car into an unbelievably cramped parking spot. Then she flipped open the folder, taking out photos of the crime scene. Stewart Larrabbee lying on his side, his eyes open. Three gunshot wounds, including one in the groin. A little too personal,

Emma told herself. Did you really do that to a stranger? Not unless you had something against the whole subspecies. Then she cooled herself down again. After all, Loretta could have come through the door shooting wildly.

Clearly, Maples had been coming up the stairs with her gun drawn, ready to assist her partner. She'd gotten off one round, splintering a doorframe. Three photographs caught her in various angles, sprawled on the stairs. The towel had been bunched against her neck. In the photos it was dark with blood. She'd bled to death in under three minutes.

Emma shoved the photos back inside the manila envelope and stepped out of the car. She tried to imagine Loretta bending down to minister. Why bother? But, then, was there logic in any of it? Emma remembered what Dawn had said, about the girl committing public suicide. Maybe that theory had legs.

A baby-faced patrolman stood in front of the door at 101 Stanton, looking seriously annoyed.

"Emma Price," she said, sticking out her hand. He looked down at it as if she were extending a bribe and he were scrupulously, white-knight honest.

"The least you could do is be punctual."

Emma apologized profusely. Ten minutes was hardly a lifetime, but she knew he was responding to who she was, who and what she represented. He walked ahead of her up the stairs and through the door, then let it slam in her face. She shoved it back open and tried to keep up, taking the inside steps two at a time. On Loretta's landing there was the sweet, pungent odor of hot dogs steaming. Her stomach clenched, reminding her of that interior tenant.

"Damn," she said, under her breath. When this was over, she'd have to make an appointment. A quick D and C on Friday and then a good night's rest. She'd be good as new, right as rain. Sure, Emma thought, shaking her head at the ridiculous naiveté. She'd had an abortion as a teenager and even then it had hardly been simple. Now she had Liam. Older, and supposedly wiser, Emma told herself. Right! It was going to be a hell of a lot harder to excise an embryo having brought one to term.

Patrolman Janus was fiddling with the lock, then the door swung open. He bent down, raising the yellow crime-scene tape. She did the same, then joined him inside the apartment. He swung the door closed behind them both, and leaned against it. Janus had a shorter than regulation haircut and there was a sprinkling of hair above his top lip. Emma thought he didn't look old enough to even be a high school graduate. But she had grown to distrust her views on this point. Since hitting forty, she'd found it harder and harder to guess anyone's correct age. The world divided into two even spheres, those under the Big Four-O seemed to be lost in a quagmire of eternal youth, those over, teetered on the brink of oblivion. The sight of herself in the mirror the night before had stunned her so completely that the next morning she'd avoided looking at herself. As if I really am a vampire, Emma thought.

The remains of a meal were still on the table, calcifying: chicken bones, a side order of half-eaten mashed potatoes. The chair had been shoved back as if Loretta were only taking a break.

It was a small apartment; half had been given over to sustenance, half to relaxation. An old velvet sofa sat at one end. In front of it, a coffee table that looked like a freebie lifted from the garbage. Emma flipped through the array of magazines on top, *People, Vanity Fair.* The bookcase was filled with paperbacks, and also held a small color TV. A closer look showed Loretta's literary taste to veer between science fiction and gothic horror; the complete works of Stephen King, William Gibson, even a sidetrip into the nineteenth century, *The House of the Seven Gables* and an oversized volume of Poe. "The Pit and the Pendulum," Emma thought, realizing that the club could have been named with this in mind. Perhaps that also explained Loretta's attraction to the place. Indeed, thinking back, she had noted enough boys in English vamp, enough girls with dark rings around their eyes. Though the Goth look had not exactly prevailed.

The bookcase also held a small stereo system and a collection of CDs; mostly grunge music from Seattle's heyday, Hole, Nirvana, and lesser lights along with lighter fare, the entire works of Ani DiFranco.

Janus had seated himself at the table and was busy writing. I'm supposed to assume he's keeping track of me, Emma decided.

She moved on, into the bedroom. The size of a large walk-in closet. It held a full-sized mattress, a small table, a dresser. And a painting. At first glance one thought of O'Keeffe, the cactus flowers painted lush, red hot in the center, the outer leaves trimmed in smoky gray. A road in the desert curved through a host of blooming cacti. And the main focus, a circle of ravens pecking at something stretched out in the middle of the road. On closer examination, the body of a naked woman was revealed, blood trickling from the side of her mouth. Underneath, in yellow script, the artist had written ROADKILL and beneath that, the sloping signature. Emma had already guessed. It was Penny Strider's work. Just acquaintances? Like hell.

Pulling open the top drawer of the dresser, Emma found a large collection of black lace underwear, immaculately folded. In the next drawer down, short sleeved T-shirts and two black sweaters. The bottom held three pairs of stovepipe black pants.

She spun around the room, then headed for the closet. No door, just a sheet hung up to divide it from the living space.

Three dresses, one plaid and two in basic black, all short enough to skim the top of the thigh. The shoes at the bottom were black as well, platform-heeled and square-toed, with zippers on the sides.

"Ready?" Janus asked. He was rubbing his chin hard. Emma thought wickedly that that might be his way of encouraging facial hair to grow. Even so, with his sort of pug nose, the sprinkle of freckles, he'd look eternally young. He'd get carded until he went gray. Of course, it reminded her of Will. Just two years before, they'd stopped into a liquor store on the Cape and the girl had asked for his ID. Will had been thirty-eight years old at the time. And Emma had been so envious. She, who'd never been carded, even when she was thirteen, sneaking into Max's Kansas City to see the Dolls.

"Give me another few minutes," she said.

Janus whistled pugnaciously, but he backed away and Emma pulled out the evidence list. The department had retrieved the murder weapon. They'd also taken the blood-stained shirt and pants, the towel, and a list of pharmaceuticals, none of them apparently illegal. Penicillin and tetracycline, plus a small container of Zoloft. The doctors who'd prescribed the drugs had been noted as well. For the Zoloft, a Dr. Carolyn Reynolds. Emma made a note to check on her. Perhaps this was how Loretta had gained her aversion to headshrinking. Heading into the bathroom, she pulled back the shower curtain, emblazoned with a map of the world, and found a pristine tub. The sink was another story, a rust-colored stain had been left around the plug. Loretta had said in her confession that she'd tried to wash off the blood. She'd changed in here, too. The garbage can on the evidence list had come from the bathroom.

Emma opened the cabinet. The shelves were bare, but pasted on the interior wall, a veritable photo gallery. A baby girl, bouncing in her mother's lap, who must have been

Loretta. Then Loretta, close enough to teenage to be recognizable, with her arm slung casually around another girl's shoulders. Her friend had hair that was naturally blond, falling in a shoulder-length wave. Finally, three color shots snapped inside one of those three-for-five-dollars booths. Loretta, in what Emma knew was her current incarnation, pressed eagerly, face up to the camera lens. The woman with her had long red hair, a pert nose, freckles, and green eyes of all things. An unconscionably Irish face.

There was a crackling sound from behind, then the police radio blurted out some demand.

"Listen, I've got to go," Janus called out.

Emma reached out and unstuck the tape, sliding all the photos into her pocket. Then she turned, offering a furtive, guilty scan of the doorway. Janus was still in the living room. She could almost feel the hot breath of his impatience on her shoulder. When she stepped out, she found him waiting by the door.

"You and your partner responded to the call," she said.

"We did," Janus said, then added his unsolicited commentary. "I don't know how you people live with yourselves."

"The call came in at 1:47, shots fired."

"The neighbor called it in. A Ms. Peterson." They were outside Loretta's door by then, ducking under the tape. He pointed down the hall. "4C."

"The front door was open downstairs?"

"Peterson buzzed us in."

"She told you where to go?"

"She told us her floor. She'd heard shots and claimed she was afraid to step outside her door to check."

"You found Maples first."

He was heading for the stairs.

"Did you know either of the officers personally?" Emma

called it out after his departing back. He turned to face her then.

"I knew Stew."

"Loretta Picard was inside her apartment when you came up the stairs. The door was shut. How did you know who had been doing the shooting? Did the neighbor tell you?"

"Stew was lying in front of her goddamn door. You have the photos and I'm not on the witness stand, so don't even start with me. You're gonna ask if she invited me in? Try it, and I'll lose what little hold I've got on my temper now. You fucking people. Jesus. You expect us to do our jobs when you're the ones in trouble."

He turned and stalked away, muttering under his breath. Emma waited until she heard the front door slam, then headed for Peterson's door. She rang, but there was no response. She tried again, then sighed, scribbling down the name for her contact list. Backing away, she tried to decide. Did you have a bird's-eye view of the hallway from an eyehole that far up? And hearing shots, would you go check or cower in your bedroom? It depended, she supposed. Most people were curious, but were they curious to the point of insanity? The woman could have looked, could have seen something. She'd been interviewed, of course. Emma knew that she had forsworn any further, keener knowledge of the events that seem to have transpired right across the hall from her. She'd be back. She'd have to have her own talk with Ms. Peterson.

Heading down the stairs to her car, Emma tried to replay the sequence of events. Loretta shooting Larrabbee first, then taking out Maples. Why not try to run? Why go inside her apartment and shut the door? And why that pathetic attempt to hide the weapon in the garbage can? That alone was proof that Loretta hadn't thought the attack through. Then

Emma flashed on the painting hanging above the bed. Road-kill, she thought, as she opened the car door and checked Penny Strider's address. She tried Strider's number again. Fifteen clicks indicating new messages stacked into a hold-ing pattern. Emma shrugged. She had intended a trip to New Jersey that day to check up on the aunt and the cousins, plus a stop at Loretta's former high school. But by then it was nearly one o'clock.

Proximity is all, Emma told herself, getting into the car and making a quick U-turn. Penny Strider lived between Av-enues A and B on Fifth. The trip to Jersey would have to keep. Three pigeons fluttered up, hovering above her wind-shield. Roadkill, she thought to herself, remembering the cactus-ridden cabinets in Bea's apartment, the coyotes crawling over the sinks at the Pit, and the dead woman bak-ing in the desert sun.

17

Bea's sister Ana hadn't been able to give him much, the one solid lead, Chazz Perry's possible mode of employment. Apparently, Perry had been into computers and working for some Internet startup. A brave new world, Laurence Solomon told himself, leafing through the Yellow Pages.

Laurence used computers the way most people his age did, with total ignorance. He was accepting of their existence, grateful that they made certain tasks noticeably easier, and damned if he was going to ever be made truly dependent. He was, in fact, pretty damn suspicious of technology in general. The way the world was becoming smaller, squeezed tightly onto an electronic highway.

On his twenty-second follow up call, he hit paydirt. The man at the other end was a personnel manager at Logitech who'd gotten the faxed sketch Solomon had been sending out with his morning coffee. "Chazz Perry? The name doesn't ring any bells," he said. And Solomon was ready to hang up the phone when he heard some throat clearing. "Who does these sketches for you, anyhow?" the guy asked.

"What do you mean?"

"Don't you think it's weird how every single one of those guys looks the same? The same knit caps, the same scruffy facial hair, that same grim look. Don't you think there's ever a bad guy out there, happy he did the deed? You know, like George Clooney's character in *Out of Sight*."

"Actually, I remember Jennifer Lopez," Solomon said, willing to be entertained. "That might have explained Clooney looking so satisfied."

"Now *there's* a woman."

The voice was a little high, a sign of youth, Solomon decided. The whole world taken over by infant armies. When had the worm turned? Suddenly, they were the ones inventing, the ones believing their inventions would prosper. Meanwhile, jaded ancients kept trying to talk them down from the great starry heights. Tried to break their spirit the same way our folks tried.

"This guy here was Caucasian, blond hair, blue eyes, three earrings in his right ear."

"Ruby studs," Solomon said.

"Ruby studs." There was a pause. "A good-looking guy, though, right? The kind girls die for?"

"Yes." Solomon thought how appropriate that question was. "You're thinking of someone," he added, ready to nudge this along.

"I might be. Charles. Charles, Chazz. Could be the same. Murray, not Perry. Did some freelance work for us a couple of months ago. A real whiz kid."

Solomon checked his watch. "What say I come down?"

"Guess that could work out. I can hook you up with Martine. She hired him for the job." His voice dropped a notch, already uncertain. "Look, he might not even be the guy."

"I don't mind taking the ride," Solomon said. "What sort of work was this Murray hired for?"

"He was a firewall expert. Martine could explain if you need more than that. Hold on a sec. I'll see if she can take a meeting."

Solomon held the line, tapping his finger and trying to stave off any excitement. It was probably a bad lead, most were, after all.

"Want some?" Ruiz doing the asking, standing at the door with a box of Krispy Kremes.

"You're going to keel over and die if you eat those," Solomon said.

"Die happy," Miguel told him and reached down, grasping one between two fingers, then taking a heady bite.

"Come by in an hour. Martine says that would be perfecto," the voice on the phone said. "Detective Solomon, is it? You got that from the Bible."

"Someone did." Solomon had a pretty clear idea of who. Some slave owner in Georgia thinking to himself here's a fine joke.

Laurence, Laurence Solomon. He was seven days old when they moved him into Ralph's bedroom. At night he thought the ocean was breathing but it was only Ralph's snores making the entire world calm. When it rained, the drainpipe had sent a pattern shivering into the wall, and Ralph was there, reading him a story with his flashlight turned on and their heads hidden under the blankets.

"I'm your temporary custodian," Ralph had said. Then one morning Laurence had been fast asleep, tucked into blue sheets on his bed and he'd felt the hand. He knew immediately what it was, the one from the movie that went out murdering women and innocent children while its owner dreamed practical dreams. Laurence jumped out of bed screaming, and realized that the hand was hard and cold and long and patterned, slithering over his body, then falling onto the carpet. The snake's mouth opened and its fangs separated, its tongue flicking out to touch his ankle.

Ralph had put a very real palm over Laurence's mouth then, and thrown him back down under the covers to get him calm. That's when he recognized the boa from Al, this old circus guy and general lowlife who rented a room in the house next door. Ralph told him how he'd snuck across the roof and down through this tiny open window, crawling into Al's room just as the sky turned crack-of-dawn purple, how Ralph got the snake out of its cage, dropping it into a backpack, and zippered it in, the snake feeling like a coil of live rope.

"They get calm in the dark," Ralph had said, reaching for the snake and putting it on Laurence's lap. "You know how boas eat their victims? They squeeze them to death. They can eat anything big, even a baby elephant."

The brothers snuck downstairs into the basement preparation room, Ralph closing the door softly behind them before turning on the light.

"Watch this," he said. Ralph was holding a second brown paper bag. He put the snake's bag down first, then reached inside, taking the reptile out to set him on the floor before opening up the second bag. Inside was a cardboard box, and inside that a tiny brown mouse.

The snake caught sight of the mouse, shivering and quaking on that cool cement floor, and slithered over to it, squeezing the life out, then unhinging its jaws and swallowing.

Laurence watched the mouse go in there and then saw its body move slowly, lodging itself somewhere in the middle as Mr. Snake rolled himself up, feeling well satisfied.

Ralph had checked the time, then whispered, "Perfect."

"Help me," he'd said and the two of them lifted up the front half of Ida Morris's coffin. Ralph hoisted the snake inside, kissing it on the head as though he were some old-time priest, then stood back looking at his handiwork.

"Come on," Ralph taking Laurence by the hand. Upstairs, Laurence sliding under his own covers and realizing he was terrified. Were they going to be caught and punished? Worse, would he betray Ralph, running to their father to tell?

"Can I come in there with you?" Ralph, already half asleep, had nodded and Laurence had crawled in next to him. Ralph's breathing lulled him back to sleep, so that just before he drifted off he felt the sea change, and his terror melted away.

The snake waited till the mourners packed the room, then came over the top of the coffin, grinning its death's-head grin. The old ladies in the room yelled that it was the demon spirit who'd been trying to pick Ida's soul clean and failed. But Arthur, of course, knew better.

"Which of you did this?" Arthur demanded. And Ralph raised his hand.

Ralph lived in a second-floor flat a scant ten blocks from their ancestral home. Laurence heard the peephole slide open.

"What's up, homeboy?" Ralph asked.

"An emergency."

"Wouldn't be here, otherwise."

The metal screen dropped down again. No further sign of life from inside. *Testing me every goddamn minute*, Laurence thought, ringing the doorbell again.

"I'm busy," Ralph yelled out. But Laurence could hear the teasing.

"Don't play with me, man." The honesty in the plea must have rung out. Locks and bars were undone. Then the door swung back. Ralph was wearing a pair of sawed off shorts. Laurence glanced down out of habit, and plain old respect. Ralph's right leg had been shot off in 'Nam and the new mechanical one he'd bought the year before looked like something out of the Terminator movies. A blast of cold air circulated through the hall and Laurence shivered. Ralph kept the place colder than the goddamn morgue.

After Ralph got his permanent official discharge, the government had spent good money rehabilitating him, teaching him all about computers. He became so damn professional, he'd been hired by the FBI. That was back when computers were supposed to be giant brains running the universe. After a while he'd gotten sick of D.C. and moved back to New York, settling in Harlem. For ten years had lived up on Sugar Hill and advertised himself as the brother with the knack, the original Internet fool.

And Ralph's Afrocentric consulting business was booming. Plenty of Def Jam contenders needed websites set up. He also ran private tutoring, teaching neighborhood kids how to one-up Microsoft and write their own programs. Ralph had named his biz, Expanding Horizons, said it was his way to give something back to the community. Laurence had to laugh, remembering all the nasty looks those old women had shot Ralph, and all the names he'd been tagged with.

"Coffee's on the stove," Ralph said, leading him back into the kitchen. "That is, unless you're ready for a serious drink." He reached out, rubbing a hand through Laurence's scalp. Laurence felt the warmth radiating out through his palm. "You're my little baby bro, ain't you just?"

"You want to take a ride?" Laurence asked.

"To where?"

Laurence got ready to tell, and felt the peace invading him. He knew that if he had been put on earth for some purpose, other than to thwart his father and cause him to crumple down in the street one morning, clutching his heart, it was for this. He was here to find a reason and debunk the history put forth by those who believed death was an ancient curse that could never be explained away or even confronted. As far as he was concerned, all death was, was another idiot who had purchased himself a lethal weapon.

18

Emma pulled up in front of a children's furniture store. The window was chock full of new-model Maclaren strollers. She knew where her own version was, gathering dust in the basement. I should have thrown it out a long time ago, she thought. I should have had a stoop sale to get rid of that, the crib, the rest of the entrapments. My life as a study, she thought, wrong moves, missed cues. What a relief to be able to unfold the slip of paper that held Penny Strider's address and set off around the corner at an accelerated clip.

The street was full of tenement housing that was now undergoing severe gentrification. A Dumpster in front of one of the buildings was filled with plasterboard, old furniture, and several greasy, outdated stoves. Workmen eating their lunch soaked in the shade in the doorway of the building. Not one of them lifted their eyes when she passed. Emma knew it was ridiculous to care. Remember how much you hated being hassled, she told herself. Well, you're finally safe. No more strange men on the subway groping for your private parts. No more horny bastards making sucking noises in your face as you walk by.

And even at her most defensive, Emma decided she had never been like Loretta. That haircut, the body language, with elbows drilling into the air. What could have been done to her that would have made her invent that pose? Plus, the pose itself was a contradiction. Clipping her hair like an NBA star. Having a dragon tattooed with its tail flicking between her breasts. If you meant to avoid notice, you turned mouselike. Loretta was playing the opposite game. Look at her on *20/20*,· demanding the world take notice. Emma went back over the apartment, so spare, so few indications of a private life except for the bookcase with its particular titles, the CD collection and finally, most particularly, Penny Strider's painting.

Stepping inside the alcove at 311 East Fifth, Emma scanned the mailboxes. Finding Penny's name, she pressed hard on the buzzer. And got silence for her trouble. Exactly what she'd expected. Still, worth a try. Having given it this much attention, she hazarded doing a little more. Luckily, she only had to check her watch three times, before a promising mark showed. Stepping inside the plate-glass doors, he did a double take when he found her standing there. Her smile was meant to disarm him, her attire meant to further reassure.

"I'm Lila," she said, putting out her hand. "It's so embarrassing, but I've been staying with my younger sister in 7B. She's gone away for the week and I seem to have locked myself out. Could you tell me how to get in touch with the super?"

"7B?"

"Penny Strider. You know her?"

He shrugged, then made a fairly obvious scan of the mailboxes. His key was already out. He hesitated, then set it into the lock, opening the door. Making her smile into a piece of honeycomb, Emma swerved around him. "Hey, wait a sec." Emma hesitated, beaming. The sides of her mouth began to ache. It will do wonders for my wrinkle lines, she told herself. "The super lives in the Bronx," he said. "But sometimes he hangs in the basement." Leading the way to the end of a dimly lit hall, he pointed to a door.

"Thanks a bunch," Emma said, and added a titter for effect. She pushed the door open and found the basement stairs. Halfway down, she paused, waiting. When she could no longer hear his footsteps, slowly, and as quietly as she could manage, she headed back up, curving her head around into the hallway. From somewhere far above, she heard an apartment door close.

Seven floors and no elevator. I thought they'd outlawed these buildings, Emma thought. Climbing up and up and up, she noted another interesting fact of pregnancy. She was dizzy and short of breath. Plus, in the last building she'd gagged because of ball park franks, here the smell of ammonia overwhelmed her.

Apartment 7B. She pressed the buzzer, no answer from inside. Across the hall, Lauryn Hill was singing about Zion. Anthem for my own time of life, Emma thought, touching her soft belly. She strode across and rang. The music shifted down a notch, then the door was pulled back.

"Yes?" A woman with short dark hair apparently standing on end and a pair of horn-rimmed librarian frames perched on her nose.

"I'm Janice Lodge from the New York City Adjustment Board," Emma said, swiftly finding the lie. "We're doing some research on the landlord. There have been complaints."

"You're kidding." The woman's nose crinkled. "I never made one."

"Actually I've been trying to get in touch with..." Emma made a show of looking for her notes and pretending to check, "a Penny Strider. We have her listed as residing in apartment 7B."

"Penny? I don't think you'll have much luck finding her. She's gone. Told me she was heading out two days ago. I asked when she'd be back and she wasn't sure. Said she'd been admitted to an art colony out in New Mexico. What did Penny complain about?"

Emma decided to hazard the most obvious guess. "She thought the rent increases were outrageous."

"That's a killer. She told me she was paying half what I pay to begin with. Always after something for nothing, huh? You'd almost think she was a native."

"She's not?"

"Baltimore. She pronounced it Bawlamer. People from down there have that weird accent. You know?"

Emma laughed. "She went to New Mexico? A nice place. I was out there once on vacation. I went to Taos. Is that where she's heading?"

"Fuck if I know," the woman said. "Or care."

"You and Penny didn't get along?"

"What would give you that idea? Me, I'm friends with all my neighbors. Even the ones that think they're God's gift to the world." A punctilious raising of the eyebrows. Emma knew there was more here but just how much could Janice Lodge, rent adjustment investigator, get away with asking? If I press more, I'll raise suspicions, Emma decided. Then thought of the photos, nestled in her wallet.

"Strider's an artist? The name did sound familiar. I might have seen her work?"

"Maybe." A shrug. An attitude of studied indifference.

"There was a redhead who had a show down in Soho. The paintings were edgy, out of control fauna. Desert settings?"

"The red-headed part is her," the woman said. "Couldn't tell you about the work."

"Thanks," Emma said, wishing she could tug the photo out now, for confirmation. Instead, she backed away.

"No problem." And the door clicked shut.

Outside on the pavement, Emma checked her watch. It was after one. Two and a half more hours of work life left before she became a mom again. She could either stay here and try to test tenants' memories or head over to the Pit. Emma had checked that morning and found out that Lisa Kravinovsky, the erstwhile keeper of the Pit's hiring and firing agenda, would be in from ten o'clock on.

At least I've gotten a jump on Reg, she told herself. Which didn't exactly bolster her confidence. In fact, she decided that her special circumstances could be as much of a hindrance as a help. She couldn't help trying to make links between Chazz, Penny, and Loretta. Which could be leading her in the completely wrong direction, farther and farther away from the Emerald City.

Emma knew she'd have to call Laurence Solomon. The best way to heave the burden off her back, was to muster troops. Go on, Em, she thought, tell him about that inscription in the bathroom stall, send him and Ruiz down to the ladies' room for the photo op. She had a stark image of portly Miguel bending over the toilet in the Day Glo stall. The thought gave her a certain vindictive surge of pleasure. And she had to wonder, what would Laurence Solomon make of what she'd found? Thinking that, the heat surged up. A woman's body was invented solely to betray her, Emma decided. How far would he have gone if she'd let him? What could they have done, there, in broad daylight in the front seat of a car? He was using you, she reminded herself. Which only prompted an even more vivid fantasy.

She crossed Second Avenue, heading west. The gate protecting the entrance to the Pit bore one of those brain-crunching, LSD-tinged designs, Peter Max gone funky. It had been pulled halfway up, but the front door was closed. Emma buzzed, then turned to admire the street traffic, the neighborhood full of post-adolescents wearing hipper-than-thou costumes. A young mother strolling along, pushing a carriage, wore a tidy outfit, gray on black with the prerequisite Doc

Martens. Bending over, she cooed to her charge. Emma felt a pang of nostalgia. Averting her eyes, she pressed on the buzzer again, then leaned forward to knock. When she did, she pushed against the door with her shoulder and it gave from the pressure.

"Hello," she called out, stepping inside, "anyone home?" Light emanated from the back of the club. Emma used this as a navigational tool. "Hello," she called again, heading toward the glow. She found the door Eliot had escorted her through two nights before, tugged it open and began to climb. Halfway up, she heard a noise, a door being shut, a breath of wind from above.

"Lise, did you get me my coffee?"

She recognized Eliot's voice.

"It's not Lisa," Emma called out.

"Who the fuck is it, then?" He emerged from the darkness, stopping inches away from her. "You! You're fucking unbelievable!"

"I was looking for Ms. Kravinovsky. Bill told me to speak with her."

"So how'd you get in?" he demanded.

"The front door was open."

"Bullshit." Eliot sneered. "You probably jimmied it. What do you want with Lise?"

"That's confidential," Emma said smoothly. Things had certainly changed since their last encounter. The escalation of hostility was more than a little surprising. And intriguing.

"Fuck that." Eliot grabbed her arm and pulled roughly on it, leading her down the stairs.

As they reached the door, a tall woman with shoulder-length dyed blond hair stepped inside, hoisting two brown paper bags.

"My God!" She jumped back. "You scared me half to death."

"I told you to lock up."

"I was just going to the deli. It's no big deal, Eliot. You're so fucking paranoid."

"Paranoid is what I should be. This is New York City, not the middle of a cow pasture."

"I grew up here. You didn't. Remember, country boy?" She dropped the bags on the mahogany bar, and stalked off.

"You're Lisa Kravinovsky?"

"What if I am?"

"I need to speak with you. I'm from Capital Crimes."

Lisa Kravinovsky shot her eyes to heaven. "I've heard about you. Bill's got a message, says we've told you enough and he's tired of being hassled. If you want anything else call his lawyer, Randolph Miller at Simpson Thacher, and work it out." Turning to Eliot, she gave the same withering look she'd frosted Emma with. "Go on, then, show her out."

And she disappeared into the bowels of the club, her heels making a staccato sound as she climbed the metal catwalk. "Just what I was doing," Eliot said, adding, "bitch," under his breath. "You want to vacate the premises? Or would you like me to start to enjoy my work?"

He reached for her arm again. As he did, she looked down at his hand, then up at the tattoo that had been inked into the flesh on his bicep: a delicately rendered lion, crouched and ready to spring.

"Have I offended you in some way?" Emma asked.

"Who said that?"

Deciding to change direction, she added, "Nice job," using her chin as a pointer and indicating the tattoo on his upper arm. "Did you get it done locally?"

It took him a while to register she was actually offering a compliment. Then he proffered the slightest flicker of a smile. A mean sort of smile, Emma decided, the kind a wolf offers before sinking its fangs in. "A guy in my hometown,"

Eliot said. "Nobody could beat him for artistry." His fingers dug harder into her wrist. "Let's go. I don't have all day." They made their way in tandem to the door and he pushed her through the half-open iron curtain.

"Eliot, listen." Emma made sure that her voice was low, confiding, even apologetic. "It's part of my job description to be a pest. None of this is meant to be personal." He had already turned his back. She stuck her hand out in a final attempt to break down his resistance. "I'm sorry if you think I acted like an asshole," she offered. He turned back to stare down at her hand and shrugged. Then a little smile crept over his lips. "What the hell." He extended his right hand to meet hers. And in the sunlight she made out the inscription on his left shoulder. IN GOD WE TRUST, underneath, rendered in pale blue, a lamb with its legs bent back beneath its supplicating body. A lamb with a tiny golden halo etched above its head.

Eliot turned away, stepped back inside the door and shut it behind him. She heard the lock click down.

And she stood there, rooted to the spot.

Lucien Agosta at the funeral. That speech he'd given with its biblical reference points. Emma backed up the stairs, then walked to the corner, glancing back every few steps to watch the gated door. Once there, she clicked on her cell and phoned the precinct. Laurence Solomon was not in. She swallowed her pride and asked for Ruiz, but he was also unavailable. She left her cell phone number and waited, keeping watch. Five minutes turned into ten. The door of the Pit closed against all comers. And Emma saw Lucien preaching to the unconverted; the lion with fur-blown cheeks, the lamb, trapped in the act of supplication. The lamb, God's own favorite son, kneeling down.

Half an hour passed. Then forty minutes. She was running out of time. Heaving a sigh, she headed to her car, started it up reluctantly, and was in the middle of the Brooklyn Bridge, caught behind a stalled car, another apparent victim of the bridge's treacherous magnetic field, when her phone finally buzzed.

"Hello," she said. At first, only static, then a voice swayed into focus.

"Detective Laurence Solomon."

She wondered how to start to tell this, how much sense any of it would make. I've got nothing tangible to go on, she decided, already feeling her assurance bleeding away. The ramblings of a paranoid schizophrenic?

"It's Emma Price."

"I knew that much."

"Lucien Agosta?"

The voice crackled back her way. "Who?"

"Beatriz's father." A smile edged into her tone. "The speech he gave at the funeral, the rant about the lion lying down with the lamb."

"I remember that. So?"

"Eliot Marshall is the bouncer at that bar, the Pit. The business card I gave you?"

"I remember that, too." Said as a dig. Emma didn't bother raising a defense. It would only waste time.

"Eliot has tattoos on his upper arms. A lion and a lamb. The lamb's got a halo."

She waited for him to get the point, to dismiss her with a laugh and tell her she was raving.

"Nice touch, that," he said. His voice had dropped into a lower register. But, surprisingly, it didn't harbor disdain. "You're coming to me with this?"

"You're an excellent detective with a heart of burnished gold. The type who guides old ladies across busy intersections."

"You really think that?"

The unstated subtext, there for her to refer to, was what had gone on between them in his car the day before. Since he'd offered the opening, she ventured on, "There is the other view. You like to keep all bases covered, like to keep control. Wasn't that why I was the recipient of your, let us say, amorous intentions?"

There was a pause, a hissing noise that might have been an intake of breath. "You think I'm that cold?"

"I'm giving you this," she said, pressing. "I could have held back, but I didn't."

"This being what?"

"We could find out," she offered.

"So noble of you," he said. "We? What makes me think you have your own agenda?"

Still, half an hour later, she'd crossed the border into Queens, and pulled up in front of a small private house on a working-class block. Solomon was waiting for her by the door.

"Down the hall to the right," the woman said. In her early fifties, she had that ageless look nuns acquire, her gray hair pulled back into a bun, the pink cheeks and muted, dove colored habit completing her disguise.

Walking down the hall, Emma noted that each room held a small TV, a bed, and a bookcase. Lucien's was last. He sat on his bed, staring into the television screen.

"One of his stories," the woman said. "He's very dedicated to them, talked to us about them last night at dinner. Mr. Agosta, Detective Solomon here wants to talk."

Lucien pulled his eyes away from the screen for a second, and blinked, then waved his hand in their direction.

"I'm busy now," he said, sticking his chin out. A woman on the soap opera was saying, "Doctor, I think you know what I'm talking about. Randolph will never fully recover." She sounded perversely pleased.

"He's been very good," the nun said. "Hasn't given me any trouble about his medication. He even got up this morning and helped out in the garden. What I tell him is, everything's up to you, isn't that right, Lucien?" She got no acknowledgment. "I'll leave you with him, then," she added, backing away.

"It's not as bad as all that," the doctor on the soap opera offered.

"What a crazy that woman is," Lucien said. "She bugs me all the time, asking how I feel." He didn't turn their way again. Emma noted that he'd shaved. Standing this close, he was gaunt, almost skeletal.

"This is the good part coming," he said. "This one here, she's going to tell him how she's always loved him and only him alone. How the whole world through, there's not another man that makes her this kind of happy. And he's going to tell her how he feels the same exactly. Then they're going to mess with each other right in the next room while her husband's lying there. Some kind of world they try to show you."

"It's to make us feel better," Emma said, taking a seat on the bed beside him. "We can pretend we'd never do the same. We can pretend we're not really animals."

Lucien offered no response. He just kept looking into the screen as if someone in there were about to tell his fortune. The woman in the soap opera was exclaiming, "I've loved you so much. I was afraid to tell you." Emma noted that the doctor's eyes were glistening and he had Grecian Formula hair. Some stylist's idea of a distinguished gentleman.

When a commercial came on, Lucien turned, and even smiled.

"How you doing, Mrs. Price?" he asked.

"You remember me?"

"Sure. I know everything there is to know about my Beatriz."

He leaned over to the bedside table, then pulled the drawer back and took out a pack of LifeSavers. He held it out, an offering. "Want one?"

Emma nodded.

"What color?"

"Lime?"

"I'll take a look." He unrolled the whole pack, then handed her the solo green.

"Mr. Agosta, we need to ask you some questions about Bea," Solomon said.

But then the commercials were over and the doctor had returned, kissing the soon to be bereaved wife passionately. Lucien sighed. Emma recognized that sound. It was the sound that covered the loss of everything.

"You followed Bea," Emma said. "She used to tell me about it."

"Used to complain, you mean," he said, looking her way again. Emma nodded.

"Someone had to watch," he explained, sounding more fatigued then belligerent.

"They go out into the world and what can you do for them after that?" Solomon offered.

Lucien nodded. "Here's the stupid part," he said, motioning to the TV. "This man here, the one who's sick, is a homo. His boyfriend's going to come into the room and find the wife with the doctor. The way these people go, it surprises you. But then, if you look back at the Bible, it was always the story. Sodom and Gomorrah. Now that was a lesson." He sounded world-weary, and about as reactionary and irrational as the next religious zealot. Bea had seen him as a burden, an embarrassment. Emma could certainly understand that. But there was a part of her that felt compassionate nonetheless.

"You say to yourself, is this the world," Lucien added.

"Mr. Agosta, when was the last time you saw your daughter?" Solomon asked.

Lucien shook his head, waving the question away.

"Mr. Agosta, what do you think happened to your daughter, Beatriz?" Solomon reached for the remote and clicked the television off.

"What do you people want?" Lucien demanded, suddenly enraged.

Solomon simply folded his arms, waiting.

"The lion and the lamb," Emma offered. "What was that about, Lucien?"

"I don't know a thing." The words were stubborn. But he suddenly looked terrified, shrinking back onto the bed. This is what he has left, Emma decided. Moving around inside his head are all the things he didn't do that might have saved her.

She reached out and put a hand on his shoulder. And he didn't shudder her off. "We need to know what you saw," she said. "You know why? Because I care about Bea and so does Detective Solomon. It's why he helped you get this place. It's why he's here now, with me. He needs to know. And Bea needs you to tell us."

Lucien's body was shaking. "Oh, you've been a bad bad boy here," he said to Emma, then broke free. He stood and began to back away, but she came over to him and placed her hands on either side of his face.

"Lucien," she said, "Nothing bad's going to happen." She was close enough to taste his breath. It was sweet from the candy and underneath it sweeter still, like something was rotting. "Were you waiting outside her building that day?"

"What day? I don't know my days," he said, but he stayed there, momentarily steady in the traces. "Monday or Tuesday or Wednesday or Sunday."

"It was the very last day you ever saw her walking down the street in front of you," Solomon said softly. "It was the last day she was alive."

"I'm crazy," Lucien said and then he started to cry. "Who's going to listen to me? But a girl should listen. She should listen to her papi. Beatriz never wanted to. Said I was stupid and why didn't I go away. Said she wished I was dead. Is that any way to talk to your papi? Then this other one came and made the lion open his mouth and tell me how I should be ashamed, that I was nasty and dirty. Me! The lamb just sits there and the blood goes dripping down its neck. Abraham gave his firstborn son, Abraham did that." He shook his head. "I used to work construction. People used to give me respect."

"The lion and the lamb, he showed them to you."

"He said God seared his flesh. He told me it was a sign, said he was the real prophet, and how I was no one. Nothing. Said I was crazy and even my daughter knew it." Lucien pursed his lip and made a stubborn face. "I told him different, but he just laughed."

"The lion, was it on his arm?" Emma asked, touching the skin directly below her shoulder.

Lucien nodded.

"A big man?"

He nodded again.

"What color hair did he have?"

"Brown, maybe even black. Dark. And he was angry. He snarled at me like a dog."

"Did Beatriz get into a car with him?"

"Not him. The one who was always with her, the one with the blond hair. The dark-haired man said he'd meet them later, after we spoke. He got up close and started hissing. There was fire in his mouth. That was why I ran. Ran away and hid when I should have stayed there. When I should have helped her." Lucien sat down again, then began to rock back and forth. He started moaning. "What am I good for?"

"There was nothing you could have done," Emma said softly. She reached for the television and turned it on. "Thank you, Lucien," she added and she leaned over, kissing him on the top of the head simply because it was the only blessing she had to bestow.

Emma followed behind Solomon's car to the BQE, then over the Brooklyn Bridge and onto the island of Manhattan. As she pulled off the bridge, her phone buzzed. Solomon told her Eliot had left the bar and was headed for home.

Twenty-first, between Seventh and Eighth. Two off-duty cops in T-shirts, blue jeans, and heavy high tops stood in front of an apartment building with their arms crossed, in bookend poses. Emma spotted Ruiz. He was purchasing a Jamaican meat patty from a street vendor. Ambling up, the patty nestled in his right hand, he offered Emma a companionable nod. "Good to see you," he said, sounding amazingly sincere.

They stepped inside the lobby and Ruiz pressed the super's buzzer.

"No need to spook him," he explained to no one in particular.

The super was a man in his early forties with a close-cut buzz who wore old work pants. They were held up by an extension cord. Emma assumed this was some sort of fashion statement since his tight-fitting undershirt revealed a buff physique and his hair was dyed an ethereal platinum blond. Ruiz went downstairs with him to seal the exits. She and Solomon took the elevator up. It creaked ominously as they ascended. And took a long time to release them, the door emitting a sharp, high-pitched whistle as it pulled back to reveal a bouquet of dusty dried mums in a white china pot sitting on a bleached wooden table. Solomon pressed the buzzer. And waited. No answer. He buzzed again.

"All that prep for nothing," he said. "The guy probably stopped for lunch." He fiddled with the door handle and the door miraculously eased open. "Ali Baba and the forty thieves," he said.

"This isn't good." Emma was thinking about the odds of this happening, an unlocked door twice in the same day in this city. The crime rate hadn't dropped that dramatically.

The apartment was painted a stark white. Framed pictures on the walls; advertisements for photography shows, Brassai and Cartier-Bresson at MOMA, Diane Arbus's Halloween twins. The living room could have been decorated direct order from Preferred Seating, with a leather couch, two leather sling chairs, and a glass coffee table sandwiched in between. The plank floors were scraped clean and varnished. A forty-inch TV on a stand took up one entire living room wall. It was like a condo, no debris apparent anywhere and no sign of current habitation, no magazines, no books, no newspapers.

"I need you upstairs," Solomon said into his walkie talkie. "You hear me, Miguel? The other guys. I want them to stop everyone who's coming in and out. Get their ID. If they can't produce any, hold them. Call the precinct for more backup and get the meat wagon, we have ourselves a stiff."

Emma tried to step past him but he blocked her way.

"What do you want to go in there for?" he asked.

He shook his head and maybe she was a stubborn, willful child, because, when she craned around, she was greeted by what was left of Eliot seated on the bed, his back propped up against a rattan headboard.

"The gun was stuck in his mouth. Whether he pulled the trigger or someone else did it?" Solomon shrugged. "You can still smell the cordite, so this was recent. You okay with this, Emma?"

She nodded, then pressed her head against his chest, closing her eyes.

19

Regina Dawes was a heavyset woman in her midforties and Laurence's favorite ME. He loved watching her use those large, efficient hands. They could coddle the world, Solomon thought. Gina was discussing the entrance and exit wound, how the bullet had sped through the back of Eliot's head, then imbedded itself in the wall. One of the guys from the Tenth dug it out and bagged it. As a matter of professional courtesy he handed it over for Laurence to examine a snub-nosed bullet from a small-caliber weapon. The gun had been shoved right down Eliot's throat and was also available for further inspection once Gina pried it out of Eliot's hand.

No note, but that wasn't especially significant. The only reason Solomon had even a second of doubt was because of the circumstances.

Right now, across town, Ruiz was attempting to gather some more information as to that woman Penny Strider's current location. He'd called in the news that after insinuating himself inside the apartment by use of the super's master key, he'd discovered an empty nest. Solomon did trust Miguel enough to hope that he wouldn't destroy evidence. As for any more subtle clues, he knew he'd be heading there himself just to make sure all the bases got covered. Thank God, Emma Price had checked the time and found herself wanting, that way he'd avoided the unpleasantness, avoided pointing out how none of this was her domain, how the pursuit was now *his* in every aspect of its unfolding glory.

He knew he hadn't seen the last of her, and he doubted whether she'd made every detail available. But she'd told him enough for a start; Penny Strider's designs showing up at both Bea's apartment and this downtown club; Eliot's apparent hostility and his anxiety when Emma mentioned Chazz Perry's name; Penny Strider's disappearance scarcely twenty-four hours after Bea's death; plus the message on the bathroom wall at the Pit echoing the lines scrawled on the back of the business card. And the *pièce de résistance,* Loretta Picard's ownership of a Strider masterpiece.

It was his turn now, up to him to suss out the links. And he had his own knowledge to throw into the mix, Chazz Perry aka Charles Murray's field of expertise put into proper English thanks to Ralph's UN-worthy interpretive skills. "The kid's a hacker," Ralph had explained. "This here is his day job maybe. He builds firewalls, develops codes for them, and preps himself in the process. One thing feeds the other."

"Firewalls being?"

Ralph offering him his own version of in-the-know condescension, a frosty smile, a flintlined tap of the eyebrow, the imperious, older brother gesture. Eternal, Solomon thought. "Firewalls. Ways to make it impossible to break inside and steal the business's secret information. High-tech locks, you get?"

He got. Information flooding in, none of it making any sort of seamless, perfect sense. No signs of a struggle in the apartment. The bedroom, immaculate except for the mess left behind when skull and brains had smashed into the wall. Only one set of fingerprints on the gun that Solomon assumed would turn out to be Eliot's own. Plus, it was hard to imagine someone being able to force such a muscular guy to stick a small-caliber Luger down his own throat. Though one thing being a cop had taught him was, anything was possible. Still, he'd be surprised to discover Eliot had a history of profound depression.

Everything in the room was being bagged; a glass at the bedside table that was empty and stank of liquor, a *Penthouse* magazine encrusted with blood, on top of that the deceased's set of keys with a key chain that read HAWAIIANS DO IT BETTER. The boys were being careful, flicking paintbrushes across the floor to try and find stray hairs. Meanwhile, as he did the spring cleaning, Andrews from the Tenth was jawing at him, complaining about how his youngest son didn't want to even go to college, and was taking time off to find himself. Andrews said he'd be damned if he was going to support some slack-mouthed kid. No, he was not about to hang a roof over the kid's house and slave some more just so this kid could go experiment.

Andrews always wore that permanently exasperated look. Solomon nodded, companionably. No sense in throwing in how Dawann was earning straight A's at Miami University's six-year med program. He rarely spoke of his own personal pride. It was enough to know that things were good. It was demeaning to use your own homefront progress as a weapon. Solomon pretended to listen, using the time to look around again. Now that the fingerprint boys were done, he could open every closet and cupboard, noting even more clearly the absence of a life. In fact, those tattoos on Eliot's upper arms were about the only personal touch he could find.

The bedroom was spotless, but the rest of the apartment was hardly as tidy, a light coating of dust on the glass coffee table top, dirt on the windowsills, and a few soiled dishes in the sink. Then the crew from the coroner's office bagged up the body and carted it away. They had to lean it on its side to get it into the narrow elevator. Once the body was gone, it was easier. Solomon didn't think it was just the physical proximity. The corpse being there meant the soul was still held in place, keeping the cord tucked tight between the *is* and the *was*.

He scrutinized. He tried to imagine. The glass could have been washed out, refilled with a little coating of liquor, then set down. A nice friendly drink turning into something sinister. Still, why go to so much trouble? Because suicide shouldn't raise a host of questions. So why now? The pressure, Solomon decided; that steam driving the pistons. Penny Strider's flight coinciding with Beatriz Castillo's demise. Then Eliot becoming one of the dear departed. Whoever was behind this was spooked. If it was the disappearing Chazz, then he had to have something large in the works to be taking all this trouble to tidy up. And Solomon reminded himself how anxiety often led to carelessness. Go on, he thought. Do it, Mr. Cool. Fuck up. Drop the ball. Do us all a favor.

"What is it with people?" Andrews was complaining. "Stick a gun in your mouth and make a mess for everyone. Whatever happened to doing things the old-fashioned way? Pills. A little booze. Then lights out."

"That's the only question you've got?"

"What's your beef with me?" Andrews gave him an annoyed look.

"What about personal effects?" Solomon said.

"Maybe he's not the type who needs possessions. There are those types, what's the name? On the tip of my goddamn tongue."

"Ascetics?"

"Leave it to you to know. You're looking for reasons? Maybe he just moved in."

"He's been here over a year."

"Then he was probably remodeling." Andrews yawned to display his lack of interest. Solomon understood, Andrews was a type. Like Ruiz really, a beat cop admiring the shape of his pension.

But, hey, not even a *TV Guide* to go along with that forty-inch screen. And only a few clothes, two summer-weight Italian-cut suits, a shoe rack with four pairs of shoes, shined and ready for service, one pair of Nike Air Cross Trainers in a size twelve.

The lion and the lamb, let me lie down in that valley.

Solomon looked over this and decided what was in evidence was a life that had been scrupulously hidden.

"You think he whacked himself?" Andrews asked.

"Do you?"

"Don't get hot with me. I thought you might be in the know."

"I was only trying to interview the guy."

"For what reason?"

"From your mouth to God's ear? I tell you and then?" Solomon asked. One of his cardinal rules was, never give anything away for free.

"My problem here is, a guy sticks a gun in his mouth, there's got to be some motive."

No date book. No notes scribbled on a pad by the phone. He'd offered Andrews a suggestion, that was plenty, considering. Andrews apparently realized he'd get no more. "You finished here or what, detective?" he asked.

It was stone still, and pitch black. Solomon moved forward gingerly, as the door clanged shut behind. He put his hand out for assistance. Then a voice said, "Up here." Suddenly lights flared on. Enough to blind you with, Solomon thought. When his eyes recovered, he made out a man, waving to him behind what could only be described as a parapet.

"There's a door behind you."

He found it. Climbed up to the second floor. Bill Weston was waiting. Into a private office, where Solomon assessed the man. Beanstalk-tall, rangy, the skin on his face pockmarked from a childhood case of acne. And the stink of herb.

"Here's what we have on poor Eliot." Weston was thrusting a manila envelope across the desk, and staying pointedly on his feet.

Hoping I'll vacate the premises if he makes me feel less than welcome, Solomon thought, shattering those hopes by taking a seat in what looked like the most comfortable chair in the room, a plush, blue velvet number. Breaking open the flap on the envelope, he found one single employment sheet listing home address, phone, and Social Security number. No prior places of employment. No life history.

"This is all you have?"

Weston sighed. "We're trying to cooperate, detective. Eliot was a member of our family. It's been quite a shock." Only Weston didn't look shocked, he looked stoned, slightly glazed eyes, a mouth that curved into a half-moon grin.

"Come on, Mr. Weston. First this Picard girl turns out to have the wrong ID. Then someone else you hire has no work history at all? You do operate this as a business?"

"Eliot came to us with excellent references."

"Which were?"

"I'll get you the information. It will just take a little time." Weston shoved his hands into his pockets.

Solomon decided to put his annoyance on hold. "So when did Eliot start working for you?"

"I don't keep dates in my head."

"Then who does?"

"Lisa Kravinovsky. She's down the hall, the office to the right of mine as you leave. I asked her to wait in case you needed to speak with her." He waved his hand, attempting a royal dismissal. But Solomon just crossed his legs, getting more comfortable.

"So what were Eliot's responsibilities?"

"Keeping the right company in, the wrong company out. If issues came up, working on our behalf to resolve them."

"The club bouncer."

"An inelegant term."

"And you saw each other every night?"

"We did," Weston admitted.

"Did the two of you talk?"

"We chatted. Nothing of a personal nature, of course."

"So if you were to offer me an adjective to describe him, what pops into your head?"

Weston pursed his lips, considering.

"Sunny? Morose?"

"You're asking whether I'm surprised he took his own life? Eliot always seemed at ease, but then, why would he bother to confide in me? I was his boss. You can spend a great deal of time with a person and still not know them." Weston offered a serious, thin-lipped expression to accompany this pearl.

"Who were Eliot's friends?"

Weston shrugged. "Look," he said. "It's been hard enough staying open since that Picard girl went mad. The newspapers have been having a field day. As if tending bar means you've been an undue influence on our clientele. It's the American disease, affixing blame."

"I would agree that you've had more than your share of bad luck," Solomon said evenly. "A man might start to wonder if you didn't bring some of it on yourself."

Weston raised his eyebrows. His face pursed into mean-
ness. "Just what does that mean?"

"You might want to reexamine your hiring practices, for
starters."

"A lovely recommendation. And I'm sure it comes from
your long experience, detective." Weston's voice was brittle.
"This horror has got nothing to do with what you term 'hiring practices.' Metaphysically speaking, people kill themselves every second of the day."

"The philosophical defense?"

Weston came around from behind the desk, the smell of
marijuana searing the air between them. "What am I being
accused of?"

"Nothing."

Weston wrinkled his lips as if he'd recently ingested
something bitter. Me, Laurence thought. Because he was being stonewalled, and he couldn't begin to guess why.

"I've told you all I know," Weston said.

"Not even the name of one friend?"

Weston's arms stretched out to embrace the entire ocean
of possibilities, then dismiss them.

"What about Penny Strider?"

"Penny?" An utterly derisive snort.

"You do know her?"

"Of course. You're imagining her and Eliot? Who could
have given you that idea? Eliot Marshall was an oaf. A thug.
A bully. Whatever brain he was born with got blasted apart
by those steroids he ingested."

Things have taken a turn, Solomon thought. A second
ago, Eliot was the salt of the earth.

"Indicating that Penny Strider was his stellar opposite?"

"Absolutely, Penny's a complete dear."

"So she's a friend?"

Weston narrowed his eyes. "What's that to do with you?"

"Her name's come up."

"Where?" Weston waited, tapping his fingers on the desk to show his own impatience.

"You hired her to do the club's decor, didn't you?"

Weston gave a curt nod.

"Did someone recommend her?"

A flick of the salamander-like tongue.

"Why would you need to know?"

"As I said, her name's come up. We'd like to ask her a few questions, get a few details ironed out."

"It sounds like she's been avoiding you."

"Not exactly. Apparently she's taken off on a trip to some artist's colony. We haven't been able to find out the name. You wouldn't know where we might reach her?"

"No, I wouldn't have a clue."

"Would you know someone else who might help us out?"

Weston kept his mouth shut.

"Chazz Perry?" Solomon asked.

No sign that the name registered.

"Charles Murray?"

Nothing again.

"See if you can rack your brain," Solomon said. "I'd appreciate you trying to come up with some friends. Friends of Penny. Friends of Eliot. See if the name Chazz Perry starts to ring a bell, or Charles Murray. Try making a list. Put some phone numbers on it. Call your lawyer if you want and let me know the upshot. I'll be back to you about it in the next couple of hours."

"Is that all?" Weston asked.

"For the moment," Solomon said, standing to take his leave.

"You forgot to tell me something else, detective," Weston said, leaning back in his chair and folding his hands.

"What's that?"

"How you've only got my best interests at heart."

Lisa Kravinovsky was keeping busy, a double-entry notebook open next to her. One hand was adding up columns of numbers. Solomon admired her poise, her buxom physique. And her blond hair done up in a fashionable French twist.

"Going over the books?"

She looked up, grinned slyly, and said, "This is homework."

"For?"

"I'm in the MBA program at Pace."

He handed her the bio. "Is this really all you have on Eliot Marshall?"

She studied the sheet. "Not much there."

"Your boss told me you were in charge of hiring the employees and checking their work backgrounds."

"Is that what I do around here?" She raised an eyebrow. "Those Brits, always passing the buck. Eliot met Bill at the World Gym. They were doing free weights together."

"No references asked for?"

"And none received. Bill's a very fluid guy."

"I noticed. Did Eliot ever talk about where he'd worked before?"

"Once. I asked and he said he'd spent the last few years out West in cow country. And how living there bored him to death."

"Did he mention a specific state?"

"Maybe Montana?" Said as though he were in a position to offer some firm agreement. "I could look at a map."

"What about his background? Any siblings? Near and dear relations?"

"We never went there," Lisa Kravinovsky said.

"You weren't close then?"

"We kept different hours. I'm a day hire, he was on the late shift. And when we overlapped, we didn't exactly go in for heart-to-hearts." She wrinkled her nose for emphasis.

"Then he wasn't your type of guy?"

"Eliot was the show-me sort. Show me yours and I'll show you mine. Not that I mean to speak unkindly of the dead," she added, crossing herself. "I just want to be clear. After all, you are an officer of the law."

"Did he have a girlfriend?" Solomon asked, ignoring the flirtatious look she'd sent his way.

"According to him, legions. Guys like that love to inflate their world. Then it up and explodes. So, as for names, he was never that specific." For the first time, she sounded uncertain. "Look, Eliot wasn't exactly Einstein. I think of suicides as people who worry and that wasn't one of Eliot's major faults. All for one and one for all was more his motto." A jar of hard candy sat on the edge of the desk. She opened the lid and offered one. Solomon shook his head.

"You were with him earlier today. What was his mood?"

"Obnoxious, as per always. He got mad at me over not locking the door. I was only outside for a second. I mean, no one's going to come walking in here off the street."

"He didn't seem more nervous than usual?" Solomon asked, noting silently that, of course, someone had walked in on him, Ms. Emma Price.

"No."

"When Officer Ruiz called, you said Eliot had left. Can you tell me exactly when that was?"

"I went out to get lunch about one, and when I came back this bitch was here. Said she was working for Loretta. Maybe you should call her up to check?"

"Why don't you approximate," Solomon said.

"It was only about twenty minutes later. He called up to say he was going."

Solomon remembered Emma telling him how she'd stood watch. "Is there a back door?"

"Sure. We're pros at fire safety. Goes out onto East Fourth."

"Was he usually here during the day?"

"No."

"And he didn't give a reason?"

She shook her head.

"He didn't by any chance get a phone call?"

She shrugged.

"Or make one?"

"How in hell would I know? I'm not keeping tabs on him, all right? That's not what I'm paid for."

Solomon made a mental note to check the phone records himself.

"So you're paid to do the books. And I assume you make out the paychecks?"

"That's right."

"Did you handle payments to Penny Strider?"

"Where are you off to now?" She looked around the room as if someone out there could provide the answer.

"Did you cut her a check?"

"I suppose I must have." Lisa peered at him. "What's the game plan, Lieutenant?"

"Detective."

"Maybe I can see the future." She had mischief in her eyes. "You start off with Eliot, then go to Penny. You're talking two different continents."

"How was Strider paid? You do have her Social Security number?"

"Look," Lisa said, smiling a little too happily. "There's no use pretending to search. I'm not here to waste your time.

Bill paid her out of his own personal account. In cash. I warned him, but he wouldn't listen. It was Strider's idea and he went along with it. Bill has always had certain weaknesses. Bill thinks she's his little discovery, genius in the making. He's always going on about how one day we were going to say we knew her when. As far as I'm concerned, she was the divine princess of attitude. Red hair flowing down her back, dressed all in black so you would have thought she'd been in mourning in the womb. When she talked to me, it was always me supposed to click my heels and say *jawohl*." Her shoulders rippled, an elegant, sensual shrug.

The woman's lethal, Solomon thought, marking her down as the perfect snitch. Still, her venomous description had the ring of truth.

"Then what could there be between Eliot and Penny?"

"Nothing at all. I've already told you."

In that, at least, she was in concurrence with Weston.

"Do you know a Chazz Perry?"

"Nope."

"A Charles Murray, then? Tall, blond, three ruby studs up one ear. According to women in the know breathtakingly handsome." He pulled out the artist's rendering. She bent down to study it.

"Not by name, but I do know this guy. He'd hang at the bar with Loretta. And believe me, the drawing doesn't do him justice. He even took my breath away. But don't get jealous, Lieutenant. I like men of a more mature persuasion."

"He and Picard were close?"

"Thick as thieves." She winked again, cementing the implication.

"How about this guy and Penny?"

"She'd love how she's the center of your world." Lisa Kravinovsky stretched her arms, displaying her ample cleavage. "It may surprise you, but I don't spend a whole lot of time following other women's progress in a crowd."

"You would have noticed the two of them talking?"

"I might have."

"You noticed him and Loretta."

"'Cause that was obvious."

"You hired Loretta."

"Bill said that, too? No way is he going to stick that one on me."

Solomon didn't respond, letting her think whatever she needed to.

"He did it. Penny Strider's rec. Penny sent the girl in looking. I told him she was going to be trouble. Poor old Bill." She lowered her voice as if she were imparting a secret. "I have a feeling the powers that be are going to be asking him to take a long, long leave of absence."

So that's it, Solomon thought. All this honesty comes from her angling to fill the void. He handed Kravinovsky his card. "If you think of anything else."

"Thanks." She read it over carefully. As she did, her lips moved slightly and he caught sight of the tip of her pink hungry tongue.

"The name of the town he hailed from, that sort of thing. If you come up with something specific, give me a call," he said.

"I surely will," pausing for emphasis here, then continuing, "Lieutenant."

She'd call. It was not something he looked forward to. A certain type of woman, he thought, or was it a certain type of person? Ready to disembowel her familiars, lining up heads for later springboard use.

Solomon headed downstairs. Inside the ladies' room, he banged open the door to the second stall.

AND TRAVELLERS NOW WITHIN THAT VALLEY,
THROUGH THE RED-LITTEN WINDOWS, SEE
VAST FORMS THAT MOVE FANTASTICALLY
TO A DISCORDANT MELODY;
WHILE, LIKE A RAPID GHASTLY RIVER,
THROUGH THE PALE DOOR . . .

He pulled out his pocket flash. Collecting evidence in the bathroom, that pretty much said it all about this case. "Through the pale door." Solomon had a vision of everyone he knew vanishing into that ghostly territory, swallowed, then changed, the same way Beatriz Castillo had been.

Then he flashed back, finding Emma Price as she stood next to him in Eliot's living room, laying out all she knew in a tidy bundle for him to scoop up. Two skillful liars, that's what we are, he decided. But he also reminded himself of that prickle that rose under his skin, coursing through his body as he watched her, savage and revealing, a fever that had already made its own indelible and original mark.

20

Emma made it back just in time. She stepped out into the schoolyard, and Tony raced up, demanding money for ice cream. She gave it over gladly. He tugged on Liam's hand and then they both sped off. As they did, a truck backfired and Emma lunged after them, meaning to slam them onto the ground. Then she pulled up short, realizing where she was, and she looked around to see if anyone had noticed. Another mother on the other side of the playground was staring.

It had been years since she'd witnessed something as graphic as what she'd seen in Eliot's bedroom. The sight was not something you got used to. But with practice you could at least bury it away. Another thing I didn't miss about this job, Emma thought, as she heard Suzanne's voice, calling for her.

"Damn." Her heart sank to the ground and began to tunnel for cover.

As Suzanne came up, Emma made a search of the cracked pavement, looking for her still-pumping organ.

"World to Emma," Suzanne said.

The boys returned. Tony was busy demolishing the four tiers of a rainbow-colored Popsicle Rocket, and Liam was working on a Flintstones push-up bar that had been dyed an obscene orange. The color was washing off onto his tongue and smearing the corners of his mouth.

"Em, are you all right?" Suzanne was not going to give up. The boys spotted some friend and took off. Emma sucked in a few small breaths.

"I can't do this," Emma muttered.

"Do what?"

Emma blinked. When she did, she saw Eliot's bedroom, everything neat, immaculate, except for the tattoo of blood on the headboard. Why? Why would anyone? It was an innocent schoolgirl's voice asking. She didn't believe for one second this was a suicide. Beatriz wasn't even first on the list anymore, no, Stewart Larrabbee and Cheri Maples had been given that honor. But none of the deaths made sense. Roadkill. Emma imagined Loretta lying there on the highway with that flock of ravens feathering the air above. Loretta as victim. A fairly unique point of view. Plus that other nagging detail, the photograph she'd recently liberated from the bathroom cabinet. No way she should have slid it out and jammed it into her pocket. She'd told him almost everything, but she hadn't had the nerve to offer that. Too many embarrassing questions would have been forwarded, along with the one she asked herself when she ran out of excuses and avoidance techniques. Why? She had no good answer.

Unfortunately, her best friend was still standing in front of her, demanding clarification. Emma opened her mouth and found she still had the capacity to surprise herself.

"I'm pregnant, Suze."

"What?" Suzanne seemed to think her own hearing was at fault. She shook her head hard, like a distance swimmer clearing water from her clogged-up ears.

"I'm pregnant," Emma said again firmly, deliberately. "I'm about to bring another child into this world."

"God." Suzanne's mouth hung open, then closed softly. "He left because you were pregnant? What an absolute bastard."

"Will doesn't know," Emma said. And then added, defiantly, "He's not going to."

"How are you going to manage that?" Suzanne asked. Then a trifle too complacently, she said, "You couldn't have an abortion."

"And why not?"

"Em, come on!"

"Don't tell me you've turned into one of those pro-life lunatics."

"It's not that. This is Will's baby. I'm sure he'll do the right thing."

"Which would be what, exactly?" Emma said. "I've thought this over, Suze," she added, wondering, as she said it, if that were true. Suzanne reached out to take Emma's wrist in her hand and she pressed down, making a physical plea. Emma shook her head firmly. In doing so, she felt her own sorrow inflate, pumping carbon dioxide instead of oxygen, poisoning the arteries, and savaging her heart. "Can you stand it if I ask you a favor?"

"Of course," Suzanne said, her anxious look belying that claim.

"Nothing criminal," Emma said, hoping the joke would offer reassurance. "Please don't tell anyone. I know it's unfair to ask. God, who keeps a secret these days?"

Suzanne stood there, apparently considering the request, which forced Emma to do the same. Not just unfair, she decided, but totally unrealistic. Suzanne would tell Al immediately, because theirs was a good marriage in which the minutiae of people's daily lives were fodder for discussion. And Al and Will were still good friends, so he could hardly be expected to keep this secret for long. From there? The whole world blasted apart, Emma decided. Still, Suzanne might wait, given the tenor of this last entreaty. *I just need a head start,* Emma decided, and felt palpable relief when Suzanne nodded.

"Thanks," Emma said fervently.

The boys were waiting for them at the corner. "Want to blade up to the Promenade?" she asked, hearing the telltale chirp in her voice. Perkiness was not an adjective anyone had ever used to describe her personality. Another sign of how I'm teetering on the brink, she decided. "You go on home," she added to Suzanne. "I'll take care of them." Then she actually reached out, giving Suzanne a shove. "I'll be fine," she added.

Reaching her own door, Emma shut her eyes, trying to reconstruct the world. An elm tree forged skyward, shedding bark. A blue Thunderbird was parked illegally at the hydrant. Traffic whizzed by. Still she couldn't resist the other images flooding in: "Hate" carved into Loretta's scalp; Cheri Maples's sprawled form embracing the stairs; the tattoo of blood on the wall of Eliot Marshall's bedroom. Emma looked up and noticed the clouds overloaded with heat. She told herself that her child, whom she loved more than anything, waited for her in the hallway. And for that second, she let herself go weak and imagine another possibility, a reconstructed life where there was room for more. Shoving her hands down into her pockets, she surreptitiously rubbed the corners of her stomach, mouthing a tender goodbye.

Late afternoon slid into early evening, a breeze pushing the humid air away as the three of them coasted down Smith Street. The boys were so adept they could avoid most pedestrian traffic. As they stopped at the corner of Atlantic in front of the dive shop, waiting for the light to change, Emma glanced in the window. She and Will had strolled by, pausing to fantasize about a blissful island vacation. So many ideas they had never gotten around to pursuing. Vacations usually ended up becoming a few weeks on the Cape or weekends at his mother's house in Rhinebeck.

Were we too cautious, Emma wondered? Was that one of the flaws? It hadn't bothered her. But she knew something as banal as this could be added onto Will's list. In fact, Will, tooling by here, could look in the window and imagine himself diving down to coral reefs, rousting unknown denizens of the deep. He might tell himself, *she* was what prevented me. He probably has a hundred entries, Emma thought, and knew each one had claws sharp enough to torture and shred what was, at best, a flimsy covering.

Tony skated ahead. Emma reached over and grabbed Liam's hand. "Miss Labadie is so cool," he said. "She told me I can do advanced math anytime I want. Tony and I were doing this program on the computer, plus we played this round-robin soccer match in gym. Tone and I were on the same team and now our record is six and oh."

"Great." Emma looked him over with wonder. "You're incredible, Liam," she said, hearing the sorrow topple out of her voice. She hugged him, and that was all he could bear.

"Mom, let me go," he said, twisting away and racing to catch up to his friend.

They bought pizza on Montague Street, then skated to the Promenade to eat. The first bite didn't agree with Emma but she still used it as medicine, chewing carefully and forcing herself to swallow. Look at all these people, she told herself; this couple who look as if they're straight out of a Gap ad; those two women, also a couple, with the taller one leaning in for a quick kiss; this elderly pensioner sitting on a bench having a conversation with an invisible friend; and this homeless man searching for buried treasure in the trash. Terrible things happen every day, but no one seems to care. The world just moves on, regardless.

The boys finished eating and roared off, narrowly avoiding an elderly woman with a cane clenched in one hand. Her nurse glared their way, cursing. Then they pulled up short.

"What?" Emma asked, coming up to join them. Then realized. Will's new apartment loomed up. And Liam was now paying dutiful homage. "Dad lives there," he said, pointing.

Emma's lungs fluttered against her ribcage, and her throat constricted. She fought for control, but remembered Liam rhapsodizing about the view from Will's living room, how you could see the Manhattan and Brooklyn bridges and ID all the boats docked at the South Street Seaport.

There's a future where we'll act mature and reasonable, she told herself, and tried imagining that day when her anger would be dulled, worn to a small, fierce flame, and after that, snuffed out. Except she couldn't. How did anyone manage? How did they capitulate, then forget? Suzanne's right, I'll never be able to keep this secret, she thought. In fact, I've already failed. So I'll abort this child, then end up brandishing the choice and using it as a lethal weapon.

"It's so cool up there," Liam was saying to Tony.

Emma squinted at the window. Above them, the sky was starting to crease, going soft and orange as the sun sank low over the western banks of the Hudson. The setting sun reflected off the glass, blinding her. Tony rolled off on his fleet feet, but Liam waited beside her.

"When are you going to make up with Dad?" he demanded.

"We've been over this," she said, exhausted at the prospect of what lay ahead.

"If you don't make up with him soon, I'm going to go live with him."

"You will not! Don't say that, Liam."

"But I want to. I'm going to have my own bedroom. He's going to buy me Sega Dreamcast. He's more fun than you ever are."

"Liam, please," Emma began.

But he set his shoulders and skated away. Catching up to Tony, he whirled his best friend around. The two of them laughed so hard, they doubled over. Then Liam threw her an angry look and the boys turned the corner. Chasing after them, she spotted Liam stopped at Will's new front door.

"Wait up," she yelled, to no avail. They were inside, the door slamming shut in her face. Searching the alphabetized list, she found "Price" written in elegant script. When she pressed down, a woman's voice demanded an identity.

"My mistake," Emma said, feeling chastened. She pressed down on the buzzer again.

"Stop playing games." The same woman's voice.

Emma drew back, as if stung. "I'm looking for Will," she said, swallowing hard, then gathering courage. "It's his wife."

There was a pause. Then the door was buzzed open and she raced down the hall only to find the elevator was already ascending. On its way up to the tippy tip top, she thought grimly as she waited impatiently for it to return.

The elevator disgorged an elderly woman who gave her a keen once-over. Emma offered a haughty look in response, then rolled inside, pressing seven.

Liam and Tony were standing at the door to Will's apartment, staring at a young woman who had on a short plaid miniskirt and a skintight black T-shirt with VOODOO emblazoned on it. The finishing touch was a pair of Birkenstock sandals.

"Hello," Emma said, coming up behind Liam. When she put her hand on his shoulder, he flinched and pulled away.

"Jolene," the girl said. She *was* a girl, up close, nowhere near the icy precipice of thirty. Emma felt her lips curl back into an evil, feral grin. She warned herself away from the murderous thoughts she was having. Think of innocence, she told herself. Think of Will, the Will Price you know. Only that was ridiculous, Will was no different from the rest of the bastards. He was a man. The 48 percent of the human race who simply couldn't help themselves.

"I was telling Liam his dad should be back soon. Will just went out to get some groceries. He was going to make us a little dinner. We had some work to do." Jolene stuttered over the last part and let it sink down to the floor. "I'm a producer," she added.

"How nice for you," Emma said, truly sorry that words could not kill, or at least maim. "We'd better go. We don't want to intrude. Isn't that right, Liam?"

He avoided looking her way, but did spin around and glide down the hall with Tony at his heels.

"I'll tell him you came by," Jolene said gaily. As if this had all been her greatest pleasure. Which was probably true enough, Emma thought bitterly.

"You do that," Emma said. If a snake had slithered out, wrapped itself around Jolene's ankles, then sucked her down into the private little hell she'd issued from, Emma would have been the first to applaud, then tamp the lid on permanently.

To think I was imagining a moment of forgiveness, she thought. That bastard. That motherfucking bastard.

Once inside the elevator it was impossible to know what to say. Liam's eyes had flooded with tears. Stupid, she thought. That's certainly what I am. Foolish. Idiotic. Not to mention naive!

Out on the street, two black kids were passing, wearing the down ghetto outfit of the moment, baggy pants, underwear riding above the waist, wraparound shades, and bandannaed back hair. As they walked by she heard one of them saying, "Suckah!"

* * *

Liam kept half a block between them all the way home. She wanted to call to him and get him to wait, telling him how none of this mattered. She dearly wanted to lie. But didn't dare. He'll have to live with this, she reminded herself. Then added, under her breath, "so will I."

When they got to the corner of Smith and Bergen, he bolted.

21

Solomon had a vicious headache. He downed three ibuprofen, bone-dry on his tongue, then walked up the seven flights to Penny Strider's place and found Miguel looking even more mystified than usual.

A one-bedroom, the bed wearing sheets and a plump comforter. There were nails in the wall and dirt marks to show how, at one time, the room had been a veritable portrait gallery. Miguel had been thorough, every drawer pulled out to reveal the achingly empty interior, trash cans emptied and plundered.

"Long red hair, freckles on the bridge of her nose, a spider tattoo on her upper arm. All that's from the woman across the hall. Right now, she's down at the station helping Deedee with a sketch. Think we could call up *America's Most Wanted?*"

"And say what?"

"That's your department. You're the one with the serious smarts."

Solomon went over and pulled up a window. He felt briefly comforted by the cityscape outside. But his temples were throbbing and the steamy, ozone-ridden air in the room wasn't helping.

"I sent McCarthy down on the sly with all the prints," Ruiz said. "He got them to Pat. She said she'd run them, but only cause it was you, asking." Ruiz gathered up a box of Dunkin' Donuts Munchkins that rested on the table, and made a tching sound in his throat. "Ready to head out?"

Solomon held up a traffic cop's paw. Then he made another circuit of the two small rooms. Into the bedroom, pulling back the shower curtain to reveal a classic old-style claw-foot tub. He dragged a finger across the empty bookshelves and lifted up a slight layer of dust. He tried to set this next to what he'd learned at the club, Penny Strider's close relationship to that Brit manager. Picard working the bar and her own intense interest in the vanished Chazz. Penny's designs in the bathroom, and his own snapshot of the inscription Emma Price had discovered. None of it clicked. In fact, all of it seemed like makework, leading nowhere. Turning back, he began to count the outlined spaces on the wall. Twenty-seven in toto. The girl was a little too damn prolific.

Then he looked down at the floor and noticed the picture-perfect sheen.

"Where did she do the painting?" he asked, meaning it as a rhetorical question.

"Hell if I know," Ruiz muttered. "Maybe she used a dropcloth."

But Solomon was scanning the walls and floor again. "No sign of paint splattering anywhere."

"So maybe she was a clean freak."

Solomon discounted that. There had been dust on the bookcases, and on the dresser. A thin layer of mildew in the bathtub.

"I'd say she has a workspace."

"Lar, it's after five," Ruiz said, smiling gingerly. "Me and Diane we got this thing planned. My *tio's* sixtieth. Got the roast cooking now." He sniffed the air as though he could inhale that fine, rich odor, as if it were wafting in on the wind, this far north.

"Five's the time people are coming home from work," Solomon said. He went over to the kitchen, threw open the cabinets to discover nothing inside. "No one saw a moving van pull up?"

"The woman across the hall saw her leaving. Just like Price told you."

"She's the only one with any information at all. What did this Strider woman do, live out of a backpack?"

"Maybe so, people do crazy things."

"Of course, you've got to get home," Solomon said.

Ruiz gave a sigh of relief and collapsed the half-eaten box of doughnuts under one arm, heading for the door. He tugged it open and stepped out, only seconds from a clean getaway.

"Kind of too bad, though," Solomon added, and subdued the laughter that ached to accompany this statement. Miguel had frozen just outside the door, his face hidden from view. It was just as well, considering. "First Castillo drowning when she couldn't even swim a stroke. Then that muscle-bound Eliot sticking a gun in his mouth. Now this Strider woman cutting out, with her friend Chazz one step ahead. Like they're pretty much mocking us, don't you think? When what are they but kids, really. Barely grown. Half-pint, half-assed babies." Solomon left it there for a moment, let the significant pause infect the atmosphere.

"So what?" Ruiz said. Sullen didn't do justice to the way the words were phrased.

"You saw that *20/20* interview with Picard?"

He stepped back inside and threw off a curt little nod.

"Luck walking out of their lives. Acting like it could have been anyone she took down. You. Me. Anyone. And guess what? Back at the bar I find out she and Chazz were friends. Maybe even more than friends."

"You don't know what you're doing," Ruiz said. "This is gonna have serious ramifications."

"With Bernardino, you mean? Not if we stay one step ahead. And if we don't, I'll take the fall."

Ruiz rolled his eyes, pleading with an eternally unvigilant God for help.

"Aren't you even curious?" Solomon asked.

"No," Miguel said. He heaved a tired breath to show the burden he was carrying, and studied his hands for a long, long while. An eternity later, he spoke. "All right. I'll stick around another hour, make one more canvass. Ask about whether anyone knows where she did her painting. Will that satisfy you?"

"You're a sweetheart," Solomon said and made sure to keep the smiling to a bare minimum.

"Don't get personal." Ruiz offered a bemused look that did make him seem charming, even boyish despite his girth. "Want one?" he asked, offering the half-filled donut carton.

The chocolate nugget was mercilessly sweet, but Solomon cut the taste with a cup of New World coffee. Traffic was brutal, another repair job on the bridge. The way the infrastructure in New York was crumbling, it hardly seemed worth the money spent. But it did give all those drivers surrounding him time to work their cell phones. He did the same, putting in a call to a friend at Rikers, because a visit with Loretta Picard was definitely figuring in his evening plans.

So by the time he made it back to his desk, it was seven. Running Marshall's S.S. number through the computer, he got precious little. Born and bred in Wichita. He put in a call to the local constabulary and was hooked up to a Stephan Lind who said he'd be willing to try and track down Marshall's nearest and dearest. The second he hung up, the phone rang.

"This guy I found says she had a place out in Brooklyn somewhere," Ruiz said. "That's the best I can get for you and I tried information, there's no listing in the borough under her name."

"Thanks, bro."

"I'm not your bro and you got a bug up your ass with this one. Now I'm going home."

So it was all his. The evening taking shape, starting with the trip to Rikers. He picked up the sketch of Charles Murray aka Chazz Perry, then set it down on his desk next to Deedee's vision of Strider. Then he scooped the two of them up and slid them into the Castillo case file, dropped it into his briefcase, and reached for his car keys.

"A guest for you, Solly." Bernardino's face stuck in through the half opened door, looking a little too happy for him to find comfort in the announcement.

The man was broad-shouldered, wearing a taupe double-breasted suit. He had an abundant head of pearl-white hair. "O'Donnell, Office of Enforcement Operations," he said, extending his hand. "I'm here about Eliot Marshall."

O'Donnell took the only comfortable chair and settled in. Noblesse oblige, Solomon decided. A man so used to creature comforts, he didn't stand on ceremony. "You found the body."

Solomon nodded, working double time in an attempt to keep up with this because it was the Office of Enforcement Operations's sworn duty to supervise the Federal Witness Protection program. It meant you usually didn't meet the sons of bitches face to face. They were bureaucrats for the most part, their major task to green light prospective applicants, then provide the regenerated witness with a clean identity. Plus, testifying in front of Congress whenever the program was taken to task.

The U.S. Marshals were the ones handling the grunt work. It cracked Solomon up how Hollywood made Vanessa Williams into the typical protected witness with Schwarzenegger as her bodyguard. Every protected witness Solomon had come across had been either a former felon or a certified loser.

Eliot in the program? It made perfect sense. The absence of a personal touch, the negative résumé. Had he told his new boss anything about his status? Had it been one of those tit-for-tat favors? Or was Weston beholden to someone else?

"Why were you at Marshall's place?" O'Donnell asked.

"I was looking to talk."

"About?"

"The weather."

"Solomon." Bernardino shot him a harsh look. "We're co-operating with the feds on this one."

The royal we, Solomon thought. "And what's your personal interest?" Solomon asked, directing the question to O'Donnell.

"He doesn't have to explain to you. Just answer him," Bernardino said. And the *you* stood in for a curse word.

"Lieutenant." The voice was modest, heavily Southern. A white boy in his fifties, handsome enough, broadened by age and lack of exercise. Solomon had always detested white Southerners. They reminded him of Big Bull Connor and his pack of German shepherd dogs. And he couldn't imagine that O'Donnell was going to prove to be an exception. "Just give me a simple answer," O'Donnell said, offering an ear-to-ear grin. So they were supposed to be good ole boys together. Bernardino licked his lips, but, amazingly enough, managed to refrain from speaking. He grunted, though, a barnyard sound. A pig, Solomon thought, about to drop down and roll in a big vat of shit.

"Am I the only one here that's going to have to pitch around without a flashlight? It just doesn't seem fair." Solomon met O'Donnell's eyes and saw the flicker of interest.

"What say I speak with Detective Solomon in private?" O'Donnell said. Bernardino shook his head.

"Anthony, why not let me deal with this." O'Donnell was standing, his physical presence alone said, go.

"You're sure, now?" Bernardino asked.

"Positive." Bernardino actually looked hurt, almost doleful. It seemed as though he were about to draw himself up on his high horse. But then he deflated. "Okay. All right," he said. And slunk away.

There was a measured silence as, down the hall, they heard a door slam shut.

"So he hates your guts," O'Donnell said. "Has he got a reason?"

"He might. Not one he's discussed with me."

"Hardly makes for the happiest work environment."

"I'm not complaining."

"Maybe you should." O'Donnell eased one big leg over the other. "You might find you get some sympathy."

"From who, exactly?"

O'Donnell opened his hands, as if to say, let's just see. "What say we start again." Then he reached inside his vest pocket and took out a business card. He slid it across the top of Solomon's desk. Solomon looked down at the fine print; MALCOLM O'DONNELL, ASSISTANT DIRECTOR, OFFICE OF ENFORCEMENT OPERATIONS. Assistant Director, meaning second in command. Solomon looked back at the outfit, reassessing the price tag on the suit, and noting the shoes this time, not department-issue patrolman's black, a buttery color, elegant, yet traditional. The same might be said for the man.

"You were questioning Marshall in connection with what?"

"A case I'm working on."

"The name of the case?"

Solomon waited him out.

"I'll need your case file," O'Donnell said. "And all your notes."

"Because?"

"You've surely figured that out. Eliot was one of ours."

"So you're assuming he didn't take his own life."

"I'm not assuming anything. Assumptions are a waste of time. I'm simply covering my bases."

"He must have been a prize witness if you're bothering to investigate."

"You don't think we take care of our own?"

"I don't think D.C. usually gets the call."

This time, it was O'Donnell who was silent. Then sighed, as if at some patent stupidity. "What case is this you're working on?" he asked. And asked it as if he knew the question would be answered.

Provenance, Solomon thought, a big word for the little I've got. Still, he saw the boardwalk that morning, waves tugging across the wet slats and Bea's corpse waiting, as patient as a lover. The only thing to do was to buy himself some time. It meant throwing this man a bone. "I wanted to ask Mr. Marshall about Beatriz Castillo."

For a millisecond, O'Donnell's smile evaporated, then reemerged, even more brightly lit.

"What questions were you going to ask?"

"How well he knew her. The girl's dead. She drowned off Coney five days ago." Solomon had a feeling this wasn't news to O'Donnell. He decided to see how far that knowledge stretched. "Marshall was seen heading for the beach with her."

"So?" His expression offered nothing to read this time.

"The girl couldn't swim. She was phobic about the water."

"And she drowned. Is there any reason to believe it wasn't accidental?"

"I can't say that."

"Were there signs on the body?"

"Nothing obvious."

"This eyewitness who saw the two of them together knew Marshall?"

Solomon nodded.

"On a friendly basis?"

"On a need-to-know basis," Solomon said.

"And all this is in the file?"

"Absolutely."

"Which is where?"

Solomon's turn to stonewall. But he made sure his eyes didn't sway to the stack of papers on his desk. Or the attaché case that he'd slid the file down into, right before he grabbed up his keys. The case that now jostled his feet, buzzing, it was that impatient to announce its own presence.

"I give you five, and you wrap this up for me." O'Donnell stood, reached out a hand. Solomon took it and felt a slight dampness in the palm. "You should remember what I told you before, detective. Sometimes when you tell someone about a problem you're having, they can surprise you."

The carrot and the stick, Solomon thought. But he nodded and smiled, drowning the "yassuh," but doing the physical rendition of supplication, which was, of course, just what the *man* expected.

"The girl drowned in rough water. Hell, Olympic swimmers would have had trouble that day. Probably someone dared her to go in. Could have been Eliot. Kids do crazy things."

"You're telling me," Solomon said. He noted O'Donnell's

description of the surf. Nothing he'd mentioned could have prompted that reference.

"So we're on the same page with this now, detective," O'Donnell said.

He nodded again.

"Then I'll go tend to your boss." A wave of the hand. The man stepped into the hall and actually had the temerity to wink. Solomon stood up and shut the door. Amazing! God made some people truly ignorant.

22

"Liam, my man."

Chazz was offering the high hand. But Liam couldn't help but notice his hair. Last week it had crested into white-blond waves and now it was plastered down straight, jet black. He looked past to find Bea. No sign.

"What's doing?"

"Not much," Liam said.

"Heard about your dad. That's rough."

Chazz's hand was reaching out, tapping him on the shoulder. "It sucks," Liam said, the bad word used deliberately. He felt good saying it. Looking out through the chain link, Liam caught sight of a ferryboat passing, white surf behind it, stripping the water.

"Want one?"

Chazz offered a cigarette. A pack of Camels. Liam shook his head.

"Isn't Bea coming?"

"Sorry, bud. She's busy. Sent me instead," Chazz said, then added, laughing, "What am I? Chopped liver?" Chazz's hand coming out again, gently knocking his chin.

"It's not that." The disappointment stinging, though.

"I know, I know." Chazz sucking in on the cig, watching the big ships chug past. "But maybe later we can all meet up."

The green car was new. Inside, on the front seat, there was a box of Milky Ways, with the top bent down, waiting.

"Don't stand on ceremony," Chazz said. He didn't. Then

they were on the highway. To the right, the football field of
blue water that was the Red Hook pool.

"Could you call her?"

Chazz looked over. "Call Bea?"

"Just to ask."

"She knows you're here with me," Chazz said. "She'll try
and get away. She's doing some family shit." Chazz was fiddling with the radio. "Listen to that!" he said.

"That's Smash Mouth."

"The worst sort of retreads."

Liam looked away quickly. It wasn't cool to like them.
But he did. He sang the song on the sly, "somebody once
told me the world was gonna roll me, I ain't the sharpest tool
in the shed." Chazz tamped out the cigarette, lit up another.
It took a second for what the sweet smoke was to register.
Then Liam giggled.

"What?" Chazz asked.

"That's a blunt you're smoking."

"True. True enough." Chazz grinned. "You want some?"

"No way!"

"Why? You buy into that line they give you about drugs?"

"I just don't."

"Okay, all right. So how'd you know what I was smoking
then?"

"Cause my dad smokes out back. My mom told him he
couldn't do it in the house."

"You ever find his shit?"

Liam nodded.

"Ever try to smoke some yourself?"

"No," Liam said.

"Good for you, then," Chazz said, and he laughed even
harder.

The embarrassment came over Liam in a rush. Now
Chazz knew that he was a virgin. He shifted in his seat, felt

it stick to his bare legs. His blades rolled out along the carpeted floor, then back.

"So your dad pulled a fast one on your mom?" Chazz's hand was out again, touching him on the shoulder, giving a squeeze. "Don't worry, Lee, my man. Happens to the very best. My dad booked when I was four. Just took off with a suitcase. Told me, 'bye sport.' I guess he didn't want to get overemotional about leaving his only son."

"He never came back?"

"Nope. Filed for a divorce. Didn't even fight for custody. A beautiful person, my dad. A real gem."

"You never saw him again?"

"Saw him plenty, him and his lovely bride. On holidays they'd have me over. Really nice, her family would show up and my dad's. Even got a stepsister in the bargain. Wasn't I the lucky one?" He made a face to emphasize. "So who do you hate the most for screwing things up, your dad or your mom?"

"I don't hate anyone," Liam said. Only, it came out wrong. It was like he was begging. Begging to be believed.

"Right. I'll bet you want them both dead."

How did he know? All night long it was a pitched battle, going on after his mom thought he was asleep. His eyes came open and stayed glued to the ceiling. First, it was his dad, flipping over on the highway, glass shattering, blood everywhere. Then his mom shoved onto the tracks and the F train running her over. The thought should have made him cry. But it didn't.

"Why shouldn't you want them dead, huh? They've made your life miserable. People don't think." Chazz asked the wind. It howled through the car, shivered around Liam's shoulder, tugged at his shirt sleeve.

Liam studied the darkness, studied the cars passing, then

inched his eyes back to find the clock ticking away. It was late.

"I should go home," he said.

"Is that what you want?"

It wasn't. What he wanted was Bea. He wanted to tell her everything. Hear her say, "Liam, is that really how it was?"

"Where's she gonna meet us?"

"Here," Chazz said, pointing at the exit sign.

"Coney Island?"

"That's right." There was the sound of screeching tires, which was their car, making a hard right and speeding down the exit ramp. They drove past the aquarium, went three blocks more and there was the horseshoe entrance to Luna Park.

Everyone was dressed for a hot summer night in shorts and sleeveless tank tops. They passed the Funhouse where his dad had taken him. Inside, the dark clung to your body, cobwebs clutched at your hair, and a woman's voice howled. He'd only been five. He'd started crying pitifully. And his dad had had to run him back out. "What in hell were you thinking?" His mom asking. His mom grabbing for him, hugging him hard for comfort. "Moron!" Said under her breath, but loud enough for his dad to hear.

"Two tickets, please."

They were going to ride the Cyclone. He wanted to explain to Chazz how rides made him sick. Dizzy. But that wouldn't be dope. That wouldn't be the thing. And then he was in the seat and the metal bar was clicking down. This girl sitting in front was laughing so hard, she doubled over and started gasping for breath.

"What's up, cuteness?" she asked, turning around, and looking at Chazz.

He didn't say. She pouted, then nudged her friend.
"Snob."

He looked over and saw that Chazz was crying. He was staring straight ahead, and there were tears on his cheeks. Then
he lifted up his hand and wiped them off.

The cars lurched forward. Liam shut his eyes, but that
only made it worse. And they were going up and up and up.
They were at the very top of something and then, suddenly,
they were tipping down. His stomach dropped away. He
screamed, but they were already at the bottom, then soaring
up again, dipping, curving, lurching right like they were going to take off and be airborne. Chazz had hold of his hand.
Chazz was squeezing it. And Chazz was smiling. Another
curve and a whoosh of air, cold, then hot again, and Liam
heard laughter, thought maybe it was the girl, then realized it
was his own voice. Laughing, laughing hard and long because all he could see were stars and the thin sliver of moon
up above, the earth spinning below, then dropping away into
the darkness.

"That was awesome."

"That was the bomb."

They sat on one of the boardwalk benches, eating. Liam
had blue cotton candy, a hot dog, a Coke.

"It's after eleven," Chazz said. "I'd better get you back
home."

"So she's not coming." He couldn't help sounding disappointed.

Chazz stood up. "Let's go, kid," he said.

Liam peered into the crowd. There were girls who looked
like her, drifting past, but each one had something wrong.
The forehead. The shape of the eyes.

* * *

He pulled the seatbelt on and as he did, remembered how the metal bar had felt, jammed in, making a line on his stomach. And he felt the car rolling forward, felt his stomach lurching as they twisted toward heaven.

There was a buzzing noise. Chazz reached into his pocket and pulled something out. A phone. A pink phone. It was Bea's pink phone.

"Yeah, it's me. Who else did you think it would be?"

So it was Bea calling. She was going to meet them, after all. Liam sighed out his love. And his relief.

"Can I talk?" he asked. But Chazz looked angry, shook his head hard, then put his finger up to his lips for silence.

"There is just no fucking way," he said into the phone, looking out at the road and rolling the wheel back and forth under his fingers. "Yeah, I know you're worried. You think I'm not?" There was a long pause. "I'll make it, if I have to." He clicked the phone off, threw it down in disgust, then looked at it as if it were growling, exposing its fangs.

"That wasn't Bea?"

"That was no one," he said. "No one who's mad. Mad as the mad fucking hatter. But does it matter, cause here I am, little Lee. Here I am, because I'm a fuckup." Chazz gunned the engine, and they changed lanes, passing a bus with an Indian's head sketched on it. Mohawk Trail Lines. "Bea's dead, Liam. She died over a week ago. Got pulled under the surf and drowned. That's her phone, which is, pathetically, the only thing of hers I've got. See what a fuckup I am. Not that you want to know. Sorry, Lee. Sorry I had to be the one to give you the bad news. But that's what comes of having boneheads for parents."

The car was slowing down. They were pulling off the road, bumping up on some pavement. Chazz was tugging him close.

"It sucks, it really does," Chazz said.

His face was burning, he couldn't see. Then he realized why. Now he was the one who was crying.

"It's okay," Chazz said.

No it wasn't. Bea kissed him when she put him to bed and there was this smell when she walked out of the room, cut roses, lingering. She told him it was because she used toilet water. He'd thought it was a joke, but then, one day he saw a bottle for sale in the drugstore around the corner. Liam wanted that smell to come back right now, flowers, fresh cut, seeded on his tongue.

They would play X-Men together with Bea on top of the star fort, defending. Raining down invisible missiles on him when he tried a sneak attack and the missiles exploding, pow, pow, pow, flames and smoke so thick that everyone was blinded.

It was Bea laughing at his pathetic jokes.

"What's a Band-Aid you put in the freezer used for?"

"A cold cut."

"Why did the boy put his dad in the freezer?"

"To make an ice pop."

"Knock, knock."

"Who's there?"

"Ella."

"Ella who?"

"Ella Funt."

He was coughing, choking. Chazz patted him hard on the back.

"Here we go," he said. The car bounced back onto the roadway. The lights of the city startled him, coming up dead ahead. He turned to the right and found his own reflection, trapped in the window glass. Outside, people were coming home, stepping inside just as the trees started hissing, and the ground swelled up, making great earthquake waves. His mom stood out on their stoop right now, looking for him in every single direction while the tidal wave filled up the playground, drowning the slides and the jungle gyms, then poured up Court and up Smith, on its way to the corner of Bergen.

Water, water, everywhere.

Squeezing his eyes shut, he saw Bea. She was out in the ocean. There were needle-thin ships, white ocean liners steaming by while she called for help. Then he was diving off the side of the boat, doing a triple twist like those Olympic divers. He was pulling her to safety, swimming back to the ship, while people waved at them from up top.

"You're wishing I'd left you alone, aren't you?" Chazz said. "I should have, too. But I called in and heard your message you'd left for Bea. I just thought maybe. Someone should be there. Someone should come."

Liam's eyes were still shut. But he could feel Chazz watching. "Bea loved you so much, Lee. It was just like you were her very own."

Heading down Smith street past a barricaded lot full of cars. Cruising past the International Grocery, where a bunch of men stood on the corner, a tossed bottle sailing out into the street, shattering. Then harsh laughter.

Liam had been five when he'd asked if she would marry him. And Bea had said, "yes," then she'd told him everything had to be done proper. Tony as the judge. Cecilia and her twin sister, Emily, the witnesses. Bea wearing a sheet pinned to her shoulders for the train, making her veil out of a piece of curtain lace.

"Now you say, will you take this woman to be your wife, to have and to hold until death do you part."

Then they both said, "I do," and she bent down to give him the wedding kiss, smooth and wet on the lips. Which was supposed to be forever.

"Liam," Chazz said. They were only two blocks away from his house, waiting at a red light, the motor humming underneath like some perfect beast. "Don't be mad at me."

He wanted something. Liam felt the tug of it. They always did. They wanted you to say it was okay, how you'd be fine. But it wasn't fine, nothing was. He wished he had a bomb. He'd stick it right under the seat when he stepped out and back away and watch the car explode, see the white heat shimmer out, watch the car tossed into midair, then sailing back down to earth, twisted, flaming.

He curled his hands into fists.

They drove past the schoolyard.

And he wished, more than anything, to send himself back through time.

Two weeks before, Bea had picked him up. She'd bought him an Eskimo Pie, then they'd taken the bus up to the park where he'd gotten soaked in the sprinklers. She'd spread this red-checked tablecloth on the ground and set a feast on top of it. They'd played Twenty Questions, charades, until they were groggy. Then waited there for the moon to shine out of the corner of the evening sky.

"Shoot the messenger," Chazz said, under his breath. "Shoot the motherfucking messenger."

The light changed. They were halfway up the block. He saw his mom out on the stoop.

"It wasn't my fault," Chazz said. "It just happened."

"How?"

"Calm down, would you?"

Liam felt the tears coming again.

"Bea was special," Chazz said. "Why else would I bother with you?"

Liam reached for the door handle, pulled it up. Chazz grabbed onto his shoulder.

"Shit. Lee, I didn't mean it like that."

"You did so!"

He felt old, saying it. Then he shoved the car door open and ran. His mom was standing at the foot of their stoop, waiting, her hand shading her eyes like an Indian scout.

"Mom," he called out.

"Liam?"

Her face was all twisted up. Had he made her get old that fast?

"Thank God. Where were you all this time? I was beside myself."

He fell against her and turned his head. The green car drove on. He watched it pass, but Chazz wouldn't even look his way.

"Please don't do that to me again," she was saying, "I couldn't bear it."

He couldn't believe it. She was already forgiving him. He understood suddenly, what he could do to her. It made him feel strange. Then sad.

"I won't," he said.

"You'd better not." She stood up. "Get inside." He headed up the stairs ahead of her, and kept the smile tucked away. An invisible acknowledgment of her weakness and his new-found power.

23

Standing on the top step, Emma Price fumbled with the keys. Liam, next to her, shifted from one foot to the other. Then a whistle stiffened his cheeks. "Where did you go?" she asked. So much anger in her voice, and underneath that, the fear. That profusion of images, tamped down for so many long hours, now rose up to confront her. They were graphic, physically sickening.

"I went to Matt's to hang."

"And didn't choose to call?"

Liam pouted. His lips slung down. Sheer torture. The other memory tugged her hand down, kept the blow she wanted to register at bay. Her mother's face as she listened to someone on the other end of a transatlantic call. The blankness. All it took was a second and you crossed over, taking up permanent residence in another, harsher world.

"I'm sorry for what went on this evening," she said. "It's a mess."

His eyes flickered up at her. She saw his own anger burning in them.

"I wasn't with Matt," he said.

She bent down then, took his shoulders in her hands, the keys brushing against his flesh, unintentionally. He winced.

"Where were you, then?"

"With Bea," he said. His voice was fierce. It made her rock back on her heels.

"Of course you weren't." The response too defensively swift.

"I was so with her. Call her if you don't believe me." Brash. Defiant. And she saw where they were waltzing to next. Liam's shadow flung back down the brownstone steps, predicting the future. He would become that taller, thinner stranger. And then? He would walk away. Emma understood. This trainwreck was her life.

"Bea's gone," she said.

"No." But his voice shook.

"Someone told you, didn't they?"

She saw in his eyes that they had.

"Oh, Liam. I've been such a terrible mother."

He didn't argue. So she stood up again, and opened the door. He slid inside and ran up the stairs, ran away, yet again. She heard the door to his room slam shut and stepped forward, meaning to pursue. Then found she was afraid. So this is what it means to lose your nerve, she thought. And a self-pitying smile flitted over her lips. Then she heard a car door slam. Heard footsteps closing in behind her.

"Emma." Will's voice, calling out. She didn't turn, simply stepped inside her house and closed the door firmly against him. Closed it in his face, she thought, smiling meanly. He still had the key. She slid the police lock into its holder.

He knocked. Rang the bell. Knocked again.

"Emma, please!" Bound to wake the neighbors. Or the dead. She sank down in the shadows.

Blind. That's what she'd been. That girl. Standing there at Will's door and taking obvious pleasure in pointing out what should have been obvious, what must have been obvious to everyone else. "Jolene." She said the name several times, let the sharpened edge nick the skin, then draw blood.

From above she heard the creak of Liam's door opening.

Looking up, she found him bent over the railing to watch. This. The greatest show on earth. Two dumb, demanding parents.

Will's key was in the lock. The door opened, and stopped at the length of the chain.

"Let me in," he hissed.

His hand came in to grapple with the metal links. She thought that if she had an ax, she could use it now, to sever the digits.

Which wouldn't be fatal.

"Oh, hell," she said under her breath, and stood up. "Back up, asshole."

She showed herself. They were face to face and when their eyes met, his cheeks turned bright red. Not, she knew, from exertion. He backed up slowly. She closed the door, left it there for a long enough time to make it into a warning, then undid the chain and opened it.

He stepped inside. His hands crossed over his chest, an involuntary motion of protection and then, suddenly they flashed down to protect the most vulnerable part of all.

She began to laugh, and couldn't stop. The laughter choked her. It made her eyes well up. She leaned against the wall for support.

When she was able to finally still the insanity long enough to spit something out, she said, "You really are a bastard."

Waiting in the kitchen for his return. She heard muttering from upstairs. The sound of shoe leather creaking the floor. Then all that stopped. She sipped her decaf and wished for a mixed drink instead, one of those concoctions provided at beach resorts, complete with a heavy dose of rum and a snappy pink umbrella, shading the carcinogenic cherry from the sun's harsh rays. She heard the stairs creak as Will descended and braced herself. Had it only been two weeks since that flight home? Time flies when you're having fun, Emma told herself. She heard him pause, heard the shift as he came around the back of the stairs, and made for the kitchen. There had been times in their married life when she'd waited for him here, with the lights purposely shut off, waited in the dark while he coaxed Liam into sleep.

But now, he was only Will. What a child deserves, Emma thought, what a parent is able to provide. What a gulf there is in between.

"I hear you met Jolene."

As if this were cocktail party banter. She felt the laughter welling up again.

"I should have explained," he added.

"I should have guessed." She turned, leaning against the sink for support and couldn't help flushing, because looking at him what she saw was Jolene's pert face, her irretrievably younger frame. "I guess I gave you a little too much credit," she allowed. "Thinking you had an original reason."

"Not guilty of that." Looking up she found he had his hands raised as though he were under arrest and she was the guntoting sheriff. What a comedy of errors, she thought to herself. Here we are, Liam's parents, his and someone else's too. "You poor thing," she whispered.

"What?"

She could tell he hadn't heard, but just assumed she'd muttered an insult. And she knew she couldn't explain now. It was late. And she was years too tired. To confess that she was pregnant? What scared her most, she wondered? Then knew. That Will would be decent. That he would come crawling back, pretending Jolene was just a momentary mis-alliance, a slip from the path of righteousness and true regard. We tell ourselves there are good reasons we harbor our affections, Emma thought. We mount up reasons. But in the end there's no way to explain who we fall in love with, or why. No way to justify it, either. Love, the most mysterious impulse of all.

"I'm sorry," Will said. He took a deep breath, apparently gathering his strength. She knew he was about to tender an explanation. She didn't want to hear it. She already understood. He believed Jolene would never plague him about the weight he'd gained, the way he'd forgotten to replenish the milk when it was done, leaving the nearly empty carton in the fridge, a glowing signpost pointing to his incompetence. And Jolene wouldn't finger his dirty clothes when they piled onto the spare chair, or chide him when he forgot open school night. Petty details. Things that often enough didn't signify. But in their case, symptoms of something larger and ultimately more insidious.

"Don't." She put up a hand to stop him. "It won't fix anything," she added and saw relief scripted on his face.

That flight home, barely a week ago. Will might have been in midair, over Cleveland, listening to the engines hum while the stewardess passed by, offering drinks and solace. Will could have smiled her way. He was so agreeable. Good sweet Will. He never looked as if he could hurt a soul.

This hurts. It surely does. And in the end, it will hurt Liam more than either one of us.

"He said he knew Bea was dead. So I agreed to it. And then I realized, he'd been bluffing. Part of him didn't actually believe it till then."

"And?"

"He cried for a while. I put him to bed and rubbed his back. Finally, he fell asleep." Will sighed. "It sounded stupid when I tried to explain. Keeping her death from him as a way of protecting him. The whole thing sounded stupid when I said it." Will paused. "And selfish," he added. "I guess I do see that now."

Emma nodded. Waited for him to take his leave. But he

was waiting, too. For what, she wondered. What in hell does he want from me now? Then she realized. He still needed her permission. "Thank you, Will," she said, and couldn't help feeling a certain pride in self, as he turned away, accepting this, her final offering, with alacrity.

24

"Loretta." Solomon extended a hand. Loretta Picard stared down, her nostrils flaring. "I'm Detective Laurence Solomon."

"Pretty damn late for a social call," she said.

"This won't take long."

"Then why couldn't it wait till morning?" She snorted. "I have a lawyer, you want to talk to me, talk to her first."

"I've spoken with someone from your lawyer's office. A Ms. Emma Price."

Loretta folded her arms, refusing to take a seat. "So what did she say?"

"That I should meet with you."

"Why would that be?"

The lies just flowed. He'd agonized on the drive; should he give Emma a call? The second after O'Donnell stepped out of the office, Solomon had reached for the briefcase and taken the back stairs down to the lot, then gunned the engine, heading north to Rikers. What had he been hoping for if not a way to make himself into a player? And how would he explain that in a way that would be convincing enough? Emma would never cooperate. Why should she? This was one situation where his interests and hers diverged so completely.

Solomon observed the fauna in front of him. Picard's hair, with that shaved-in RAGE. Too much of an affectation, he decided. You try to convince the world to back off, and it turns into an invitation. Even a dare. The kind O'Donnell was offering. The smart thing? To cut bait. To turn tail. To run. Solomon admitted it was a shortcoming. Because the harder it got, the more he slogged uphill. Even though he saw how unlikely success was. That despite the Bible's optimistic teachings, David using one little rock to take Goliath down.

"Bring any presents?" Loretta asked.

Solomon shunted a pack of Marlboros across. She tapped one out, stuck it in her mouth, then leaned in for a light.

"You'd be more comfortable seated," he told her.

"I'm just fine."

"Beatriz Castillo?"

She didn't blink.

"You do know the name?"

She shook her head.

"Funny."

Loretta Picard leaned against the wall, smoking. She eyed him as if he were the lethal member of this party of two. "That's it?" she asked.

"You're an art lover?"

"Me?"

"You."

"I'm afraid to answer on the grounds that it might incriminate me." A cynical smile pierced the air.

"But you invest in fine art."

"Do I really?"

"You own an original oil painting."

"I don't remember inviting you over for a viewing."

"That's what happens," Solomon said. "You decide to go kill two cops and suddenly your privacy gets shot all to hell."

"Poor pitiful me," she said. And blew out smoke rings to show how much that hurt.

"So where did you get the painting?"

"I bought it."

"From the artist?"

"Could be."

"How much did it cost?"

She scratched her head. "I forget."

"Did you go to Penny Strider's apartment to pick it out?"

Loretta's nose twitched, rabbitlike. She rubbed her hand against it. "She showed me her slides," Loretta said. "Used to bring them by the bar, just in case."

"So the two of you were friends?"

"Me and Penny?"

"You and Penny."

"Friends don't charge other friends money," Loretta said. Her eyes made a circuit of the room. "We knew each other to say hello. That's what you came up here to ask? About me and my art investments?"

"What about you and Chazz Perry?"

Loretta blew a wreath of smoke into the air, then raked what was left of her hair with her free hand. "I don't know who you mean."

"Charles Murray?"

She offered the most noncommittal of smiles.

"Sit down," Solomon said. She didn't budge. So he got up and crossed the room. She waited till he was up in her face, to blow the smoke out. He grabbed her by the shoulder and pinched his finger into the lean muscle.

"Hey!"

"Sit the fuck down!"

Her voice was as clean and as cool as his. "Want to kill me? Go on. Do everybody a favor. If not, get the fuck away from me."

Solomon loosened his grip, then let go. She rubbed the place where he'd bent his fingers in. "Nigger bastard," she said evenly.

"White trash bitch."

She laughed.

"That's right, I am," she agreed.

"Chazz was a pretty good-looking guy."

Outside the chicken wire, the moon broke through a strip of clouds, throwing down a thick shaft of light. It moved across the floor, licked at the table legs, then darted up and over the top.

Loretta dropped the cigarette and ground it underfoot.

"I'm going back to bed," she said.

"Why'd he pick Beatriz Castillo? Why not you?" Solomon put on his best game face and leaned in so close he could smell the tobacco on her breath. "Eliot told me to speak with you. He said you could tell us anything we needed to know about Chazz."

"Eliot?" She laughed meanly. "Eliot Marshall. What story is he making up now?"

Solomon heaved an internal sigh. She was apparently unaware that Eliot was one of the dear departed. "Sure you don't know this Chazz? Blond. About six one. Three ruby studs in his left earlobe. And one special distinguishing feature. A little tribal dog carved right above his pubic hair. That was his real crowning touch."

"Never met him," Loretta said. But her eyes narrowed. There was a flicker of doubt. The dog, he thought, that diary entry indelibly etched. Thank you, Bea.

"You mean Eliot was wrong? You mean Chazz didn't let you get that close? He said you two were thick as thieves."

Loretta was watching him, but her arms folded over her breasts defensively. He thought he could see the beginnings of pain glistening in the corners of her eyes.

"Poor Chazz. Someone stuck a gun in his mouth and pulled the trigger, blasted his DNA all over the four walls. Eliot went pale when we showed him."

"God. Oh, God." She whispered the words like a solemn prayer.

"I guess he was supposed to be some kind of warning. Was he playing out of his league? Mrs. Price thought I should stop by and see if you could help me out with the particulars. We need to find the next of kin."

Her face was truly pale, almost spectral. He thought how curious pity was. Larrabbee and Maples hadn't courted her special sympathy. In a world so littered with corpses, empathy carried only so far.

"Through the pale door, right, Loretta? Is that how the ghosts get through?" Solomon's hand was jiggling. He forced it to behave.

"This is wrong," she insisted.

Solomon held his breath as she paced the room, hesitated, apparently staring at nothing, then slid down into a chair. He sat down opposite her, waiting. Finally she looked up at him, begging silently for a reprieve. And he shook his head.

"No joke," he said.

Loretta knotted her hands. "Chazz was a decent guy," she said. And her mouth trembled. She leaned over, running her fingers through the shaved scalp, then sat back, questioning that merciless deity, "What's really the point? What's the fucking point of anything?" She studied her hands, then the wall, then sighed heavily.

"What was Chazz into, Loretta?"

"All you people ever do is ask questions." She sounded world-weary, permanently jaded. "What good's it gonna do for you to find anything out now?"

"You people?" Looking around behind him for the invisible backup. Then he saw. The intensity of her assault indicated a personal relationship with the deceased. Something she'd denied. Still, it was worth asking. "You said you didn't know Larrabbee or Maples. Was that true?"

She sighed again, and her shoulders sagged. "Larrabbee had some deal with Reynaldo, the guy who owns the bodega around the corner from the Pit. The two of them used to hang out and shoot the breeze. When I'd walk by, Larrabbee used to say good evening, tip his little blue cap. Then one day, it was pouring and he asks if I need a ride."

"And you took him up on the offer?"

"Sure I did." Her eyes were pinching the memory down. "Got into his little blue chariot. All goes quiet on the western front. Then we're almost home and he starts in with the questions. Where am I from? How am I managing? He's bugging me out with questions. Sounds familiar, right? We pull up to my stop and he takes out this photo of his daughter, says how he's been watching me and I remind him of her, she's from his first marriage, and her mom doesn't know what to make of her cause of the purple streak in her hair and the nose ring. I'm like, oh too bad."

Solomon set the scene for himself, dark inside the patrol car, and outside on the street, the lights shimmering because of the hard rain.

"So, I don't know. He seems harmless enough. And he's there, you know. Convenient. It becomes this kind of regular thing. He's always on his best behavior. He's got me believing in him, okay? I mean, isn't that how they teach you in that police academy? Get the snitch's trust first, then try and cut the deal." Loretta offered what was supposed to pass for a knowing look. What it looked like instead, was a kid's face, deflating, when he'd caught his betters in a lie. "We were talking about our musical tastes. He's telling me how he's partial to all that soft shit. Mariah Carey. The works. I'm goin' on and on like an idiot, thinking he wants to know about all these bar bands that I'm into. And then he throws in the wrench. How he's heard something on the street about these IDs being sold. How good they are and he hears the person does anything you want. Birth certificates. Passports even. Anything you need forged. That stops me cold. But he doesn't seem to notice. He just says, Loretta honey, you have to tell me. And he puts his hands on my shoulders, then stares deep into my eyes, like he's my romantic champion. Tells me how all he wants to do is take care of me and proceeds to stick his tongue down my throat. When I try to get away, he puts his hand around my neck to stop me. Says he can 'cure me' of my affliction." Her nails tapping the top of the metal table. Solomon noted the bronze paint, little curved shivs covering the tender tips of flesh. "What a line to start with, me reminding him of his daughter! You think he went and tried that on with her?"

"What's this got to do with Chazz?"

"The Pale Door. It was Chazz's business. He could get you anything you needed. He had the right world view, you know. How no one should be held back by what they couldn't control."

"You mean like being underage."

"Yeah. I don't get why someone would kill him for it, though."

"Maybe he sold IDs to the wrong party?"

She shook her head, apparently studying the quandary.

"So you went after Larrabbee to help Chazz out?"

"Did I say that?" She glared at him. And Solomon decided to sidestep, for the moment.

"Why then?"

"Because he was an asshole, all right?"

"That's a reason?"

"It's the one that comes to mind."

Going nowhere here, Solomon told himself and decided to switch gears. "What about Eliot?" he asked.

"What about him? You mean asshole number two, right?" Then she narrowed her eyes. "What's he laying on? I bet he tagged you with that story of his. Made himself out to be some fucking hero."

Solomon tried to look as knowing as possible.

"He told you how he was living out *America Undercover*, right?"

"You mean, that he was in the Witness Protection Program?"

"All part of the package, right? Such a big, mysterious hunk of a man." She eyed him. "Hey, it's not true, is it?"

Solomon sat back, as silent as a monk.

"Damn. And all we did was make fun." She giggled slyly.

"How did Chazz's business operate?"

"Word of mouth."

"Only his? No partners?"

She cast her eyes down then, studying the pattern on the tabletop. Her hand rested gingerly on the metal surface. Then her fingernails took over, making a rat-ta-tat machine-gun sound.

"Penny Strider?"

"No fucking way!" Such adamance. "Not Penny." But more like, don't go there, than an honest denial.

"Penny's disappeared. With Chazz getting murdered, it could make a good friend feel concerned for her safety."

Loretta shifted in her chair. There was a sheer wind blowing through the room, sending the hairs on the back of Solomon's neck shivering up. How to dig out the lies from underneath the truth? "What about Cheri Maples?" he asked. "It was her first day out on the job. You couldn't have known Cheri."

Loretta met his eyes for a long, long while. And then, something passed between the two of them, he felt it, the same way he'd felt the shiver entering his body. "Ever been in love, Mr. Solomon?"

"Yes." He agreed too quickly. Which bred her automatic distrust. And he knew better. To get, you had to be willing to give. Solomon forced himself to take a hard look back. The mother of his child, Niala. Red-haired, light-skinned, foxy. He'd loved her hard and well, for a few years. Then shifted his attention. Combing through his memory, he found a succession of women. Infatuation. But that wasn't love. It wasn't the way one person took hold so that your entire life became a mission. Who had he really loved that way? His son? A cleaner, more reliable sort of affection. His father? A love born of fear, then tempered with anger. Ralph? Something smooth, filed down by years of dependency and trust. There weren't many people who you could even hope for that with. And then it came to him so hard, his eyes stung from the impact. Emma Price. You don't know, he told himself. He dismissed the what-might-have-been, knowing that he had savaged all of it now.

"I don't know," he said. "I just don't know."

"Well, then, you really *wouldn't* understand."

"You're saying you and Larrabee?"

She snickered. "Don't you listen?"

"Who then, Chazz?"

Loretta shook her head. "Love sucks, right? That must be what you tell yourself. I guess you're right. I mean, my own experience isn't exactly a testimonial."

"Who, then?"

"Don't you even think you're missing out? Not a little?" Loretta said, avoiding the question.

Two could play that game. He kept quiet, waiting for the rest.

"Of course, who's to say. Maybe you're the one who's smart. Love. What's it add up to? Sure, everything's great for a while. Everything's peachy. But then there's always that minute when something gets messed up. After that..." Her eyes were averted, pondering the result. "I guess it's like you've bought this piece of crap dress just cause it made you look fine. Then one day, there you are, walking down the street, and the fucking thing shreds. It falls off you. Leaves you a regular bare-assed wonder." Loretta made a face. "That's me. Empress Loretta in her brand-new clothes."

It had to be Chazz. Solomon played out the rest. Loretta taking out Larrabbee in a misguided attempt to protect Murray. Loretta proving her devotion in the stupidest possible way.

"You get so low, you think you can't sink any further," Loretta said. "There's a door down there and you want to open it and slide through and disappear. You know why? Because certain people make you promises. People give you all sorts of ideas. Then they turn around and blame you when you believe them. You're the one who's pathetic, wrong-headed, stupid. You're the number one reason they're gone. You're worthless and anyone in their right mind should have seen that all along. In fact, it's a wonder they ever started with you." Loretta winced. "Why'd that girl have to come running up the stairs? You tell me." Her eyes clouded over like she was stepping back in time. "All I could think of was 'pull the trigger.' And then, there she was begging me. So I went and got the towels and tried to help her." Loretta raised her head again to meet his eyes. She said the rest as if it were a warning. "It was different with Larrabbee."

"Just exactly how?"

"Don't you listen to anything? He was an asshole."

"You kill off every asshole in the world, who's left?"

"Now there's a point." Loretta laughed. "He deserved it," she said. "Saying that shit about his daughter to me. Trying to make me think he was being my friend, sticking his nose in. Saying he was going to offer me the cure." Then Loretta's voice wavered. "But her. She was the afterthought. I mean, just when you're thinking the hard part is over, the wrong damn person comes waltzing up and ruins everything. You know what she asked me? 'Why?' I didn't have a reason. Was I supposed to say something lighthearted like, 'shit happens?' " Loretta leaned her head on her hands. "Stupid. Stupid. Stupid," she said under her breath. "Sometimes you want to take everything back including the minute of your own fucking birth."

Late night in the Rikers parking lot. Laurence Solomon worked at making an assessment. So Chazz was the one dropping the IDs? It added up to a big round zero. So the girl was crazy and lovesick. Over Chazz? She'd acted upset when he lied and said Murray was dead, but he couldn't imagine describing someone you'd fallen that hard for, so blandly. "A decent guy," she'd said. What more did he know then? There was, without question, an easier way to go. Beatriz Castillo's drowning, an accident. Charles Murray running out of shame. Penny Strider, right this minute, working on a canvas out in Taos. Eliot Marshall done in by his own big mouth.

It made sense. Except for one thing. O'Donnell. Why come north for Eliot Marshall? Unless ... what if Marshall wasn't the only one they'd lost?

He reached inside his jacket pocket for the phone and didn't even have time to press in the number, when it buzzed.

"Yes," he said.

Twenty minutes later, Solomon stood in the parking lot at the far end of the Brooklyn Navy Yard. A dog's-eye view of the river. Across, on the opposite shore, those gleaming office towers. Three police cars and the coroner's wagon were grazing together. Inside a green Ford Taurus, a body was slumped over the steering wheel.

"A man for all seasons," Ruiz said, handing him the wallet. Inside, a host of IDs. Charles Murray's driver's license being, in this case, the most germane.

25

Nine A.M. found Emma Price tunneling under the Hudson. Emerging into the white heat of Jersey, she was temporarily blinded. As Emma drove past some of the ugliest landscape on earth, the radio announcer claimed they were entering the second heat wave of the summer. Great belching smokestacks with fumes pressing out and a haze coloring the air. She drove west. Passing Newark, she noted several new office towers rising up on the left-hand side, a not too subtle contrast to rows of abandoned project buildings on the right. Taking a left onto 280, she was suddenly protected from suburban streets by white cement walls. At exit fourteen, she made a sloping right and pulled to a stop at a traffic light. New construction on either side, townhouses so generically pure they really could be anywhere, then strip malls; ShopRite, Barnes & Noble, the Gap, the Home Depot.

Loretta's aunt lived in a split-level on Leslie Lane in Little Falls. Emma had to pass Marcia and Sally and Nathalie to get there. A developer with purely female progeny, now immortalized. Pulling into the driveway, she noted the venetian blinds shifting, then shivering down.

Before her finger touched the buzzer, the door pulled open.

"I'll say one thing, you're prompt." Brittany Manners sounded more than a little disappointed. Stepping inside,

Emma noted that the woman was well over the desirable body weight for her short frame. A double-knit suit with a shapeless skirt only enhanced her bulk. Her hair was blow-dried into a blond bubble, her eyes ringed with black eyeliner. More than anything, she resembled a monstrous rodent.

"So what's so damned important?" Meaning the early morning phone call, the request for an interview Manners had very reluctantly complied with. She backed up to stand by one of the two couches that made up the living room furnishings. They were both plaid. Directly between them, a high-gloss coffee table held neat piles of reading material, *TV Guide, Woman's Day.* The walls were graced with dried floral displays and motel-quality seascapes. Taking a seat on the couch, Emma felt the wiry cloth scratching through her thin linen skirt.

"I've got ten minutes." Manners snorted, as if for emphasis.

"They're lovely arrangements."

Manners looked mystified. Emma waved her hand at the four walls.

"Thanks." She laughed. "I got them on special at Costco."

She offered a baleful stare. Emma made a show of getting her notebook out and retrieving a pen from her bag. And Manners tapped her toe on the floor to indicate the passage of time. Emma had hoped for an ingenious opening line. Even if she'd had one, it wouldn't have mattered. Might as well cut to the chase, she decided. Her most fervent wish? An emergency airlift of some quick-brewed espresso.

"I've been going over my assistant's notes," Emma said. "You spoke about having a conflict with Loretta."

No answer. Just more foot tapping.

"Could you clarify what that conflict was about?"

Manners moved her gaze so that it rested on the view available out of the bow-shaped picture window. "Nope."

Emma smiled cautiously and reached into her purse to take out the transcript.

"Your exact words are, 'I wasn't having her back here again.' We'd like to know why."

"You can like to know all you want. I've said my piece."

"We'll subpoena you."

"Says who?"

"Was the fight about your sister?"

"No means no. Don't you get it?" But a stubborn twitch had developed under Manners's eye. It was something, the way the skin jumped out every few seconds, as if an insect trapped underneath were lunging, desperately trying to secure its freedom.

"Loretta's a troubled girl. Did she provoke you?"

Brittany Manners opened her mouth. Emma had a moment of hope, but then she shut it, zipping it up tight.

"I understand you may not like her."

"You understand?" The look came after. Then a plea for divine assistance, her eyebrows lifted toward the heavens. But her foot had stopped tapping.

"We don't have to like our clients. We have to represent them. And in order to represent them, we have to understand them."

"Good luck understanding her."

"Did she do something wrong? Or was it what she said? Was that it? Did she say something that provoked you?"

"She might have." Manners eyes narrowed. "I don't see why you don't go straight to the goddamn horse's mouth."

"I'm hoping to find out from you, and judge whether it's pertinent to the case."

"She's a goddamn freak of nature," Manners said. Actually, she muttered it under her breath, and glanced down at her watch. "I'm late for work." Moving toward the door, she nudged Emma with her eyes. As Emma stood, she found relief on the other woman's face.

Emma cast about, desperately, for some other possible diversion, then saw the perfect target. A small table by the wall was littered with gilt-framed portraits of the family. She sidestepped over as behind her Manners made small huffing noises, like a rhino pawing the ground and preparing to charge.

Pick wisely, Emma told herself, reaching out for the framed picture of the two sisters. Marie, Loretta's mother, had clearly been the winner in looks, buxom and flushed, with a kindly, lopsided smile. In front of them, their assembled children. Four tow-headed boys in descending ages and two girls, one blond, one auburn-haired. Emma recognized Loretta. A slightly more grown-up version of the mom and smiling tot boosted from Loretta's bathroom cabinet. And the blond-haired girl also looked familiar. The blond in the other photo Loretta had stashed there. In this family portrait, Loretta was turning to greet her flaxen-haired companion. The other girl's eyes had crinkled up in responsive joy. Brittany Manners's youngest had her arm slung around her cousin Loretta's shoulder. They were aiding and abetting each other in the crime of youthful enthusiasm.

"Animals, all of you," Manners said as she strode over and reached out to grab the photograph away. "I don't give a shit what happens to her. And I don't want to hear another word from any of you, ever again. I'll tell you what I told that bastard from the DA's office. Get out of here and don't come back."

Except that the expression on her face belied this statement. Anger and grief weighted in equal measure. She clutched the picture to her chest, using her free hand to give Emma a fervent shove.

* * *

Outside, Emma sat behind the wheel of her car. Ten minutes before, Brittany Manners had closed her front door, locked it, and headed for her Ford Explorer. Crossing to the driver's side, she'd caught sight of Emma, offered her the finger, then had gotten in, revved the motor and sped off like a bat out of hell.

Not exactly making best friends here, Emma noted silently.

"Not animals, vultures," she added aloud, managing a slightly bitter laugh. She felt sorry for Brittany Manners, sorry for the mess that was her family. But it was hardly going to deter her.

As she attempted to find her way back to the main road, she got lost in a web of girls' names, Ginger, Holly, Bridget, before finally coming to the end of the development. She crested a hill, and looking down, saw a reservoir dappled with geese, the trees surrounding it all dark green. At the furthest edge she saw salvation, a neon sign advertising TED'S OLD-FASHIONED DINER.

Inside, she found all the familiar odors: fried eggs, burnt toast, and underneath the acrid smell of ammonia. Working the counter, a woman with a face that had outlived Father Time, a bulldog complete with a nest of wrinkles around the chin. The peaked cap only added insult to injury. Her name, Trudy, was scripted above her left breast.

"Can I help you, dear?"

Emma glanced up at the photograph of a coffee cup, covered in Reddi Whip and advertised as Fresh Cappuccino.

"Two black coffees," she said.

"That sort of morning, huh?"

Emma nodded. The cups came quickly and she downed them in descending order, then followed the signs to the restrooms, and after that to the phone booth, where miraculously there was a phone book ready for perusal.

The doors to the high school were locked. The voice over the speaker asked who she was. Emma told them and was buzzed in. She bypassed a shiny new metal detector in the middle of the hallway. At the main office, the secretary pointed her in the right direction.

The halls were eerily quiet. Then, halfway to her destination, she was stunned by an ear-splitting beep. Classroom doors slammed open and the hallway flooded with teenage bodies. Leaning against the wall to save herself, Emma admired the youthful bodies. In the rising crescendo of laughter and greedy talk, she found herself wondering, how had Loretta fit in? Where were her compatriots? This student body was so white bread, the dress code basic Tommy Hilfiger. No ghetto wannabes. The few cases of big-toothed bells, neatly ironed. And barely making a dent in the preponderance of plaid, girls in short-short skirts and flesh-fitting Ts who looked decidedly anorexic.

Another beep. They were gone.

At the end of the hall, Andrew Tax's office. Lodged in the corner, a poster of Lauryn Hill gracing the door, her thick hair pushed inside a rasta cap, her eyes half shut as she achieved performance bliss. Emma knocked and a mellifluous voice said, "Enter." So she did. Inside, the cubicle took the word "mess" and knocked it on its ear. Piles of books and magazines dwarfed the human resident. Not a tough feat, considering. The man greeting her had sandy blond hair and a goatee. It took her a second more to realize he was standing. She took his hand.

"Emma Price," she said.

"Andrew Tax."

The voice was the problem. From the phone she'd developed an image of a man of more than mature years, a large-featured, barrel-chested guidance counselor. Yet here was someone in his early thirties, someone who was ridiculously diminutive.

He lifted a pile of newspapers and she took a seat. On the bulletin board behind him, a girl in karate uniform was photographed in battle stance. The caption read, A GOOD OFFENSE IS ALWAYS THE BEST DEFENSE.

Words to live by, she thought.

"Ms. Picard's file?" He handed it over. Opening the thin manila folder, she found two sets of grade sheets covering Loretta's ninth- and tenth-grade years. Reasonable marks; a B average with a few As sprinkled in for flavoring.

"What else can I help you with?" He asked this easily, genially.

"Did you ever have to counsel Loretta?"

"Counsel her?" Was it some oath of office they took that forced them to answer everything you asked with another question? "She did speak with me, yes."

"What about?"

"Unfortunately, that would be confidential." He didn't make it sound unfortunate at all.

"Was she referred by someone else in school?"

"Was she referred?" He stroked his incipient beard for a while. "No."

"She came to see you because she was upset about something, though."

"She might have."

"Mr. Tax, you did agree to speak with me."

"I did agree, yes."

Emma leaned in. "Then I would really appreciate it if you decided not to waste my time."

"Why do you think I'm wasting your time?"

"Why do you think I can't recognize a stall when I see one?" she countered.

His eyes twinkled. "Okay. Ms. Price, is it?"

"Emma," she said.

"Okay, Emma, dear." She decided to let him get away with this. His diminutive stature made him too easy a target. Clearing his throat, he gave a halting cough, then added, "Loretta felt underappreciated."

"By who?"

"Well, coming as she does from a dysfunctional family . . ." His voice trailed off.

"Everyone's family seems to be dysfunctional these days," Emma said.

"You don't mean that, I'm sure." His eyes narrowed into a beetlelike warning. "Her mother was a substance abuser. I'm sure you know she met with an unfortunate end. And her father? Well, he was never an issue."

A succinct description. Emma nodded, hoping for more. "Loretta felt lonely, isolated." His professional judgment.

"In other words, she didn't fit in. Did she have friends?"

"Not many," Tax said. "She often complained of being overlooked." Then he offered a mischievous grin. "She's taken care of that, now hasn't she?"

A theory. Murder as a play for attention. And Emma decided she didn't know enough about him or his relationship with Loretta to discount it out of hand.

"You mean she suffered from low self-esteem," Emma said.

"Perilously low," Tax agreed.

"What did you tell her?"

"Certainly not to go out and get a gun."

"I wasn't accusing you."

Tax shrugged. "The fact is, I feel miserable about Loretta," he said. His expression was surprisingly sincere.

Perhaps the glibness was simply a professional foible. Tidy analyses were often the province of mental health professionals. That, and a knowledge of psychopharmaceuticals. Loretta's Zoloft prescription sprang to mind.

"The more you tell me about Loretta, the better help we'll be able to offer," she said.

"That's my line." His laugh was high-pitched, nervous. "She was extremely depressed. I'm really not equipped to deal with the sort of anxieties she was expressing. I referred her to a colleague."

"Who was that?"

"Dr. Carolyn Reynolds."

Bingo, Emma thought.

"Dr. Reynolds is in New York," Emma said.

"Then you've spoken already."

This would require a certain sort of leap. And one Emma felt confident enough about making.

"Yes," she said, pulling out her notebook. "But Dr. Reynolds was a little vague about the exact date of referral."

Tax reached down, shoved aside several piles of papers and retrieved a brown leather notebook. Opening it, he scanned the pages, using his second finger as a divining rod. "Here it is," he said. "June 28th."

Two months ago, Emma thought. "So you and Loretta had kept in touch?"

"Actually, no." And he shook his head fiercely, physically defining the negative.

"You mean, from tenth grade until this summer, you had no contact at all, then she calls up, out of the blue? What did she say?"

"I suppose it can't hurt to tell." As if he were asking an unseen audience for permission. Even as his eyes locked on to Emma's. "Loretta was desperate. She said she needed to talk. She'd had certain emotional setbacks. And I gathered there was no one else to turn to."

"You gave her Dr. Reynolds's name and number?"

"I'm a high school guidance counselor. I'm not equipped to deal with this." Excusing himself. And apparently feeling he needed to proffer the excuse. "I called Carolyn and explained. I was relieved to hear Loretta had made an appointment."

"Did you and Dr. Reynolds ever have occasion to discuss the case?"

"Heavens, no!"

"Even now?"

No answer. How could they have resisted? Emma had spent her own time in therapy, had used them as professional witnesses. And she had come to a rather unfair conclusion, that psychotherapists, psychologists, psychiatrists all chose their professional path for one reason. A fascination with their own foibles. Which made them, ultimately, more fucked up than most of the rest of us, Emma decided.

"Mr. Tax, do you have any idea what precipitated this crisis for Loretta?"

She saw he did.

And also saw he wasn't going to tell. There was a knock on the door, a curly-haired girl peeking in. "Mr. Tax?" A crestfallen look when she found him occupied.

"Vera. Just wait. I'll only be a minute more."

A minute or two, Emma thought, hearing the door slide shut. "This obviously has a bearing on her state of mind at the time of the murders. It can help her, Mr. Tax."

"I'll think it over," he said. Which meant he'd be phoning his lawyer for advice. Standing, then coming around the desk, she realized he only reached to her chin.

"Loretta was lonely here," Emma said. "What about her cousin?"

"Faith? They were friends, of course. But hardly contemporaries. A two-year gap. Means a lot when you're a teenager. Faith didn't even start till the year after Loretta left."

He wore blue jeans, held up with a belt. The buckle was emblazoned with a turquoise-and-silver eagle. "It's been a pleasure," he said, as Emma stood. She opened the door and he put his hand on her shoulder. "By the way, Faith transferred last year. If you want to see her, you'll have to take a trip over the hill. She's an independent minor now. She lives in Montclair."

Eleven thirty-eight. Recess outside Montclair High. The differences between the two towns was readily apparent. Lots of black-and-white-skinned hip-hop party boys. And a whole selection of uniforms, jocks, plus girls and boys with streaks of blue in their hair wearing bell-bottoms wide enough to trip the owners. Plus a truly familiar blast from the past, a young girl wearing a peasant blouse.

Once again Emma made it past the metal detectors unscathed. Then the school secretary led her down a confusing maze of hallways to the lunchroom, where the noise was as overpowering as the smell of bad cafeteria food.

Faith Manners was all grown up. Her blond hair had been cut short and it stuck up in swatches. She had a nose ring, plenty of black eyeliner, and dark brown lipstick. On the outskirts of Goth, Emma decided. Not quite ready to take the plunge yet. A tattoo of a serpent made a nice touch, standing in for a bracelet.

Emma handed over a card. "I work for Capital Crimes in New York. We represent your cousin Loretta."

Faith gave a studied lack of response, finishing her drink, a chocolate milk of all things. Then, standing slowly, she yawned as if this were the most boring thing she had ever encountered.

Outside the school, rows of stone benches curved to form a mini-Coliseum. Faith clambered up to the top and took a seat. Emma labored to join her. At the top, she found herself wheezing pitifully.

"So," Faith said, lighting a cigarette and inhaling deeply. "What are you coming to me about?"

"As the lead investigator, it's my job to find as much information as possible. We need to formulate a defense."

"You're trying to stop them from frying her."

"Yes," Emma said. "To put it baldly."

Faith threw the cigarette down, half finished, and stamped on the butt. Then she stuck a piece of gum in her mouth and chewed hard. "Who told you where to find me?"

"Andrew Tax."

"Andy's got that shrink thing down, doesn't he? You say, good morning, Mr. Tax. He says, 'are you having a good morning?' Like you should answer him with fully operative sincerity."

"I also spoke with your mom."

"You did, did you?" This got her full attention. Faith blasted Emma with a toothy smile. "And how did that go?"

Emma thought it expedient to do a quick sidestep. "You're an independent minor. That takes work."

"It's not so bad, if you have the right lawyer."

"Why go to the trouble?"

"You did meet my mom?" Faith squinted, looking past Emma.

"So I would assume the two of you don't get along?"

"Let's just say we've reached a mutual impasse," Faith said. "Anyhow, I thought you were here for Loretta."

"I am. But I'm also curious."

"Curiosity killed the cat. Look, they didn't agree with my lifestyle choices. She didn't agree. Does that tell you enough?"

Emma shrugged.

"So, when you asked my mom about Lore, did she tell you how she was Satan's spawn?"

"She didn't mention it."

Faith let out a cackling laugh.

"What's your mother got against Loretta?" Emma asked.

"Lore didn't tell you?"

Emma shook her head. Faith grunted. "Hell," she said. "And I guess my mom didn't either. But I'll bet she couldn't help letting something slip. Why else would you come to me?" Faith fixed her eyes on the far and furtive distance. "My mom and Marie were real close. Like this." She twisted her fingers into a knot to illustrate. "Even with Marie's problems. And did she have them! Aunt Marie was always going somewhere for an answer. AA. Alanon. She even went through this religious phase. Used to come over and burn incense. Got my mom to 'om' away with her. It was a hoot. You'd come in and the two of them would be doing these maneuvers. Looked good on Marie. But my mom, she's built like the side of a house." Faith's voice drifted off. Emma waited, afraid to nudge for more. Faith spit the gum into her hand, then rolled it up in a tiny piece of paper and flicked it off. "Hard to say why people do what they do, huh? I guess they're all crazy." Faith leaned back on open arms, as if considering. "You know how many times Marie tried to kill herself? Three before she made it work. My mom was there at the hospital those other two times, pumping out her stomach, telling her off. Saying all this shit, like you gotta live. You gotta try. My mom was always dragging her back to the land of the living. Like this is such a wonderful place."

"Better than the alternatives."

"Your opinion," Faith said dryly. "It wasn't Marie's."

"Even so, you've got centuries to be dead in," Emma said.

"A long fucking thing, eternity." Faith cackled again. Then she punched Emma in the forearm lightly. "You've got some humor, you know?"

"Thanks."

Faith was interesting. Smart. And angry. That potent and all too familiar combination.

"It was just a week after the funeral. We're all sitting down to dinner and we can see how Mom's chewing on something else. Everyone's looking nervous, just because. I mean, when she goes off, she's vicious, you know? And then she starts muttering things and cursing under her breath. My dad doesn't have the nerve to say, 'what?' No one does. Dessert comes. Apple brown Betty, I guess. Or fruit cobbler. And my mom stands there, with the plate in her hand and says, 'murderer.' She says it right to Lore. Lore looks up and then pushes her chair back. And my mom goes off while the rest of us sit there with our jaws dropping open and my dad, he doesn't ever say a goddamn word. My mom slaps her hard on the cheek and Lore puts her hand up and starts to cry, then stops herself and my mom says, 'pervert. Don't you ever set foot in my house again.' "

Emma had the scene there, engraved in her mind. And couldn't find the less than subtle thread. "Pervert?"

"Loretta was doing it with Ms. Elgin, the language arts teacher. Some kid came up on them over at the reservoir and snapped a photo of the two of them kissing. Next thing you know, it's indecency and loose morals and Ms. Elgin's being fired. Then bing, bang, boom, Marie's gone. My mom decides two and two makes five. I mean, what the hell does she care, Loretta's life is already in the toilet, so why not make it even worse." Faith stood and grabbed her bookbag. "You see Loretta..." And the expression on her face went soft for the very first time, "give her my best. Ask her how it would be if I came over for a visit."

Next stop, Rikers. Yes, she and Loretta were going to have another little chat. Inside her car, Emma checked her voice mail. Dawn had called three times.

"What's up?" Emma asked.

"You tell me," Dawn demanded.

"I'm in Jersey. I've been interviewing the aunt and the cousin."

"Do you know a Detective Laurence Solomon?"

"I might," Emma admitted, wincing internally.

"You might, huh? And in what goddamn context?"

Emma opened her mouth to reply, then shut it tight, sensing that Dawn didn't want her to go on.

"He got in to see Loretta Picard last night on your say-so. Now she's hysterical. Says she won't talk to you or anyone from the office. You better come down here and fix this, Emma."

The phone clicked off, defying her.

And to think I felt bad about squirreling those photos away, Emma thought. Getting into her car, she slammed the door so hard, the metal body rocked.

26

The desk sergeant directed her upstairs, past old induction posters with THE FORCE WILL BE WITH YOU as a caption. A burnished uniformed recruit saluted underneath the six-inch lettering.

She didn't bother knocking, just thrust the door open. Solomon turned to confront the violator. Finding her, his face showed relief.

"Emma."

The way he said her name. As if it were the answer to some difficult question. And it stopped her in her tracks. She swung her head around, wondering if someone else was behind her, widening his scope of reference.

"How dare you go to see Loretta without asking me!"

The mask slid on. His eyes narrowed. He inhaled and stood, seeming unnaturally tall, even threatening. Another trick, she decided, as she stepped forward to confront him.

"You used my name!"

He drew a breath, and seemed to steel himself, then said, "That might have been a mistake."

"Might have been?"

He seemed to be studying her, over distance. When he spoke again, the tone he chose to use was ingratiating. She found this eminently insulting. "Sit down. Let me explain."

"I'll stand," she said.

"Suit yourself."

He slid past her to shut the door. There was a second of

contact. Emma drew back. And he sighed. That world-weary sigh men gave when the women of the world confronted them. A sigh that meant, I'm doing my best and how can you blame me for it? Emma slapped him on the cheek as hard as she could. He grabbed her hand on its trajectory back down, pinching with his fingers.

"Sit down!" At least he didn't sound comforting now. She still refused his offer. "Woman, what in hell do you want from me?" He released her and backed away, then lifted a folder off his desk and opened it, fanning photographs under her nose. "Here," he said. "Look at these."

She looked down at the photographs of a crime scene: the first one showed the victim; a male Caucasian with blue eyes and dark hair. He was in the front seat of a car, driver's side. One shot to the forehead, execution style. The next, a closeup, showed the damage on impact, the back of the skull and headrest both split apart. Then exterior shots; a green Ford Taurus.

"I don't know him," she said.

"But you do," Solomon insisted. "Meet Charles Murray aka Chazz Perry, Beatriz Castillo's one and only. Cantas ID'd him. The hair's a dye job."

"I see." Emma took the seat now, lifting the photos to scan them again. "Where?"

"The Navy Yard parking lot. A sculptor who works out there found him, a little before two. Said he'd gone out for a drink at midnight and the lot was empty. When he came back, he noticed the car."

"Isn't there security?"

"A gate to gain entry. But the guard goes off at nine. Afterward, you have to press in a code." Solomon reached inside his billfold, freed up a business card, and dropped it on top of the sheaf of photos. "Also, this gentleman paid me a visit yesterday. Wanted me to know that Eliot was one of theirs and to keep my hands off."

She read the words several times, before they registered. "You mean that Eliot was in the program?"

"Something Loretta knew. As did plenty of other people. Apparently he boasted about it. Loretta also told me Chazz was the one doing the IDs. He did hers. Larrabbee had gotten wind of the business and was asking questions." Solomon paused, then he opened his desk drawer and took out the mini recorder. He slid the tape into the palm of her hand. "It's all here. The entire interview," he said. "I didn't make a copy."

As if this could appease her. The betrayal. And it wasn't just the way he'd used her, possibly even used up her chances with Loretta. It was more than that. It was Chazz. Losing the chance to do what? To accuse him? To force him to explain? Because someone had to explain. Otherwise what was there to take away except an image of a mean-spirited God, pulling the strings from on high?

"I've got a theory," Solomon said.

"Which is?"

"I've done some checking. Eliot's the third loss for the program in less than two weeks. Up in Fall River, there was a morning hit-and-run. And out in Nogales, a woman was killed during a carjacking."

"That's no proof of anything."

"No proof. But why else is O'Donnell up here? They don't send someone like him to take care of the Eliot Marshalls of the world. He's got to be doing damage control."

"Let's say you're right, it still gives us nothing," Emma said. And she looked past him, to find the assembled factory buildings. A muffled shot. Then a car door slamming. Out on the East River, white caps betrayed those treacherous currents that could tug you down for good.

"Murray was a computer whiz. What if he knew Eliot was on the level? What if the two of them cooked up this scheme to break inside and sell off names?"

"Oh, please. That's ridiculous. This is a government agency. I have the same low opinion of bureaucracy as the next person, but I'm still not going to believe there weren't safeguards in place to prevent that from happening."

"The entire Witness Protection Program is entered on a computer database," Solomon said. "I spoke with someone who knows all about this and he told me that hackers broke in three years ago. It sent them into a frenzy, moving people in the dead of night all across the country."

"If that's true, they must have made sure it could never happen again."

"He also explained that that's not possible. Any computer database can be broken into no matter how many firewalls you put up."

"Oh, really?" Emma offered her most potent look of disbelief. "Who's this expert you're talking to?"

"My brother Ralph."

"Your brother." Somehow the fact that he'd called in a relative made it even more absurd. "So why is Charles Murray dead? And what happened to Bea? If Murray's the brains..." Her voice trailed off. She knew the answer, of course. "What did Loretta say?" she asked.

"I was trying to tell you. Murray was the one who sold her the ID and Larrabbee started to ask questions about him. Apparently, according to your client, Larrabbee also made sexual advances. She rejected them, rejected him. But it obviously made her angry. Listen to the tape," he said.

The way he stared. It didn't make her uncomfortable. She let herself register that fact.

"Funny how Loretta put it," he said. "She told me when he

kissed her he told her he could cure her. But cure her of what?"

"Being gay?" It was an exchange program. And Emma saw that the time for resistance was past. She took out her wallet and set out the last shreds of incriminating evidence. "I'm assuming the redhead is Penny. And the look on Loretta's face says it all. Deeply infatuated."

"Have you ever been in love?"

"You're asking me?"

"Your client asked me," he said. The tone of self-satisfaction. The whole thing coming together for him. This man! She turned away and brushed against a stack of neatly arranged files. They fell on the floor and she leaned over to get them, and as she did, saw that she'd also brushed the photos of the crime scene onto the floor. She stood, holding them in her hands, and stared down at them, because something was in there, tugging at her memory. She shut her eyes, trying to find it. And cursed as it disappeared for good.

"Emma." She felt his hand on her arm. "Are we friends?"

"We can't be friends." Her eyes sprang open. The image had been there, tugging at her. Now it was certainly gone. "Damn it," she said, under her breath. And then realized it was time.

The sound of whirring dying out as he leaned over to take a kiss. He was kissing her hard, and with the sort of desperate longing she couldn't bear. And couldn't bear resisting. She raised herself up to greet him, finding something violent underneath. Her need for this to happen. Her greed. His hand slid over her breasts, rubbing the top of each nipple, escalating the tugging down below. She pushed against him, angry again, even vicious. You never know anyone, she thought, least of all yourself.

The knock saved them. They sprang away from each

other. He was actually blushing. She laughed gaily in the face of all that entailed.

"What?" Solomon said gruffly.

"It's only your roomie." Ruiz's voice from outside.

Charles Murray's mother sat at a metal table in interview room B. She was a thin woman, with steel-gray hair cut in a bob. A doughnut and coffee had been placed next to her right arm. They sat, apparently untouched.

Poor thing, Emma thought, because the central fact of this woman's existence had to be overwhelming.

What could you really say to her? So they told her to sit. To make herself comfortable. They offered coffee, doughnuts, bitter herbs.

She'd come straight from the morgue where she'd identified the body. Now they were about to strip away what few shreds of dignity she had left. Emma watched through the double pane of glass as Solomon stepped into the room and proffered a hand, cupping the woman's in his own. He told her that he was sorry. Lies unfolding in layers.

I kissed him. I wanted to kiss him and did. The first man who's touched me since Will. Twelve years. I'm crazy. Pregnant and crazy.

Emma felt lightheaded. She leaned against the glass. Would this woman look up at the mirror? Would she even imagine she was being observed? After all, who would care to observe her when she was simply another bereaved parent, this her new natural habitat?

"What happened to my son?"

"That's exactly what we need to figure out," Solomon said. As if it were a problem they could work on together. Scratch down the numbers. Do the complicated math. Then add up all the columns and *voilà!*

"Detective Ruiz?" She turned to look askance. Miguel Ruiz had taken the seat next to Solomon and folded his arms over his chest. He looked profoundly uncomfortable.

"I told Mrs. Murray the deceased was found early this morning," Ruiz said.

"But what happened?" She said it again, made suddenly ferocious.

"Your son was found seated in a vehicle in the parking lot of the Brooklyn Navy Yard. There was no sign of forced entry to the vehicle. There was no sign of a struggle. He was shot once in the head with a small-caliber weapon. Right now, we're assuming he knew his assailant."

"Knew them? What do you mean?" She looked confused. She looked to Ruiz. But he was keeping busy. Shifting his hands. Patrolling the room with his eyes. "Are you trying to tell me something?" As if she were deaf, and nobly aware of her handicap.

"What we need most here is your assistance," Solomon said. "Anything you can tell us."

"But of course I'll help you. Of course I will, yes." Were they the ones who needed reassuring? That's how it is, Emma thought. Pretend, because it's your only defense. This is happening to someone, anyone, else.

"When was the last time you and your son were in contact?"

"The last time?" Her eyes shone when she said it, and her voice was taut. The thinking back seemed a physical strain. "It must have been Thursday of last week. He phoned me at work."

"Did he say anything unusual?"

"No." Said peremptorily. "He asked me about the weather. It was a joke of course. Baltimore was built on a swamp. It's been the most maddening summer I've ever experienced. The mosquitoes are so thick at night, even with the spraying. I'm surprised there hasn't been some horrible malaria epidemic."

Solomon waited. Emma knew he wanted her to remember, to realize. The last time, the very last time I spoke to my son. The moment that would eclipse everything else. The moment she'd have to depend on and reinvent countless times to insure her sanity. Did he really sound normal? How could he have sounded normal? Was he only pretending? Telling me that everything was good and decent and fine. Because look. Look where I am! Look where he's brought me. Would you just look at what he's done?

"Mrs. Murray's a librarian," Ruiz threw out.

"Head of Library Services," she said, correcting him. "At Johns Hopkins University." This part was clearly a badge of pride. The slight haughtiness of manner, reinstated for a moment. But then her expression changed, the confidence dissipating. "Charlie asked about work. I told him, 'wonderful.' And we laughed. He understood the humor." She sounded wistful. "I do like my job, after all. But no one ever believes me. They think, a librarian, what could be more devoid of interest?" The shadow of a smile passing over her lips, then fading away. "I told him about Sid Bramley. Poor Sid. Moved to Florida and a week later had a heart attack on the golf course. Now Linda's at a loss, wondering what on earth she'll do with the apartment. You work your whole life, and then retirement comes and you don't even get God's grace to enjoy it."

"I really am sorry to press," Solomon said. His hand went out to touch her shoulder. "Was that all the two of you talked of?"

"Yes, yes it was." Such a small voice. So beaten down.

"Just a few more questions."

She looked up at him, seemingly encouraged. Was he saying the ordeal would be over soon? Then she could get back to her life. "Go on," she said.

"When did you see Charles last?"

She seemed to make an internal countdown. "Perhaps a month. He came down to stay for the weekend."

"And?"

"And?"

"How was he?"

"What does that mean?" She shook her head. "You tell me my son's been murdered. How am I supposed to understand these questions? Charles was happy. He was alive."

"Mrs. Murray, this was no random shooting."

"Then you tell me, who killed him?" Her staid demeanor was gone. She pointed her finger, shook it at Solomon. "That's your job, isn't it?"

"Did you know Beatriz Castillo?"

"Castillo? Beatriz Castillo? Is that someone you suspect?"

"That's the woman your son lived with."

"But he didn't live with anyone," she said firmly.

"Yes, he did. He shared an apartment with Beatriz Castillo." Glancing down, he added, "396 Fifth Avenue. Brooklyn. That was his address?"

"Of course it is. Was." Her voice faltered over the change in tense. Precision had defeated her.

"What was your son's phone number?" Solomon pushed the pad over to her side. She didn't reach for the pen. "Can we get you something, Mrs. Murray? Some water, perhaps?"

She shook her head. "Charles used one of those portable phones. That way we could always be in touch. I worried, of course. All those reports of brain tumors." She licked her lips, rubbed one hand hard against her cheek as if eradicating a smudge. "Some things are meant to be private."

"You mean you didn't know whether he had a girlfriend?"

"I never asked him about it. Charles is a wonderful boy."

"Did you know any of Charles's friends?"

"Of course." This was said defensively.

"Did you know a Penny Strider?"

Another complete blank. Solomon's sigh was almost palpable. "It would be tremendously helpful if you could stand to put together a list."

"I don't see why..." She stopped herself again. Grief stricken. And completely lost. Emma understood. She'd had no choice but to let him become a stranger. In the end, you took whatever your children offered. And told yourself you were lucky.

"He talked about his work?"

"Of course." But she was so completely uncertain by now. "Charles had an amazing mathematical mind. He did so well at Hopkins. I'd thought physics. Something abstract."

"Your son worked with computers."

"He designed systems. It paid handsomely. He told me that." She said this last with a renewed burst of defiance. "You know what Professor Frederick said about my Charles? He said he could do anything. And a compliment from a man like that is worth its weight..." She stopped then, frowned, and stared balefully at Solomon. "I'd like to go."

"Of course." Solomon stood and offered her his hand. She pointedly refused, walking stiffly to the door.

What had they learned? Another mother who had been swaddled in naiveté. Another mother who relieved her suffering by staying pointedly unaware.

Emma stepped into the hall and then, there it was. She saw a flash of green. The car stopping at the light. Liam turning toward it and the look on his face as the car swung past. He knew the person at the wheel. A green car. A Ford Taurus.

* * *

Recess. The cement outpost crawling with pint-sized escapees. Liam was playing a game of horse. She watched him make the shot and then slap Tony's hand, watched him do that victory twirl. This display of confidence suddenly seemed foreign, even suspicious.

"Liam," she called. He turned, found her.

"Mom." The voice was sullen, the shoulders slanted down. He had been the same that morning when she dropped him off.

At the far end of the playground, squads of climbers braved the old fashioned jungle gym. Emma remembered how she had always taken preternatural care. "Don't fall," she'd say, before she even let him try. And she'd stand close, just in case, hoping that in saying the worst, she could manage to usurp its power. "Beatriz's boyfriend," she said. "Chazz."

His eyes dropped to the ground, giving him away immediately. How had she missed this? How many other things had he hidden from her successfully? She saw her own accomplishments added up: smoking pot with her friends, cutting class to feed the pinball machines, hitching rides on the interstate. But after all, she'd learned deceit from the master, her sister Rosa.

"You knew I'd be angry."

"Bea asked me not to tell."

So he had been protecting someone else. That was how it always was, after all. Emma saw their future mapped out. The ground done in bas-relief with muscular mountain ranges rippling. His resistance. Her pursuit. His bad behavior. Her intimate knowledge thereof. "You were with Chazz last night?"

He looked away. And she saw the distance he would travel by plane or boat or car, dusty roads full of cattle in the morning, sunrise over the Ganges, sunset on the beach at Paradise

Cove, places where the heat was ferocious, or where ice chips doubled as pillows. You ran from your parents as you ran from your past, and yet... No matter where he went, he would always be tugged back. That catgut cord would bind them together.

"I'm not angry," she said, bending down in front of him. "Liam. I need to know. Was he the one who told you Bea was dead?"

Liam nodded.

"Where did he take you?"

"To Coney Island," Liam said. Then his face brightened. "I went on the Cyclone. It was the bomb."

She saw what he would become. A different boy, less timid, more boldly defined. Emma knew how she must appear to him. Every loss of temper, provoked, every savage mistake, intentional. What can I do, she wondered? Nothing. Nothing to be done at all. So she kissed him, tugged him into her arms, and held on for as long as he would let her.

27

Inside the prison, the heat was truly unbearable. As the guard led Emma through the cell block and up the two flights of stairs, she felt the sweat begin to pool on the back of her neck. Under her arms, the linen fabric felt cool and damp as it clung to her skin.

Loretta's cell was at the very end of the hall.

"Picard." The guard offered her last name, said it like an admonition. "A guest." Something Loretta was aware of already. Emma had been pointedly turned away. And had persisted in her determination to at least see her client.

The door slid open and Emma stepped inside. The cell was no bigger than a closet. So much for the luxurious quarters some proponents of tougher jail time imagined. Loretta was the only occupant; the one window perilously high, tiny, and matted with chickenwire. The light cast through was permanently, almost maddeningly, diffuse. Loretta lay on the bottom bunk, her arms folded under her head.

"I didn't send that detective up here."

No sign she'd been heard. No sign of anything. Leaning on the far wall, Emma inhaled her own odor; a dankness. Not fear, she decided, frustration. One of life's little ironies, how, without Loretta's abridged confession, she would never have known what questions to tender.

Emma reminded herself how she'd never really had this girl's trust. So the claim that she'd now lost it seemed more than a little bogus. And she couldn't blame Solomon. She

completely understood what had propelled him north. In
this, his self-interest and her own desire to make good for
Beatriz jibed.

Emma reached into her pocket, pulled out the tape
recorder, and set it down on the floor between them. She
flicked the switch. Solomon's voice, a full-fleshed baritone.
Loretta reached up then, and covered her ears. Like children
might, pretending they couldn't hear the lecture.

"Don't listen, then," Emma said, turning off the tape. She
picked up the tape player and dropped it on the mattress.
"He swears he only made this one copy." Emma stepped
back, achieving the illusion of distance. "You did know
Beatriz."

No response. But no refusal either. Was this progress?
Emma wondered.

"Bea worked for me. She was my son's sitter." Emma
studied the rise and fall of Loretta's chest, the rhythmic rise
and fall. "What luck for you." Reaching into her back
pocket, she extracted the wallet, flipped through to find the
two photographs she'd stripped from Loretta's bathroom
cabinet; that toddler bouncing in her mother's lap, Faith with
her munificent smile. Stepping over, she fanned them in
front of Loretta. And finally got a response. Loretta grabbed
them. And Emma gave way.

"I saw Faith this morning."

Loretta's eyes shut, firmly. Emma stepped back. Time
moved forward on a deliberately efficient tangent. I've either
got all the time in the world or no time left at all, Emma
thought.

The floor was imbedded with years of filth. She sat. Light
fell in tiny dappling squares, marking her legs. Emma considered Andrew Tax's theory, Loretta as the ultimate petulant teen. These murders committed to draw attention to her
plight. In a way he was right. But only in a way.

"A world full of creeps," Emma said. "All of us out for ourselves, right? Self-interest rules. I'm the one who's supposed to dig up every shred of evidence that can save your life. And here I go, working this other agenda. Which I forget to inform you about. No wonder you're pissed off. There's nobody out there for you, is there? No one you can really be sure of."

"So why don't you get the fuck away."

"I can't."

Loretta's eyes snapped open. She sat up to further her accusation. "Sure you can. Go on. Leave."

"I need you, Loretta. It's the only way I can manage."

"Right! You need me. I'm supposed to care."

"Did I say that?" Emma smiled a mischievous smile. "I'm not asking for your sympathy. I'm only asking you to be smart. Think about yourself, for once."

"Bullshit."

"Is it?" Emma was transported back to that cool autumn day. Dawn's office in Trenton. The way Dawn sensed her own incipient weakness. And played to it.

Loretta tucked in her legs, backed up so that her eyes were the thing most visible. She looked trapped back there, an animal caught in its darkened lair.

"Larrabbee was asking you questions. He wanted to know about Charles Murray's business. He thought he was only asking you to give that up. Pretty stupid, really. But then, he made certain false assumptions."

Again, no denial.

"Did you ever take the antidepressants Dr. Reynolds prescribed?"

A long, long pause. Then Loretta's voice, croaking out an answer. "I guess I did, for a while."

"But you stopped. Why? Were you feeling better?"

"Feeling better?" A choking sound after. "You ever take that shit?"

"No, I haven't."

"Well, don't. It's like, there's you and..." Loretta lifted her hands out into midair, "there's everything else. Everyone else. There's this big space between you. You can barely see where they are."

"How long before you stopped?"

Loretta had bent her knees in completely, hugging them to her chest. "Maybe a month."

"Did you go back, tell her it hadn't helped?"

"Why would I bother?"

"I guess you wouldn't. Love's the biggest bitch, isn't it? How long were you and Penny involved?"

Nothing. But Emma had perfect faith. She had the hook sunk in tight. Invisible. But someplace where all it would take was one sure tug to establish her mastery.

"She got you that job at the Pit. How long were you with her before that?"

"What the fuck do you want?" Loretta was up. Was in her face. Emma didn't back away. The looks exchanged more practiced from her side. Years of subway staring contests. The fury in Loretta's eyes when she saw she would lose. And then, a shove, so hard, Emma fell back, saving herself by putting out her hand. A mistake, the pain smashing through her wrist as she avoided contact with the metal bed-frame.

The guard was inside, reaching for Loretta, grabbing her arms. No resistance there. Just the same sullen look of defiance she'd had sketched on her face before. Emma rubbed her wrist. Felt it go numb. "Don't!" she said firmly. "We're fine. We're really fine."

The guard gave her an incredulous look.

"I'm fine," Emma said again. She braved a conciliatory smile.

"Suit yourself." The woman stepped away, stepped outside again, leaving the sting of her incredulity behind.

They were both standing, Loretta refusing to meet her eyes. "Bea talked about you," she said. Emma felt the air freeze around her. She had the temptation to hold her breath so she could treasure this moment. And Loretta's suddenly stark humanity. "Bea loved your kid. Said how he was so easy. Me, I told her I could never do that kind of job. Said I wouldn't have the patience." Loretta's smile was wistful. And she did look up now, offering the gift of personal contact. "Bea liked those sweet drinks, Singapore slings, mai tais, little holidays, I call them. Chazz was lucky to have her. You know?"

"I know," Emma said.

"But then, that's how it is. Some people get lucky. The funny thing with me and Pen. It started off, she was after me. She'd show up where I was waiting tables, and give me all these lines. Try to get me to go with her to a concert, or out for a drink."

"How long?"

"Over a year."

"Why did it end?"

"You think I know? She wanted out, I guess. Said being with me was turning into a punishment for her. Said she only wanted to be fair. Faay-uh." The second word an imitation, Penny's Southern drawl.

"When Larrabbee asked about the business, he didn't know Penny and Chazz were partners."

"For fucking ever. He was her prom date in high school. That was how far back they went." Petulance in her voice. And a hiss coming after. The sort of warning a snake gives, before unsheathing its jaws. "Pen was the one with the ideas. And he was Mr. Execution." She laughed then, miserably.

Emma was trying to keep track. Penny Strider's prom date? Then Murray's mother had lied. But why? The woman's act had been so damn convincing, too. Then Emma saw another way out, that whole country of the disappeared. Chazz Perry had, after all, been Charles Murray at birth. So why couldn't Penny Strider also be an alias?

"Chazz tried to warn me before it happened, you know. He'd say little things about her. And I told myself he was being mean. Or jealous. You can say you're like brother and sister, but some brothers and sisters..." Loretta's face was dark. "After she broke it off, Chazz said to me how I shouldn't be sad. He said it was really a good thing, said Penny wasn't capable of knowing how great I was. How I'd find someone better and to just hold on. I guess I couldn't listen. I've never been too good at taking advice." Loretta's eyes flickered. She wore a tortured smile. Which didn't hide her weariness. Her body hung down, exhausted. To climb up on that cross. To stick the nails in yourself. Eternity was a long time to reflect on that one moment of stupidity. Because, even when the whole world was supposed to be watching, there was always someone averting their eyes.

"Where is she?" Emma asked.

"Who?"

"Penny Strider. Where has she gone?"

"You think she'd keep in touch with me? You think she'd talk to me, after this? I mean, I ruined everything for her, didn't I? All her big plans. She probably thinks I meant it to work out this way."

"You were only trying to get Larrabbee off her back."

"Was that what I was doing?" Loretta shrugged. "You get these plans together. You think if you just do this one thing, they'll see. See how you're worth something really. See how important you really are to them. You make this shit up for yourself." Loretta's hands fluttered up. "Real stupid, is what it looks like now. Me, the world's number-one moron. Most people who lose it, they go shoot up a bar. Or take out some kids who were mean to them up at their high school."

Emma set her hand on Loretta's shoulder.

"How come you're not disagreeing? I thought you were on my side."

"I am."

"Yeah, right!" But she let Emma's hand rest there, all the same.

Outside, in the parking lot, waves of heat pounded out. Emma boosted the air conditioning, then called Solomon. And found him in transit. He'd been at Penny Strider's studio, high above the Brooklyn Navy Yard parking lot. And come away empty-handed.

So she offered him a gift. The knowledge thus imparted, she set off. And was halfway over the Brooklyn Bridge when the return call came in. They'd found Murray's mother at the morgue and she'd denied the existence of said Penny Strider. Yes, he'd taken someone to the prom. But the girl's name was Amanda, not Penny.

"You're sitting down, I assume," Solomon said.

"Yes."

"In your car? Tell me when you hit a red light."

"I'm there now," she lied, already buzzed by the elation in his voice.

"The girl's last name? It's O'Donnell. Amanda O'Donnell. And Malcolm O'Donnell, our OEO buddy? That's her dad. I already called D.C. He's been on sick leave for over a week. So that visit he made yesterday? They're denying all knowledge. Looks to me like the man's flying solo."

28

"Over here." Solomon had grabbed her arm, and was tugging her through a side gate, flashing his badge. There was no way they could miss that four thirty-eight commuter flight to Baltimore.

"Here you go." He shoved something her way. Emma realized it was a ticket for the shuttle. Her death warrant.

Sure, once she'd loved to fly. Now she couldn't figure out why she'd ever believed in the invulnerability of man and his inventions. Her stomach was churning. She fought the bile back, fought to stay calm.

And pronounced herself a miserable failure.

Forty-eight airborne minutes. Truly an eternity, what with this panic seeping into her bones.

"What's wrong?"

"Nothing."

"You sure?"

Why were they going again? Oh, that's right. Because Solomon had this crazy notion that they were going to find Mr. Malcolm O'Donnell at home. That he would open the door and be so impressed by their diligent pursuit, he would offer up his daughter. And himself.

"You didn't have to come."

"Yes, I did." She'd suggested the Metroliner. He'd told her the plane was faster. And sounded so impatient, she'd seen this as her only chance. How absurd. If Malcolm O'Donnell was involved, if he hadn't come north to attempt to find and then protect his daughter, he was hardly going to be hanging around his house. And if he was as in the dark as they were, this wouldn't lead them to Penny. Amanda. Whatever her goddamn name was. She had to be across the Canadian border by now. Or crossing the Atlantic.

They moved down the entryway, the gangplank, she thought, and onto the plane.

He was living in a dream world. They both were. Because no incriminating evidence had been found at Eliot's, or in Charles Murray's car. What did they hope to charge Penny with when, and if, they came upon her? Selling scam IDs? Solomon's information about the Witness Protection Program was, at best, hearsay. As for that business, all they had linking her to Murray was Loretta's statement. Hardly the sort of solid evidence needed to bring an indictment. Hardly enough for a search warrant.

Talk about flying by the seat of your pants, Emma thought as they stepped into the plane. Which was terrifyingly small. Two rows with three seats on each side, crammed in.

"What happened to first class?" she asked, feeling unbelievably brave to squeak out the words.

Solomon smiled gaily. Another sign of his incipient madness. She stared down at her boarding pass, and realized that the panic was so virulent, she was unable to read the seat numbers.

"Here we are," he said.

Row 7A, a window seat. She stared at the EXIT sign above the window, then down to the handle. Told herself all she had to do was pull it and slide down the automatic chute to safety.

"Ladies and gentlemen, the captain has put the seat belt sign on. Please put all carry-on luggage into the overhead compartments ..."

Packed in like sardines. Emma was glad she hadn't taken the middle seat when she saw their traveling companion: an overweight man in his midforties who was already sweating profusely. Solomon's lips curled downward as the man sat down with an oomph, the upper half of his body obliterating the armrest.

"You're sure you're okay?"

She couldn't even lie. She was past that. Way past it. She felt the plane shiver and quake. Then realized they were taxiing down the runway.

Prepare for lift-off.

Emma dug herself into the seat and closed her eyes. The metal body shivered and for that furious second, it seemed as if nothing would be accomplished except misery, that the bolts would come undone and they would be thrown outward by some tremendous centrifugal force, but then, of course, they were airborne. The nose pointed up, the body swung to greet it, and she felt her stomach tilt with it, felt her stomach curse and uncurl. Her fingers tugged down under the seatbelt, tucked inside the waistband of her pants. And then, she felt Solomon's hand around her arm. What a tender smile.

"What?" She heard herself, ferocious, belligerent... terrified.

"We're not going to crash," he said.

"You go ahead and believe that."

Then knew she was being unfair. How could he have known when she didn't tell him. Frailty. Something to be tucked away, out of notice. He was trying to be kind, after all. Emma reached out, covering his hand with her own, and giving it one quick squeeze. It seemed a superhuman effort to manage. She let go and turned away, to stare out the window at that disappearing landscape, the bas-relief map of her home town.

And allowed herself to recognize how, the first time, too, Dawn's request had come when she most needed a diversion. It had been barely seven months after she'd lost her sister. Rosa. Every time Emma flew she imagined Rosa's last moments. And wondered, had she been brave?

Losing her changed everything. How could it not? Nothing was the same once you'd lost a child. Emma saw her mother as she'd looked once, efficient, professional, standing on the steps of the school she'd founded, waiting for the children. Louise Cohen at forty, wearing jeans, a sky-blue linen shirt. Grasping a cigarette between two fingers, and puffing on it in her fervent, distracted manner. She'd started the school to support them, when Sy was blacklisted for party membership. Louise as jack-of-all-trades, carrying her tools across the grounds to fix the broken pipe in the concrete swimming pool, repairing splintered window frames.

The plane banked right, then dipped. Emma clutched the hand-rests, hard.

Her older sister Rosa was nineteen. She was coming home from her first year of college. And Emma waited anxiously for her return. Told herself there'd be plenty of time to sneak into the Ransoms' pool at night, or ride their bikes down by the railroad tracks and pick those massive bouquets of cattails. Only Rosa went south instead. To Mississippi. Clouds of nightsticks raining down on the Freedom Riders' heads. Her sister one of them. Then came Schwerner. Chaney. Goodman. The perilous wait.

"Those boys are dead." Louise said it one night, as the three of them watched Cronkite. Sy shook his head hard, hissed at her for quiet. But her mother was adamant. "Your daughter should know. You should never lie to a child."

"Will it happen to Rosa?" Emma heard her own voice asking.

"Rosa will be fine." Sy patting her on the head. Children always know, Emma thought, remembering how she'd turned to her mother, how Louise had sighed and exchanged a conspiratorial look, the two of them attesting to his incipient blindness.

Late August. Rosa making her triumphal return on the back of a boy's motorcycle. Emma had so admired that boy who had thick brown hair and a little beatnik's goatee. Rosa spilled out everything; how the voter registration drive went, how people shot at the houses where they had been staying, and the local police chief trailed them around town, how the people who let them into their homes were the kindest, gentlest, creatures on the face of this earth.

"Creatures?" Sy's voice heavy with sarcasm.

"You know what I mean, Daddy."

"I wish I did."

The boy opened his mouth to defend her. And that was the end. He was sent packing.

That night, the four of them had nestled in front of the huge fireplace with no roaring fire inside. Emma had leaned back against her mother's legs and let Louise stroke her hair. Sy tried to touch Rosa, but she pulled away. Emma saw her father's face twist up, saw him turn away, embarrassed. Then he'd said, "Rosa, darling," using a toastmaster's voice. "The kind of bravery it took to do this. All I can say is you have made us very proud."

From the window of the bedroom she and Rosa had shared, she'd watch the lights of Palisades Amusement Park with its giant saltwater pool, beckoning. Rosa took her across every summer, and they spent hours on the rides, Rosa next to her, holding her hand and screaming with glee as the roller coaster took off, jumping over mountain-high curves. Emma had always known where she could go for comfort. Turning, she could always find it in her sister's eyes.

* * *

But Rosa fled. She was in California. She was teaching at a grade school in Chicago. She was back at school to improve her range. (Her words, Emma thought.) She was at Oxford. Her parents were so proud. They boasted to everyone.

Emma? She wrote religiously. And Rosa returned the favor. Whenever she had unfolded a letter, Emma had held her breath, shivering in anticipation.

The last letter had arrived just two days after the plane crash.

I'm going north, Emma dear. We're going to look at a small place here because Pierce keeps saying we have to decide. And part of me wants to give up. But then I think about Dad's face when I tell him. Even though I'm tired, Em. Tired of doing, tired of working at making a difference and telling myself how selfless and good I am when I'm just the same shitty know-it-all I always was. When it's my way of being special. Is that fair? Good, bad, indifferent. What does it matter? I see myself taking up gardening, or knitting after the baby. I tell myself I could be the almost perfect mom. Pierce wants to get married. And I keep telling him no. Then I wake up in the middle of the night, and look over at him and hate him and love him and wonder why I told him in the first place, why I'm torturing myself. I start crying and you know, Em, this is some sort of pit I've descended into, only there's no happy ending. No one can hear me, I'm that far out on the moors. No one's out there about to throw down a rope and drag me up to safety.

Emma hadn't told them afterward. It would have been too much. Losing Rosa killed them both, anyhow. Louise, wasting away, then dying of lung cancer, just two years after her older daughter's death. Sy, going in his sleep only a year later. A massive heart attack.

Looking down, Emma admired the outlines of the Atlantic coast. Twenty-eight minutes they'd been up here. It was positively unnatural. She glanced over. Solomon had opened a magazine. And was apparently deeply engrossed.

The Atlantic. The same ocean she'd crossed the year after Sy's death. It had been her thirtieth birthday present to herself. Will and she had been together two years by that time. But she had gone alone. January in London was chilly and damp. She'd met up with Pierce at a small restaurant near Notting Hill Gate. And he was nothing at all like the one she'd imagined; a short, dark haired man, slightly overweight and decidedly nondescript. "I liked your parents so much that one time we met," he'd said.

They began, grudgingly at first, then with real fervor, to talk about Rosa. Pierce recalling their first meeting at Oxford, how they'd shared a tutor, how the man had been an unsufferable and pedantic oaf. And, of course, how brilliant Rosa was.

"She'd love to conduct an argument," he'd said. "Start off by playing devil's advocate, taking his side of course. She'd be turning the screws so slowly he never even felt them pinch. Poor bastard. Your sister was merciless." The lunch was entirely amiable. Then, as Emma reached for the check, Pierce touched her arm and said, "The thing is, if she'd never met me...it might never have happened. Do you think? I mean everyone's life could be so damned different. We could all avoid trouble, if only we knew."

"Don't be silly," Emma said. Which was a fairly weak response. How many times had the same thought crossed her mind? Asking an impervious god why Rosa had had to meet that man, why she'd had to fall in love, get pregnant, let him, of all people, get her into trouble.

"What if she'd missed the flight entirely? What if she'd gone back home in the fall the way she meant to, instead of staying here? What if..." But of course, then he'd had to stop, not knowing how much more Rosa had shared with her younger sister. Emma didn't enlighten him.

"It doesn't matter," Emma said, hearing the falseness in her own voice.

"Of course it does, everything matters." Pierce stood, shook hands briskly, as if he were trying to avoid contagion, and strode off.

Emma had spent three more days wandering the streets, visiting all the tourist attractions, washing down her misery with tea and bad food. Then, finally, she'd taken the night train north. Beautiful up there at the crash site, even in the middle of winter, the landscape full of purples and faint blushing reds. No traces of Nessie, but there had been several boats out on the surface of the water. Emma had stared out, trying to find Rosa, and found, instead, heather growing near the edges of the water, trim lake sand, birds wheeling above her head.

She'd taken Dawn's offer that first time because she needed to matter to someone. Her mother, Louise, had shrunk down by then, going from a slim, reliable woman to someone whose hair had lost its luster. Her father, once charmingly distracted, seemed impossibly distant. The stories they told, and every conversation turned on them; bent on immortalizing Rosa, on making her into an icon.

Emma knew why. Some parents soldiered on. Some were better at pretending. Because this wasn't something you recovered from. The fact of your loss, hiding back there, waiting to whisper all the terrifying possibilities, a copper band squeezed tighter and tighter, torturing the heart.

Emma saw Carmen, crumpling on the ground at Bea's graveside. And then the plane lurched to the right. She looked out the window and discovered thick gray clouds all around them, rain streaming down the double-plated glass.

"The captain has turned on the seat belt signs, ladies and gentlemen."

The captain's voice cut in. "Ladies and gentlemen, we are going to be experiencing some turbulence. I want to apologize in advance for the inconvenience."

A flash of lightning.

And terror gripped her again. I'm going to fucking die up here, Emma thought. Not up here, no, down there. Down there on the ground. The two of us. Me and this child of mine, together.

Realizing the ultimate joke. This, the ultimate diversion. Because she was now fiercely, ferociously protective.

The plane dropped down, roller coaster swift.

I won't have it, Emma decided. I absolutely don't agree. Not here. Not now. Not fucking now!

"How are you doing?" Solomon asked. She registered the question. As she did, she realized with a rush of relief that they were still flying. With shudders and swings, but still apparently airborne. This happens every day, a hundred times over, Emma told herself, and the pounding in her body began to subside. She looked around the cabin, then back at him.

"You said we weren't going to crash."

"It's a safe prediction. Worst-case scenario, you won't be able to call me on it." He grinned. "So how are you, really?"

"As good as one could expect," she said. "Under the circumstances."

"Would you like to fill me in on what those circumstances are?"

"Later," she said, wondering if she'd be able to keep this promise.

Solomon admitted a working knowledge of the geography. "I had family here," he said. She didn't ask for specifics. Instead, she stared out the window at the passing scenery, a harbor crowded with redone factory buildings, the highway skirting the city so that, from above, you could only see glimpses of the Federal-style housing stock. They turned off and curled around a park, then a small shopping district, and made a right. A nineteenth-century vision of suburbia, this neighborhood made up of sweet Victorian homes.

"The tony section," he said.

She had gathered that. Perfectly combed picket fences. Houses large enough to house the most extended family. The cars in the driveways telling the rest of the story; BMWs, Benzes, and late-model Volvos.

O'Donnell lived at the very end of the block. His house hardly the biggest, but large enough. And boasting a circular drive. The storm was over, the sky full of sprinting cumulus clouds. Stepping out of the car, Emma admired the yard. Two weeping willows, an oak, a maple. Well-kept garden stocked with hollyhocks, roses, and late-blooming Stella D'Oro daylilies.

Up the steps. Solomon pressed the buzzer. Emma hugged herself, feeling the aftershock of those deep dips the plane had taken. Her right ear gave a stuttering pop. Deaf, but not deaf enough to miss the sound of footsteps. Then the door was pulled back. And there he was. That white-haired Southern gentleman. She gasped. Then cursed inwardly at her weakness. But his smile was amazingly disconnected. She realized he didn't recognize her. But he knew Solomon.

"Detective, don't tell me you were in the neighborhood."

He stepped back. They walked inside. The decor was heavily Victorian, fruit-laden wallpaper, brass sconces, plus an ornate wooden sideboard. Framed family photographs hanging on the wall. Portraits of this man with his red-haired, blustery cheeked wife, the wife holding a bouncing baby girl in her arms. Then the girl as a teenager, kneeling next to a soccer ball in uniform. The girl again, this time perhaps eighteen, a gray silk prom dress clutched under her shoulders. Her face bent toward the camera, the look in her eyes vivid, almost sultry.

"To what do I owe the pleasure? Your lieutenant sent you all this way to hand me the case file?"

"Hardly."

Each man taking the other's measure. Emma standing behind Solomon, watching the mental duet. Malcolm O'Donnell wore a casual, stay-at-home outfit: khaki trousers with a striped short-sleeved shirt open at the neck. One nervous twitch presented itself, his hand dancing to his head, tapping back any stray hairs that might have tried to escape.

"Come, sit down." He led them into the living room. Window treatments to the right. Ethan Allen to the left.

"Your office called?" Solomon asked it, a rhetorical question. O'Donnell's whole demeanor said he was fully prepared.

"They did. Can I get you something to drink?" He nodded toward Emma. Then his eyes closed in a little. Memory nudging. She didn't want where they'd met before to register. Not when their disadvantage was already so apparent. "Yes, that would be wonderful."

Into the kitchen where bar stools sat at a long counter. Next to the stove a collection of knives were imbedded in a wooden block. Copper pots hung from great black hooks overhead. He opened the double fridge. "Juice? Soda? Iced tea?"

"Iced tea would be wonderful."

"And you, detective?"

"Nothing."

So he poured her a glass. Handed it to her.

"Thanks," she said.

"My pleasure."

Back into the living room again. She sipped at her drink, then set it on the table, coasters provided. A glance at Solomon showed his expression wavering between annoyance and disgust. O'Donnell was in the easy chair, sitting with crossed legs. He said not a word.

It was up to Solomon. And there was no way to prepare for this, no way to know the right words. Emma felt sorry for him then, because defeat was already evident. Why begin? Because if you didn't, you'd wonder why you hadn't tried. And once you tried? You invented a scenario where everything would come out beautifully. You lied to yourself and stuck yourself up, a target to be skillfully picked off by the next available marksman.

"Where's your daughter?"

"My daughter?"

"Amanda. Where is she?"

"I can't imagine what business that would be of yours."

"Can't you? What were you doing, jerking me around yesterday? What were you up to?"

"I was doing my job."

"No, you weren't," Solomon said. "You've been on sick leave."

"I've been on leave. No one said I was ill."

"And?"

"I'm sorry, detective. I'm not at liberty to tell you any more than that."

"Where's your daughter?" Solomon stared at him. "Are you harboring a fugitive?"

"Now don't be ridiculous. My daughter isn't a fugitive."

"If I tell you she is?"

A biting laugh. That said he knew everything they knew. And more.

"I would beg to differ."

Going nowhere, fast. Emma leaned forward, coughing to break into the standoff. "I'm sorry," she said. "I was wondering if I could use your bathroom."

His eyes flashed her way, retreating a little from the anger. "Certainly." He ushered her out, pointed the way down the hall to the kitchen. Then stood there, as if he would monitor her time. But Solomon was waiting. Measuring between the two, she saw he knew which one would be more dangerous. She heard him leaving, as she shut the door. Emma sat there, waiting until his steps disappeared. Inside that tiny room, she glanced out the window and admired the backyard. A well-kept lawn with patio furniture at the far end. And an old carriage house, the left-hand door standing open to reveal a late-model Lincoln. A right side closed off. Emma stepped out of the bathroom and considered what possible course of action she could take now. She wanted, more than anything, to get past the living room and head upstairs for a look. But there was no way to manage that without being spotted by O'Donnell. Solomon's voice was loud. And testy. "You come marching in. Making me look bad. And then I find out you don't even have the authority. I want to know why."

Emma stepped back into the bathroom. How much more time could they have, before he threw them out? With no search warrant. And O'Donnell's apparent assurance. He must have gone over the various possibilities in his mind,

long before she or Solomon had arrived. He knew so much
more. Knew what this was about. And what was at stake.
Emma glanced out again, and reregistered what lay behind.
That carriage house. The closed door. The one thing
Solomon had learned from the caretaker was that Amanda,
Penny, whoever she was, had taken preternatural care, coming in last Friday, crating up all her work, and carrying it off
in a rented truck. The paintings weren't small enough to
cram into a bedroom. Emma made her way down the hallway and stepped through the back door, smelling the overpowering odor of roses in bloom. They hung on the side of
the house, climbing and overloading a trellis. Above her, the
sky was turning violet. A breeze had come up. It made her
shiver. She moved quickly down a stone path. And sidestepped in, past the Lincoln. Then sighed. Because there
they were, stacked against the far wall. Thin wooden crates
holding someone's precious life's work.

Emma walked over to the crates, touched the top of one
and began to count, got up to thirteen when she heard the
creaking. Where? Heard it again. Coming from above her
head. She slipped past the parked car and out, then around to
the back, where there were steps, after all. Up to the second
floor. The door firmly closed. So she knocked. And in a second it was pulled back. There she stood. Surprisingly small
and slim. Wearing cut-off jeans, a man's T-shirt, no bra, because her nipples were outlined, clinging to the fabric. Her
red hair had been braided carefully, wound up around her
head like a crown. Frida Kahlo-like, Emma thought.

"Amanda," she said. And stuck out her hand. "Emma
Price." The woman looked down, then rubbed her own hand
against the side of her pants. Yellow paint came off. She took
it, held on for a conditional second.

"Are you now?" she said. Her eyes already greedy, rav-
aging Emma's face, scouring it with the sort of determina-

tion Emma found familiar, but hardly comforting. Amanda O'Donnell leaning on the side of the door. Behind her, a painting set on an easel. Already, busy at work. The background done. Had it been prepared in advance? So Emma hoped. A cold gray sky with dark waves beneath it. The furious sea at night.

Emma heard them coming across the lawn to find her. O'Donnell's voice raised out in warning. As if he had to. This daughter of his so beyond him. Beyond all of them. Smirking, actually smirking now. Her eyes wrinkled at the corners. The laugh so interior, so personal, and so omnipresent. Wasn't there something to say? Something that would fix the blame where it was meant to go? What did you do? Why do it? Neither question important enough to matter. Because if it had been, she wouldn't be standing here now.

"Mandy, don't say a word."

Amanda O'Donnell flung her eyes, in one critical, scathing glance, over the three of them. Such magnificent contempt. "What could I possibly have to say?" she asked. And stepped back. Then, studying the canvas, she leaned over, and took up her brush.

29

It was a physical response, Emma's hand making the statement after the word had died on thin air. The *no* verbalized afterward, a reflexive argument against the unfairness of it all. How could they expect that she would walk away? Instead of backward, she moved forward into the room to confront her. She wanted to say something stupid, like "not so fast," or "don't even try."

But, of course, her progress was ignored. The brush raised instead, delineating the space between them. Amanda's head averted, her body flexing. She knows who I am, Emma thought. The stance said more. How, who, and what she was would never matter. Arrogance as bliss.

Emma's hand snapped down on Amanda O'Donnell's shoulder. Emma meant to turn her around, to face her and squeeze an answer out. Amanda's hand grabbed onto her own, dragged it off, and then Amanda pushed her hard, saying "Get off me," as though she were some lethal insect raised up to sting. The push so strong that Emma lost her balance and went crashing back; she put her hands out to save herself, of course without thinking. The piercing pain again as her wrist buckled.

"God!" Tears started in the corners of her eyes.

Emma sprang back, rubbed her wrist, and let go immediately. It was broken. She had to kneel, stars reeling in her head. The pain so fierce.

Amanda retreated. And looked to her father.

"What?" Amanda said. Annoyed. All this simple inconvenience. Emma caught her breath, jabbed at the pain, and shoved it back into the outer reaches of consciousness. Then worked to see this as what it might become.

"It's my wrist," Emma said. And held it out for inspection. Solomon bending over to minister.

"Can you move it?" As though this were a sporting event and she was the wounded player. Emma tried, failed, then shook her head.

"Bad luck." The kind of thing a coach would say. They exchanged a quick look. She knew he saw it, too; time stretched out now. The action frozen. Bending his head around to O'Donnell and asking, "You have anything we can wrap it in?" Then wrinkling his forehead, as if thinking through the rest. "Maybe we should call an ambulance."

"Right! Like she's having a heart attack." From Amanda. The heart attack part of her wish list.

Solomon's retort just as wry. "Or the police. What do you think, Em? Would you consider pressing charges?"

Emma nudged her body back until she felt the wall behind her, then shut her eyes, consciously heightening the effect.

"You're not going to faint on me now," Solomon said.

"Puh-leeze." It was Amanda protesting. "She's faking it. Don't you see that? It's all an act. She's not hurt at all. Plus, she was coming at me." Directing the next part of her volley to Emma. "You touched me first..." The sneer in her voice even grander. "She's not hurt at all. Dad..." Said with a whine. "Dad."

Solomon's hand was on her shoulder. Emma opened her eyes again.

"What garbage." From Amanda.

"Quiet." It was O'Donnell senior's voice. "Be quiet, Mandy." O'Donnell moving closer, then reaching out a hand. Emma taking it, standing up, and working as she did to avoid any unnecessary movement. Even the breeze, pressing against her flesh, made her wrist throb.

"What do you want?" O'Donnell asked. He was staring at her, his curiosity apparently fully intact.

"Why did you come to New York?" Emma asked.

"Eliot Marshall..." But then his voice trailed off.

"Your daughter was acquainted with Mr. Marshall."

"I don't know what you mean."

"Of course you do," Emma said.

"What's wrong, you don't believe my dad?" This from Amanda. The belligerent look on her face echoing her tone.

"I've spoken with Loretta Picard."

Solomon cleared his throat. Emma understood. He was warning her to go slow. But it was too late for caution.

"So who's that?"

"You don't even read the papers, then?" Emma responded.

"Why would I? All they print is bad news." A serpentine smile, her tongue fluttering at the corners of her mouth, then vanishing.

"You got her the job at the Pit," Emma said.

A fairly long pause. Then Amanda's response. "Oh...that Loretta."

"You and Charles Murray were also friendly."

"Yeah, we were friendly." Amanda sighed dramatically. "Really bad about Charles."

"His mother called," Malcolm O'Donnell offered, a little too quickly. "So terrifically upsetting. Charles and Amanda have been friends since grade school."

"Like brother and sister," Emma said.

Amanda nodded, carefully.

"You look really broken up," Solomon added.

"I sure am." Amanda O'Donnell stepped back then, and Emma moved forward. She noted the canvas, skillfully rendered: a bleak midnight sky. In the upper left-hand corner, a tiny sliver of moon.

"Detective Solomon has been trying to contact you for several days," Emma said.

"Several days? I've been here," Amanda said.

"Since?" From Solomon again.

"Let's see." Counting off on her fingers. "Last Friday night. I drove this rented truck down with all my shit."

"Why?" he asked.

"Why what?"

He didn't answer. She surveyed the room, her eyes passing quickly over all three of them, and on to the roll of canvas that lay in the far corner.

"Because," she said. "I needed to work. You said you talked to Loretta. Well, think how it's been since she lost her fucking mind on me. Think about my side."

"Your side?" Solomon said.

"I mean, you never know what someone's really like. All I say is that I want a little space and she goes nuts. Starts following me when I go out. Starts accusing me of all sorts of things."

"Like what?" Emma asked.

"You know what. Cheating on her. When I wasn't. But I saw it was time. I had to go. So I told her that. And then the drama really started. She'd show up in places when she knew I'd be there. Look mournful, like I'd gone and snuffed out her soul. You know what I mean, don't you? Misery personified." Amanda swung her head from Emma to Solomon, then back. "She writes me all these letters, sends me e-mail. I'm suddenly the crucible of her whole life. Great! Just great! So I'm already making plans to get away. And I'm ignoring her big time because what else can I do. Which makes her even more frantic, I guess. Next thing I know, she's taking out these two cops and being dragged off to jail."

"Which should have solved your problem," Solomon said evenly.

"No way. I've got work to do. A show coming up. How'm I gonna get that done?"

"You came home so your dad could protect you?" Emma asked.

"I came home for some downtime," she said.

"Why tell people you were going to New Mexico?"

"To throw them off the trail. Hey, the last thing I want is to be involved." Throwing up her hands then, as if in disgust at her own innocent plight. Stepping back to stand next to the open sink. Emma wondering how much of this had been stage-managed; the pressed-out oils laid out on a table, the canvas freshly dabbed.

"You and Charles Murray were business partners," Emma said.

Amanda shook her head, as if weary of fools.

"What sort of business is this you're referring to?" Malcolm O'Donnell asked.

"The Pale Door. Your daughter and Murray sold fake IDs. A little sideline, some spare cash for the two of them."

"Who says she was involved?"

So here it goes, Emma thought. Murray. They'll hang the whole of this on him.

"Where's the name from?" Emma asked.

"Pale Door. Charles always loved Poe," Amanda said. "He got it from his favorite poem."

"Poe." Emma flashing on the selections in Loretta's bookcase; Poe's collected works, along with modern gothic masters.

"How about you? Are you a fan of the gothic?"

"How nice of you to ask about my literary taste." The humor in her eyes, sheer mockery.

"The two of you were partners," Emma said.

"I'm afraid not."

"You should be afraid." From Solomon. Emma knew he was seeing the game plan.

Emma switched her focus to the father. "Your daughter's an innocent victim of circumstance?" she asked.

"I don't understand what you're referring to."

She turned back to Amanda then. "Why don't you tell me how Bea got in the water?" she asked.

"Bea?" Then a shrill laugh. And a stony silence.

Emma knew that here was the moment. A small victory but something, if she could make her worry. Perhaps, in worrying, stumble. In stumbling, fall facedown, scraping herself against the unforgiving pavement.

Emma turned back to Malcolm. "You came to speak with Detective Solomon about Eliot Marshall because you were afraid the computer system in the Witness Protection Program had been compromised. You were afraid someone had broken through the firewalls, correct?"

"Incorrect. My sole concern was Marshall." Curt. The next words would be, time for you to go. Get the hell out. Good luck and damn good riddance.

"So you and your daughter have never been estranged."

"Of course not."

Back to Amanda. "You and Eliot and Charles had this great idea, right?" Emma said and stepped in closer, stabbing distance. "You'd break inside the agency computer. You'd do it for fun, just to see if you could. And how to start? Why not with your dad? Your dad must have a computer in his office, with a modem attached. Maybe even a dedicated line, right here at home. You never thought Charles could really do it, did you?"

Amanda's face didn't offer any clues. Too late to worry, Emma told herself. Besides, I'll never get another chance. Unfolding the story. Testing it against all possible variants.

Not a possibility. The buzzer had sounded. The next contestant was being ushered out. "But then Charles got inside. And better yet, he broke the code. Was it having Eliot that helped? His new Social Security number and name, must have been some sort of tag line?"

No answer. But her audience was certainly riveted.

"So now the stakes were even higher. Whose idea was it first? Eliot's? Or maybe yours? Why not try and sell off some of the names? Who was going to know? I mean, who would have thought you'd get as far as you did, right? Everything was going along so smoothly, wasn't it? Except I guess for Loretta losing her mind about you. But even that worked in your favor. Larrabbee had been after you and now he was no more. Plus, she's put away for good. You couldn't have counted on the glitch, but then, no one ever does. It was Charles. You never thought he'd be stupid enough to tell anyone else about this. But he did. Told his girlfriend. Was it a confession, or just a confidence he was sharing? Was it pride in his grand achievement? Too bad that she decided she wasn't about to let it happen. There are always a few things you don't expect."

"That's what makes life interesting," Amanda said.

"Bea wouldn't have gone near the water. Someone threw her in. Was it Charles? Did he do it for you? Or just because he was afraid of being caught?" Emma searched for the answer in her face. And then remembered. Eliot had been with them that morning, as they drove off. "It was Eliot, wasn't it? Not Charles at all. Eliot did the dirty deed. For you? Or just for himself? Afterward you had to tidy up. Eliot. Then Chazz. You don't have to say a word. Just give me one wink if I'm warm. Two, if I'm burning hot."

She didn't wink, instead she laughed, ferociously.

Malcolm O'Donnell stepped forward. Emma thought he was going to reach out and shake his daughter. But it was a different sort of revenge he was after, grabbing onto Emma instead. And by her bad arm, shaking the wrist.

"Let go." Solomon's voice. Detective Laurence Solomon with his gun unholstered and at the ready. O'Donnell slowly disengaged.

"I'm calling the police," O'Donnell said.

"Then I'll have to tell them how your daughter assaulted my partner. You know how we boys in blue love to hate the feds, so why don't you just go ahead and call." He holstered his gun and stepped back.

"Was there some clause in the contracts?" Emma asked. "Eliot's looked like suicide, and the other two? A hit-and-run and a carjacking? Did you make that a requirement? Or was it just luck of the draw?"

"Luck of the draw," Amanda said. "Now there's a stupid phrase."

"Mandy," her father hissed.

"Why stupid?" Emma asked.

"Because nothing's about luck."

"Why did you kill Chazz? Was he threatening to turn you in? Was it about Bea? Or was it just so you could pin the whole of it on him? Is that what it's all about?" Emma scrutinized Amanda, trying to decide as best she could. "Does your father buy in to your story? Or is he part of it, too?"

"How dare you!" Malcolm O'Donnell said.

"How dare *you*," Emma responded without even looking his way. "Who knows, Amanda, maybe it will work for you. I'd like to tell you you'll feel sorry. I'd like to imagine you have a conscience. But I'm too damn old to pretend."

"You're really that old?" Amanda said.

A sharp look exchanged. Emma had known, all along, what their chances would be here. Amanda's eyes narrowed.

She pressed her hands deep into the pockets of her blue jean shorts.

And Emma turned to Malcolm O'Donnell.

"Bea phoned to tell you," Emma said. "I'd like to think it was already too late."

He looked physically stunned. She'd trapped him in a lie, after all.

"Remember me now?" Emma asked. "396 Fifth. You held the door. You were going out. I was on my way inside. We exchanged pleasantries."

He looked her over again. A flicker in his eyes, denoting memory.

"And then, there you were at Bea's funeral. Were you paying your respects? Or were you looking for Charles?"

"Out, please. Now."

"By the way," she said, turning back to Amanda one last time. "It was kind of Detective Solomon to call me his partner, but not entirely accurate. I'm that investigator, the one working for Loretta. And Beatriz Castillo worked for me. She cared for my son. Strange world, huh? Luck? Fate? Who really knows." Emma backed up then, holding her arm as steady as possible. "It's my job to find reasons," she said. "There are always reasons. But thank God I never make the mistake your dad's making here. Thank God I never confuse the reasons with the excuse. Because there's no excuse for what you've done, Amanda."

Down the steps. Across the lawn. Into the car. Solomon starting the motor. The two of them pulling away.

"Amazing," he said. She didn't know if that was bad or good. And didn't care suddenly. Dizziness. Nausea. Her hand lay nestled in her lap.

"I need a doctor," she said. Having never fainted, it was

certainly strange, pretty much the way it was usually described. The world spinning. The currents tugging you away. "The only thing is," she said. Then lost the train of thought. Her eyes were firmly closed. Which didn't help. "Laurence."

Heard him say yes. Felt him touch her forehead. The only thing real now, the throbbing. The fierce stabs of pain.

"They'll want to take an X-ray maybe. You've got to tell them."

Leaning in again. "Yes?"

"Tell them I'm pregnant, would you? Please promise me you'll remember."

30

So ridiculously dramatic, Emma thought. She studied the cast the doctor had attached to her wrist. They'd called in an orthopedist, once Solomon relayed her condition to the resident on call in the emergency room. The woman who'd arrived had sounded knowledgeable enough, opting for this flexible restraint and adding an admonition to have it looked after on Emma's return to New York. The parting quip, "better safe, then sorry."

Then Solomon had gone, wielding her insurance card.

Emma decided he'd left her alone, to give her a chance to ponder her own stupidity. Leaning her head back against the wall, she studied the various confessions of the day. Loretta's, Liam's, and, of course, her own.

Then the door opened. "Let's go."

Solomon wasn't furious. But he was detached. Kept sneaking looks at her, as if she were a new subspecies. As if he were taking mental notes.

Down busy hospital corridors. Out the exit door with a whoosh. Into the car. Still no conversation.

Solomon unfolded a map, studied it, then put it aside. And they drove off.

Pulling up to Budget car rental, in a slim fifteen minutes. "We're not going back to the airport?"

"I'm not crazy."

"I certainly didn't mean to imply that."

But he was stepping out, and closing the door. She fol-

lowed meekly behind, waiting while he dealt with the paperwork, then called a cab. No further talk ensuing on the way
to the train station.

"I'll get the tickets," he said, nudging his chin toward a
bench. She took a seat and watched him stand on line.
Watched as he worked his way up to the clerk, then came
back, offering her a ticket. "We'll make the 8:18," he said.
"It gets in at 10:37. Want some magazines?"

She shrugged. He was already off again, surveying the
newsstand.

Emma reached into her purse and retrieved her mobile
phone. She dialed by holding it steady between her knees,
and jamming the buttons with her index finger.

"Suze?"

"You're back?"

"Not yet." In the background, the sound of a blaring TV.
And Liam's voice, offering the play-by-play. Jeter takes a
ball. "I'll be home by eleven, maybe eleven-thirty."

"That's okay. He can sleep over." The pause meaningful
enough.

"I'm sorry, Suze . . ." Her voice trailed off.

"What for?"

The loudspeaker cut in, announcing the 8:18. Emma was
glad she didn't have to explain. Instead, she signed off and
looking up, found Solomon, waiting.

"Ready?" What merciless consideration he was showing.
Walking with her to the train. Finding them seats. Letting
her in first, then handing her the magazines: *Vanity Fair,*
People, the *New Yorker.* Something for almost everyone.

"I'm going to the bar car. Can I get you something?"

"Could you please stop!"

"Stop what?" The raising of the eyebrows. The incredulous expression on his face.

"Being so goddamn solicitous."

"What would you prefer?" A courtly tone. When what she observed was a man bent on torture.

"A seltzer," she said, pointedly looking away.

An hour later, he returned. They were passing through Wilmington. He handed her a cup with ice and untabbed the can, then poured the foaming liquid.

"I shouldn't have told them what we knew."

He nodded calmly.

"You have every right to be angry."

"You did what you had to do. And it wasn't what we knew, after all. It was a theory. Your theory, not mine."

"Even so, I ruined your chances."

He looked as though he were examining this option carefully, as if it were a precious object recently purchased, and he was studying all its elegant, defining contours. "I never thought my chances were particularly good."

"Then why were you so adamant about going to Baltimore?"

"Actually, it was the only idea I had."

"A last-ditch notion?"

"Perhaps." Solomon extended his hands, then his body. Comfort only in the eye of the beholder.

"You're angry because I didn't tell you I was pregnant before?"

"No. That's certainly not any of my business."

She looked away now, feeling the blush spread across her cheeks. "But it would be, if we got involved with each other."

She reached out with her good hand, to grab onto his arm. He'd done the same, only a few hours earlier, a generous offer of encouragement. He gave her hand a clinical look.

"You keep too many damn secrets," he said.

She pulled away quickly. Reaching down, Solomon found a copy of the *Baltimore Sun* and unfurled it.

Emma was left to examine the passing scenery: houses stuffed with lights, the late-night sky violet thick, darkness wrapping them as they moved north. They traveled through suburban fields, through woods, and into the swampland of New Jersey. Not one word more was exchanged. Nothing till they'd disembarked from the train and were standing on the platform. Then Solomon's offer came. "I'll get you a cab."

Emma didn't even bother to verbalize her refusal. She shook her head grimly and took off.

Her chariot south moved swiftly. Each time they soared over a bump, her wrist ached. Emma jammed her teeth together, in self-defense.

Eleven twenty-eight when she rang Suzanne's buzzer. Suzanne coming out in her silk kimono, seductively unfurled at the breast. Suzanne asking, "What happened?" Now there was a story.

Interior. Suzanne's kitchen. An oak table piled high with unanswered mail. Suzanne clearing a place and offering a glass of tap water. Saying, "Tell me everything." And after Emma told her all phases of the criminal investigation, after she sat there, with Suzanne encouraging her to say more, nodding her head as though she understood every facet, the question was simple. "Have you told Will?"

"I'm only just back," Emma said. Then saw what was meant. Added, "Oh. You mean about that."

"Yes. That." Suzanne studying her. Appraising her.

"I'll talk to him tomorrow."

"And then?" Suzanne looked so pathetically hopeful. "You're keeping the baby?"

"Yes."

"I knew you would." Suzanne's expression said the rest. What she hoped would be the next step. People were so unreasonably optimistic. "It's going to be hard for you, Em. Hard for Liam."

Emma sighed, the air rolling out to fill the room. "Women do it all the time. I'll have to manage."

"This might shake him up. He might realize..."

"Realize what?" Emma felt the weariness overtake her again. "Listen, could I sleep upstairs tonight?"

"Anything. Anything you need."

Suzanne came over to her then, and took hold. Held on so tenderly. It made Emma gasp.

"You've told Al," Emma said.

Suzanne nodded.

"I expected you would. Shit, maybe I even hoped he'd break the news to Will and save me the trouble. How is it, that I find out at this late date I'm the coward?"

Suzanne stepped back, her eyes flashing. "You? You're the bravest person I know."

"Hardly."

"Yes, you are, Em. Indefatigable."

"That's not bravery, that's stupidity," Emma said.

"What about Will?"

"What about Jolene?" A flicker in Suzanne's eyes. "Jesus, how long have you known?"

"Only since yesterday."

"And Al? His buddy Al?" Emma was surprised at how the fury rose up. Indefatigable, she thought. Not a bad adjective. "We don't tell each other everything."

"One of you doesn't." Emma started to laugh and found she couldn't stop. Or didn't want to. Suzanne hugged her again. Who needs the comfort now, Emma wondered. But let Suzanne do it, all the same. After she'd gained control again, she untangled herself, breathed a hoarse breath, and added, "It's not about what went wrong. It's about what didn't go right."

"It's about men and their fucking needs," Suzanne said, grunting afterward to remind Emma of the porcine root of her complaint. A further surprise.

"What happened to contentment? Where's that Zen way of being?"

"Will turned into an asshole, yes or no?"

"Yes . . . and no. The truth is we stopped caring enough to look at what was wrong. And if you don't look, how can you fix it?" Emma reached down and lifted her empty water glass. "To men and their fucking needs," she said, starting to laugh again. Suzanne lifted her own, a wine glass, still half filled.

"To men," Suzanne agreed. Then drank. Emma turned, heading for the stairs. A short climb to the guestroom where merciful sleep could finally overtake her.

"One more toast," Suzanne said. Emma was about to protest but Suze had already raised her glass. "To us. To us women with our endless complaints. Because why complain unless you believe that nothing is beyond repair? So, to us."

"Yes, to us," Emma said. "To women and their cockeyed optimism."

31

Solomon left a message on her machine the next morning while she was out. No investigation would be forthcoming from the feds. And they were denying any knowledge of losses in the program. As for the lab reports? Marshall's was classified. And they'd gotten all the work back on the crime scene with Murray. No traces of DNA, no stray fibers anywhere.

She called him back and got Ruiz, who told her he'd be glad to deliver a message.

The talk with Will was done face to face. By the time it occurred, at two-thirty that same afternoon, she felt remarkably dispassionate. She heard his key in the lock and went to greet him. Offered him a drink as he came in the door.

"What sort of drink?" he asked.

"Something strong."

"And why would I need that?"

"Because we're going to have a baby."

She watched him get it. Watched his face turn color, as he stood there in the hall. Watched him as he set his keys down on the sideboard, instead of back in his pocket where they belonged. "This isn't some kind of sick joke?" he asked, because he had to. What else could he do, considering?

She nodded. "I meant to tell you before."

He was smart enough to see, by then, what before meant.

"That night when I came home. Sweet Jesus, Em, why didn't you?"

He stepped through the open door and into the living room. The painting her old friend, Grace, had given her for her fortieth hung above the fireplace. Two children playing at war. One held a saber, the other a revolver. Their mating dance was done at a healthy distance.

Will took a seat on the couch. Then he put his hand down next to him, tapping the pillows.

"I wanted you to know. It doesn't change anything between us," Emma said.

"Of course it does."

"No. I thought that it would, but it doesn't. It just makes it more complicated." She offered a wan smile for his benefit. "But we're both adults, aren't we? We can figure out the logistics."

"Em..."

"Listen, Will, you were willing to leave when it was just Liam. Why should it make any difference, now that there's another child involved?"

"God, you are cold."

"I don't think so. I'm just being realistic." She didn't point out how he'd encouraged this trait. Instead, she sat and admired him for what he appeared to have become. Someone she'd once loved. Reminding herself of that helped her to temper the anger. This can't be about the Jolenes of the world, she told herself. This is only about you and Will.

"What if I ask you to reconsider?"

What if? "I already have," she said, then reached over, took his hand and held onto it, feeling a sudden surge of tenderness. "We'll work it out." He didn't agree, but she ploughed ahead. "And then the three of us will sit down together. We'll both tell Liam."

"You mean you haven't done that yet?" Spat out at her like a curse. So much for a reasonable ending. He stood up, backed away from her, and was out the door, slamming it behind him.

Emma told herself he'd calm down. And went to work on the next matter at hand. Which was Loretta. By the end of the next day she'd beaten down the door at Dr. Reynolds's office and gotten the woman to say she was willing to be deposed. That, plus Andrew Tax and Loretta's agreement to let their own specialist examine her, gave Emma a little sliver of hope. Meanwhile, on Long Island, a husband poisoned his estranged wife and her parents at a reunion dinner. The Nassau County DA said he was prepared to level capital indictment.

Friday. Will's call came. She didn't know where he'd gone to talk it through, but he sounded reasonable enough. They would go to the doctor's office together, when he could. He would be there at the birth. She assumed he was hoping to insinuate himself back into her life. But she didn't disabuse him of that notion. Instead, she said yes to all. And they decided the best thing to do was to wait for the amnio before telling Liam.

That Saturday, after Liam fell asleep, she called Solomon at home. A machine picked up, his voice, fractured by the wires. She didn't bother to leave a message.

Emma told herself she wasn't waiting. She reminded herself to grow up. A crush, a faint schoolgirl hope. The sort of thing she had long ago sworn to abandon.

Alone.

Days when everything was fine. When she picked up Liam at school, walked him home, and let him lope upstairs ahead of her, disappearing. Days when she made them both dinner. And afterward, as he took a shower, she heard him singing inside while the water beat down.

"Time to put out the light."

"Mom, can I have some fruit?"

In the kitchen, Emma, disemboweling an apple and a peach, then bringing them upstairs. Her pharaoh. Her supreme ruler. Reading to him from Harry Potter while he ate. Understanding this was the stall. Understanding they were cooperating in it together. Harry who had been born a great wizard. His parents were, of course, dead. His life was amazing, profoundly different, and original. His life was surely his own.

Liam finished his snack. And Emma clicked off the light, then leaned over to kiss him.

"Would you rub my back?" A younger child's request. He fell asleep as she rolled her hand down. And Emma found herself wondering, yet again, how many years the two of them had left. Soon he would resist so thoroughly, believing that he had already stopped needing her. And wasn't that the day she swore she was preparing for? A day she dreaded and hoped for, in equal measure?

Late September.

Then October.

And then All Hallows' Eve.

It was a surprisingly mild afternoon. Emma's mission, taking off from work to find Liam the perfect wizard's robe and wand. One of those crisp fall days when the sidewalk glitters, when the city shines. Emma bought Chinese pork buns from an outdoor cart, then headed north, making for the largest costume store in the city. The sun fell in slices through the canyons the buildings created. It was another one of New York's finest hours.

She took a side street, cutting ahead of the late-afternoon walking traffic. At a bistro that expanded onto the sidewalk she bought a triple cappuccino. And kept on. Another side street boasted an elegant hat store. The creations veered from the outrageous to the ridiculous. Still, she stepped inside and when the woman, overly solicitous, asked if she could help, Emma didn't flee. In fact, she bought a fedora and set it on her head. That would be her costume. Then she set out again, a hard right down a narrow, cobblestone block. Halfway down, a banner proclaimed APPARENT ART. Emma glanced at the painting in the window. It showed a primal assault, Noah's ark with a hole broken into the hull and the animals pouring out, greedily attacking a bearded man, his wife, and his four blond-haired daughters.

The artist's name simply confirmed what she already knew. Penny Strider: A Life in Progress.

The paintings were obscenely large.

Painting number one was titled *Mi Amor.* A flock of crows rising above a city street. And a girl taking a walk with her pet. The girl's white-blond hair had been violently sheared off. Tucked behind her, on the dark street, her four-footed accompaniment, a red-toned dragon flicking its tongue. The night sky was painted so lightly, it was as blue as day.

Painting two bore script as well as a printed title underneath. THE THINGS WE DO FOR LOVE. The same girl, surrounded. A Western-style shootout with the posse in pursuit, except this was a modern bunch of sheriffs and deputies. They wore the uniforms of New York's Finest. Two of them lay dead on the ground; a woman and a man. And around them the crowds had formed. Gamblers and ladies in hoop skirts leaned over the railing of the saloon, named, of course, the Pit. Tumbleweed sailed by. Painting three. A naïf sea. Sharks ripping apart the water. And two odd additions. A lion's head poking above, with its brown mane intact. And a lamb, stretched out on its back, its eyes tightly shut. In the middle of the painting the real action. A different female figure, held just under the curve of the water by a man in a wet suit. The victim's short dark hair was slicked back. Emma read the title aloud. "HOW THE LION MAKES PEACE WITH THE LAMB."

Painting four. A desert landscape, studded with cacti. Wolves and hyenas crowding around the centerpiece. A human figure hung on a cross, like Jesus. A nude, blond-haired man with three ruby studs. Next to him, on the ground, clothing laid out for display, black jeans, a white sleeveless undershirt, a pair of black Beatle boots, and a pink Nokia phone.

Dying to Know U.

Emma made the call. Then stood outside for a little while more. But it was getting late. She had to go. She found the costume store and bought a bright scarlet cape.

Five o'clock and she was at school, picking up Liam from aftercare. He chattered on about his day, and she didn't listen, working out how to frame the question, then realizing there was no good way.

"I've been thinking about Chazz," she said. Which made him go silent, made his face darken with worry. "How did he find you that night?"

"I told you. I called Bea."

"But Chazz showed up. He was checking her messages?"

Liam shrugged. How could he know anything, she told herself. Stupid, on your part, to even think he would. And what a sense of relief. The air she'd held onto, whistling out.

"He was using her phone," Liam said. "You know. The one we gave her for her birthday."

Her turn to stop. To turn. To stare down at him.

"Using it? How do you know?"

"He had it with him. He got a call on it. I thought it was Bea calling up. I guess that got on his nerves cause he told me then."

"Told you she was dead."

Liam nodded. His bottom lip was beginning to tremble. I have to ask him the rest, she thought. Then thought again. "Liam, it's all right," she said. And wondered where this lie had been dug from. It wasn't all right. Not at all. She was pledged. She'd have to dredge up whatever answers there were. She'd have to offer him up as a potential witness.

No.

No fucking way.

She bent down, put her arms around him. "So you had a good day at school," she said. No answer. "What did Mrs. Leonard say about your drawing?"

He smiled then, his tone was abashed, but pride colored his face. "That it was the bomb."

"Now that's some fine compliment."

Ten o'clock. Liam in bed. And Emma downstairs, pacing. Thinking about those paintings. Why do them in the first place? The one of Bea drowning had been sitting on her easel that day. Why display them? Arrogance? Guilt? Both in equal measure?

It would be Halloween the next day, no holiday she preferred more. Bags holding spectral lights. Goblins and witches walking the streets of the city undisturbed. Emma looked out the front window of her house. Two boys stood on the corner, smoking and talking trash. Their body language said it all. The hips stuck back. The chin pressed forward.

To the right, down the street she knew so well it was strangely exhilarating to find that late-model Volvo pulling up, and Solomon exiting by the driver's side door.

He crossed the threshold and as he did, offered her a look that roved over her face, toyed with her shoulders, and moved dramatically down her body. Nasty, she thought, nasty and perfect, all at the very same time. "So you got my message," she said.

"Listen," he replied. "Listen, Emma..."

Was it the beginning of an apology? Or simply an offer? The way he said it. So polite. So formal. Emma found she had to comply. Tilting her head and holding her breath, she heard the sound of someone's front door, opening and closing, the squeal of brakes as an out-of-town motorist narrowly avoided hitting a teenage girl. And she heard the girl say "goddamn," heard the fear in her voice when she realized just how close she'd come to annihilation. Emma heard someone moan a moan that was clearly sexual in nature. She heard the sound of pages turning in a book while a mother read to her child, and she heard the sound of wooden blocks clicking together as the child built the perfect castle. In the back room of that same apartment, an elderly man unscrambled the events of his complicated day, telling someone long dead the perfect story.

All of this occurring while he stepped inside her house, shut the door behind him. He put down a briefcase. In the vestibule, he reached out and unbuttoned the top button of her blouse, letting the fabric slide down. He put his hand inside and held it there against her skin. He slid his hand down further, making a practiced move, releasing her bra. She laughed at the ease and her laugh changed everything. You could taste summer and thunder, a warm wind whipped rain in the air. You could imagine the clean light after.

He undressed her slowly, deliberately, pressing her back into the hallway and then, into the living room, and there on the floor they knelt down. He was kissing her, pressing his tongue into her mouth, then into her ear, and she wondered what she was doing with this man.

"Here," he whispered. He leaned over and took her right breast in his mouth and sucked hard until the nipple ached. He let go and did the same with the other one.

He moved his hands down her body slowly, evenly, surely, to where she would have begged for him to touch. She began to shiver and he pushed hard inside of her as she reached out to meet him.

When they were finished, when he'd pulled away, he lay down on the rug beside her and held her hand loosely, the way a friend might. Then he leaned on his elbow and moved his fingers down, to outline her face.

"Does this mean you've changed your mind?" Emma asked.

"About what?"

"About me."

Solomon studied her. "I don't know that my mind needed changing."

"Only suddenly I'm not intimidating?"

He laughed. "Frustration was a better definition of the emotion."

She looked him over then, assessing as best she could. "And what about you, Laurence? You're saying you've got no complications of your own, no twists and turns?"

"There might be a few."

She lay back then, and stared at the ceiling. "You went to the gallery?"

"I did."

"What are your thoughts?"

"My thoughts? The woman has talent. She knows how to put together a story."

No point going on. Not if she really believed there was a future. She put her hand up to quiet him, to get his full attention. And when she had it, said, "My son was with Charles Murray the night he was killed."

"What?" Solomon sat up. Stared down, incredulous.

"He was upset with me. He ran off, called Bea and left a message. We were stupid, trying to protect him. We didn't tell him Bea was dead."

"I see." The incredulous look had drained away. And here was a surprise indeed. Because the look on his face was gentleness personified.

"That pink phone, the Nokia in the last painting, wasn't some idea she came up with. It was Bea's phone. A gift from me. Murray had Bea's phone with him the night he was killed. Liam said he got a call on it while they were together."

"You know the number, of course."

She nodded.

"I'll get the phone records."

She saw the calculations being made. And didn't have to wait too long to get the rest.

"There was no phone in the car with him. No personal effects at all, except that wallet."

"Whoever killed him took it."

"I've been thinking all along, she'd paid someone off to make the hit," Solomon said. "She could have done it herself."

"Or she could be laying the blame somewhere else," Emma said. "What about her father?"

"They're not going to hang onto something incriminating like that. The phone's long gone."

"But the calls could tell you something."

"They might."

"There's only one other thing," Emma said. "If you ever need Liam to testify as to what went on that night, or that he saw the phone in Murray's possession, you'll be out of luck."

"You're kidding."

"No. He's not going to do it. And if you think he is, then we never even had this conversation."

"Em... how do I know what I'll find? You can't mean that."

"But I do."

"Hey, I understand that you don't want your son involved."

"No. You're misunderstanding me, Laurence. It's not what I want. He's not going to be involved. If I have to call you a liar in open court, I'll do it."

"Why did you tell me about this, then?"

She had the answer, prepared weeks in advance. "Because I was tired," she said.

"Tired?" But he nodded then. And smiled, the twinkle reaching to the corners of his eyes, where, she noted, small wrinkles occurred. "You want me to promise. I really can't promise..."

Was it just last Halloween? Beatriz Castillo stepping out onto the stoop to pose. Will at the bottom of the stairs, holding the camera. Liam had been a prince, and Bea, his warrior princess. Her dress, cheap silk from Chinatown. Her eyes made up with dark slashes and blue shadows. Bea held his hand and Emma tucked her arm around the two of them while Will snapped the shot.

Emma thought of Bea stepping out into the harsh summer light. Bea feeling guilty because Eliot had just made her papi run. Guilty and dirty. And secretly glad.

Inside Chazz's car, Bea juicing up the radio while Chazz settled his hand around her shoulder, the big man discussing his plans, telling her how he and Penny were building a cathedral together, a cathedral made out of peasant gold.

Had Bea shivered that day? Had she recognized God's breath, offering her a warning?

Because that day Eliot had taken her into the water. Bea, clawing at him, as he did it, her fingers not even scraping against the neoprene wetsuit.

"I'm sorry," Emma said.

"Don't be." Solomon's face still graceful in the half light. "Of course your son comes first. I wouldn't have expected anything else."

Into the bathroom where Emma washed her face. "I'll just be a minute."

She climbed the stairs to check. Liam sleeping fitfully, clutching the sheets to his body. Liam groaning once while he slept, then turning over. The shadows tossed by passing street traffic curled through the blinds. One of the things she liked was how this house never really got dark.

Because real darkness still unnerved her.

In that other house the trees had whistled as the river swept by. When her parents turned off the lights, you couldn't make out your own hand, held inches from your face. And Emma had heard the sharp-nosed witch coming. The scratching of nails was her making her way out of the cupboard. Emma had thrust her head as far down as she could, way under the covers. She'd counted by twos and crossed her fingers.

But then, the sound of the door, creaking open.

"Em, are you awake?" It was Rosa, crawling into bed beside her, Rosa's flashlight beam breaking the darkness apart. Rosa had two oranges to share and a bowl for the rinds. She uncurled the skins so they could feast together. Then Rosa told her the story of the river horse and promised, "I won't go till you're asleep."

* * *

Emma leaned over Liam, offering her own sort of benediction. She checked the time. Almost two. And she hadn't heard the front door close ...

The Joanna Brady Mysteries by
New York Times Bestselling Author

An assassin's bullet shattered Joanna Brady's world, leaving her policeman husband to die in the Arizona desert. But the young widow fought back the only way she knew how: by bringing the killers to justice . . . and winning herself a job as Cochise County Sheriff.

Available wherever books are sold or please call 1-800-331-3761 to order.

JB 0202